THE
HEIR
OF
WAR
RISES

EIGHTH CIRCLE BOOK 2

THE HEIR OF WAR RISES

KATERINA SPEERS

For Noelle. You are all the best parts of me.

CONTENT WARNING

Please note this book contains subject matter that may be difficult for some readers, including discussion and/or description of death, torture, bullying, alcohol, drugs, violence, profanity, sexual situations and mention of sexual assault. Proceed with caution if you choose to enter the world of Elysium.

OLYMPIA

FEEL RIVER

LAKE INFINITY

SELESTE

BOSSENA

OSTA

AURORA

MORYON'S MOUNTAINS

TURSK

AVONON

AGRABODA

GULF OF HEROES

LASTEIKA

VILLADELLE

PYRGOS

ELIS

PERA

MESSENE

PYRANOS MOUNTAINS

THURIA

LAKONIA

CHEVALA

IBROS

SPARTA

CAST OF CHARACTERS

COMPILED BY YOURS TRULY, CROAK

Terena Luca - the main character, arguably. It's me, I argue.

Gabriol "Croak" Luca - Terena's handsome younger brother

Sonah Yahn - Terena's twin but strangely, four years younger...

Hermes - Olympian god with anger issues.

Daris Antonius - Commander of the Liodari. Not trustworthy. But the heart wants what the heart wan—ouch! Stop!

Rydon of Decu - mercenary and a Eudaemon, which is fancy for "immortal guardian". Croak is his best friend.

Gabriol of Rois - another mercenary. Amazing hair. Tall.

Ormano "Orry" Peredor - Cleric, so, boring as fuck, but Terena finds his research valuable. Croak's best friend.

Lerek - that's right! He's alive! Crown Prince of Heylisia.

King Altos - King of Sparta.

Pytho - oracle. Seems nice but has really strange eyeballs.

Migela - assassin. Mute, but funny as shit when you understand the hand gestures she makes.

Vassori - tracker. Xoran's sister. Very cute in a scare the shit out of you kinda way.

Xoran - Captain of the Imperial Guard to the Emperor of Heylisia. Not a good guy. Slimy.

Melanos - a god and a very cool... god. Gigantic.

Bethana - a nymph and Melanos's ladylove who was cursed by Poseidon and turned into a serpent.

Jason - heroic, Liodari, and newly appointed lieutenant.

Fane - former Liodari now just an average Spartan soldier.

Leander - Heylisian Riverman, where Heylisian officers send their psychopaths.

Cassandra - a seer. Came from somewhere called Troy.

Duke Ovenno - Sonah's pretend dad. Not a good guy. At all.

Galen - Duke Ravos. Asshole.

Solon - Emperor of Heylisia. Evil if evil were a person.

High Cleric Christos - claims to be pious but really, an asshole.

General Peleon - brother to the emperor and the general of his armies. Need I say more?

CHAPTER 1

OLYMPIA

Ormano Peredor scribbled furiously, glancing back and forth between the scroll he was referencing and his notes. Shuffling aside one of the many papers strewn across the table, he frowned in concentration as he searched for the one he needed.

"Any luck?"

Startled, Orry spared a glance at Terena Luca strolling to his side, her hand tucked into her belt as she looked at his work.

She must've just come from training, Orry thought when she leaned against the desk. Her sable hair was in its usual style, secured high on her head so the mane hung down to sway gently as she walked, but there were strands loose and a flush of color high on her cheeks. Snow had melted on her leather breeches, leaving behind dots of moisture, and her fur-lined boots were wet when she crossed her ankles. Her hazel eyes narrowed as she looked down at the scrolls in front of Orry.

"Nothing yet," he muttered as he dipped his quill in the ink, careful not to drip any on the ancient scrolls. Hermes had presented Orry with the scrolls when he'd first arrived, months ago.

Orry was searching for anything he could find on the Shroud of

Faybhen. He'd yet to discover how it opened a portal to the Olympian gods.

A month after Terena and Croak arrived, Orry was still no closer to discovering the shroud's secrets and his frustration was eating at him.

"What's this?"

Orry glanced at where Terena's hand was settled and he did a double take as she lifted it, frowning at the ancient words.

"Careful!" he snapped and swatted her hand with the feathered end of the quill.

She bent closer as he casually read the dead language and grinned.

"This," he said, "is a fascinating story I'd not heard before. It is of a goddess we never knew existed, at least, not in Heylisia."

"What goddess?"

"She had many names. I saw a reference in one of these scrolls to her as Até, but this text refers to her as Kaïra. The God of Ruin. Her power was so terrible, even the other gods feared her. Except Thanatos. The God of Death loved her and they were to marry, but she was killed."

"What? How?"

Orry shrugged. "It doesn't say. Only that Zeus defiled her corpse, stealing one of her emerald eyes and fashioning it into an amulet he then gifted to a mortal. A shepherd. The goddess had many powers, the most insidious allowed her to invade the minds of mortals and gods, twisting their desires and ambitions to cruelty, depravity. The affected would turn on one another, becoming so corrupted they destroyed their families.

"Kingdoms were ruined, generations wiped out. She could do this with the gods too, but she was not malicious. Although that's a guess on my part, with what little is written of her. And while she never threatened the King of the Gods, Zeus was not happy there was someone out there with this kind of power, something that could be used against him.

"Thanatos, of course, thought it was Zeus behind her murder but Apollo put an end to the rumors with his gift of foresight. But his visions could not find the real culprit. Didn't stop the God of Death from raging when Zeus used the goddess's eye as an ornament for some random mortal. He was broken by her murder, and to have Zeus use her eye for a trinket and gift for a mortal was something Thanatos could not forgive. In his grief over her loss and fury at Zeus for his callousness, the God of Death altered the power of the amulet."

"Well? Don't keep me in suspense."

Grinning, Orry turned back to the wonderful scattering of texts across his workspace. "He made it so even those who did not have bad intentions would have their minds corrupted if the shepherd willed it. The halls of the afterlife filled with so many souls, at one point the Olympians convened about taking the amulet back. They were overwhelmed with prayers from their people, begging the gods to do something about the shepherd's power. He took over a kingdom, but I cannot find which one."

"Did Zeus get the amulet back?"

"He did not," a deep voice called out, startling them both.

Orry tensed as the trickster god, Hermes, lounged against the doorway to the library, his arms crossed at his chest. As usual, he wore a black silk tunic opened to reveal the golden skin of his chest, his black leather breeches tucked into the immaculate boots laced to his calves. His blond locks were pulled back and tied at his nape. Hermes watched them with a slight frown.

"Did you know her?" Terena asked, waving a hand at the papers before Orry. "The God of Ruin?"

"Aye," Hermes said. He pushed away from the door, strolling toward them with his arms still crossed. "She was lovely. Spent much of her time alone, though. None of us wanted to be anywhere near her. Not because she was an asshole or anything. But the power she wielded made us leery, lest Zeus think we were plotting his demise."

"And yet," Ren said, moving away from the table as Hermes neared, "Thanatos was the only one among you who didn't care about that. I find that interesting."

"Find it interesting all you want," Hermes snorted as he looked down at the ancient pages. "But I daresay, even you, niece, would quake before Zeus."

"So who killed Kaïra?"

Hermes shrugged. "We never found out. Shortly after, war broke out and then we were banished."

"And what of the shepherd's bloodline?" Orry asked, twisting in his seat to face Hermes. "What kingdom did they rule?"

Hermes spared a glance at him as he picked up a corner of a parchment near his hip. Dropping it back onto the table, he sighed. "Olethros. Tinos was the shepherd-turned-king. The first and only of his line to have the amulet. He was killed during the war, that I know." He clicked his tongue and looked over at Terena. "I don't know what became of the amulet, obviously. We were no longer around to care."

"So it could still be out there?" Ren asked, her hazel eyes narrowed.

"Possibly."

"And where was Olethros located? Perhaps we can trace the king's lineage and see if we can find the amulet." Orry looked up at the god with barely concealed excitement.

Hermes winked. "Olethros is now called Metilai."

TERENA LAUGHED.

Of course.

Dropping her chin, she grinned as she closed her eyes and shook her head.

"So, it could be in Emperor Solon's vaults as we speak?"

Hermes waved a hand dismissively. "If it was, I'd imagine Solon would've used it by now. He's been rounding up trackers who all possess amulets of power. And I do not believe he's descended from Tinos's bloodline. From what I've learned of his empire, that region's been conquered several times before Justinian the Fair took the crown and Heylisia was born."

"Right," Orry murmured. He was picking at his fingernails, biting his lip in a way Terena knew meant he was deep in thought.

"This arrived just now," Hermes said after a beat. He held up a folded slip of paper between his fingers, his aquamarine eyes on Terena.

Straightening, Terena took a step toward Hermes and snatched the missive, squinting at the words. Her eye twitched as she read. When she was finished, she lifted her gaze to find Hermes smiling faintly back at her.

"When do we leave?"

Orry turned, his eyes moving back and forth between Terena and Hermes. "What's going on?"

"Sonah's in Sparta."

Orry's brows shot to his hairline. "That's... what you expected, right?"

"Aye," Hermes said without taking his eyes off Terena. "We will leave in the morning."

Terena's pulse thrashed as she struggled to maintain calm. "Good. I'll be ready."

"I've already sent a note back confirming we're on our way. The cleric stays here until he figures out how to open the fucking portal." His gaze shifted at last to Orry.

Her friend visibly deflated. "I'd like to join you," Orry said, his eyes shifting to Terena. "Please? I've never been to Sparta, and perhaps the king would let me see—"

"I need you here to finish your studies," Hermes interrupted in a tone brooking no further argument.

Terena gave Orry an apologetic shrug.

"Go find your brother," Hermes said as he strode away. "He needs you."

"What did your men do now?" Terena grumbled as she strode after him.

"You'll see."

CHAPTER 2

SPARTA

Sonah Yahn stared at Crown Prince Lerek of Heylisia as if she'd seen a ghost.

He *was* a ghost.

He had to be.

Prince Lerek was murdered on his terrace in Metilai seven months ago.

And Sonah should know; she was accused—along with her sister, Terena Luca—of his murder.

Clutching the towel tight in her shaking hands, Sonah took a few tentative steps toward him.

"Prince Lerek?"

"Aye, Sonah," he said, with the same heartbreaking smile she knew so well. "It's me. I heard you were back here and thank the gods, I found the right tunnel exit this time."

"Tunnel? Prince—"

He came at her so fast she gasped as he threw his arms around her in a fierce embrace. Sonah froze, then lifted a hand to his back in a feeble attempt at a hug. Her mind struggled to keep up with reality. She trembled, and Lerek's arms tightened.

Dropping a kiss on her head before pulling back, Prince Lerek grinned at her, his brown eyes swimming with unshed tears. He swallowed a few times and chuckled.

"I didn't think I'd see you again," he said, his voice gruff. "Where's Terena? Is she with you?"

Sonah's stomach fell. She felt like throwing up. Images of Terena fighting Daris Antonius in Messene over what Sonah had told her flashed behind her eyes.

She was an idiot. And she should've kept her big idiot mouth shut.

"No, Prince—"

"It's Lerek, Sonah. For the millionth time."

"Lerek," she said and cleared her throat. "No, Lerek. By now, she's with the new king in the north."

He seemed dejected at her answer. She reached out and grabbed the sleeves of his tunic. When his cheeks colored, Sonah fumbled at her towel and ducked back into the bathing chamber.

Snatching her robe from the chair near the tub, she called out apologies to the prince. After cinching the sash tight around her waist, she smoothed her hair and walked out of the room to face him.

"What happened to you? How are you not dead?"

He looked the same as he had all those months ago, except his hair was much shorter and he wore the clothes of a Spartan courtier.

Then it hit her.

Isher. Isher is dead.

Sonah shook. The blood leeched down her body and she felt cold. So horribly cold.

"Gods," she whispered, shaking her head as the tears Lerek had held back finally fell. Sonah choked on a sob and Lerek rushed forward once more. He held her close as she cried, thoughts of Isher throughout the years flooding her mind, tearing at her soul. Her knees buckled and Lerek bent with her, cradling her as she kneeled on the floor and sobbed.

At length, her trembling settled, and she hiccuped as she pulled back to look at the prince.

"Was it... was it Daris? Was it Daris Antonius that killed him?"

"No," Lerek rushed to respond. "No. Gods, Sonah. There's so much to tell you. I fear I don't have time—"

"We have time!" she cried, her fingernails digging through the silk of his sleeves. "I need to know! I made a terrible mistake, Lerek, and I need to see if I can make it right!"

"Sonah, you were bathing," Lerek said and looked pointedly at the robe barely covering her.

Sonah's cheeks heated, and she pulled back, scrambling to her feet. She looked around frantically but Lerek turned his back.

"I'll let you get back to your bath," he said in a loud whisper, "but I will be back at midnight. Try not to fall asleep."

Before she could respond, he stalked toward the large gilded armoire opposite her bed. Sonah's mouth dropped when she noticed the doors were open. Her dresses were shoved to one side and a panel at the back hung open. She gawked as he pushed the panel back and stepped inside, shutting it firmly without a backward glance.

Sonah stood rooted for a long time before she lurched forward, touching the panel that was now just the back of her armoire.

As she felt around for the seam, a loud knock sounded at her door. Frowning, Sonah ducked out and took a step toward the sitting room.

"Yes?"

"Lady Sonah, King Altos requests your presence at dinner," the muffled voice of her guard, Jenos, replied through the thick oak.

She rushed into the sitting room and opened the door a crack. Peeking out, Sonah smiled when the guard stepped into her line of sight. "Thank you, Jenos."

When she made to close the door, Jenos reached out, his weathered hand curled around the wood. He looked down at the marble floor before he lifted his light blue eyes at her with a frown on his lined face. "Apologies, lady, but this time you are to come dressed... appropriately. The king has guests."

"Do you know whom he hosts?"

"Aye, lady," he said in a low grumble as he shifted his feet.

Jenos was much older than most of the Royal Guard, and when he'd first been assigned to her, his sheer size and frightening visage had kept Sonah from befriending him. But she'd soon realized he was little more than a giant puppy; his scarred countenance and big warrior's body hid a soft heart. She often wondered if King Altos knew her better than she realized.

It was clear, seeing him shuffling uncomfortably before her, whoever King Altos was entertaining was not to Jenos's liking.

"If you cannot say, I will not force you," Sonah said softly, and from the way he rubbed the back of his neck, Sonah knew she'd guessed correctly. Reaching out, she laid a hand on his vambrace and smiled. "Do I have time for a quick bath?"

Jenos lifted his blue gaze, his cheeks flushing deep red beneath his salt and pepper beard. "Aye, lady," he said in a rough voice. He ran a hand over the short grey hairs atop his head.

Sonah gave him a wide smile and thanked him again before shutting the door with a soft snick of the latch.

Turning back to the large sitting area of her rooms, Sonah leaned back against the door and closed her eyes.

Dinner with the king and mystery guests.

And a midnight meeting with a dead man.

Great.

STANDING TALL WITH JENOS AT HER SIDE, SONAH unclenched her hands once more. She hated how her body unconsciously betrayed her anxiety. Puffing out a breath, she pushed her shoulders back and lengthened her stride.

Jenos slid a glance at her.

"All right, lady?"

Sonah didn't look at the warrior, but she moved closer to him. "Aye, Jenos. Thank you. Just a little... it's been a while since I've worn dresses. I'm a bit uncomfortable."

"If it's not too bold to say," he replied in a low voice, "you look lovely."

Surprised, Sonah stumbled as she looked up at the old warrior. He shot his hand out and gripped her elbow so fast she knew no one watching would've seen her misstep. She silently thanked Altos again for Jenos's companionship.

"Thank you," she mumbled, then looked up at his stoic face. "Thank you, Jenos."

He nodded without looking at her, but she saw the color creep up his neck.

They arrived before the doors to the king's private dining room and Sonah blinked. She'd only ever been in this room for dinners alone with King Altos. When he had entertained guests in the past while she'd been in residence, it was always in the main hall next to the throne room.

The doors opened, and Sonah took a deep breath. When she caught sight of the king seated at the head of the large table, she strode in, chin up and shoulders stiff.

Her eyes shifted to the man who rose at her entrance.

Sonah balked.

Her throat tightened and she took a reflexive step back, stumbling into Jenos.

A woman she knew very well sat regally next to the man on the king's left, her eyes the same piercing dark brown Sonah had seen every year at the abbey for the first ten of her life before being sent to the White Palace.

She looked away from Sonah, her eyes falling to her plate.

The man standing stiffly beside the king, wearing a dark velvet doublet with a high collared tunic and satin breeches, stole her breath. His pale face looked even more colorless as he stared back at her through small brown eyes beneath a heavy brow.

Duke and Duchess Ovenno.

The people who'd pretended to be her parents her whole life.

COME BACK TO ME.

Daris Antonius shook his head for what felt like the hundredth time that day, pacing the small study he used as his office within Arestia Castle.

He'd had another awful night; sleep eluded him until the small hours of the morning when he was roused by his lieutenant, Jason Sotoris. The same dream he'd had since that day in Seleste a month ago haunted his sleep last night. Terena wrapped in his arms, sated after a night of passion. The last night before everything had gone to hells. In his dream, she nestled against his neck, her lips brushing the whorl of his ear as she whispered those words, over and over.

Come back to me.

Daris had taken to working himself to the bone during sparring sessions or out on scouting missions so as to fall into bed too tired to dream.

It failed every time.

Muttering to the gods about how much he needed to rest without Terena harassing his sleep, Daris stopped his pacing to scrub a hand down his face as he awaited the arrival of King Altos. Rubbing absently at the damnable ache in his chest he couldn't seem to soothe, he paced the confines of his study.

Compared to the king's rooms and the rest of the castle, this room was bare. There was a large round table to hold his maps and papers, and a small hutch where he kept some of his personal books and items. There were only enough chairs for himself, the king and one of the other officers in Altos's armies that would sometimes occupy the room. No curtain decorated the lone window overlooking the training yard and barracks.

The king had told Daris they'd meet after his dinner with Duke and Duchess Ovenno. Daris had fumed at being surprised by their visit, having had only a few days notice from the Spartans patrolling the eastern border. Even then, the king had warned him to say nothing to anyone until their arrival, especially Sonah.

Not that Sonah was speaking to him.

She'd made her opinion of him known—loudly—most of the trip back from Seleste. He'd tried to see her once more while at the castle, to no avail. The handful of messages he'd sent to her rooms were returned unopened and with messages of her own that made Jenos, her guard, color and stutter when he'd been forced to repeat them.

Daris cursed. He resumed his pacing, his thoughts once again occupied with the duke and his unexpected visit. Daris had warned King Altos there was no benefit to Sparta for the duke's visit. The only motive Daris thought made sense was Duke Ovenno planned to use Sonah. For what, though?

A knock sounded at his door, and before Daris could answer, his lieutenant, Jason, entered. His hair was mussed and clothes mud-spattered. He scowled as he caught Daris's eye and shut the door before cursing under his breath.

"What is it?"

"Heylisia's legion from Elis has crossed into Ibros. They're headed south."

Daris roared, swiping a hand across the table. Paper scattered and rained onto the floor with his uncharacteristic loss of control over his emotions.

Fuming, he ran a hand through his hair, cursing when it snagged over the ties to his eyepatch. Turning away from Jason, he adjusted it before glancing at the Liodari. "Find Captains Athanasi and Leonidas. I want them here within the next ten minutes."

"Aye."

"Jason."

His lieutenant turned back.

"Ready the men to ride out. I'll speak to the king after his dinner. I have a feeling Duke Ovenno travelled with the legion. And if I'm right, he's once again sided with Emperor Solon. I need you and the men ready in case they're here for Sonah."

Jason stilled at Sonah's name but recovered quickly, nodding as he strode for the door.

Daris closed his eye.

He was in for a long night.

CHAPTER 3

SPARTA

Sonah's head pounded. She was sure the throbbing at her right temple was fast enough to burst a vein. She stared at Duke Ovenno as she struggled to still her trembling.

"Sonah! Come, please, join us," King Altos said with a smile more like a grimace. When Sonah turned her gaze to him, she noted how stiff he seemed, how tight his face.

She jerked out of her trance when she felt Jenos's hand at the small of her back.

"Lady?"

In silence, she moved on leaden legs, her steps heavy as she made her way to the table. With his guests already seated, Sonah was unsure of where she should sit.

Duke Ovenno stepped behind the chair at King Altos's right side and pulled it out. The loud grating of the chair against the marble floor made her flinch.

Looking to the king for help, Sonah soon realized none was forthcoming. Altos dropped his gaze, his lips pinched as he stood, waiting.

Sonah walked until she stood beside the seat Duke Ovenno was still holding, her eyes not daring to meet his. When she moved to sit, she shuddered as he pushed the seat in for her.

Her eyes lifted to meet those of the duchess. The woman's face
was ashen. Her hand shook as it lifted her crystal wine glass to her
pinched ruby lips.

"Now," King Altos said brusquely after taking his seat, "as Duke
Ovenno is still your... guardian, he and the duchess have come to
take you home."

Sonah blanched. Cold flashed over her and the blood left her
face.

While she'd been the Royal Taster to Crown Prince Lerek during
her time at the White Palace, she was thought to have been Duke
Ovenno's daughter. Now, months after the assassination of the
crown prince—no, it had been Isher who was murdered—the ruse
was no longer necessary.

So why come here? Why continue this game?

"To that end," the king continued after an awkward pause, "you
will return with him—"

"What?!" Sonah shot to her feet, her chest heaving as she stared
in horror at the king. "You would—"

"Silence!"

Sonah stood for a long moment after the king's bellow, then
quickly sat. She alternated between fear and rage. She had not gone
so far as to think of him as a friend, but she had thought King Altos
would at least have fought harder for her. But he seemed more than
fine with handing her over to the very man who had set her up as a
pawn in a madman's palace.

The quiet thickened as Altos gestured for the servants. Sonah
fumed, the sounds of plates and glasses and cutlery filled the taut
silence around them. With their work completed, the servants
vanished, save for a footman standing far enough behind the king's
chair as to be out of sight.

"Dear Sonah," Duke Ovenno said, his booming voice making her
cringe. "I regret I was unable to come to the White Palace after..."

Sonah lifted her eyes enough to glare at King Altos, who was
watching her with a glare of his own.

"You continue this—" Sonah flung out a hand, almost knocking over her water glass. She righted it and turned her glare from the king to the duke. "You continue this *farce* even now? I will go nowhere with you." She turned her narrowed eyes to Altos. "I hope—"

The king stood so abruptly his chair crashed to the ground before a servant scurried over to pick it up. Sonah flinched but otherwise did not back down.

"If you'll excuse us, Ovenno," King Altos ground out. Pulling Sonah's chair out roughly, he seized her wrist, all but dragging her out of her seat. Sonah gasped, her face hotter than the sun as she rushed to keep up with the king's stride.

She hadn't been looking where he led. Thrusting her into a room she'd never been in before, Altos slammed the door shut before rounding on her with fury blazing in his eyes.

"There's more going on here than just Duke Ovenno coming to Sparta," Altos seethed as he stepped dangerously close to Sonah. She had the wherewithal to shrink back. "You *know* I am aware they are *not* your parents. I had hoped you'd also know I would never put you in harm's way. You are very important to me. To Sparta. But I need you to play along so we can find out what exactly is behind this unexpected visit. Why he'd have the audacity to come here in the first place!"

Sonah was taken aback by the fury punctuating his words. She'd known the king long enough to form an opinion of the man she believed was shared by all who knew him.

This was not that man.

Altos must've seen something on her face because he blinked as if waking from a trance and took a step back. He ran a hand over his mouth and took a deep breath. "I need you to play along. And I need you not to defy me in front of them. You will not like the conse-quences, Lady Sonah. I promise you will not."

Sonah's eyes stung with tears, turning the king's face blurry. She gave him a curt nod. An endless moment later he turned, cursing under his breath as he strode to the door, yanking it open with enough force, the wind from it cooled Sonah's hot cheeks.

Quickly wiping the few traitorous tears escaping her control, Sonah rushed to follow the king.

As Sonah retook her seat, she dared a look over at him. King Altos was a master of disguise. No longer the wrathful sovereign he'd been a moment before, the man at the table now looked jovially over at his guests and gestured for them to eat.

Across from her, the duke began to eat as he spoke of how happy he was to see Sonah again. The conversation made her ill, as did his stupid smile.

"Sonah," Altos said, his voice kinder than his countenance, "your... parents will remain at Arestia for a few days before you all leave together. I will have Commander Antonius and a contingent of his men escort you back with the duke and duchess when it's time to leave."

"That's not necessary, Your Majesty," Duke Ovenno said with an oily smile. "I've men of my own capable of escorting us. As you know."

The king's smile could wither freshly budded wisteria. When he deigned to respond, his words were harsh.

"If I trusted your men over mine, I wouldn't need to send my best warrior to protect Lady Sonah. You've proven once you're incapable of guarding her." His lips twisted in a derisive smile, Altos lifted his wine goblet in a mock salute. "It wasn't an offer, Ovenno. It is my command."

Sonah barely heard. The loud buzzing in her ears had taken over almost all of her hearing. She sat there, numb, her eyes dropping back down to her plate filled with food that made her nauseous. Her lip curled as Duke Ovenno chimed in, his loud voice grating on her nerves.

Sonah looked across at the duchess. She swore she had seen sympathy there before the older woman dropped her gaze.

"May I be excused?" Sonah asked abruptly, interrupting the duke.

Sonah did not wait for King Altos to respond before she pushed away from the table. "I feel terribly ill."

Color bloomed in the king's neck and cheeks, but he waved to Jenos, who came quickly to her side. Catching her elbow in his large hand, he guided her away from the table.

As they made their way to the doors, Jenos grunted. "That was not wise."

Sonah was beyond caring. She needed to lie down for a bit.

And prepare for her midnight meeting with Prince Lerek.

DARIS WAS HONEST WITH HIMSELF THAT THE TENSION WITH HEYLISIA AND being surprised by the simpering duke and his wife were not what bothered him.

It was that gods damned dream.

It had been over a month since the events in Seleste. Longer since Terena had fought him over his betrayal. And while he hadn't killed Prince Lerek, he hadn't told her about his role in those events.

She had every right to be angry. To hate him.

He hated himself for it.

The door swung open behind him and Daris turned, with rage at the intrusion ready to be unleashed on whomever made the unfortunate mistake of bothering him.

He stopped cold when King Altos entered.

The king paused when he saw the look on Daris's face. He glanced at the scattered papers, then back at Daris. Closing the door behind him, the king turned with a scowl.

"I need you to ready a company of your men," he said, stepping further into the room. Daris straightened. "The duke will leave in two days' time, and you are to go with them."

Daris remained silent as he watched his king.

"As you'd thought, they've come for Sonah Yahn," the king added, his hard eyes narrowed. "There's been another development."

"You've heard already?" Daris asked, crossing his arms across his chest. He trusted Jason's discretion and would not suspect him of circulating the news of Heylisians moving through Ibros. He could only assume it was the scout who'd returned, but he was still annoyed word had spread before he'd had time to plan a response with the other officers.

"Heard what?"

"Heylisians have crossed into Ibros. The duke forgot to mention it?"

The king's face darkened. "That insolent weasel. No, he failed to mention an army at his back. Fuck."

"What did you mean, then? What other development?"

"I received word from the northern king yesterday," King Altos said. "I put off responding, but with Duke Ovenno's arrival and demands, I'm glad I did."

"What'd he say?"

"Either the Fates play games with us, or the plan is unfolding as it should," Altos said absently. He turned back to face Daris. "The king is on his way here. For Sonah Yahn."

Daris smothered the curse burning the back of his throat and closed his eye for a beat before responding.

"Terena?"

"He did not say. I will send him a note after this, but I cannot think of a way to stall the duke until the king's arrival. Duke Ovenno is still under the impression we do not know who Sonah really is, and I've done nothing to disabuse him of the notion. So here's how we'll play it to our advantage. I've told him you'll be joining Sonah as her escort. Pick ten of your best to go with you. I want to know what that fool is up to, and with you in his castle, you can monitor him and his dealings as well as protect Sonah."

"And the army in Ibros?"

"Let me worry about that. Your concern is Sonah."

"Sire, I don't think—"

"You are Sonah's guardian," Altos said, narrowing his dark brown eyes. "You will go with her. If I can convince the King of Olympus to send Terena Luca after you two, Sonah will never reach Ovenno."

Daris's heart stopped, then sped up painfully. Carefully schooling his features, he stayed silent as he waited for Altos to say more.

The king looked at him for a moment before he nodded and turned away. He walked to the window and stared out, his back to Daris.

"It is not going well for them," Altos continued. "I believe the duke and his allies seek to use Sonah for the same purpose as us."

The king turned back to him and smiled at the look on Daris's face.

"Aye. I believe they wish to bait Terena to their side. To lure her into their war against Emperor Solon. To use gods to fight against the emperor's growing power. Somehow, he has managed to find gods of his own."

"Impossible," Daris said before he could stop himself.

"That was my thought as well," Altos said with an arch of his eyebrow. "And yet the duke brought news of a situation prompting his journey here."

The king paced back to the window and stared out in silence. Daris waited, fists clenched at his sides.

"The emperor has reclaimed Ravos. Duke Ovenno was not forthcoming with details, except to say the emperor sent General Peleon to treat with Duke Ravos. It was a ruse. The general had someone with him who had powers similar to Terena. This... god, was with Peleon. They were sent with a message for Duke Ravos's allies."

"What message?"

Daris felt a prickle of unease slide down his spine as the king shook his head.

"Duke Ravos was the message. He was dumped outside the gates of Calla. Ovenno's men found him after the morning shift change."

Daris's blood went cold. Calla was the capital of Ovenno. If Solon's men could get that close to the duke and not be seen...

"They killed him?" Daris asked, steeling himself for the answer.

King Altos rubbed his eyes with his thumb and forefinger, then opened his bloodshot eyes, staring at Daris with resignation.

"They melted his face. The duke said they didn't even know it was him until after the healers revived him. He told Duke Ovenno the emperor has gods fighting for him, and that they are coming for him and Duke Aurora next. He died shortly thereafter."

There was a loud ringing in Daris's ears. A long time passed before the king spoke again.

"We have to send Sonah with them, Daris," Altos whispered. "We've no choice now. The northern king has threatened war if we do not return Sonah to him and Terena. I'd rather he visited his wrath on Solon than Sparta. You will go with Sonah, ensure her safety. I don't want Duke Ovenno getting any stupid ideas about leveraging her for amnesty."

Daris opened his mouth to speak but Altos held up a hand to stay him. "Terena will come for her, Daris. I want you there when she does."

"She hates me," he bit out, his eyes on the ground in frustration.

"Aye, well, hopefully some of what she felt for you before remains and she'll listen to you when you explain about Lerek. It's time. We've no choice."

CHAPTER 4

OLYMPIA

Croak stayed close to his sister as they rounded the corner and saw the men milling about in the main hall of The Keep. She'd found him yesterday moments before the blood rushing to his head made him pass out.

With Rydon and Gabriol's help, they'd lifted him back from the battlements where Hermes's scum had ambushed and hung him over the wall upside down. Croak had screamed his head off, panicking when the rope slipped. His heart had lodged in his throat as he'd tried to remain still so as not to further tempt the Fates. A lifetime later, he looked up into his sister's grim face and cried with joy at seeing her—and being rescued, of course.

Hermes's idiots had laughed at Croak when he followed his sister into the dining hall. They weren't laughing when she left, though. Hermes had berated her for unleashing her fury on his men, one of whom lost a leg during their argument. She'd pushed back, telling him they'd started it by picking on Croak, although he took exception to the 'picking on' part. He was certain he threatened their masculinity with his own virile personality and lashed out like a bunch of babies.

Or perhaps it was the innocent prank he'd pulled on them with the snake he and Orry had found in the old ruins outside the palace.

Hermes looked up as they arrived and he motioned for Terena. Croak hurried to stay close, casting a scathing look at one of Hermes's men who had the audacity to smirk at him. His black eye and split lip made Croak feel better, though.

"Another message from Altos," Hermes said when Terena stopped beside him.

"What now?"

The god's usually smiling countenance was no longer on display. He looked annoyed as he thrust a crumpled note at her. "Duke Ovenno is in Sparta, asserting his parental rights. He wants Sonah to go back to Ovenno with him. The king suspects it has something to do with Emperor Solon putting pressure on the provinces no longer under his control."

"So we go to Calla," Terena said as she handed the message back to Hermes.

"No." He stroked his chin and turned away. "I will still take my army south, for Sparta. You take Gabriol and Rydon and go to Calla. Take Migela too," he added, motioning to the tall, Offeni assassin who'd joined them a fortnight ago. Migela strolled up, her hand on the hilt of her sword as she smiled grimly at Terena.

The raven-haired Offeni wore all black, her hair long on the right side while the left side was shorn to the scalp. Her nose twinkled from the jewel through her left nostril as she tilted her head and signed in greeting. Migela was mute, her tongue taken when she was a child during an invasion that killed her family. She was now one of the deadliest assassins on the continent and Croak was glad to have her on their side.

She was also a little sweet on a certain cleric.

"It'll take them a few weeks to get there," Terena said after she acknowledged Migela. "Why don't I go south with you and we can intercept them?"

"I need you to do something else for me," Hermes said distractedly as he nodded at something one of his men whispered in his ear.

Turning back to Terena, he said, "I want you to find a tracker that has... eluded some of my finest mercenaries. One of my scouts found her in a village west of Vesala. I was going to put it off for now, but since that's where your sister's headed, I thought it best to send you now."

"If your man found her, why can't he bring her back?"

Hermes sighed dramatically. "Because she gave him a message for me. She will only go with the Royal Tracker."

"Me?"

"I assume that's who she meant," Hermes sang out sarcastically. His goons chuckled as Hermes turned to leave. Terena dogged his steps just as Rydon and Gabriol descended the staircase to their right. Croak caught Rydon's eye and strolled over to him.

"She said it like that? She called me the Royal Tracker?"

"Aye."

"What's going on?" Rydon asked as Croak neared. He didn't stop and Croak jogged a few steps to keep pace with him as he and Gabriol followed Ren.

"We're going to Ovenno," Croak said, failing to keep the excitement from his voice. "The duke went to Sparta and is taking Sonah back to Calla with him."

Rydon started, his steps pausing as he glanced over at Croak. "No."

"Aye," Croak grinned, "and now Hermes wants Ren to find a tracker for him. Who is also in Ovenno."

"Fuck," Gabriol muttered, wedging his big body between Croak and Rydon, forcing Croak into the wall. He mumbled curses under his breath as he ran to Rydon's left.

"Why this tracker?" Ren called out.

Hermes turned. "I was told she would help us."

"That's great Hermes." Ren laughed. Spreading her arms she asked, "Help us how?"

Ignoring her, Hermes smiled as he added, "When you have Sonah, meet me in Metilai. I'll expect you there by your nameday."

"What?" Ren scoffed, striding after Hermes. "Why Metilai? You never said—"

"I told you we were taking back what is ours," the god replied after he'd mounted his warhorse. Resting a hand on his thigh, he scowled down at their little group. "Destroying the empire was always at the top of my list. After getting your sister back, my plan was always to attack Metilai."

"And what of the shroud?" Ren sounded exasperated as she flung out her arms.

In the month they'd known Hermes, the god had spent most of his time training Terena to use her powers. While she'd grown in her abilities, especially the closer she was to her nameday, he was cagey with details surrounding the Olympians.

Especially her father, Ares.

"Hopefully, the cleric figures it out. We'll be back for him when the time comes. But Solon and his empire need to be dealt with first."

"Hear, hear," Croak called out and stamped his foot. Rydon threw a grimace his way as Gabriol smacked the back of his head.

Hermes turned his mount and looked at Ren over his shoulder, grinning. "I thought you'd be pleased! You'll be back with your sister in a few weeks and by the time you ascend with all your powers at long last, you'll have revenge on the man who almost killed you."

"There's war all across the eastern side of the continent," Rydon called out, stepping up to stand at Terena's side. "And you want us to head right into it? At least give us a host of soldiers to travel with us."

Hermes looked down at Rydon in disbelief. His hellion of a horse snorted and Croak swore the puff of vapor was smoke from the fires of Hades rather than the cold.

"You travel with a god," Hermes spat, his jovial expression at odds with his harsh tone. "You yourself are immortal. Soon you'll have another god to travel with so believe me, Eudaemon, you're in a much better position to traverse this continent than I am."

Gabriol snorted and Croak let out a disbelieving chuckle. The god pretended at humility about as well as a viper pretended at being docile.

"Two months," Hermes said as he pointed at Terena. "I will see you in Metilai. Bring the tracker with you when you find her."

NEAR VESALA, OVENNO

A week later, they arrived at the village outside of Vesala where Hermes said they'd find the tracker. The stars emerged and shadows gathered as the night deepened. Terena slowed as they neared their destination.

The rundown looking building did not resemble any tavern Terena had ever frequented. In fact, it looked deserted. No one stood outside and there were no sounds coming from within as she, Croak, and Rydon, stopped in front of the abandoned watering hole. Migela and Gabriol were on watch, standing on either end of the empty street, hidden in shadows.

"Did we make a wrong turn?" Croak asked as he swiveled around, looking up and down the street. The buildings on either side seemed just as rundown, seedy in a way that spoke more of criminal activity rather than despair and poverty.

Terena glanced around, her eyes narrowed as she took in their surroundings. "Stay sharp," she murmured, clapping her brother on his shoulder. "Someone's watching us."

Rydon scowled as his hand drifted to the broadsword at his side.

"Should we leave?" Croak's voice was barely above a whisper, but Terena heard the panic beneath.

"We'll be fine," Rydon muttered, arching an auburn eyebrow and lifting his chin at Terena. "We've got a god with us. And I'm immortal."

"God or not," Croak sputtered, stepping closer to both his sister and Rydon. "She's still months away from her nameday. When she ascends, I'll rest easier about visiting establishments such as this."

"I told you to stay behind," Terena hissed as she cast him a baleful glance before walking toward the rotting wooden door of the tavern. According to Hermes, this is where his mercenary had seen their quarry.

"Aye, and what would I do sitting back there with only Orry for company?" Croak grimaced. "I'd go mad within a week."

"Shut your hole," Rydon growled, grabbing Croak by his cloak and dragging him along.

Terena put her hand to the door, then pressed her ear against it. Hearing nothing, she pulled back and lifted her hand to knock.

"Don't do that!" Croak whispered loudly.

Ignoring her brother, Terena's tentative knock barely reached her ears.

Yet she heard the soft snick of a lock disengaging. Glancing over her shoulder at Rydon, Terena stepped back, her hands settling on the hilts of her short swords.

The door opened a crack. Heart thudding against her ribcage, Terena waited, stiffening her frame. Seconds passed, but no one showed up on the other side as the door remained ajar. Twisting her lips, Terena puffed out a breath in annoyance and pushed open the door.

Pitch black enveloped her as she stood inside the entryway. She could not tell if the room was large or not, if there was another room beyond where she stood at all.

Rydon's breath tickled her cheek as he leaned close. "What do you think?"

"Reminds me of another tavern you and I went to a few months back," she muttered. Terena pulled her swords from their scabbards slowly so as not to make a sound. Gripping their leather-bound hilts, she hefted them as she took cautious steps deeper into the darkened interior.

A grunt followed by a whimper from behind them made Terena whip her head around, only to hear Croak cursing under his breath. Rydon cuffed him, slapping a hand over her brother's mouth to stop another cry escaping his lips.

"You've come a long way for me," a disembodied voice said from above.

Terena craned her neck. There was nothing to see in the void.

"Do you think it wise? Hunting someone with no wish to be found?"

Terena remained silent. Her feet whispered across the ground, putting distance between her and Rydon.

"Has he even told you why he seeks me?" the voice continued, now in front of them.

Terena heard a gasp behind her and turned. Rydon swore, his sword lifted as light flared around them.

Her face darkened as Croak was brought forward, eyes wide in his ashen face. A dark-skinned woman with light brown hair plaited over her shoulder had one arm banded around his stomach, the other lifted to where she held a dagger with a curved edge to his throat. A small gold loop winked at them from the woman's eyebrow as she turned her lips to Croak's temple.

"If you leave now, I won't skin this little one. And you'll tell your god I want no part in his plans."

Rydon snarled and made to lunge at the woman, but Terena stayed him with an arm flung out to his chest.

Without breaking her stare, she said in a calm voice, "If you do not unhand my brother, now, *I* will skin *you*."

The woman's lips stretched into a wide smile. "Aye. I believe you. So we can agree to leave each other alone?"

"I was told you asked for me."

"By whom?"

"You asked for the Royal Tracker," Terena replied in a clipped tone. Spreading her arms out, she grimaced. "Here I am."

With that, the woman released Croak, who stumbled forward. Rydon grabbed hold of his jerkin and yanked him to his side, his sword still held aloft.

The woman kept her dark eyes trained on Terena, the smile still in place. "I'll admit, I did not think Hermes would send his best."

"I am not his best," Terena ground out, her body vibrating with violence. "I am his equal."

The woman blinked, and for a moment so brief it could've been a trick of the eye, Terena swore she saw confusion cross her sharp features. When she tossed her head back and laughed, Terena almost snapped.

"No, goddess, you are not."

To Terena's surprise, the woman sheathed her curved dagger and covered her heart with her hand.

"You have no equal."

CHAPTER 5

SPARTA

Moonlight streamed through Sonah's bedchamber windows. Despite the sharp bite of the winter winds, she liked them open. It was the only light she would allow, so anyone who passed her rooms would believe she was asleep.

When Jenos had left her at her door earlier, she had bid him good night, claiming a lethargy she was very good at faking. The old warrior had nodded and left her reluctantly. He remained outside her door as always.

Sonah paced through her bedchamber and out into the sitting room. The dying embers in the hearth glowed softly as she passed. Turning, she made her way back into her bedchamber as the doors of her armoire creaked open. Jumping at the sudden movement, Sonah pressed her hand to her chest and held her breath.

Lerek's smiling face looked up at her as he hopped down from the wardrobe.

"Gods, Prince Lerek, you gave me a fright," she whispered as she exhaled.

Dusting off his grey breeches, she noticed how casually he was dressed. She'd never seen Prince Lerek looking anything less than royal. He could be a stable hand the way he was outfitted.

"Were you expecting someone else?"

"What? No!"

Lerek grinned at her. They stood in silence for a moment before Lerek launched forward and hugged Sonah tight to his chest. Sonah's squeak was smothered in the prince's chest and for a few seconds she stood stiff in his arms. Then she relaxed, inhaling deeply. He smelled of sandalwood and spices. Like home.

She sighed. Not home, she supposed. Rather, her former prison.

They spoke at the same time.

"Sonah—"

"Lerek—"

Lerek pulled away and grinned at her. "You go first."

Taking a few steps away, Sonah glanced out toward the sitting room before turning back to Lerek.

"We need to leave. I had dinner with the king tonight. Duke and Duchess Ovenno are here. King Altos is making me go back to Ovenno with them and—"

"Your father's here? Perfect! Let me go—"

"No!"

Lerek stilled as she grabbed hold of his forearm. She cursed herself for being too loud and stood a moment in silence, listening for Jenos.

When she was satisfied, she turned back to the prince.

"If Duke Ovenno's here, he can help us, Sonah," Lerek hissed.

"You don't—" She shook her head and tried again. "There is much I need to tell you, Prince Lerek."

"It's just 'Lerek' to you, Sonah. And I have much to tell you as well."

"You go first."

He frowned at her, and after a moment's pause, gave her a curt nod. Striding toward the armchair next to her bed, he dropped onto it with a heavy sigh.

"I had a plan," he said, his eyes rising to the ceiling. He laughed. Sonah moved to the bed and sat as she regarded him.

"I thought I was being smart. Careful. It all seemed perfect in my head, you see." Lerek rubbed a hand down his face. "All I needed was something plausible, something my father would agree to, in order for me to leave the palace. When word came to us of the new northern king, I thought it a blessing from the Fates."

Sonah twisted her fingers in her lap. "I don't understand."

Lerek smiled sadly. "I planned on switching places with Isher, Sonah. So I could leave and be with Terena Luca. I love her. I've always loved her. But my father had other plans for me and I had to do something."

Sonah's head snapped up. She gaped at the prince. "What?"

"I'd been planning for months. I told Isher about it the last time he was at the White Palace and after much arm-twisting, he agreed to help. I bided my time. And just when I'd given up hope of figuring out how to get away, my father hands me a reason. The new northern king.

"I had the steward, Solarus, speak with my father about sending me north to meet with the northern king. I knew if it came from his steward, my father would be more open to the idea than if I'd gone to him directly.

"When he sent for me to tell me of his plan to send me north, I could barely contain my excitement. But he wanted me to leave the very next day. I had no time to let Isher know, so I sent a note telling him to meet me in Laurica. I tried stalling, but all it bought me was a few hours. The morning of our departure, I received a note from him saying he was already on his way to Metilai."

Lerek must've taken Sonah's dumbfounded expression as amazement, or awe at his ingenuity. He smiled at her as if she was not completely horrified by his stupidity.

"You..." Sonah covered her mouth. She couldn't finish the sentence. She wasn't entirely certain she wouldn't leap off the bed and strangle him. Because of him, Isher was murdered. Because of him, she and Terena had been accused and dumped in the dungeons.

Terena was tortured because of his ridiculous plan.

Sonah shook with the force of her rage.

Lerek's smiled faded as he watched her.

"Sonah, I did not know—"

"That your actions would cause Isher's murder? That I would be accused of conspiring with traitors? Or that Terena—"

"The only one who knew of my plan was Duke Aurora!" Lerek hissed, shooting up from the chair. "I thought he'd betrayed me, but King Altos insisted that was not the case. Someone else within the palace must've known of my plan. And even the duke's and Sparta's involvement. Someone with access.

"Originally, Isher and I were to switch places the morning of our departure. He would act as me, traveling with the convoy, while I stayed behind as him. I planned on leaving for Aurora the following evening and sending for Terena when I arrived. I even had a priest waiting in Avonon to marry us!"

Sonah jerked upright, shushing Lerek as she motioned wildly with her hands. Turning away, Sonah looked toward the door to the sitting room, waiting for Jenos to storm in at any moment.

When that did not happen, she folded her arms at her chest and turned back to the prince. In a loud whisper, she asked, "How are you here, then? If Duke Aurora betrayed you, why was Daris Antonius involved? Why bring you here?"

Lerek sighed and his shoulders slumped. "King Altos insists the duke did not. Betray me, that is. Aurora had gone to them with my plan. He wanted the firstborns out of the palace and saw this as his chance. I cannot blame, him, of course. He is—was—a good friend and I tried to protect his sister, Analise, as best I could. But he wanted her home, away from my father.

"You, more than anyone, know best the life of a palace taster. My father may have thought it would keep the provinces in line, having their firstborns at the palace, but they were—are—angry. I guess none of them were ever truly a friend to me. It killed Duke Aurora thinking about his sister in danger every day. I'm sure you felt the same. And I am sorry it never crossed my mind to think you might be unhappy there."

Sonah ducked her head. She'd hated being the Royal Taster. But she hated the isolation even more. For whatever reason, she never fit in. Perhaps it's because she wasn't really a firstborn.

"So the duke went to King Altos with a bargain," Lerek continued. "According to the king, in exchange for help getting the firstborns out of the White Palace, Aurora gave him something the king's been searching for for years. The duke used my plan as the distraction he needed for Daris and his men to smuggle the firstborns out. They were going to drug Isher with a sedative that would put him in such a deep sleep, he'd appear dead. And since my original plan was to switch places with Isher, the Liodari planned to smuggle me away, along with the firstborns, during the funeral for Isher. King Altos assured me there was no plan to kill Isher, only to give the appearance of his death. And while I was taken away with the firstborns, Isher would miraculously rise from the dead. As me."

He dragged a hand through his hair, displacing his carefully coiffed locks.

Sonah watched the guilt and remorse chase each other across his face.

"Why was Daris even there? Why didn't Duke Aurora send his own people?" Sonah shook her head. She lifted her hands to her temples. "I don't understand any of this."

Lerek dropped his head back, closing his eyes with a deep sigh.

"I only know what King Altos shared with me. That Aurora went to him to ask for his help. So the king sent his Liodari. They had someone on the inside to put the sedative in Isher's drink and put my clothes on him."

"But you invited me! To your rooms! I had a missive right after dinner, requiring my presence because you were having drinks with your brother."

He looked up at her, one hand outstretched as he beseeched her. "That was not me, Sonah! I swear on my life. I did not write that missive."

Sonah shook her head, tears threatening once more and she shut her eyes tight. When she could speak without fear of her voice breaking, she asked, "Then why is Isher dead? How did the plan go awry?"

"I do not know for certain. I remember Terena screaming at me and the Imperial Guard taking me away. The Royal Physician gave me a sedative and I was left alone to sleep. When I awoke, we were on our way to Aurora. I wasn't told of... I wasn't told about Isher until after we'd arrived in Avonon.

"Daris said he'd had a man stationed near my rooms, to keep an eye on me. The man reported back to him of your arrival, and Daris became suspicious. He went to my rooms himself to investigate and found the guards slaughtered. Then he found us. Someone else was there, he said. He saw Isher... he saw someone hooded, standing over me and when he rushed toward me, the person fled over the balcony. I'm not sure how anyone could've survived a fall from that height, but there was no word of anyone being found dead from a fall, so..." He sighed and looked over at her. "They snuck me out with the firstborns the morning of the... execution."

Sonah inhaled raggedly, her throat clogged with emotion she tried to control.

After a long silence filled only with the sounds coming from the fire in the hearth, Sonah hugged her arms close to her body and looked into Lerek's eyes.

"So here we are," Sonah said with a sigh.

"Aye," Lerek replied, shoulders slumping.

She narrowed her eyes. "The fact remains, both Duke and Duchess Ovenno are here and Altos has agreed to let them take me with them."

"That's good!" Lerek said, pouncing forward with a vicious smile. "Find a way to tell your father about me and—"

"He's not my father," Sonah grumbled.

"What? What's that mean?"

"He's not my father, Lerek. He never was." She heaved a sigh. In a lower voice, Sonah said, "I couldn't tell you before. I couldn't tell *anyone*. I'm an orphan. Duke and Duchess Ovenno found me at Lethe Monastery when I was an infant. They used me. Presented me to Emperor Solon as their own. I was to act as their daughter or the duke would have the abbot and monks at the monastery killed."

"Oh, Sonah," Lerek sighed, raking his hand through his hair as he turned away. He muttered curses, pacing before the window.

With a frustrated sound, he flew toward the curtains and yanked them across the window. "Damned cold, even here in Sparta!"

Long minutes passed in silence, thickening the longer it stretched.

"I can't go with them, Lerek," Sonah whispered. When he remained silent, she glanced up at him. He watched her with big brown eyes and she shook her head, dropping her gaze. "I can't. I can... leave word with them about you if you'd like. But I cannot go. I need to find Terena. And she's with the northern king."

Lerek darted toward her, his mouth dropping open. "She is? Then I'm coming with you. We'll go together. We'll leave tonight!"

"Tonight?" she squeaked loudly. Clamping a hand over her mouth, she cast a look at the doorway again before moving closer to Lerek. "We cannot leave tonight! We need to prepare! We need food, supplies! Do you know how long the journey is?"

After a moment, Lerek nodded, stroking his chin as he paced away. "Aye, you're right."

"You've never been outside the empire," she chided softly. "When we were on the run, we spent most of our time in the woods, sleeping on the ground with nothing in our bellies sometimes. And we had warriors with us! And Terena! I love you, Lerek, you know I do, but you are no warrior. I don't think I've ever even seen you wield a sword. You'd be even less useful than I am."

"Fine," Lerek said through gritted teeth as he glared at her. "What do you suggest, then?"

"I need to think," she muttered. Sitting on her bed, she chewed on a fingernail.

"How long do we have?"

When Sonah cast him a sour look, Lerek gestured impatiently. "I mean, how long before you're to leave with Ovenno?"

"Oh. Uh, Two days, I think."

"We'll need horses," Lerek mumbled, pacing before her.

"Aye."

"And food, of course."

"Ugh! Stop! I said I'm thinking!"

Lerek's eyes widened, and he stared at her as if she'd suddenly grown a second head. She spared him a glance.

"What?"

He shook his head slowly. "You've... you're different. You've changed since..."

"Aye," Sonah said.

They were silent once more while Sonah thought about how to gather the supplies they'd need for their journey. They'd need coin as well, which would be more difficult for her to figure out.

"Could we perhaps send word to Terena? We could have her meet us somewhere."

Sonah was about to rebuke him for interrupting her thoughts when she caught his hopeful expression. An unwanted thought snuck its way into her head and she blanched.

While Sonah was certain Terena would be glad of Lerek's... resurrection, she wasn't sure how much to tell Lerek about what had happened since Isher's death.

So she said nothing.

"We can send word to her when we get out of here," she demurred, fidgeting.

"Fine," Lerek said with a nod. "But if Ovenno is to leave in two days, we need to be gone by tomorrow. Do you think you can get what we'll need?"

"Wait, you're not going to help?"

"I can't, Sonah! They barely let me out of my rooms except for meals and to walk around a private courtyard. I'm kept away from everyone. The only reason I found out you were even here is because one of the guards gossips. That's how I knew you and Terena were here months ago."

"Why are they still holding you? Have they said?"

"Not entirely, no. King Altos said it was for my protection, since there are traitors in the White Palace, obviously. Whoever it was meant to have both me and my brother killed. The king has tried more than once to convince me to agree publicly I am with Sparta. He thinks it will convince the rest of the provinces to secede from Heylisia if I challenge my father for his throne."

"Why don't you?"

Lerek gaped at her. "I may have disagreed with my father on many things, especially his strange obsession with conquering Sparta, but that doesn't mean I would depose him! He is the rightful sovereign of a mighty empire. He is my father! I will not go against him, now more than ever. He's lost one son already. And there are traitors in his court. He needs me."

Sonah sighed and closed her eyes. "Then why would you agree to go with me to Terena?"

"Because I love her," he said vehemently, with a fire in his eyes she'd not seen before. "I love her and this time, nothing will stop me from being with her."

I can think of one thing, Sonah thought with a sigh.

CHAPTER 6

NEAR VESALA, OVENNO

Rydon's gaze swiveled between Terena and the strange woman. Croak shuffled at his side and Rydon tightened his hold on the boy to stay his movements.

"You know who I am?" Terena asked, putting her swords away. The woman they'd been tracking, a tracker herself, lowered her arm to her belt, tucking her thumb beneath the leather.

She seemed relaxed for someone a hair's breadth away from being gutted by a god for threatening her brother.

"I do," the woman said, but did not elaborate.

"Then you know why we—"

"Hermes too afraid to do his own dirty work?"

Rydon scowled. He opened his mouth to give her a good dressing down when Terena laughed.

"So you know him?"

The tracker woman chuckled. With a shrug of her shoulders as she spread out her arms, she took a step closer to Terena. Rydon tensed.

"I haven't had the pleasure, no. But if the last two mercenaries he sent were to be believed, he's, and I quote, 'an all-powerful god who would not demean himself to come after scum trackers himself'. After I sent the last one back to him with one less hand, I thought he'd get the hint I do not wish to be bothered."

"That was you?" Rydon asked harshly.

Again, the tracker shrugged.

"I enjoy my privacy, merc. And I've had enough of men trying to control me." Turning her gaze to Terena, she added, "I thought by asking for you, he'd lose interest. I didn't know you were with him."

"How is it you know who I am?" Terena asked.

The woman canted her head, regarding Terena for a long moment. "Let us just say, I know someone with a vested interest in your ascension."

"What's that mean?" Croak asked at the same time Terena asked, "Of whom do you speak?"

"But even for you, God of War," the woman continued, "I will not bow to Hermes."

"Why do you call me that?"

Even as the woman smiled, Rydon's hand settled on the hilt of the sword, his grip tightening as he shifted his legs wide.

"I'm an admirer." The woman shrugged. "Soon, everyone will know of you."

"I am a daughter of Ares, aye, but please call me Terena. And you've not answered my question. I can count on one hand the number of people who know who I really am."

"Two. Two hands." Croak said, holding up his hands. He shrugged. "Maybe three."

"Either way, the word is out. Especially for someone as interested in you as I've become."

"What's your interest in me?"

"It started with Metilai, as I've said, but when I heard Ares is your father, well... I had to meet you."

"Why?"

"I have a proposition."

"Here we go," Croak muttered.

"What do you want?"

"If you promise I won't be forced to bend the knee to Hermes, I will come with you."

"Why now when you were so reluctant earlier?"

"I didn't know it was you when you found me. So I've changed my mind."

"In exchange for what?"

"A drink. Have one drink with me. If you still enjoy my company in the morning, I will join you."

"Ren—"

"A drink it is, then," Terena said, frowning at Rydon as he moved closer. She turned back to the woman and waved a hand. "And you will not bow to Hermes. I vow to you, if you come with me, you are my sword, as Rydon here is. He is—"

"I know who—and what—he is," the tracker interrupted quietly.

The air thickened with something Rydon could not name, the hairs on his arms standing on end. Her next words almost stopped his heart.

"You've yet to find Sonah Yahn, I see."

Rydon did not need to look at her to feel the tension wafting off Terena. Her voice held a note of steel in it when she spoke.

"What do you know of m—of Sonah?"

Instead of replying, the woman stared at Terena for several long, uncomfortable seconds.

Terena took a step toward her.

"Peace, Terena," the tracker said, raising her hand in a placating gesture. "It was merely an observation. She is still in Sparta, then?"

"What do you know?" Terena asked in a deadly, soft voice.

"Speak fast," Rydon growled, his hand flexing as he adjusted his grip on his sword. "Or you'll leave this place without your tongue."

"Relax, Eudaemon," she sighed. "I'm sure Sonah Yahn wishes to be reunited with her saviors as well. But we should find her before Hermes does."

"What?" Terena exploded, taking a giant step toward the woman, so she stood less than two feet from her. "What do you know? Stop being so fucking cryptic!"

"I apologize, goddess," the woman said as she bowed her head in supplication. "When you're hunted all your life because you carry—" The tracker pursed her lips before she finished. "Well, you more than anyone would know what it's like. You learn early to guard your tongue."

"And still she says nothing," Croak huffed, raising his hands to tug at his hair. "Clever, this one."

"We need clever," Terena said, eyeing the tracker with a calculating gaze.

"That role is already filled, sis," Croak said. "Might I suggest—"

Before he finished, the light snuffed out and they were once more shrouded in deepest black. Rydon cursed and heard Terena gasp beside him. Something whispered past him, a soft breeze fluttering across his cheek.

Mere seconds passed before a light glowed somewhere behind him and Rydon grimaced when he saw the tracker had once more moved to Croak, her left hand holding the back of his head and her right resting on his chin.

"There are many ways to be clever," the woman crooned in Croak's ear. The boy quaked in her arms.

Terena had her swords out, but the woman shoved Croak away with a soft chuckle. "Cleverness doesn't only mean witty."

Croak stumbled away as Terena scowled at the tracker. "Do you always play with your food?"

The woman winked. "Not always."

"Was that you? With the darkness? Are you a god?"

The woman laughed. "I am no god. But aye, the dark was my doing."

"How?"

"She's a cypher," Rydon snarled.

The woman inclined her head and narrowed her black-rimmed

eyes. "Indeed. So," she spread her arms. "Are we to banter all night, or may I buy you that drink now?"

Croak perked up despite the woman's treatment. "Do you know of a place other than this shit hole?"

"Oh, my love," the woman answered with a wicked gleam in her hazel eyes making Rydon tense. "This here is for the City Watch. It's a performance. A trick. Come, I'll show you the real tavern."

Rydon traded a look with Terena, but Croak marched after the woman, clearly disregarding how she'd threatened him twice already.

Not for the first time, Rydon lamented the state of Croak's priorities.

THE TRACKER LED THEM TO A SIDE DOOR ON THE VERGE OF COLLAPSE. WHEN she held it for them, Terena paused. Croak had no such qualms as he immediately shifted sideways to squeeze through the opening. As soon as he disappeared, a faint glow illuminated the passageway.

Shrugging at their reluctance, the woman followed Croak, leaving Rydon and Terena to decide.

"We're either going to our death or salvation," Rydon muttered as he stalked toward the door.

"I hope there's wine, either way," Terena replied.

Beyond the door, a steep set of stairs led down, the passage lit by a lone torch in a sconce at the bottom. Neither the tracker nor Croak were below, only a metal door with a small hatch surrounded by large rivets.

Rydon banged on the door impatiently. The hatch slid back and a man's dark eyes peered back at them.

"Aye?"

"Really?" Rydon scoffed. "We're with the boy and the woman who just came through."

"Who?"

"Don't test my patience, scum," Rydon growled, gripping the opening as he leaned close. "You won't like—ow!"

The man slammed the hatch shut on Rydon's fingers. He yanked them back with a hiss as the door opened to reveal the woman grinning beside a laughing Croak. The man holding the door open cast them an evil smile, his scarred face macabre in the flickering light as he gestured with a mocking bow for them to enter.

"Everyone's a fucking jester today," Rydon grumbled as he slammed his shoulder into the man on his way past. Terena bit her lip and ducked her head as she followed. Sounds reached her then, a low buzz building in volume and, as they went deeper into the dark, tight corridor, they settled into a cacophony of voices, music, and laughter.

Terena moved to Rydon's side, her mouth falling open at the scene before her. A large, open room with booths, tables and a large, circular bar in the center greeted them. Candles of all sizes dotted the room, leaving some areas in darkness.

"I've traveled through Ovenno before, but I've seen nothing like this," Terena said to Rydon, raising her voice and pressing close to be heard over the noise. There were so many crowded within, she worried she'd lose Croak in the crush. She tugged at Rydon's sleeve and moved through the bodies, weaving her way around a man whose large belly pressed uncomfortably into her back.

"Oh, you are lovely," a rough voice growled in her ear and Terena shivered in disgust. Before she could tell him to fuck off, Rydon shoved the man in the face. Others protested in the man's defense and Terena surged forward, itching for a fight.

As the crowd undulated back, Terena went for her swords. The tracker popped up behind the offender right then. Without a word, everyone around her backed away, creating an opening in which

Terena was able to breathe in air that was not body odor and stale ale.

With a tilt of her head, the tracker motioned for them to follow and as they passed, the crowd gave them a wide berth. No longer bothered by patrons, Terena's gaze darted around, noting the hard men and women, their stares filled with all manner of malice as Terena passed.

They moved slowly toward the back, then the woman veered to the right, where a man stood before an arched doorway. Pulling back on green velvet curtains, the tracker laid her hand on his arm as she went inside. Croak followed as if he'd known the woman all his life.

Terena didn't notice Rydon had stopped in front of her and smacked right into his back.

When she looked up to see what had stopped him, her heart dropped to her belly.

Sitting on a plush sofa of red brocade with gold rivets, his arm stretched over the back, Xoran, Captain of the Imperial Guard of Heylisia, lifted a crystal goblet of wine and grinned.

CHAPTER 7

Croak balked at the man who'd once been under the command of Croaks' father before his untimely death. Shock had dulled his instincts, but he quickly recovered, snatching his sword out of its scabbard and dropping into a fighting stance.

After his initial shock, Xoran's loathsome face stretched as he grinned and he watched them for a long moment. He had the gall to take a drink of his wine. The scabrous dog acted as if he had no care in the world.

"You picked the wrong tavern, Xoran," Terena snarled at the soldier, her face livid.

"Not from where I'm sitting," the asshole replied. Croak wasn't sure what he liked less about the man, his rat-like face, or his raspy voice. It sounded like something he affected to sound dangerous, but all it reminded Croak of was their old cook who smoked at least fifty bossena smokes a day.

Xoran set his goblet down with more care than the vessel

warranted and narrowed his dark eyes at Terena. "Perhaps it is you in the wrong tavern?"

"Stop posturing," the tracker muttered, moving to Xoran's side, one hand digging into the pocket of her leather pants.

Taking a seat on one of the sofa's arms, she tossed a coin on the table near Xoran's wine. The captain flashed her a grin as the woman crossed her arms at her chest with a scowl seeming more good-natured than angry.

"What the fuck's going on?" Croak looked between the tracker and the captain. "You know each other?"

"Did she not say?" Xoran laughed, his face transforming slightly to look more like a dog crossed with a rat. "Vassori's my sister."

Croak was certain the same stunned look on Terena's face was mirrored on his own. Rydon looked just as flummoxed.

The woman, Vassori, shared a grin with Xoran. The captain settled back on the sofa, his white teeth a deep contrast to his swarthy complexion.

"Sister? You look nothing alike!" Croak said, his voice shrill in his ears.

"What's the matter, Croak? You don't think she's as pretty as I am?"

"I thought Serephina was your sister?" Croak replied with a mulish mien as he regarded the captain warily.

Vassori snorted while Xoran grinned. He winked at the tracker. "Serephina's a lover. Never my sister."

"You fucking snake," Terena hissed, hot color flooding her face.

Croak smiled. It would delight him to no end to see his sister tear the bastard's head off.

The captain shrugged, not realizing how close to death he stood. "I needed a way inside and Serephina was more than willing to oblige. Of course, I had to put up with her incessant whining about how it should be her son on the throne rather than Empress Adanna's, but that only proved another useful bit of information I've been able to use against the little imbecile."

"You're not taking me back," Terena said, inching forward to stand slightly in front of Croak. "You'll die before that happens."

"Stand down, Luca," Xoran sighed in a bored voice, waving one of his burn-scarred hands. "I'm not here to take you back."

"What is this, then?" Rydon growled, his voice low. Croak knew from experience it did not bode well for the snide captain.

"I have a proposition for you," the captain answered, his black eyes not wavering from Terena.

"Another proposition? You and your sister are indeed cut from the same cloth." Terena asked.

At the same time, Rydon shouted, "We don't want shit from you!"

"How'd you even know we'd be here?" Croak asked. "Do your spies extend to Hermes's court?"

"Court! Ha!" The tracker, Vassori, snorted. "He's got nobles now?"

"I meant that... figuratively," Croak grumbled.

"The how isn't as important as the why," Xoran drawled. He dipped his chin and looked at Terena again. "Isn't that so, goddess?"

"Are you going to tell us, then?" Terena spat. "Or are you going to sit there all night looking pleased with yourself? What do you want?"

The captain clicked his tongue and dropped his gaze. Lifting his goblet to his lips, he looked up at Terena over the rim and said, "Vassori will pledge her sword to you, and only you. In exchange—"

"Vassori already said—"

"I said I'd come with you," Vassori interrupted. She moved her knee to nudge Xoran's. "But I will not pledge to you until you've agreed to my brother's terms."

"Let's go," Terena muttered, sheathing her swords and motioning to Rydon and Croak with her head. Rydon backed away, his sword still out as he watched the captain and the tracker. Croak shook his head, putting away his sword as he stepped back to follow Terena.

"Would you listen if I told you I can get Sonah Yahn back to you?"

Croak closed his eyes and tipped his head back.

"Terena—" Rydon started to say, his hand splayed on her bracer but she put her hand over his, her eyes on Xoran's rat-face.

"You think to manipulate me," Ren said quietly, her words carrying an edge of power she'd only begun to show in recent days. "You cannot. Even as we speak, Sonah is on her way here. I will find her in Calla, soon."

Terena pivoted, and Xoran's next words made Croak groan.

"Aye, you'd find her. But perhaps you'd rather not see Commander Antonius. I know you two were... something. And now..." he shrugged again, the smug bastard.

Croak swung around to his sister. "Don't listen to this snake. He's feeding on your—"

Shutting his mouth before he could finish, Croak felt the rise of a very telling blush heating his face and he ducked his head.

The quiet settling after his outburst made Croak keep his head down, shuffling his feet until Rydon glared at him. With a scowl that would have had Croak running for his life a few months ago, Rydon turned back to Ren.

"The boy's right," he said, his low voice menacing as he turned a baleful look toward the captain. "Do not trust this man."

"You know nothing about me," Terena seethed. "And you have nothing to offer."

"I know you and the commander had a falling out," Xoran said as he shrugged. "I only wished to spare you a reunion."

"And what spares us from you?" Croak asked with a scoff.

"You don't have to trust me," Xoran said with such innocence in his eyes, Croak almost fell for it. "I will return Sonah Yahn to you. If I do not follow through on my side of the bargain, not only will you have Vassori's sword, you'll also have the item I need you to find."

The smile on the captain's face made Croak gag. Xoran leaned forward, resting his forearms on his knees as he watched Ren.

"Before the Immortals War, the King of the Gods gifted a very rare emerald amulet to a young man. Zeus had come to earth to woo some human, I guess, but came across the man instead, a shepherd, somewhere in what is now Heylisia."

"Are you going to tell us a bedtime story, Captain," Rydon snarled as he shifted his weight, "or are you going to get to the fucking point?"

"Let him finish," Ren said without looking away from the odious captain.

"The point, my dear Eudaemon, is that Terena, while no longer the Royal Tracker, is still, in fact, a tracker."

"You want me to find this amulet?" Ren asked with a bland expression that did not fool Croak. The corner of her lip twitched.

"Aye."

"No."

"No?" Xoran frowned.

"I will not find this amulet you seek. Or rather, the amulet *Solon* seeks. I'm not giving that megalomaniac a weapon he can use against me and mine."

"The amulet is not for Emperor Solon."

"So you say."

"What can I do to convince you?"

"Nothing," Croak snorted.

"You have a tracker. Let her find it." Terena said, waving a hand at Vassori, who continued to sit on the sofa arm as if it were the most comfortable place in the room. She tossed something into her mouth every once in a while as she watched them speak.

Croak's stomach growled in response. Would it be disloyal to grab some food while they chatted?

"I've been looking," Vassori said in a wry tone. "But then—"

"We need your help to find it," Xoran interrupted. Croak noted the look passing between him and the tracker with interest. She ducked her head and tossed another nut or whatever in her mouth.

"You get Vassori's sword and Sonah Yahn," Xoran went on, his voice so syrupy sweet it grated on Croak. "All I ask is that you find the amulet for me."

"It is useless to you," Rydon replied. Turning to Terena, he said in a lower tone, "They cannot be used by anyone outside of the bloodline it was gifted to."

"Ah, you know your cyphers," Xoran said with a grin.

Croak rolled his eyes.

"This is true," Vassori said. "It cannot be used by anyone other than the bloodline of the shepherd Zeus gifted it to. But we do not want to use it."

"Then why not leave it where it is?" Croak asked, looking between the two. "If it's lost, no one can use it."

"Because the emperor is looking for it," Xoran said with a laconic lift of his shoulder.

"Ah ha," Croak snapped his fingers. "There it is."

"I thought you said—"

"Emperor Solon *is* looking for it. I told him I would get it for him, but I will not give it to him," Xoran ground out. Croak could tell by the little tic at the corner of his lips he was losing patience. His dark eyes narrowed, and the cruel mask he'd always worn in front of them over the years finally fell back into place.

"You must think me a fool, Xoran," Terena chuckled, "if you believe I will find it for you now. I'll get Sonah on my own. And you can keep your tracker."

"Wait!"

Terena turned back toward the door, motioning for Rydon and Croak to follow, when Vassori called out. Croak glanced over his shoulder to see the tracker standing now, her hand in front of her and panic on her face before she schooled her expression.

"I will pledge my sword to you without your help finding the amulet."

"No."

"Please!" Vassori's plaintiff cry stopped them all. Rydon's lips were still firmly pressed together, letting Terena deal with the woman. Croak folded his arms and watched the performance.

"Vas—"

"No," Vassori batted Xoran's hand away and he sat back on the sofa, staring at the ground while Vassori rounded the table to stand before Terena.

She dropped to one knee.

Croak's mouth fell open, and he swung his head to Terena. She stood straight and stiff, her eyes on the woman kneeling at her feet but with a look on her face Croak had only ever seen on Solon's face.

And on Hermes.

"I have no right to ask this of you," Vassori said, her head bowed, "but please let me pledge my sword, my life, my death, to you. I do not ask for anything in return. I wish only to serve."

"Why?" Rydon asked.

There was a beat of silence following his question.

"Because you will lead us when the war comes."

"Heylisia's already at war," Croak said quietly.

"What war is coming?" Rydon asked.

"Vas!" Xoran's face was thunderous as he stood, his hands clenched and his eyes spitting fire.

"You know," Vassori said, lifting her head at last. Her face had such a vulnerable look, Croak shifted uncomfortably.

"You know," she said again, more forcefully. "The oracle told you. 'Leading the gods to glory'."

Terena's face lost all color. Rydon swore under his breath. Croak felt dread slide down to his belly.

"The second Immortals War is coming," Vassori whispered, as if she wished not to be overheard by the Fates. "And if you're leading the gods to glory, I want to be at your side."

CHAPTER 8

SPARTA

Slipping away from Jenos was the most challenging part of their escape. But it'd be easier to leave from her rooms rather than Lerek's. So they'd decided to meet in Sonah's bedchamber, the supplies they'd need hidden in the chest at the foot of her bed.

Sonah opened the door of her room and Jenos immediately stepped into her line of sight, a worried frown on his kindly face as he took in her pale countenance and trembling hands.

"Lady? Is everything all right?"

"Jenos," she started in her breathiest voice, "would you fetch the physician? I am not feeling well." She threw in a coughing fit to sell the ploy. "Please, hurry."

"At once, lady," Jenos rumbled and strode off.

When he'd rounded the corner, Sonah turned back and motioned Lerek forward. He had a large sack slung across his chest, his thick wool cloak hiding his simple tunic and leather jacket. He wore the same grey breeches she'd seen the previous night. Sonah reached out and pulled his hood to cover his copper-brown hair. If they were stopped, he'd look like any other Spartan at first glance.

Snatching her cloak from Lerek's hands, she quickly fastened it and tugged up the hood. With a jerk of her head, Lerek moved out of the room, and Sonah closed the door silently.

They headed down the opposite hallway Jenos had taken, moving swiftly on silent feet, ducking into an alcove to hide from a couple of roving guards. When the hall was clear, they scurried down a few flights of stairs and through corridors leading to the servants' quarters.

"Wait!" Sonah hissed when Lerek was about to head right into a group of maids carrying empty plates toward the kitchens. She grabbed the back of his cloak and hauled him back, her arm pressed to his chest as she peered out.

"Now," she whispered, her shoulders hunched as she hurried around the corner. Hidden in a deep recess of the stone wall near the arched doorway leading to the kitchens, an old wood door was the only thing standing between them and freedom.

Sonah pushed the door, cringing when it groaned. She stopped to look over her shoulder, waiting a beat to be sure they hadn't been discovered. When no one came running, she tugged on Lerek's sleeve and they slipped through the door.

Not bothering to close it, they ran in a crouch, hugging the stone wall to their right. They followed the wall until they reached a dip and dropped down.

"Where—"

"There's a ladder a few yards ahead and we can climb up to the top of the wall," Sonah panted as they moved.

"And then?"

She didn't answer until they'd reached the ladder. Taking a closer look at it, Sonah worried it wouldn't bear their weight. Well, maybe hers. She looked from the ladder to Lerek, then back again as she chewed on her lip.

"And then, Sonah?" Lerek prodded, grabbing hold of her arm and giving it a shake.

"Then we drop on the other side," she hissed.

Without looking at him, she clambered up the ladder. Behind

her, she heard Lerek's muttered curse before he climbed up. Sonah looked down over her shoulder when she heard a gasp and the crack of wood.

"Lerek?"

"I'm fine," he whispered.

Turning back, Sonah climbed and crouched at the top, waiting. She scooted back so he'd have room to step up.

Sonah's chest squeezed. Looking down into the black abyss on the other side of the wall, she frowned.

"How far down is it?" Lerek gasped at her side.

She looked up at him to see him scowling down at the endless darkness beyond.

"I... I think not far?"

He shot her a look of disbelief. "What's that mean? Is it a foot? Two? Ten?"

"I'm not good with distances," she mumbled. "Or numbers."

He scoffed.

"Do you have a better idea?" she seethed. "I've had a day to scout out an escape route. This is the best I found. It's not far down. I don't think the drop will kill us."

"You don't—" Lerek sputtered and then cursed under his breath.

"Ready?" Sonah asked a second before she lowered her legs on the other side. She looked up at Lerek's alarmed expression and pushed off from the wall.

Her heart rose to her throat as she fell. Seconds later, her feet landed. She fell to her knees and cried out, falling awkwardly onto her right side, her thigh smacking against the cold grass and bracken.

"Come on!" she called up to Lerek, even as her feet and knees ached and her thigh burned from the fall. She moved back when she heard Lerek's movements above. With a loud *oomph*, he landed and rolled, knocking into her. She fell back onto her bottom, trying to stop her momentum with her hand stretched back. She cried out when her hand twisted and a razor sharp pain shot up her forearm.

"What the fuck, Lerek!" Sonah clutched her bruised wrist to her chest as she glared up at Lerek's shadowy form. He bent close and helped her up, mumbling apologies.

"Now what?" he asked when they were both upright. Sonah looked around, blinking to adjust to the dark now that the torches on the other side of the wall no longer lit their way.

"We continue down this slope and it'll lead us to the gate near the stables," she answered as she turned to start down in that direction. Lerek followed close behind.

"We're going to steal horses?"

Sonah's face twisted and she exhaled in frustration. "No. That would almost certainly ruin our escape. We won't be able to get horses until we're out of Sparta."

"How long will that take?"

Sonah muttered to herself about patience and the uselessness of spoiled princes.

"I don't know, Lerek," she said through gritted teeth. "I told you, I'm not good with stuff like that. Just follow, all right?"

A long time passed as they continued down the mountainside. They took it slower when the decline steepened, ducking low so if they slid, they wouldn't go careening to their deaths.

When they finally stepped onto a cobbled stone path, Sonah breathed a sigh of relief. She looked back at the prince and flashed him a quick smile.

"See? Not so bad."

"Aye," he whispered, smiling back at her.

Shouts reached them a few minutes later and Sonah grabbed Lerek's cloak and ducked behind bushes near the large stone steps leading back up to the castle. They crouched low, huddled together as a group of soldiers rushed past, torches held high. Sonah waited another minute to see if anyone else followed. Satisfied no one was near, Sonah darted out of cover, Lerek close behind.

As they neared the gates to the castle at the bottom of the mountain, Sonah turned right.

"We're not going through the gates?"

"Go ahead if you want to get caught," Sonah sneered. Without a backward glance, she continued, feeling along the stone until she found what she was looking for. The grate in the wall was old and worn but still intact. Turning, she motioned for Lerek to come closer.

"Can you pull this out?"

"With what?" he asked with a quizzical frown.

Sonah pulled a face. "With your hands."

Lerek scoffed. "I don't think so."

"Well, can you *try?*"

"Gods, Sonah! When we get out of here and are somewhere safe, you really need to fill me in on what happened to you since Metilai!"

"Agreed. Now get this open."

Lerek shook his head, then grabbed hold of the bars and tugged, his feet sliding on the dewy grass. When the grate didn't budge, he braced his feet against the stone and tried again.

"Here," Sonah said as she reached for the sack around his shoulder. Rummaging around, she frowned until she caught something and grinned.

"Aha!" she held up a long iron bar with a hooked end at him in triumph.

"What's that?"

"It's a fire poker, Lerek," she said. Gods, was he really this coddled? To not even know what a fire poker looked like?

"Sorry," he mumbled. "It's dark out."

Sonah twisted her lips, thrusting the poker at him. "Use this. I brought it for protection but maybe we can use it to loosen the bars."

Lerek snatched it from her hands with a scowl. After a few awkward attempts, the grate gave and yanked part of the way out of the stone. Lerek repositioned his feet against the wall and gave it another pull, flying onto his back when the grate gave way.

Sonah gasped excitedly, and grabbed Lerek's cloak. "I knew you could do it! Now, let's get the fuck out of here!"

"W<small>E CAN'T FIND THEM</small>, Y<small>OUR</small> M<small>AJESTY</small>," C<small>APTAIN</small> A<small>THANASI SAID WITH A</small> scowl.

Daris swore and glanced at King Altos.

"Fuck!"

The curse was uncharacteristic of the king, especially in front of his men. His face turned a deep scarlet, and his eyes narrowed as he looked around, his gaze landing on Daris.

"They can't have gone far," he snarled. "Find them. Put the prince in a cell and bring Sonah Yahn to me."

"Aye, Sire," Daris said and made to turn when the king grabbed his arm.

"Do it quietly," King Altos seethed. "I don't want the duke getting wind of this."

Daris looked at him for a long moment before giving the king a curt nod. Altos released him and Daris strode away, his men following.

When he was a good distance from the king, Daris said over his shoulder, "Jason, you and Michael head for the Champion's Gate. I doubt they'd be stupid enough to go out that way, but you never know. Trojus, you're with me."

He turned as the men moved off. When Captain Athanasi came out of the doorway, Daris stopped him.

"Have your men watch every stableyard in the city. If they're on foot and have already made it out of the city limits, they'll be easier to catch without horses."

"Aye, Commander," the captain said.

Daris's pulse raced as he descended the staircase and strode across the grand foyer. At that hour, there were few courtiers still milling about, their hooded eyes and slurred speech testament to their evening's revelry, so he and his men were largely ignored.

He knew the whispers of Sonah's departure would circulate soon enough, despite King Altos's wishes. While Sonah had kept to her rooms, the servants were very aware of who she was and their tongues would soon whisper in the ears of those servants in the pocket of some of these courtiers.

He hoped they'd be back before those whispers found the duke and duchess.

CHAPTER 9

NEAR VESALA, OVENNO

Terena could not speak for the giant knot in her throat. She stared down at Vassori, the woman's hazel eyes bright with zealous fervor. The fact that this woman knew what Pytho had told Terena was not the only thing bothering her about this conversation.

The man standing behind the tracker bothered her more.

"Your sister wants to side with gods in a war that might not ever come to pass," Terena said flippantly. "Yet you've still not said why you wish to find the amulet for yourself and not your master."

"Emperor Solon is not my master," Xoran bit out, his face a storm of anger. As if reading her thoughts, he scrubbed a hand down his face. When he regarded her again, his mask of indifference was restored.

"I have reasons to do so, which do not concern you. I have not lied to you. I will bring Sonah Yahn to you in exchange for the amulet. And Emperor Solon will never see it. I swear on—"

When he stopped abruptly, Terena cocked her head. "Aye? You swear on..."

"Xoran," Vassori chided, turning her head long enough to glare at her brother before she turned back, earnest once more. "I beg you, goddess. Do not turn me away. I will be your shield when you need it, your sword when—"

"Yes, yes," Croak scoffed, sauntering closer to them. Terena arched a sable brow at him. "We are all her shields and swords. What else do you bring to the table?"

A fraught silence followed his question, and Terena saw Xoran tense.

"Vassori," he whispered. She did not turn to look at him, but she canted her head at his plea. "Do not. I beg you."

"Listen to your brother," Terena said when the silence continued. "I do not need your sword. I have Rydon—"

"And me."

"And an Olympian god with an army of ten thousand men that grows every day." Rydon added with smug satisfaction.

"Hermes is the trickster god," Xoran fumed. "Do not think because you're a god he will not use his clever tongue to deceive you. Has he told you what happens when you reach two and twenty? What happens to your eudaemon?"

"Aye," Terena said, glaring at him. "He's told me I will become immortal and my powers will manifest fully. And Rydon will be mortal once more."

"Rydon?" Xoran sneered. "What of Commander Antonius of the Liodari?"

Croak made an unpleasant sound, but Terena ignored him. She cursed inwardly at how the heat rushed to her neck and face at the mention of Daris's name. Pretending a calm she no longer felt, she shrugged.

"What care have I of the commander?"

Xoran laughed, his face incredulous. His sister hissed at him but the captain was very animated, crossing to Vassori's side with manic glee.

"Your care, goddess, is most definitely with the commander. And if Hermes told you this one is your eudaemon," he jabbed a finger in Rydon's direction, "then he's already spun lies for you."

"Speak plain," Rydon roared, his face a deep red. Spittle gleamed near his mouth where the hairs of his beard shook. "What is he lying about?"

Xoran seemed to revel in the moment, his chest puffed out as he shifted his gaze from Terena to Rydon. "You are not her eudaemon. Daris Antonius is."

Stunned, Rydon gaped for a moment before erupting. He lunged for the Captain of the Imperial Guard, his hands fisting in the man's tunic before Terena and Vassori could think to stop him.

"Rydon! Rydon, stop!" Terena yelled over Vassori's shouts. Behind them, he heard Croak's distinct laughter. Vassori had a hand wrapped around Rydon's wrist, tugging ineffectually.

It was Terena's voice, close to his ear, a breath away from Xoran, who calmed him.

"Rydon," she whispered. "If it's true, it changes nothing. You are for Sonah, and I am glad of it. I am glad, do you hear me? I cannot think of a man more worthy to watch over my sister. Do you hear me?"

"What?" Xoran whispered, his mouth dropping open. "What— Sonah Yahn... is your sister?"

Looking between the two of them, understanding dawned and his expression changed to awe.

"And a god. How?" Xoran's face went through a range of emotions finally settling on satisfaction, a smile blooming as he turned to Terena.

"Shut the fuck up," Rydon growled, his face so close to the captain, spittle landed on the man's nose.

"It makes sense now," Xoran continued.

Clearly, he had a death wish.

"What makes sense?" Terena asked with a sigh, her hand still on Rydon's shoulder.

Xoran turned to his sister. Her hands covered her mouth and she stared back at the captain with wide eyes. "Emperor Solon has been looking for Sonah Yahn for months now. I didn't know why he wanted her and not you."

"Fuck," Croak said behind them.

"Of course he wants her," Rydon snarled. "The man is so hungry for power he'd use a child to further his interests."

Chest throbbing where his heart clearly wanted to escape his ribcage, Rydon's breaths were coming in hard and sharp. He calmed slowly, still clutching at the captain, whose eyes were now narrowed in a way that made Rydon's eye twitch.

"You didn't know? About being her eudaemon?" Xoran asked, incredulous. A look of pity passed through his eyes before he smiled. "And here I thought you, too, were keeping secrets from the goddess."

"Stop calling me that," Terena muttered, yanking on Rydon's wrist. He finally let go, allowing her to pull him away, but he continued to stare at the man.

Terena looked at him a moment more before turning to Xoran, her eyes gleaming. "You lie. You lie because Hermes himself made Rydon my eudaemon."

Xoran stared back at her, his lips falling to a frown. He wagged a finger at her. "He made him the heir's eudaemon."

"What?" Croak asked.

Rydon blinked at Xoran. "Aye. And Terena is—"

"Not the heir," Terena sighed, her hand drifting to Rydon's bicep. He swung around to look at her, his heart heavy.

"What?"

"I don't understand," Croak said, moving closer to Rydon's side.

"I... didn't tell you about my conversation with Hermes when we first arrived in Olympia," Terena replied. Her hand slipped off Rydon's arm and she brought both hands to her face as she shook her head.

"That was... that was over a month ago!" Croak cried out, arms spread as if he was the wronged party in all this.

"It just—it slipped my mind!"

"What? How the fuck—!"

"Croak, please," Terena groaned, finally dropping her hands. She turned to face her brother. "I have a lot on my fucking mind these days and the order of my birth was really low on that list!"

"Well, what do you think now?" he asked, exasperated, as he motioned to Rydon with his palms up.

"How's that possible? You're older—"

"We'll speak on it more later," she replied through gritted teeth, giving Rydon a pointed stare.

"Terena, I—"

"You're wasting time," Xoran cut in. "The emperor tasked Duke Ovenno to return with Sonah Yahn. He has something he's holding over the duke. I know not what, but he agreed to hand her over in exchange for something. I am to meet them in Calla and escort the lady back to Metilai."

"What could Solon have over the duke to make him do his bidding?" Rydon pondered.

"As I said," Xoran replied, cutting him an insolent glare, "it matters not, because the emperor has no plan to give it to him. He ordered me to bring Sonah to the White Palace. Duke Ovenno was never going to get back whatever it is he'd exchanged Sonah's life for."

"So your plan is to what, hold my sister hostage for an amulet?" Ren's face closed up as she stared at the captain.

"I do not wish ill on your sister, I truly don't. But if I'm to betray the emperor, I at least deserve the amulet in return for my trouble."

"This is bullshit," she said and turned, striding for the door.

"I'm going with you," Vassori said, moving toward Terena. Her brother reached out, grabbing hold of her wrist.

"Vas—"

"You're playing with a god right now," Vassori snarled, yanking her wrist away. "How fucked up are you? Do you know what she can do to us?"

"Believe me," he griped, "I do know. I was there when they were about to execute her."

"Oh, aye, let's bring up *that* joyous occasion," Croak scoffed.

"The duke's allies have retreated to their own provinces. He is all alone against Emperor Solon right now. In case you haven't heard, Colinas fell a fortnight ago; The emperor sent Duke Ravos to Calla with half his face melted off. Duke Ovenno's facing annihilation if he doesn't bring Sonah Yahn back from Sparta. The emperor promised to do worse to him than Duke Ravos if he failed."

Rydon could feel Terena stiffen at his side with each word from the captain. Her face turned ashen and a deep scarlet in quick succession.

"How do you know this?" he asked.

Xoran's lip curled. "You're not too bright, are you? I'm his fucking Imperial Guard Captain." He shifted his eyes to Terena. "I can get her for you before Ovenno takes her out of Sparta. I have men already in place."

"Why are you here?" Terena said, pushing gently on Rydon's shoulder. Rydon retreated a step, allowing Terena to fill the space in front of Xoran, her eyes flashing as she glared at the captain. "You're his fucking Imperial Guard Captain," she mimicked. "So what are you doing in Ovenno and not in Sparta yourself?"

"Solon's dog has a very long leash," Rydon growled, his eyes burning into Xoran.

"I'm here for *you*."

"Ah! The truth at last," Croak laughed harshly. "Kill him, Rydon."

"Enough!" Terena erupted, her face red as she glared at all of them. "I don't give a fuck anymore about why he's here. I care about Sonah. I will find her myself."

She turned to leave and said over her shoulder, "If you're smart, you'll stay out of my way. Come near us, try to take her from me, I will hunt you to the ends of Elysium."

Before Terena took another step, Vassori darted in front of her, prostrating before her.

Head bowed and sword lifted, she said, "Take me with you."

"I do not want your brother's bargain," Terena spat, pushing past the kneeling tracker.

"That's his bargain, not mine," Vassori said as she stood. Glancing over her shoulder at Xoran, who watched them in frustrated silence, she turned back to Terena. Lifting her chin, she gazed at her with a look Rydon could only interpret as reverence.

"Goddess, please—"

"Come. Stay. I care not," Terena sighed and stepped away, turning for the door. "I am going to Sparta."

"You won't find her," Xoran called out. Terena paused but did not turn back around. Rydon shoved the captain aside as he strode to Terena's side.

"Why not?" Croak asked, popping something into his mouth as he followed in a leisurely manner.

Xoran's face went blank. When he replied, he spoke to Terena. "Because the Fates have other plans for you."

CHAPTER 10

LAKONIA

At midday, Sonah and Lerek spotted a small village where the coin Sonah had pilfered from Jenos was enough to secure them two horses.

Lerek had hidden beneath his hooded cloak while Sonah negotiated, the stable master nodding enthusiastically at the sum, even throwing in a dagger after Sonah had asked where she might procure one. She was still uncomfortable around the beasts, but at least this one listened to her, and it seemed docile enough.

When they'd reached the main road outside the village, they'd continued west, sticking to the less populated paths.

"Wouldn't it be quicker using the Greek roads?"

"Aye," Sonah called back. "Quicker getting caught. We stick to these paths and shelter in the woods as much as we can. If we keep going west, there's a forest we can hide in for days. The woods are dense enough to keep us well hidden."

"West?" Lerek looked around as they rode on. "We're going east."

"What?" Sonah pulled on the reins and the horse slowed to a stop. Resting one hand on her hip, she frowned at her surroundings. "Are you certain?"

"Aye," Lerek said with a sardonic lift of his lips. "Can you not tell?"

"I'm not good with that stuff," she grumbled.

"Well, now that we've determined we are, in fact, going *east*," Lerek said with exaggerated patience, "where do you suggest we go from here?"

Chewing on her lip, Sonah thought for a few seconds before she brightened, snapping her fingers and pointing at Lerek with a huge grin. "We'll be in Ibros soon, if we're not already. We head north until we get to Thuria. I have a friend up there."

Lerek looked at her warily. "You have a friend in Thuria? When have *you* been to Thuria?"

Sonah shrugged, a coy smile on her lips. She made a clicking noise and her mare started walking. "I've been many places, Lerek. And my friend owes me a favor. Now, which way is north?"

Lerek pointed, and Sonah moved her horse in that direction.

They traveled in silence for the better part of an hour, and Sonah was glad of it. She'd learned a lot more about the prince in these last few hours on the run together than the last seven years in the White Palace combined.

What a difference being a fugitive made in one's character.

Dusk turned the sky into a kaleidoscope of pinks, oranges, and deep blues. To the left, the sun sank beyond the mountains and Sonah glanced over at Lerek.

"We should start looking for a place to rest for the night."

He looked over at her with a slow nod. His eyes had deep, dark circles beneath them and his shoulders were slumped. When he shifted in his saddle, she caught him wincing.

"Look," she said with a nod, "up ahead, you see that? We'll head for that copse of pine."

Sonah didn't bother to wait for his acknowledgment. She kicked her mare gently as she whispered soothing nonsense to her, and they surged forward.

As they neared the woods, the terrain sloped up, and she slowed her mount to walk uphill. Darkness descended quickly and she shivered as she looked up and around at the thick trees. It was unnaturally quiet, and Sonah braced herself as she brought her hand down to the dagger she'd strapped to her side.

"It's so quiet," Lerek said, his voice obscenely loud.

Sonah shot him a glare over her shoulder but didn't respond. Of the two of them, she was the only one with experience in the fugitive lifestyle, which is why he'd deferred to her suggestions to this point. But she wished he would step up a bit. Her insides quaked and her nerves were shot.

"This is as good a place as any to stop," she said softly. Sonah waited a moment before dismounting. Her backside was so sore, she winced with every step. There was no stream nearby to water the horses, so she walked her grey mare for a few minutes until she heard the trickle of water. Sonah called out to Lerek, then headed toward it.

Once the horses were drinking, Sonah unbuckled the saddle and pulled it off, struggling against the weight. Lerek rushed over and took it from her but was unsure what to do with it.

"Set it over there," she said with a lift of her chin. "We'll use them to lean against while we eat. I'll go gather some wood for a fire."

She set off, not bothering to look back at Lerek. Luckily, finding enough wood to burn was a quick endeavor.

Lerek came close to the fire, his face wet from the creek, and handed her his waterskin.

Taking deep gulps of the refreshing liquid, Sonah groaned. Mumbling her thanks, she handed it back to him. Crouching with a grimace, Sonah leaned back against her saddle.

A moment later, she rummaged in her saddlebags for some food. Tossing half a loaf of bread to Lerek, she grabbed a couple of apples and a stem of grapes to share between them.

"Sonah," Lerek said in a low voice. "Tell me what happened after…"

Sonah looked at Lerek a long time before she dropped her chin.

Twisting the half eaten apple in her hands, she frowned, knowing this conversation was coming, but wishing it wouldn't.

"It's a long story," she said with a sigh. Glancing over at him, she shrugged. "I'll tell you some of it, but we should really sleep as much as we can, Lerek. Our journey north will be long, and there'll be times when we won't be able to sleep much, if at all."

"All right," Lerek nodded. He shifted until he faced her. The firelight cast his face in shadows and she was thankful for it. She hoped her own countenance was hidden thus.

With a sigh, Sonah lifted her head, looking at the stars peeking through the trees. "General Peleon's men had Terena arrested. She was on the terrace, when... well, you know that part. Anyway, Captain Cortis put me in the dungeons. They thought I was part of the... assassination plot. They sent word to Duke Ovenno of my arrest, but what they didn't know is he's not my father. So of course, I was left to rot in the dungeons. With Ren."

Lerek hung his head. "How did you get out?"

"Croak. He and two mercenaries he'd hired helped us escape. But..."

"But what?"

How much to say? Gods, she wished Terena was with her.

"Look, there are many things I can tell you, but I think it best we wait until we're all together. With Terena and the others, I mean. Much of this is not my story to tell and I don't want to say anything she'll—"

Sonah stopped and shook her head roughly. Lerek was silent as he watched her.

When she didn't continue, he shifted and settled back against his saddle.

After a while, he asked, "How is she? I mean, how was she, when you last saw her?"

Sonah laughed darkly. "When I last saw her, she was screaming and shooting arrows at the Liodari when they carried me away."

That was the truth, at least. To say more would mean she'd have to talk about Daris, and there was no way she was going there. That was Terena territory for sure.

"I'm glad you were together," he said at length.

"Me too."

"How did you all end up in Sparta? I tried to get to you before, when I knew Terena was there as well, but I was well guarded after my failed attempt to reach you."

Sonah rubbed her eyes. Again, not something she wanted to get into.

"Terena saw the oracle in Messene. She told her to go to King Altos because he had something of hers."

"You saw the oracle?"

"Not me. Just Terena."

"How is that possible? The oracle only speaks to monarchs."

Another subject she didn't want to get into. If Lerek didn't know Terena was a god, she was certainly not going to open that bag of turnips.

She responded with a shrug.

"What was it she had to get from Altos?"

"A pair of swords."

"And then she left?"

Sonah opened her mouth to tell him no, she'd stayed behind while Terena had gone to Ibros and gotten the fangs from a mythical serpent, but that would lead to more questions, and she was tired.

"How 'bout we get some sleep, and I tell you more tomorrow night?"

He was silent for so long, Sonah took that as assent and settled down on the ground, tugging her cloak to cover herself as best she could.

"I don't know what happened to you these many months, Sonah. But you are not the same girl I knew at the palace."

She didn't know why, but Sonah felt the sting of tears and shut her eyes tight.

"No," she whispered. "No, I am not."

IBROS

They'd been traveling north for a week when they ran out of food. Sonah had not thought to bring anything to hunt with—she was no good with a bow, despite the hours Terena had spent teaching her.

All she had was a dagger.

And Lerek.

The situation was bleak.

Sighing, Sonah pulled her horse off the trail, and they walked until they found a stream. After watering the horses and filling up their waterskins, Sonah tasked Lerek with finding wood for a fire while she tried to fish. She'd tied her dagger to the end of a long branch and spent the next five minutes shivering in ankle-deep water, hoping to spear a fish for their dinner. When her attempts did nothing but soak her boots and pants, she screamed her frustration to the sky.

"If you wanted to fish, you could've just asked me," Lerek said, hands on hips. Sonah cast him a mutinous look as she trudged out of the water.

"I suppose you think you can do better?"

"I know I can," Lerek boasted, grabbing the spear from her hands. "You forget, I spent much of my childhood with Terena and Croak. Their father taught us how to fish."

"Taught you to fish but didn't teach you how to use a sword?"

Lerek gave her a sour look and held out his hand for the makeshift spear. He gestured for her to move behind him, and Sonah rolled her eyes. Watching him from a safe distance, she crossed her arms and frowned as she waited.

And waited.

He stood as still as one of the marble statues in the gardens at the White Palace. She admired the concentration it must take to be so focused, arm raised as he kept his eyes trained on the water.

As she watched, he hurled the spear, the end wobbling as it stuck in the stream bed. He strode toward it, dropping to his haunches as he yanked back on the spear and she cried out, pointing at the fish on the end of it.

With a hand clapped over her mouth, she stared at Lerek, who grinned back at her as if he'd captured the moon. Smothering a giggle, she gave him a mock bow.

"Very good, Your Highness. Tonight, we feast!"

"Well, we'll need more than just the one," Lerek said with a crooked grin. She grinned back.

"I'll go start the fire, then." Sonah turned with a spring in her step.

IT WAS STILL DARK OUT WHEN SONAH WOKE. THE FIRE HAD DIED DOWN AND the last of the embers had long since turned cold. The woods were quiet.

Unsure of what had caused her to rouse, Sonah shifted up to her elbow and looked around. A prickle of awareness made her skin rise like gooseflesh.

Then she heard it.

The soft snap of a twig behind her made Sonah scramble to her feet, her dagger out as she stood defensively. She kicked at Lerek's shoulder and hissed at him to get up as her eyes darted around the darkness.

A shadow materialized into the shape of a man and Sonah's eyes widened.

"Lerek! Get up! Get up, now!"

As soon as she'd yelled, the man rushed her. Sonah flung her dagger and was rewarded with the man's yelp.

Turning, Sonah looked for another weapon when she heard a snarl behind her and turned in time to see a man grab Lerek. Two more ran toward her.

"Grab her, dammit!"

The man in front of her clutched at his arm, her dagger embedded in his shoulder. His face was hidden beneath a mask covering everything below his eyes, his clothes so dark she couldn't tell if he was a Spartan soldier or a brigand. Either way, she couldn't let them take her.

As Lerek struggled against his captor, and the other two men circled closer to her, Sonah opened her mouth and screamed.

The man holding Lerek immediately released his hold and Lerek dropped like a stone. He covered his ears, his eyes wild as he looked up at Sonah.

The others were similarly incapacitated, and Sonah grabbed Lerek by his tunic and tried to haul him up.

Turning, Sonah crashed into the chest of one of their assailants. The man grabbed her by the tunic and slammed his forehead against hers.

CHAPTER II

IBROS

Sonah blinked away the fog in her head. Heavy lids moved as if weighed down and she pushed past the pain in her head. Her fuzzy vision cleared and she saw two figures a few yards away, backlit by the soft fire flickering off to her right. She noticed a sustained note, loud and monotonous, in her ears. Her jaw ached, and her head throbbed. She blinked harder, trying to focus.

Something was in her mouth.

Sonah tried closing her mouth and winced against the pain shooting from the hinges of her jaw and she gagged. Feeling around with her tongue, she felt something soggy and bulky. When she tried to lift her hands to feel for it, they wouldn't move. They were tied at the wrist and her arms were pinned to her sides. The bite of more hemp around her arms confirmed she was lashed to the tree at her back as well.

"—this girl for seven years, Otto," a voice was saying, the words muffled as if behind a wall, then clearer as the ringing in her ears dissipated and the words resolved into a low conversation two men were having.

Sonah stopped her fidgeting, every muscle tensed as she concentrated on the voices.

"I hear you, Your Highness," a man was saying, and Sonah heard the rustling of bramble and twigs as the man shifted his feet. "But we have orders from your father to bring her back to Metilai."

"And I am telling you I've known her most of her life and she is no more a criminal than I am!"

Sonah frowned. She knew that voice.

Lerek?

Sonah dared not move, straining to listen.

The other man sighed loudly. "That may be, but I still have my orders. If it's as you say, I am certain your father—"

"You dare deny me?"

Sonah almost smiled at the deadly drop of Lerek's voice.

"With respect, Your Highness, the emperor's orders supersede yours," the man said. Sonah felt a sudden rush of dread as she realized she knew the man's voice, too. Otto Hetteti, an Imperial Guard who served under Captain Xoran.

The Imperial Guard were always with the emperor and his family, so why was Otto here? Had he known Lerek would be here?

Sonah remained stock still as she waited for Lerek's response.

"As a favor to me then, remove her bindings. I assure you, you've no need of them."

"Your Highness," the guard said with feigned patience, "I will not give this *criminal* the opportunity to escape after we've spent many months tracking her down. It's bad enough we let a god slip through our fingers. At least now we can return with—"

Lerek's scoff was sharp and immediate. He jerked back as if the guard had slapped him.

"A god," he snapped, his voice dropping lower. "There is no such thing. There hasn't been for a long, long time."

From Sonah's vantage, she had a view of the guard's profile and saw the grim satisfaction in the smile he leveled on Lerek. "Aye. Until her. The Royal Tracker, Terena Luca."

"You're mad," Lerek said with a shake of his head. "You're— Terena Luca is no more a god than I am. Are you insane?"

"A thousand people witnessed her power in the square, the day she and this girl," the guard nodded in Sonah's direction and Sonah quickly shut her eyes. Not daring to open them lest they see her, she concentrated on their words.

"—to be executed, Terena Luca unleashed power from her hands no mortal wields. I tell you now, Terena Luca is a god."

Lerek lifted a hand as if to physically reject the guard's words. But the man was relentless. Sonah cracked her eyes to slits as he continued. "Not only is she a god, but she's now allied with the King of Sparta. Our spies within the kingdom shared how close she and the commander of his Liodari have gotten recently. *Very* close."

Sonah felt her belly drop as Lerek turned his head, sliding a gaze over in her direction. She prayed it was dark enough he could not see she was awake and watching.

After a moment, he dropped his head.

"What have they seen?"

Sonah stifled a groan.

The guard stepped closer and in a harsh tone said, "They were seen embracing. In view of our men."

Lerek stood so still, Sonah worried one touch would make him snap.

"We'll travel north to meet up with Captain Xoran and then head east. I've sent one of our men with a message so he'll know where to intercept us."

Sonah cringed at the man's words, a new fear igniting within her at the thought of the scarred and surly captain joining them.

Shifting her leg, Sonah winced against the instant rush of feeling needling her foot as it came awake. Even with how slight the movement was, the guard's head snapped in her direction, and Sonah grimaced when he frowned over at her.

"Good," Otto barked, striding the few steps toward her. "You're awake."

He bent over, untying the rope over her arms and she slumped forward. She barely sighed with relief before the man snatched the rope at her wrists. Sonah gasped as she was yanked upright. A sinking feeling came over Sonah and she wished she were somewhere she could speak with Lerek alone.

"Perhaps you'd like to hear it from one of Terena Luca's co-conspirators. She can tell you all about how close the commander and your Royal Tracker have gotten."

Sonah let out a squeak of surprise as Otto shoved her forward. Lerek caught her before she fell. With a grunt, he quickly untied the rope at her wrists. As the hemp fell away, Sonah sighed and rubbed at her chafed wrists, shooting a glare at the guard.

"Sonah," Lerek said, his voice rough. Sonah winced, unable to look at him. "Sonah, is Terena allied with Sparta? Does she... are she and the commander..."

He didn't finish, and coward that Sonah was, she waited so she'd have more time to gather her thoughts.

So much to say, but not in front of Otto. Both Lerek and Terena deserved better.

She swallowed. "So... you were dead."

Otto snorted. Lerek raised his eyes in warning before returning his stare to Sonah.

"You all thought I was dead. I understand that. But what I don't understand is how you continued to think so when it was Daris Antonius and his men who took me from the White Palace."

Sonah cringed away as Lerek's voice rose. Around them, the sounds from the soldiers nearby stopped altogether, and she realized they had a bigger audience.

Panicking about how to respond, Sonah opened her mouth to speak when shouts at her back saved her.

BOTH MEN TURNED TOWARD THE NOISE AND SONAH RAN. LEREK REACHED out, grabbing hold of her arm. In her panic, Sonah whirled, slamming her fist into the side of his face.

Stumbling in shock as she watched Lerek fall back, Sonah's mouth fell open. Otto roared and snapped forward, grabbing a fistful of Sonah's hair when she turned away, and she shrieked at the pain tearing at her scalp.

Her foot slid out from under her and she fell, screaming again as Otto's grip snagged what she was sure was half her hair. Turning to scramble up, Sonah gaped as a large animal leaped over the fire and slammed into the guard. Taking advantage of the chaos, she pitched forward, running for her life.

Branches tore at her clothes and face, but Sonah was mindless as she ran through the woods, the cries of the soldiers fading behind her. Something sounded at her back, and Sonah whipped her head around, her throat seizing as a giant shadow tore through the trees.

Sonah turned back, but her foot snagged on a root. Her momentum hurled her forward and she screamed as the ground rose to meet her. Her hands shot out to break her fall and she screamed again when her wrist snapped as she hit the ground.

Tears tracked down her face and she turned, her eyes wide and body shaking. Sonah held her broken wrist to her chest as her ribs squeezed painfully.

She had no weapon, and she was wounded.

And something gigantic was now prowling out of the shadows toward her.

A low growl sounded, and she swallowed past the thick lump in her throat, her eyes wild as she regarded the large dog salivating before her.

Sonah scrambling back. She let out a squeak as a form became visible in the mist.

Sonah's eyes widened to saucers, her mouth dropping open as the form took shape and a woman stood before her. As Sonah watched the woman kneeling before her, a shaft of moonlight illuminated the woman's face. Long black hair framed a dark face lined with ink, symbols drawn on almost every inch of it. The woman leaned forward, impassive as she stared at Sonah. Curiosity and calculation were behind the gaze of the woman before her and Sonah remained still as death, waiting.

She jerked as the dog crept closer, having forgotten the animal momentarily.

The woman lifted her hand without moving her gaze from Sonah and the dog settled on his belly, shifting his head so his snout nuzzled against the woman's palm.

The silence went on for so long, Sonah felt her pulse quicken, and she licked her dry lips. Compelled to speak as usual when she was nervous, Sonah opened her mouth, but the woman's voice stopped her.

"Sonah," she said in a voice both soft and forceful and something shifted inside Sonah. All at once, her body relaxed and her heart slowed until she felt a languid heat fill her. Her lids became heavy.

Whispers sounded all around, growing louder, pressing in on Sonah before they stopped abruptly. Her gaze still locked on the strange woman, Sonah felt at peace.

"Who are you?" she whispered.

The woman reached out and pressed her thumb to the spot between Sonah's eyes, and they slid closed.

Minutes passed, and Sonah floated on clouds soft as satin. She burrowed deeper, a groan escaping her lips as she shifted, awareness tingling over her body as she opened her eyes. Creamy light flickered in haloes from numerous candles above her.

Sonah frowned.

She lifted onto her elbow, lips pursed as she took in her surroundings. Her mouth opened when it finally dawned on her she was no longer in the woods.

"And I'm not on a cloud, either."

"No, child."

Sonah sprang upright, her head on a swivel. A soft laugh

sounded to her right. Sonah gasped as Pytho stepped forward, dropping slowly to her knees at Sonah's side.

After the initial shock of seeing the oracle again after so long, Sonah shot forward. Hugging the woman, she sobbed into Pytho's shoulder. To her credit, Pytho let her cry, tightening her arms around Sonah and slowly rocking them back and forth, whispering soothing words.

"You are safe," she said, stroking Sonah's bramble-covered hair. She shuddered and cried harder, the events of the last few weeks overcoming her in a flood she feared would break her.

A long time passed before her tears slowed and her breath settled enough for her to loosen her death grip on the oracle.

When she finally pulled away, Pytho stroked Sonah's blonde hair away from her face, wiping the tears from her cheeks as she smiled at her.

"Was it you in the woods?" she asked, sniffling. She swiped at her eyes and took in a deep, ragged breath. "I thought it was at first, but your face was darker and lined with weird symbols. And you had a dog."

Pytho's smile turned wry. "No, child. That was not me."

"How did I get here?" Sonah looked down at her wrist, marveling. "My wrist isn't broken anymore."

Pytho sat back while Sonah regained her composure.

"The future has shifted. You were to have stayed with the commander in Sparta, to await your sister's arrival and that of your eudaemon," Pytho said, her eyes on something over Sonah's shoulder.

"My eudaemon?" Sonah shifted against the pillows. "But Daris is my eudaemon."

Pytho shook her head, pressing her hands together in her lap as she turned back to Sonah. "No, child. He is Terena's eudaemon. He was always hers. Daris was marked for her, and so the Fates made it so."

Sonah's eyes darted around as she thought. "But that means... Rydon is my guardian?"

"Aye. You must now wait in Messene. A traveler wearing green robes will come to the inn. When he leaves, follow him but remain unseen."

"Pytho, I can't with your riddles today," Sonah grumbled. She moved to stand, and Pytho rose with her, reaching out when Sonah stumbled. "Shouldn't I just go back to Sparta?"

"No," Pytho scowled. "You need to follow the traveler until you find the Rivermen. They will shelter you until your sister finds you."

Sonah gaped at the woman. "Rivermen? Those bastards work for Emperor Solon! I might as well kill myself now!"

"Do not!" Pytho snapped. Sighing, the oracle leveled her strange black eyes on Sonah once more and continued. "Trust I have your best interests at heart. There are larger forces—stronger forces—at play here. Stay in Messene and find the man with the green robes. He will lead you to the Rivermen."

"And then... what?" Sonah asked, jerking her arms out and letting them fall at her sides. "How will Ren find me?"

"That's not for you to worry about. The goddess has intervened on your behalf, and now you are to do as I say."

"The goddess? You mean Terena? What—you spoke with her? Where is she?"

Impatience flickered across Pytho's otherwise serene features. She reached out, her hands wrapping around Sonah's upper arms. "Focus, Sonah. Remember what I've said. Next time you open your eyes, you will recall my voice. You will recall my words. And you will follow the traveler in the green robes."

Transfixed, Sonah blinked against the intensity vibrating from Pytho's black eyes, the determined set of her jaw. Black edged Sonah's vision as Pytho's words rattled around in her head. Sonah felt like her body was liquifying, free falling into—

CHAPTER 12

IBROS

While following Sonah and Lerek hadn't been difficult, Daris was frustrated by how often he'd seemed on the verge of catching up to them only to have just missed them.

A fortnight after they'd left Arestia Castle, Daris found their camp in the woods south of Thuria. Sticking to the uncommon trails and woods, Daris and his men managed to evade Heylisian soldiers, though not before spying a large encampment a day's ride from the border to Lakonia. Athanasi's host had proved a convenient distraction from their watchful eyes.

"Looks like we missed them by mere hours. Again," Jason fumed, kicking at the remnants of their campfire.

"They weren't alone this time," Daris said, scowling at the clearing.

"Commander," Alexi called out as Michael crouched down, pushing aside some debris on the ground.

Daris stalked over, crouching beside Michael to see what he'd discovered.

Drops of blood.

Daris rose and surveyed the area. There were signs of a struggle. A few feet away, more blood. He moved forward and saw multiple hoof prints further away and swore.

"They weren't alone," Michael confirmed, and Daris spared him a look.

"No," Daris murmured, his eye scanning the clearing. "At least ten men here. He looked up at Jason. "Take Alexi and Perikles and search the woods thoroughly."

Jason strode over. "We have to go after them. Now!"

Daris pursed his lips. "Aye. But we do not need to rush into a battle without knowing who it is we'll fight. It could be brigands as easily as Heylisians."

A hawk's keening caught his attention, and Daris lifted his head to the sky, watching as the bird soared in circles before dropping to settle on Theodoros's arm.

He frowned down at the bird's ankle and the attached missive. Carefully pulling the paper from the hawk, he unfurled it and read.

"What is it?" Jason asked as he went to stand before Daris.

"Duke Ovenno left Sparta. He found out Sonah wasn't ill after all."

"Bound to happen eventually," Theodoros muttered as he stroked a finger along the hawk's back. "Took him long enough to figure it out."

"Commander Antonius!" Michael jogged over, one hand on the hilt of his sword. He clutched something in his left hand, holding it out to Daris with a scowl.

Daris reached for it in silence, staring at the dirty cloth a few seconds before cursing soundly.

Motioning to Theodoros, Daris turned the king's message over in his hand and quickly scrawled a reply, rolling up the parchment and securing the leather tie to the hawk perched on the Liodari's arm.

When he finished, Theodoros launched the hawk, carrying his message to King Altos.

"These are Heylisia's colors," Daris said, holding up the blood stained fabric Michael had found. He shoved it behind his breastplate and turned to eye his men. "Whether Sonah and the prince went willingly with Heylisian soldiers is unclear, but we know this camp was attacked."

"We should be able to catch them if we ride hard," Jason said, his voice clipped.

Daris noted the Liodari's stiff posture and hardened features and gave a quick nod. "Aye, but there are two sets of tracks," he said.

Walking away, he gestured to the frost covered grass and leaves, disturbed by whatever had happened there. "The one on foot is alone and looks to lead west. I don't believe whoever it is is going to Sparta, so we have to assume it'll be Messene, but we won't know until we get closer. As for the other set," he motioned, stepping carefully so as not to disturb the trail, "multiple hoof prints heading north."

"If they were camped here with Heylisian soldiers, who attacked them?"

Daris looked to Michael, whose uncanny investigative abilities had helped them track Sonah and Lerek's progress thus far.

The man gripped the collar of his breastplate as he walked to the edge of the clearing. He slowed, stopping near a tree, and stared at the ground. Dropping to his haunches, he felt around the ground, then turned, his gaze catching Daris as he lifted something in his hands. Daris stalked to his side, grabbing the item he held up.

Frayed rope.

"It isn't cut," Michael said, standing beside Daris. "So either whoever was bound had removed it themselves or someone came along and undid them."

"My money's on the former," Daris muttered, his thumb moving slowly over the hemp. "If it was a rescue, they wouldn't take the time to untie them. They'd cut the binds."

"Who was tied up, then?"

Daris frowned, his eye rising from the rope to the tree. He moved forward, crouching down and placing his free hand on the damp ground where the surrounding frost left an outline of the person who'd sat there.

"Sonah," he said at last.

"Aye," Michael replied.

"What? How do you know?" Jason demanded as he strode to their sides.

Michael pointed at the ground. "The indentation is small, so either a child sat here, or a woman. And since they're Heylisian soldiers, we know they wouldn't bind their prince."

"And Prince Lerek allowed it to happen?" Jason shouted, arms spread as shock warred with rage across his face.

"I found strands of blonde hair near the fire," Michael went on, his eyes on Jason. "Enough to make me think it didn't fall out naturally."

Daris sighed and dropped his head. A moment later, he strode briskly back to the rest of his men. Theodoros brought Daris's stallion forward and Daris mounted.

"I'll assume you want to ride with me toward Messene," Daris said with a glance at Jason. He didn't bother to see whether his lieutenant agreed with him. He looked at Michael. "I'm taking four men toward Messene. You and the others follow the Heylisians."

Michael nodded as the rest of the Liodari mounted their horses and waited. Daris clicked his tongue and pulled the reins to the right.

"What do we do when we catch up to them?" Michael called out.

"Kill them all and detain the prince. I have words for him."

MESSENE, LAKONIA

Sonah jerked awake.

Panting, she looked around the room she was in, the weak light from the lone window shading the room in grey. Pushing back some of the hair that had fallen onto her face, she turned, setting her feet to the cold, bare floor.

"What the fuck?" she whispered. Bending over, Sonah rested an elbow on her thigh and covered her eyes. As she shifted her fingers over her face, she winced at the large bump on her forehead. Her wrist, however, was healed.

Had it ever been broken? Was that whole thing a nightmare?

Minutes passed before she felt focused enough to rise and face whatever was happening. As she hunted for her clothes, she recalled the escape from the castle, being with Lerek and then seeing Pytho.

Pausing as she tightened her leather corset, Sonah frowned.

Follow the traveler with the green robes.

She spotted her cloak in a heap near the door and snatched it up. Turning back to look over the sparse room, she nodded and unlatched the door. Sonah peeked out into the empty hallway before closing the door behind her.

As she descended the stairs, Sonah realized she was in the same inn she'd stayed in the first time she'd been in Messene with Terena and Rydon. And just like when Terena had reappeared after visiting Pytho, Sonah had a feeling she had the clever oracle to thank for her arrival here, too.

Jerking to a stop before entering the common room, Sonah lifted her hood when she spotted two Spartan soldiers sitting at a table near the front door. Ducking her head, she bolted forward, intent on finding the innkeeper and asking how long she'd—

Sonah's mouth fell open when she saw a portly man at the back, sitting at a table with three other men.

"There's room for you by the window," a voice said behind her and Sonah barely looked away from the man she'd been watching to acknowledge the innkeeper smiling at her.

Nodding, Sonah grumbled her thanks as he led her to a table far enough away from the soldiers she let herself relax. Her eyes remained on the big man, now laughing with his companions. He raised a hairy hand to dust crumbs off his green robes. His voice was too low for Sonah to hear.

Follow the traveler with the green robes.

"May I get you a coffee? Or some ale? We have eggs with vegetables and bread—"

"A coffee would be nice, thank you, sir," Sonah said distractedly.

Sonah turned her attention back to the green-robed man. When the innkeeper returned with her coffee, she barely acknowledged him. She raised the steaming mug to her lips, her eyes still on her quarry, then yelped.

All eyes turned to her as she shot to her feet, cursing as her hand jerked and she hissed at the burn of coffee when it splashed on her hand. Her other hand flew to her stinging mouth, her eyes watering as she set the coffee down.

So much for remaining unseen.

The innkeeper rushed over. Before he could get to her, another man was beside her. Glancing up, Sonah swore again.

Soldier.

"Sonah?"

Sonah stiffened. Her eyes widened and she twisted, blood leeching from her face when she took a good look at the soldier.

Of all the ill luck. And on her very first solo quest.

"Fane?"

CHEVALA, LAKONIA

Days after discovering Sonah's abandoned camp, Daris still had not found her. They'd stuck to the wooded areas and checked in the smaller villages as they made their way north, but no one had seen a blonde woman either alone or in the company of anyone traveling that way.

Frustrated, he called a halt an hour after dusk as they neared Chevela, a town south of the Pyranos Mountains. A few more days and they'd reach Messene, where he planned to stop and seek out the oracle's guidance if he hadn't found Sonah by then.

After stabling the horses, Jason led the way to the nearest tavern. Daris hung at the back of the group as they walked. He pulled off the leather eyepatch and rubbed at the scar over his eye. Letting out a sigh as his muscles relaxed a bit, he fitted the patch back over his eye and followed his men into the tavern.

The low murmur of conversations greeted them as they filed inside. Taking a seat at the only vacant table, Daris glanced around again, his eye narrowing as he took in the hard look of the men in the establishment. There was no laughter, no jovial conversation. Even the way they drank their ale or ate their food seemed menacing.

Something was wrong here.

"Get you anything?" the barmaid asked in the common tongue. She had a scarf over her brown hair and she scratched at a rash marring the column of her neck. Her eyes darted around, first at Daris and his men, then the men at the tables closest to them.

Daris smiled warmly at the young woman and answered her in Greek, ordering pitchers of ale for the table and water for himself.

As the barmaid hustled away, Daris sat back in his chair.

There were four men at the table to his right. All of them wore similar clothes: dark, nondescript garments and hooded cloaks. Two of them had their hoods up, even though the tavern was warmed by a fire in the large hearth on the far side. On his left, a man wearing a black kerchief on his head watched him over the rim of his tankard.

When he caught Daris's eye, he sneered at him, but didn't look away.

"It's about to get interesting, boys," Jason muttered. The others shifted, bracing for what they all knew was coming.

A moment later, the barmaid returned with three pitchers. "I'll be back with your water and tankards for the ale," she mumbled. Before she turned away, Daris caught her wrist.

"Are you in trouble?" he asked the girl in a low voice.

Startled, the barmaid looked over at him; her face was pale. She gave herself away by glancing to his left before shaking her head quickly. "No, lord. Just busy. As you see."

Daris let go of the girl and she hurried away.

Sitting back slowly, Daris shifted his gaze to his left and saw two men leaning forward, their eyes narrowed with scowls on their lips.

Daris turned his head to face them, staring them down. He kept his face neutral, unwilling to instigate, but fully prepared to engage if need be.

One man scoffed and broke the stare by taking a swig of his ale. Conversations resumed, and his men mumbled thanks when the girl returned with their tankards.

As he lifted his glass to drink, Daris caught sight of a large blond man across the tavern staring at him. Half of his hair was pulled back away from his face, making his cheekbones appear sharper. His eyes were narrowed as he stared at Daris.

Daris took a drink and set his glass down, tearing his gaze away and looked around, half listening to the conversation at their table. His gaze drifted back to the man as if by an unseen force. The man hadn't moved, his face hard and all sharp angles as he stared back at Daris so intently, Daris wondered if the man knew him.

The man who'd been sneering at him from the table next to them stood, his chair scraping loudly across the floor.

"What the fuck are you lot supposed to be? Lordlings out slumming?"

Rough laughter rumbled around them as Daris broke off his stare and turned to the man who'd spoken.

"We want no trouble, friend," Jason called out, lifting his mug. "We're tired from a long day and want to enjoy our ale."

"I wasn't talking to you, pretty lad," the man snarled as he grabbed hold of the back of Elias's chair. "I was talking to your lady friend here," he said and slapped the back of Elias's head.

As one, the Liodari bolted up from the table.

Except Daris. He'd turned his gaze back to the blond man staring at him from across the tavern. A slight smile was the only movement on his face as Daris remained seated.

"If you wish to live," Daris said in a menacing voice loud enough to quiet the men around them, "sit down. Now. Or you will have lived your last moments."

He never took his eye off the blond man. The man stared back at him, unmoving.

The man next to him made a grunting noise a moment before he came at Daris. Faster than the blink of an eye, Daris snapped up with his dagger and slashed the man's throat. He spared his victim a glance as the man brought his hands up to his neck, blood pouring over his fingers as he dropped to his knees. Elias moved when the man's body bumped against his chair and kicked him savagely away.

Silence reigned for a few seconds before pandemonium erupted. It seemed everyone in the bar ached for a fight, and the Liodari happily obliged. Daris cut through three men before rounding the table, more men streaming around him as his Liodari fought in a semi-circle behind him.

The men rushed at Daris. He forcefully kicked against one's sternum. Daris flipped his sword and swung in a mighty arc, taking another man's head clean off his shoulders.

Twisting back to face a new onslaught, Daris cocked back to smash his fist into a thug's face. A sharp whistle sounded. The attackers stopped all at once. Staggering away, the ruffians looking behind them at the blond man who remained seated.

The Liodari shifted around uncertainly, their weapons at the ready. The few remaining thugs filed back to their tables. Their dead allies were already forgotten where they lay.

In the silence that followed, Daris snapped his gaze back to the blond man, who stared back at him for a moment, his face inscrutable, before rising slowly.

Even from across the tavern, Daris could see the man was tall. While his frame wasn't large and bulky, Daris could tell he was muscular, despite being hidden beneath clothes tailored to give the appearance of a thief or ruffian. The ruse failed up close when Daris saw their quality was that of a nobleman.

Daris controlled his breathing as the man took his time walking across the tavern, his eyes still locked on him. As Daris glanced around, he saw the others watched this man with something akin to reverence.

"We've been watching you for days," the blond man said, his voice pleasant, conversational. As he moved closer to Daris, the Liodari begrudgingly cleared a path for him, as if compelled to move against their will.

Daris's eye widened as the man stepped closer. He was a few inches taller than Daris. Arms crossed, he narrowed his aquamarine eyes, regarding Daris with curiosity.

"I was disappointed you didn't notice my men," the man went on, his voice smooth like honey. "But, then again, I'd be disappointed in my men if you had."

A few chuckles sounded from the men seated around them.

"And what is your interest with us?"

"With *you*, Commander," the blond man said, his melodic voice a purr. He bent forward. "My interest is with you."

CHAPTER 13

MESSENE

Sonah's wide-eyed shock took in the broadening smile on Fane's face. How in hells was he even here? And why was he dressed as a regular soldier and not a Liodari?

Shaking her head, Sonah chanced a glance at the traveler she was to follow, who watched her and Fane with interest. She felt the blood rush back to her cheeks and she could've murdered Fane for his ill-timed interference.

Her tongue, too, was scorched and she spoke with some difficulty. "What are you doing here?"

"What am *I* doing here?" Fane scoffed, using the napkin he held to wipe the coffee on the table. When he was done, he palmed it and set his hand on his hip. "Why are *you* here? I thought you were in Sparta." As if that thought had triggered another, Fane tilted his head. "Is Commander Antonius with you?"

"No," Sonah huffed, throwing furtive glances at the green-robed man. He was no longer looking over at her, having turned his attention back to his companions. Sonah made a frustrated noise and shot Fane a mulish look. "I'm here alone."

Closing her eyes, Sonah swore under her breath. *Fucking stupid.*

Fane blinked in surprise. "Alone? No, that cannot be. You're—"

"Fane," Sonah whispered, her hand latching onto his vambrace. "Stop talking for a second. Do me a favor and please forget you saw me. I have... business here. Now go about yours."

Fane frowned and stepped closer.

For the love of the gods...

"I am not going anywhere now," Fane muttered, his light brown eyes narrowed. "What's going on? Where is everyone? Why are you alone?"

"Why are you so nosy?"

The Liodari pursed his lips. "I get that way when someone I know is alone and vulnerable and acting suspiciously." He looked over his shoulder and Sonah followed his gaze to see the soldier he'd been sitting with eyeing them curiously.

"I'm not alone," Sonah hissed, drawing Fane's attention back. "I am traveling with... that man. I woke up late, that's all."

Fane looked over at the man in question, his frown deepening. "Well, it's rude of him to ignore you—"

He made to step past Sonah, intent on the traveler, and Sonah's heart stopped. Without thinking, she grabbed his arm.

"No! Don't—don't bother him. He's with... important people. I am fine waiting. You need not concern yourself any longer. Please."

Gods, why did she have to run into a nosy Liodari on her very first solo mission?

Fane looked at her with a cocky grin, but Sonah wouldn't give in. Instead, she crossed her arms. "And where is your uniform, Liodari? Perhaps I'll tell the commander you were seen..."

The look on Fane's face made Sonah's words trail off, and she felt the shame and anger emanating from him as if they lived the surface of his tawny skin. He looked away from her, taking a step back and Sonah felt like an ass.

"Fane?"

His throat worked as he sought to find the words, but Sonah had a feeling she knew what had happened.

"After... after you all left us that... that last time," Fane started, each word pulled from him, leaving behind a scarlet blush high on his cheeks. "Commander Antonius dismissed me from the Liodari. I was sent down to the infantry under Captain Sedaros."

"What? Why?" Sonah said, reaching out to lay her hand on his forearm. "Was... was anyone else—"

Fane shook his head. He turned his gaze to look at her, and she felt a pang of sympathy at the agony in his eyes. "No one else was at fault. I alone am responsible for what transpired between your sister and the commander. I spoke out of turn and I deserved the punishment."

Sonah felt heat flash over her face and chest. She knew what he meant. She'd overheard him that night, while she'd been searching for something to clean up the vomit she'd left in the room. Jason, Fane and Michael had come back to the inn just then and spoke of Lerek's murder.

That Daris had been the one to kill him.

Knowing now it was a falsehood, Sonah felt even more guilt for her part in the affair. Not only was Lerek not dead, but Fane had been punished for revealing something that never happened. Punished severely, Sonah thought.

Not for the first time, she wondered why they'd lied about Lerek at all.

She hadn't bothered to question Lerek about it, worried he might use it as an opportunity to ask even more questions of his own. She'd fumbled the first few attempts he'd made to ask about Terena. And the way his face had contorted when he'd brought up Daris made her relieved she'd not broached the topic.

Sonah opened her mouth to say something, when the men at the far table—the green-robed man, too—rose and made their way to the door. Panicking, Sonah moved away from Fane, pulling up her hood.

"I must go," she mumbled, hoping to put an end to the unwanted meeting with the former Liodari.

"Sonah, wait," Fane called, snapping forward to grip her elbow.

Whirling, Sonah slapped at his hand, looking back over her shoulder to see the men were already gone.

"Let go!"

"You can't go off by yourself!"

"I am *not* by myself, I already told you," Sonah whimpered, clawing at his hand to release his hold.

Fane pulled close, his height dwarfing her by a foot as he glared down at her. "I don't know why you're lying, or what you're about, but I will not let you go off with those men. Not alone. If you wish to travel with them, I will go with you."

Sonah balked. "What? No!"

"Aye," Fane snarled, his face lowered to within inches. "Because I don't believe you're traveling with that man at all. I think you're following him. Alone. What kind of Spartan would I be if I let you go off after a stranger without protection?"

She opened her mouth to say something, anything, to get him to let her go. Surely, the traveler had gotten far enough away from the inn by now, following him would be that much more difficult. By the time she finished explaining Pytho had told her to follow him, she'd lose the man for certain.

Fane shut her up with his next words.

"We'll follow him together. You do not need to tell me why or what you're about. But I will not let you leave without me."

SONAH PUT A HAND TO HER WAIST, HOPING THAT RUBBING THE CRAMP forming while she struggled to keep up with Fane's long-legged strides and the man they were following would somehow make it hurt less.

If anything, it grew worse. She began to see black spots at the edges of her vision and her breaths became more labored.

At her side, Fane swore and put an arm around her waist, half carrying her as he led them around the bend where the men had disappeared.

"How are you this winded after a ten minute walk?" he grumbled as they caught sight of the travelers again. They were now in front of a stable yard, standing in a circle and laughing about whatever they were talking over.

Sonah swallowed painfully as they slowed down. Fane maneuvered them into a small opening between two buildings directly across from the stables. She was grateful for the reprieve, sucking in deep breaths as she leaned against a stone wall and closed her eyes.

"I'll have you know," she said between wheezing breaths, "that I trekked across this whole continent with no complaints from my friends. But of *course*, leave it to a Liodari to take exception at having to slow down a bit to accommodate someone with shorter legs."

"I'm not a Liodari anymore."

Sonah blinked. She watched him for a few seconds before apologizing. "Sorry. If it makes you feel any better, you are still a Liodari to me."

Fane glanced at her and she saw the color high in his cheeks before he turned away. His jaw was working overtime, but he said nothing as he continued to watch the travelers. Sonah closed her eyes.

"Let's go," Fane said in a rough voice, lightly tugging on Sonah's cloak. Blinking, she followed as he took a circuitous route to the stables.

Looking around, Sonah panicked.

"Where—"

"Do you have a horse?" Fane interrupted.

"Uh, no."

"Two," he said to the stable hand. Sonah looked after the man as he ran back inside to tack the horses.

"Did you see which way they went?" Sonah asked quietly, leaning close to Fane.

He nodded, folding his arms across his chest. His foot tapped an annoying beat.

"Could—"

"Here," he said, grabbing her hand and striding toward the man leading two horses, his sweat stained tunic sticking to his chest and biceps.

Sonah frowned as the stable hand led the smaller of the two horses over to her, a grin splitting his homely face as he proudly presented the animal to Sonah.

She stared at it suspiciously.

Not that she hated horses; she liked them fine. She didn't believe they liked her back, which was the issue.

Before she could voice a concern over the way the horse stared at her, she yelped when large hands spanned her waist and hoisted her onto the saddle. Sonah made a grab for the reins, still in the stableman's hands. The man chuckled, sharing a look with Fane that made her curse them under her breath.

Fane, of course, mounted his horse gracefully and led them out of the yard, trotting down the street in what she hoped was the direction the traveler in green had headed.

They caught sight of them every once in a while. When they did, Fane would slow, dropping back so that they would remain undetected. Hours later, after crossing into Ibros, Sonah began to despair. They'd lost their quarry. She was about to admit defeat when she spotted the trio of men fifty feet in front of them, coming into view at the bottom of a hill.

Fane must have spotted them as well, for he reached back and made a clicking sound. Sonah's horse stepped close to his side and he grabbed her reins as he turned back to where the travelers were.

"We'll stay well behind them to remain unnoticed," Fane muttered.

Sonah sat for a moment in silence before Fane made another

clicking noise and their horses set off. She hastily tightened her grip on the reins and the horse let out what seemed to Sonah an affronted snort.

"Do you not need to be somewhere?" Sonah asked after a few minutes of riding in silence. "Doing... soldier things?"

"Leventis, the soldier I was with, knows to tell our captain I was called away. He'll cover for me until I can send word again."

"Huh," Sonah narrowed her gaze at his back. As if he felt her eyes on him, he glanced over his shoulder. "Seems like a very lax team, or whatever."

"My squad is not Liodari, but we're not lax, either," he grumbled, shooting Sonah a scowl before turning forward.

"Do you still talk to any of the others?" Sonah fished, trying to inject some boredom into her tone. "Michael? Or... Jason?"

Fane winked at her.

"What?"

"I know."

Shouts sounded ahead, and Fane whipped his head around a moment before he and his horse took off. Sonah barely held on as her horse bolted after him, holding her breath as panic washed over her.

Fane had his sword out of its scabbard as they neared the travelers, two of them on the ground with arrows sticking out of their chests and the green-robed man crawling, an arrow jutting out of his calf.

Sonah's mount reared as an arrow whistled past her ear. She tumbled from her horse and onto her back. The breath knocked out of her—she couldn't move, she couldn't breathe, and her ribcage was suddenly too tight. Grabbing at her tunic, Sonah's eyes shot around, but all she could see were legs rushing to and fro.

Finally able to pull in air, Sonah turned over. Scrambling to her knees, she grunted as a muscular arm banded around her waist and yanked her up into the air. Sonah screeched, her hands clawing at her captor's arm. Pitching forward, her legs flailed as she fought to get on the ground. Barely finding her footing, Sonah went still at the press of a cold blade at her throat.

"Halt, Spartan!"

Sonah winced as the shout rang through her ears. Her wild eyes found Fane off to her left, bloodied but fighting off a soldier wearing Heylisian colors. Her heart dropped when she realized who had attacked them.

Rivermen.

When he heard the command, Fane did a double take upon seeing Sonah. The soldier he'd been fighting caught him with a punch to his jaw and Fane stumbled. His eyes filled with rage and fear as his gaze darted between Sonah and her captor.

Finally raising his hands in surrender, Fane stood still as another soldier grabbed his sword out of his hand and threw it near Sonah.

"What is a Spartan doing this far north, I wonder?" The man holding her chuckled, his nose nuzzling her throat. She jerked away, hissing. He laughed some more, the throaty sound rumbling through her body as the man held her tight to his chest. "And with such a lovely companion."

"Let her go," Fane snapped, earning him a shove from one of the Rivermen.

"I don't think I will," the man at her back said. He tightened his arm at her waist. Sonah chanced a look behind Fane and almost vomited when she saw the green-robed traveler lying on his stomach, blood soaking the bulk of his cloak over his back.

"You'd like to stay with us, wouldn't you, love?" the man whispered, his voice low and rough and seductive. Bile rose in Sonah's throat.

"I cannot allow that," a new voice said, the deep baritone making Sonah cry out in relief.

Every head whipped around toward the voice. Melanos stepped forward, his oversized frame domineering. The god wore the same long tunic and sandals he'd worn in the cave a few months ago when she and Terena had helped break the curse keeping Melanos confined inside.

The man holding her yelled to his men and they burst into motion, rushing at Melanos as she was dragged away. Fane barreled after her, but the Riverman at his side was faster, kicking the back of Fane's knee. Sonah screamed out to Melanos and Fane as the Rivermen surrounded them.

She kicked and spat, twisting and almost freeing herself, when the soldier holding her stumbled against her momentum.

Suddenly free, Sonah ran.

She'd not gotten far when she was snatched around the waist and thrown over the man's broad shoulder. His armor punched the air out of her lungs. When she regained her breath, Sonah screamed again, watching through tears as her friends continued fighting off the Rivermen.

Thrown over a saddle, Sonah immediately tried to slide off. The soldier leaped onto the horse and grabbed the back of her cloak, pulling her back. She clawed at her throat where the cloak fastenings were choking her.

With the little remaining air left in her lungs, Sonah feebly called out as the horse raced away from her friends. And any chance of escape.

CHAPTER 124

NEAR CALLA, OVENNO

The tracker had worn Terena down on their journey south to Calla. Terena had agreed to let Vassori send a note to her brother for news of Sonah's whereabouts. When they were close to the capital, Vassori had gone off alone to send word to Xoran and await his response. While they waited, Terena had sent Migela and Gabriol north to fetch the cleric. They were all to meet back up outside of the city.

Rydon had cautioned against splitting up, but Ren had told him of the story Orry had found in his research. A story of an amulet gifted to a shepherd that sounded very much like the one Xoran—and the emperor—were searching for.

Shortly before Migela and Gabriol returned with a smiling Orry, Vassori rode into their camp and pulled Terena away. As she'd gotten up to speak with the tracker, Gabriol and Migela showed up with Orry. The cleric's cherubic face was bright red from the ride, his precious tomes stuffed in a bag he clutched to his chest. After exchanging greetings, Orry made his way to the fire behind Migela, and settled beside her.

A scream tore through the encampment.

Rydon took off running, his heart thundering painfully as his mind emptied of all but getting to Terena.

When he found her, she was crouched low, her head in her hands with Croak standing near her, shoulders slumped. Vassori stood over her, a piece of parchment clutched in her fingers as she looked up. Rydon skidded to a halt.

"What's happened?" he shouted, arms spread as he stalked toward their small group.

"News from my brother," Vassori said dismissively, her gaze falling back to Terena's huddled form. Ren sprang up, her face bright red, eyes brimming with tears Rydon knew she would not shed in present company.

"He turned on us?" Rydon turned to Vassori, who flinched back at the look on his face.

To her credit, the tracker faced him with her chin lifted. "He did not turn on us. It's all part of his plan."

"Part of his plan?" Croak's cruel sneer belied his fear for his sister. "What plan calls for him to lose Sonah?"

Rydon gaped at Croak a second before lunging at Vassori. Gabriol moved to intercept him, and Croak chuckled at all of them.

"He lost her?"

"He did not lose her," Vassori snarled, shoving against Rydon's hold on her shirt. She looked over at Terena, a desperate plea in her voice. "He did not lose her, goddess. The next part of his plan would not work without first making it *look* like he lost Sonah Yahn."

"And what part of the plan is that?" Croak called out.

Without bothering to look at the boy, Vassori continued to speak to Terena.

"He cannot return to the emperor without Sonah Yahn, and he would not betray *you*, so he had a plan to make it look like they were attacked—"

"They *were* attacked!" Croak yelled. Rydon turned his attention back to Terena, who seemed at war with herself.

"Keep your fucking voice down," Rydon growled, his eyes bulging as he glared at Croak. "If Ovenno soldiers patrol nearby, you've just given us away, you fool!"

Croak flushed and dropped his head. Rydon motioned for Vassori to continue.

"He needed a ruse to get Sonah away from his soldiers, I understand," Rydon continued, stepping close to the tracker with a menacing glare. "So what happened? Where's Sonah?"

"She did not meet up with the man she was supposed to find," Vassori said cryptically. Lifting her hand, she held out the parchment to Rydon, who snatched it from her with a frown.

"What's that mean?" he asked as he scanned the missive. He shook his head, not understanding what the note meant.

"She's been taken," Terena said, her voice choking on the last word. She pushed past Vassori, her movements jerky as she quickened her pace. Rydon followed, with Croak and Gabriol close behind.

"She was not taken," Vassori was saying, jogging to catch up to Terena. "She escaped——"

"She was *taken*," Terena spat, turning on her with the viciousness of a viper. Standing toe to toe with the tracker, Terena's eyes burned. "By Rivermen. And now Solon will have her, regardless of what your brother promised."

"Mayhap that was the plan all along," Croak muttered, earning him a shove from Gabriol. Migela reached out reflexively to steady Croak as the boy looked over at them, affronted. "What? Don't tell me none of you thought of that possibility? We've known Xoran for years, and you're surprised he's gone back on his word?"

"I know my brother," Vassori argued, her breaths sharp as she raced after Terena, who'd stormed off once more. "The Rivermen were to meet up with Xoran to hand over Sonah but she escaped. He would not lie about that. He swore an oath——"

"Not to me," Terena snapped, sparing a quick glance over her shoulder at the other woman. Vassori shook off the venom in Terena's voice.

"Aye," she conceded, continuing to follow Terena. The others kept a safe distance as they listened to the exchange in silence. "Aye, not to you. But to someone he would never cross."

"Solon?" Rydon called out.

"No," Vassori growled, not bothering to look at him. She stepped in front of Terena, her hands on Ren's arms.

"He swore to—"

Before she could finish, a look of surprise came over her face and she fainted.

TERENA LEANED AGAINST ONE OF THE LARGE BOSSENA TREES GROWING NEAR the river. This time of year, their graceful branches, filled with distinctive orange leaves in the summer months, were bare. Swaying lazily in the breeze coming from the east, they resembled emaciated limbs with thin, bony fingers crackling faintly against one another. They reminded Terena of the eerie sound the incense burners made when the priests in Metilai would wave them in front of worshipers on the high days.

Shivering against both the sounds of the trees and the cold air creeping beneath her fur-lined cloak, Terena looked over her shoulder, waiting. She'd told Rydon to come for her when Vassori woke, but that was half an hour ago. Frowning, Terena turned halfway, ready to make her way back to camp, when she spotted someone coming through the trees toward her.

Croak smiled when he caught sight of her, and she relaxed her stance, smiling back at him.

"Where's Rydon?" she asked when he ambled to her side with a big sigh.

"With Vassori. She's awake but when she tries to recall what happened," he shrugged. "Nothing."

"Strange," Terena remarked quietly, almost to herself.

Croak clicked his tongue and bent over, swiping up a branch and waving it in the air like a sword. "Not really. Vassori is strange, so it stands to reason..."

Terena laughed lightly, shaking her head as she straightened away from the tree. As she walked, Croak fell into step beside her.

"Do you think she meant Hermes?" he asked as they came upon the camp. Orry was sitting beside Gabriol, blowing on a cup he clenched between his hands. As they approached, Gabriol lifted his head and gave her a slight nod. She smothered a smile when she caught Gabriol's glassy-eyed expression as he listened to Orry explain something he'd read in a priestess's journal about how the shroud opened the portal.

"I don't know who else it could be," Terena answered Croak, taking a seat on a log in front of the fire opposite Orry. "Perhaps he bound her, making her unable to say anything he wants kept secret."

"She said she didn't know him."

Terena shrugged as she stretched out her legs. "Wouldn't be the first time someone's lied to us."

Croak sat next to Orry and sighed, taking the cup from his friend's hands, despite the protest from both Orry and Gabriol.

"There's plenty to go around," Orry scoffed, even as he reached into his saddlebag for another cup. He poured the steaming brew and handed the cup across to Terena. She thanked him, lifting it to her nose and smiling as the bitter aroma made her shiver.

"The boy told you?" Gabriol asked, his voice gruff.

Terena took a tentative sip and shrugged. "He told me Vassori doesn't remember anything."

"She remembers. But she cannot say," Gabriol replied.

When Terena lifted an eyebrow, he added, "Vassori is bound by an oath to a god. So she cannot tell you more. Literally."

Croak looked over at her, twirling his fingers at his forehead as if doffing his hat. "Is the oracle rubbing off on you?" When he saw the quizzical look on Gabriol's face, Croak grinned. "Ren said the same thing earlier."

"You knew?"

Terena shrugged at Gabriol. "It was a guess."

"I wonder what god would make her swear an oath like that," Croak mumbled. "But there's only one god in this realm I feel would definitely bind someone to keep quiet about his nefarious schemes."

"That may be," Gabriol said, his voice dropping lower as he leaned forward, his gaze still on Terena. "But this doesn't feel like Hermes. She swears it wasn't, and I believe her. He wants to get Sonah back, maybe more than you do."

Terena twisted her lips at him and rolled her eyes.

"Regardless," Orry said, his gaze on his hot cup as he blew on it once more, "do we still want to find this amulet for Captain Xoran?"

"No," Ren said softly. "We go after Sonah."

"But you don't know where she is," Orry replied.

"We know where she *was*," Croak said.

"Maybe we can let the captain continue his search for Sonah while we look for the amulet?"

"If you keep saying stupid shit," Croak snapped, "you're walking back to Olympia."

"I know, I know," Orry said calmly, shifting on the log with a wince. "Hear me out, though. I believe Captain Xoran will continue his search for—"

"So? Where do we go next?" asked Rydon, appearing behind Gabriol. His deep voice was threaded with exhaustion.

"That's what we were just discussing," Orry piped up, wiping the dirt off his cup on the sleeve of his robes. "I was telling Terena we cannot find the amulet without some clue of where to start. We could've done it if we were all back at the White Palace—"

"Pass," Croak grumbled.

"Right," Orry sighed. "So, barring that, we need a seer."

"What?" Croak scoffed. "You want to go to Messene?"

"Messene?" Orry asked, confused. Croak arched a brow at him, and Orry pursed his lips before he realized what Croak meant. "Ah! No, no, we don't need an *oracle*," he said patiently. With a smile, he looked over at Terena. "We need a seer."

"There's a difference?" she asked over the rim of her cup before taking a drink.

"Aye!" Orry said, pulling his robes tighter about him as he leaned forward, warming to the topic. "An oracle sees big things, visions only Apollo can see; things affecting all of humanity and divinity. Seers tap into the magic of the world around us, the magic within the realm of Elysium, to guide their visions. They've been practicing since Hekate educated the first women. She taught them how to harness magic, how to cast spells and create potions from herbs and trees and flowers.

"The knowledge has been diluted, I believe, over centuries, especially since the emperor's obsessive search for gods."

When he finished speaking, Orry cast a look at the others, their silence expectant and their gazes entranced. Licking his lips, a corner of his mouth lifted as he continued.

"Many were killed after the Immortals War, but I've read that the priestesses, the ones who worshipped the goddess, Hekate, continued practicing, passing down their knowledge to their acolytes.

"At some point, they educated ordinary village women with their skills, and those women passed it along to their daughters and so on. As I said, it's been much diluted; I've found mentions in some scrolls of women who only cast or only create potions, many of whom are village apothecaries nowadays."

"What of seers, then?" Terena asked softly.

Orry lifted a finger and touched his nose with a sly smile. "And seers. Though, women with that gift are even more cautious than the village women who heal. The seers were among the first killed after the war. Those women were descendants of Apollo. That god never met a woman he didn't want to impregnate, it seems. He fathered demigods who had the gift of sight and from what I've read in one account from a priestess of Hekate during that time, one of Apollo's conquests sought Hekate's help to hide her daughter. She begged the goddess, offering the goddess servitude for eternity if she would save her daughter from the purge. According to the priestess's account, Hekate agreed and took in the girl, helping her hone her sight, teaching her the witchcraft she'd taught others."

"So what you're saying," Croak said loudly as he slid off the log to lean against it with a big groan. He pulled up one leg and rested his elbow on it as he splayed his hand. "So what you're saying is we not only need to find the amulet, but now we need to find a seer, too?"

"We don't need to find a seer," Rydon announced as he took a seat beside Orry. He stretched out his hands to the fire, his expression thoughtful. "The Fates are ever watchful, it seems."

Gabriol shifted and stared at him for a moment. "You mean..."

"Aye."

"Well? Don't keep us in suspense," Croak said sarcastically. "We're all dying to know!"

"I... met a seer once. Near here, in Ermanel."

"Why do I feel like there's so much you're not telling us?" Croak barked out a laugh as he winked at Terena.

"How'd you meet a seer?" Terena asked, pulling her knees closer to her body and hunching forward.

Gabriol's face broke into a big grin as color suffused Rydon's neck and face.

Running a hand over the back of his neck, Rydon stuttered.

"Can't hear you, old man!" Croak laughed.

"I said," Rydon said through gritted teeth. "I met her during a card game."

"How long ago?" Orry asked. "She could be anywhere by now."

"I'm certain she is still there," Rydon snapped. "Just as I'm certain the Fates are grinning down at us about it right now."

"So... did you leave on good terms?" Terena asked.

Gabriol guffawed, throwing his head back and holding his belly. If possible, Rydon's color deepened to a darker crimson.

"I think so," he hedged.

"Gabriol, tell us," Croak commanded, snapping his fingers.

Smothering more laughter, Gabriol ignored the glare from Rydon and looked over at the others.

"You have to understand, the woman was very beautiful, and Rydon was... smitten," Gabriol said.

Croak laughed and sat up straight, already loving where this was headed.

"I was not," Rydon ground out.

"Aye, you were," Gabriol laughed. "She bet him one night with her if he won the game. All night he'd been winning, and she'd been losing, so he readily took the bet."

"You bet a *seer,* someone who sees the future, that you would win? Are you stupid?"

Rydon's head snapped around and bared his teeth at Croak.

"He's not wrong," Terena said, grabbing the back of Rydon's cloak to stop him from pummeling her brother. "Why would you do something like that?"

"I don't know!"

"You lost, obviously."

Rydon grunted while the others grinned at his discomfiture.

"What did you bet?" Terena asked, a faint smile on her lips.

"He bet his horse, his sword, and all the money he had."

CHAPTER 15

CHEVALA, LAKONIA

"What's your interest with me, then?"

Daris watched as the blond man lifted his hand, laying a finger across his lips as he studied Daris.

"I'm curious," he said after a long pause. "She chose *you*. A Spartan. The nation devoted to our brother, whom she cannot stand." The blond man shrugged. "I wanted to see what she saw."

Daris felt something like dread slide down his chest to pool deep in his belly as he regarded the man. He remained silent.

"And then, of course," the man went on, pacing away from Daris. He turned back and looked at him as if he were a puzzle. "There's Terena."

Daris's response was immediate and visceral. He took a step forward, his lips twisting as he growled, "Who the fuck are you?"

The mood in the room turned darker. Daris saw the men previously sitting with this blond man come closer, their steps slow as the Liodari all shifted around Daris.

The blond man's smile turned calculating. Daris cursed himself for giving any advantage to this man. It was a mistake he didn't intend to repeat.

"There it is," the man said so low, Daris almost missed it. The man grinned and his face changed, affable as he wagged his finger at Daris. "You know, it baffled me she thought herself in love with a fop like Lerek. I'll admit, that alone made me question her judgement, but I shrugged it off as the... I don't know." He strutted around as though he weren't surrounded by killers and dead men. "Stupidity of youth? You see, it didn't really matter. I knew she'd meet you and fall in love with you."

Daris tensed as the blond man inched closer until their chests were breaths apart.

"Not even us gods are immune to the Fates," the man whispered, his face hard.

Daris's blood ran cold.

"I wanted to make sure you weren't another useless piece of human shit, too."

"It'll be my pleasure to gut this man for his insolence, Commander," Jason called out as his men shifted closer. Daris heard weapons unsheathe, but he did not move, his gaze held by the blond man standing before him.

As he stared back at the man, Daris pursed his lips and did the only thing to be done in that moment.

He sank slowly to one knee and bowed his head.

THE MOOD IN THE TAVERN SHIFTED DRAMATICALLY AFTER DARIS'S OBEISANCE to the blond man. The tension lessened, and the ruffians melted back to their tables while Daris's men stood in shock nearby. He knew he should have said something before he made his move.

They would understand in a moment.

The silence thickened as the seconds ticked past and still Daris remained on his knee, head bowed. He closed his eye against the throbbing headache threatening to split his skull as the blood roared in his ears. When he opened it back up, the man had moved away.

"Come with me," the blond man said and Daris rose at last. He did not look to his men as he followed behind the black clad stranger, stopping when the man gestured to a seat at the table he'd vacated.

Daris glanced at the two men who had been at the man's side and watched as they stalked away, leaving Daris alone with the blond stranger. He waited, watching warily as the man sat with a loud groan, an ash eyebrow lifting when he saw Daris still standing.

"Please, Eudaemon," the man drawled, "sit. We've much to discuss."

Daris grabbed the chair back and slid it out as he watched the man before him.

Rather, the *god* before him.

The god's face settled into a blank mask as he waited for Daris to sit.

"You know who I am?"

Daris pursed his lips. "I do not."

"And yet you bowed."

"Aye," Daris ground out. "I know enough to know you are no man."

"No, Eudaemon," the god sighed, crossing his arms across his broad chest. "I am not."

Daris waited for him to go on. Behind him, conversation broke out once more.

"I didn't expect you'd take Sonah," the god said, and Daris stiffened. "I was... very put out when only Terena showed up. But after a while I had to concede it was the smart move."

Daris's eye widened. "Are you... are you the northern king? The one called 'King of Olympus'?"

Several men chuckled. The blond man's face transformed with a crooked grin. "The very same."

"You are not Zeus."

Daris regretted his words when the god's smile vanished.

"I am not."

Daris narrowed his eye. "Where is Terena?"

"Where is Sonah?" the god countered.

"I—"

"Don't bother," he said with a dramatic sigh as he continued to regard Daris. "My men brought word of her escape. It wasn't her I was after, either way."

"Lord—"

"Hermes."

Daris felt heat stain his cheeks before the blood rushed down his body to pool like a stone in his gut. His mouth slackened.

"As I said," the god brought his forefinger to his lips before pointing at Daris. "It was you I was looking for."

"Me, lord?"

"Indeed," Hermes sighed. "And I couldn't do that until after Terena found me. Rules." He leaned forward, smiling thinly. "I admit, I am impressed the girl gave you the slip. She's not at all as I was led to believe. Neither is Terena, for that matter."

"Where is she?"

"Who?"

The look on Hermes's face made it clear he toyed with Daris. Daris's hands clenched in his lap. "Terena."

"Ah," the god sighed again as he leaned back, looking up at the timber lining the tavern ceiling. "Terena. Terena, Terena, Terena. Where *is* the beauteous Terena?" He smiled coyly as Daris felt the heat climb up his neck. "I sent her to Ovenno."

"What?" Daris exploded. "Why?"

Hermes's face closed up. "Are you not listening? I wanted to find you."

"And why was it you needed to send her to Ovenno to make that happen?"

Hermes remained silent as he stared at Daris. His lips tilted up slow as his smile widened. "Because by the time we meet up with her again, she'll have reached her majority."

Daris felt something icy slide down his spine. "She'll have her powers, then."

"Not only that, Commander," Hermes purred as he lifted his tankard and saluted Daris. "You'll no longer be immortal."

CHAPTER 16

IBROS

Sonah pulled up her knees and rubbed her sore wrists against her breeches. She glared over at the soldiers sitting around the fire they'd built a few minutes ago while she'd been trying to loosen her bindings.

It was bad enough Xoran's men had trussed her up similarly after surprising her and Lerek when they'd fled Sparta. To be caught again —this time by Heylisia's ruthless Rivermen—really chafed at Sonah's frazzled nerves.

And both times she'd been in the company of a man she'd thought might prove helpful, but in the end was no help at all.

Sonah was sick of waiting for a man to help her.

Eyeing the group of soldiers laughing now and eating—rudely *not* offering her any—Sonah rubbed her hidden wrists together, fraying the rope little by little. She winced when the friction cut into her wrists and made them raw and bloody but she kept on. Heart pounding, she muttered under her breath, willing the rope to split faster.

A lifetime later, Sonah gasped when the last of the rope gave and she looked over at the Rivermen, now settling down after their meal. One soldier, the one who had dragged her kicking and screaming to this place, had long since left the circle of men for gods-knew-where and hadn't returned. Sonah would have to be vigilant when she escaped, so as not to run into him. That left the seven soldiers bedding down near the fire.

Wiggling her legs, she groaned. They'd fallen asleep while she'd struggled with the rope. She cried out, then bit her tongue to stop herself. Sonah winced at the taste of copper in her mouth. Pins and needles overwhelmed her legs as they came back to life.

"Here," a deep voice said out of the darkness, and Sonah gasped, flinching back. Her head smacked against the birch tree behind her and she glared up at the offending male standing over her. When she saw it was the same soldier who'd captured her, she groaned.

He grinned, holding a bowl out to her. Keeping her hands hidden within her lap, she watched him through narrowed eyes as he crouched at her side, setting the bowl near her hip.

The soldier motioned with one of his hands—his fingers long and elegant for such a dirty shit—and Sonah edged away.

"Are you afraid of me?"

Sonah lifted her chin. "I am not."

He arched a dark eyebrow at her.

"You are a Riverman?"

"Aye."

"Why are you here? In Ibros, I mean. Aren't you supposed to be somewhere in Heylisia? Patrolling the rivers for hapless travelers to rob?"

The man's lips tugged up on one side and Sonah looked away.

"Ibros is ours now."

"Ours?"

"Well," the soldier shrugged, resting his face in his palm. "Heylisia's."

"How is that?" Sonah scoffed. "Ibros is independent. And they are a friend to Lakonia. Is the emperor deliberately provoking Sparta?"

The man eyed her, his gaze considering. "You know much for a sheltered lady."

"I am not sheltered," Sonah grumbled. She shifted, her legs aching, and the man reached out. Flinching back, Sonah let out a cry as the man's hand fell to her hip, only to realize he was merely lifting the bowl he'd put near her further away from her squirming.

"I am Leander."

"I don't care."

The man ducked his head. She watched him, fascinated at the way the shadows danced along his strong features, the half smile he wore covering teeth she knew from earlier were white as pearls.

Ugh! What was *wrong* with her?

"Thank you for dinner, but I won't be eating anything you or your men have prepared. We are enemies, and as such I will not make myself comfortable in your company, sir. You may have succeeded in abducting me, but I will not make it easy for you."

He laughed, and Sonah dropped her eyes to her lap, cursing her body for the shiver wracking through her at the sound. If he but bathed more, the man would be devastating, she was certain.

Gods' blood, Sonah! Stop!

"Believe me, Lady Sonah, you've not made it easy. And I'll wager those brutes you had with you are on their way to us right now, complicating this endeavor even more."

"You know who I am?"

"Aye. As does every man here."

"Then do yourself a favor and release me," she hissed, leaning forward with a mulish mien, hoping her wrath would intimidate him.

The man had the nerve to chuck her beneath her chin!

"You're adorable when your color's up, lady, even in this darkness."

"Release me! Now!"

"Alas, I cannot," the annoying soldier replied with a sigh as he rose to his full height. Sonah hated having to crane her neck back to glare up at him. "I need to keep you safe, lady. So many are after you just now. It'd be a shame to leave you at the mercy of men with ill intentions."

Sonah's brows rose to her hairline as she gaped at him. "You wretch! *You* have ill intentions! Release me at once or I will—"

"Aye?"

Sonah fumed, her eyes narrowing to slits. "I will tell my friends how poorly I've been treated, and they'll gut you like a fish."

The man crouched down so fast, Sonah jerked back.

"Your friends?" the oaf, Leander, whispered. Glancing over his shoulder, he leaned closer, his sour breath fanning her face. Thank gods he had awful breath. It made her disgust more believable. "You are fully capable of gutting me yourself, are you not?"

Sonah's scalp prickled. "What do you mean?"

He regarded her in silence. As it stretched, Sonah felt as if the man was looking into her mind and reading her thoughts.

You are ugly. You are a disgusting human being. There is absolutely nothing redeemable about you.

There. Let him read those thoughts.

The buffoon smiled at her as if he had, in fact, read her thoughts.

And saw the lie in them.

Shifting uncomfortably, Sonah groaned. Her stomach decided it wanted to be heard, letting out an undignified growl loud enough to wake every soldier within ten miles.

"Eat, lady."

"I'm not hungry."

Her stomach denied her lie angrily.

"Are you not?" he asked, his voice rough like he'd been smoking a donderis pipe the nobles at the White Palace enjoyed after dinner.

"*Now* you're concerned about my welfare?" Sonah snorted and turned her head, dismissing him.

"Eat, please. You'll need your strength."

Sonah scoffed, watching him from the corner of her eye. He was as filthy as the rest of them, as if he constantly slept on the ground.

His uniform was torn, either from the fighting earlier or some other scrap he and his men got into.

The Rivermen were Heylisia's river guard, patrolling the major rivers and tributaries throughout the empire. She'd never actually seen a Riverman in person, but the firstborns loved to share stories of them at the palace.

The only thing remotely resembling Heylisian about this soldier was his clean-shaven face. Pity he didn't splash some of the water he shaved with on the rest of him. Sonah scrunched her nose.

"I don't plan on being here that long," Sonah muttered.

To her surprise, the man laughed. She turned, blinking up at the transformation of his face as he grinned back at her.

"Whatever you're planning," he said, shifting to lean closer, his arms braced on his thighs. "Don't. These men are vicious at the best of times. You do not want to see them at their worst."

"And you," she sneered, raking her eyes up and down his body, hoping he saw how lacking she found him. "Are you not equally vicious? Absconding with a helpless woman while others fight in your stead? A vicious, lying, *thieving*, Riverman?"

Sonah felt him still, the grin fading, replaced by a cold mask of cruelty completely changing his features. His green eyes narrowed and, for the first time in hours, dread washed over her.

"I give you fair warning, Lady Sonah," he said so softly, it was almost a caress. "Do not test me. I am civil now, but I *am* a vicious, lying, *murderous* Riverman."

It was a long time after he'd gone before Sonah stopped shaking.

CHAPTER 17

CORVO, ERMANEL

Terena walked in silence beside Rydon, with Croak trailing behind. She was still angry over the news of Sonah's escape from Xoran's men, her mind preoccupied with visions of her sister alone in the woods in the middle of gods knew where.

Vassori had tried several times to reassure her that Xoran was already searching, and that Sonah could not go far on foot, but Terena was not in the mood to be placated. While they awaited an update from Xoran, Rydon had suggested they continue on to Ermanel to find the seer.

The place Rydon had brought them to was some sort of gambling den, or perhaps a dance hall for the criminal element. As soon as Terena walked in, cloying smoke surrounded her, snaking up around her head and into her eyes and nose. She coughed, looking over at Gabriol, standing beside her, to see if he was feeling it, too. There was something exotic about this place she'd never experienced before.

Croak looked gobsmacked. He stared straight ahead, his eyes wide and glassy as the smoke overtook him.

Everywhere they looked, people danced suggestively; women with women, women with men, twos, threes or more. It reminded her of when they'd first met Melanos. The way he'd entertained himself with his Relics and the ambience he'd created in his cave was strikingly similar to the establishment they were in.

"Come on," Rydon grunted. He clapped a hand on Croak's shoulder, jerking him out of his stupor. "We'll find her in the back."

While the others followed Rydon, Terena stood rooted in place, her gaze moving slowly about the large room. Someone bumped her from behind and when she turned to look, a woman was making her way past, holding the hand of a man so beautiful, Terena wondered if he was real.

The woman smiled at her and lifted her hand to trace two fingers along Terena's jaw. The man leaned over the woman's shoulder, saying something that Terena could not hear over the loud music, her heartbeat synced to the drums. He kissed the woman's bare shoulder and then leaned close to Terena, his thick lashes fluttering closed as he opened his mouth.

Terena quickly twisted away before the man could kiss her. He laughed and Terena's stunned gaze swung to the smug woman at his side before pulling the man away.

Blinking away the fog of her bewilderment, Terena looked around, passing tables where people played cards or other games of chance. She paused at a table long enough to see a woman win the card game they played, her laughter loud as the losers grumbled and moved on to another table.

Terena turned away, realizing her friends had abandoned her. Pursing her lips, she threaded her way carefully through the bodies swaying to the music. There were tables set up along the back wall where more people sat tightly together or on someone's lap.

Turning, Terena spotted Croak sitting next to a beautiful blonde woman whose long hair was a mix of curls, straight locks and braids. As she got closer, Terena saw Rydon standing in front of them with a large, tattooed man at his side.

Terena made her way toward them, her eyes on the blonde woman beside her brother when she saw the woman lean closer to Croak. She stroked his lips with her forefinger, tugging his mouth open then bent over to kiss him. When she pulled back, Croak's head fell back, his eyes closed. He slumped back onto the tufted couch, head lolling and eyes still closed.

"What did you do?" Terena snapped at the blonde woman. This close, she saw the woman had faint tattoos on her face. Three runes on her chin and a black line bisecting her lips. A star and another smaller rune marked her temple above her left eyebrow. Her eyes were more grey than blue and sparkled as if she found Terena amusing.

Rydon grabbed Terena's elbow. "Ren—"

"I asked you a question," Terena said louder.

The woman smiled at Terena. She flashed a look at Rydon then turned to Croak who was still slumped at her side. She whispered in his ear and he smiled lazily. He opened his eyes when another woman came close and pulled him up.

"Croak—" Terena started to go to him when Rydon's hand grabbed her upper arm.

"Ren," he hissed in Terena's ear. He shook her once and said, "This is the woman I was telling you about. The seer. That's Cassandra."

Terena stared at Rydon's narrowed green eyes before turning back to the blonde woman. She was watching them with a half smile as if she knew what was being said. Terena's gaze flicked to her brother being led away by a topless woman who also pulled along another man. When he passed Terena, Croak gave her a sloppy smile, his eyes glassy.

Before she could say anything, Rydon thrust her forward, his grip tight on her arm.

"This is Terena," Rydon shouted across the low table in front of the blonde woman. He let go of Terena's arm and pushed her toward the seat Croak had vacated. On the other side of the woman, a pair of men were kissing. They paused long enough to look over at Terena. One of them, a handsome man with a shock of white hair and teal eyes smiled darkly at her before turning his face back to the dark haired man he'd been kissing.

Terena sat warily.

"You are the daughter of Ares," the woman said as Rydon took a seat on the table, his knee bumping Terena's. The blonde woman bit her bottom lip as her gaze raked over Terena from her thighs to her mouth before she lifted her languorous gaze to Terena's eyes. She leaned closer, her breath a whisper away from Terena. "I've been waiting for you."

Terena jerked back.

The woman snickered and winked at Rydon. "Leave us."

Terena's eyes swung to Rydon as he rose. "I'll go find the others," he mumbled and then left her alone with this woman who was sitting too close and smelled wonderful.

The woman pressed closer when Rydon left and leaned back to whisper against Terena's ear. "Do you want to know what I've seen?"

The hairs on Terena's arms stood on end as the heat from the woman's breath tickled her ear. When she pulled back, the woman was smiling knowingly.

Terena cleared her throat and nodded. "Aye."

Cassandra reached out and picked up a glass from the table and took a sip. When she set it down, Terena saw a small bowl filled with what looked like candy. The sweets were no bigger than a grain of rice and almost all were gone.

"To see the future is to live in constant fear," the woman said, taking one of the sweets between her thumb and forefinger. As she brought it to her mouth she paused, looking at it as if it held the answers to the fate of the world. "I used to drink. Heavily. To stop the visions from invading my every waking moment. It helped dull other thoughts, too."

Terena watched the woman through narrowed eyes. She turned

to Terena and the smile she gave her was filled with so much pain, Terena felt it twist her stomach.

"Then I discovered something better," she said in a broken whisper Terena caught even over the music and conversations nearby. Cassandra turned her gaze back to the little candy she had in her fingers. "Before I tell you what I've seen, I need you to open your mind."

Terena's brow furrowed as the woman slipped the candy between her lips and leaned back, close to Terena once more. Terena's mouth opened to speak, but her throat closed up when Cassandra brought her hand to Terena's jaw and leaned in, her mouth covering Terena's.

Stunned, Terena sat there as Cassandra's tongue swept hers in a deep, lazy stroke. Her grip on Terena's jaw tightened briefly as she pulled back and pressed a soft kiss on the corner of Terena's lips.

"I'll see you when you get back," Cassandra whispered.

CROAK HAD NEVER SEEN SO MANY STARS.

And they were still indoors!

He danced, his head thrown back as the music wove around him and within him. A woman around his age danced out of his arms and another replaced her, her arms winding up around his shoulders as she pressed her generous curves against him. A few minutes later, another woman was kissing him. When he opened his eyes, he saw a man with long black hair lean forward to pull the woman out of Croak's arms. She turned, smiling up at the man before kissing him languidly. Croak moved up behind her, grabbing her hips as she writhed between him and the raven-haired man.

He'd never had a better night in his life. At least, he couldn't remember one as magical as this. His hair was plastered to his head with sweat and his clothes stuck to him like a second skin but he was loving every minute of it. He wondered if the others were having as much fun.

Croak opened his eyes and smacked the woman's ass before dancing away through the gyrating bodies. A few anonymous hands reached out as he passed and he grinned as he looked around, his heavy lids having some difficulty staying open. He'd lost sight of Vassori after finding her in a back corner devouring a woman's mouth. He hadn't seen Gabriol or Rydon in a long while.

Croak frowned.

Come to think of it, he hadn't seen Terena in some time, either.

When he'd finally reached the back of the room where he'd last seen everyone, strangers sat on the couch he'd vacated earlier. Frowning, Croak looked around, his euphoria fading as he peered through the haze of smoke and his drunken fog.

A heavy slap between his shoulder blades had him arching his back and crying out. He stumbled forward into a woman whose breasts were currently in the mouth of a very greedy young man.

"Croak!" A thunderous voice he knew too well sounded right before he was yanked back roughly by his tunic. He turned his head enough to blink stupidly up at Rydon's scowling face. "Where's your sister?"

"What?"

Croak yelped when Rydon shook him hard enough to tear his shirt. Gabriol appeared over his shoulder with an equally murderous look on his face. Vassori snuck up behind Rydon, her hair disheveled.

"Where is your sister?" Rydon growled, enunciating every word as if they were daggers he wished to stab Croak with.

Now well and truly out of his sex-fueled haze, Croak swallowed and looked between the two mercenaries and Vassori. "Ren? Dunno. I thought she was with you."

Gabriol cursed and turned. Rydon's lip curled up as he thrust Croak away. Eyeing the crowd with distaste, Rydon plowed a hole through the closest bodies blocking his path. He paid no regard to the startled or angry shouts following him, and Croak slunk by with muttered apologies as he followed Rydon.

Croak smacked into Rydon when he stopped suddenly, only to be grabbed roughly by the merc and dragged to his side.

"Cassandra," he snarled, and Croak looked from Rydon's demonic face to where his gaze was directed. He opened his mouth, but Rydon took off, his stride eating up the distance to the blonde witch, who was busy dancing between two men and another woman.

Rydon grabbed the blonde by the arm and dragged her out of her dancing orgy, her yelp of surprise swallowed up by the music. Ignoring the protests of the crowd, he forced the woman to walk in front of him, her hands flying up to claw against his hold on her upper arm. Croak scampered behind them and soon Vassori and Gabriol materialized at his side.

The shock of the cold after the warmth of the building stole the air from Croak's lungs. Smoke rose from their heated skin. His body shook uncontrollably, and he hunched over, hugging his arms across his chest in an effort to warm himself.

The blonde woman laughed when Rydon shoved her against the side of the building, sounds from a nearby tavern drifting over to them to mingle with the music coming from the dance hall.

"I left her with you and now she's gone," Rydon accused, his finger dangerously close to the woman's face. She laughed as if she had a death wish. Croak hunched further into himself.

"Do I need to be here for this?" he whined as the woman chuckled.

"Where is she?"

"Who?" the witch taunted. Croak's eyes widened and he stilled his shaking body to stare.

Oh fuck.

Rydon's eyes narrowed and he snapped his hand out, pinning the woman against the rough stone wall by the neck. She laughed again.

"Where?" Rydon asked again, his voice ominously soft.

The woman sneered. "She went for a walk."

"Where?"

"Ah," the woman said, tilting her head as best she could with Rydon's meaty hand at her throat. "Where indeed."

"Don't play games, witch," Gabriol said.

The woman's gaze flicked to him with something like surprise before she turned back to Rydon. "I don't know where."

"I brought her to you for guidance, and you—"

"I'll give her guidance," the woman spat, lurching forward enough to startle Rydon into removing his hand. She yanked on her clothes to right herself and lifted her chin. "When she returns from wherever she went, she'll have questions for me."

"I thought you'd already—"

"In my vision," the woman interrupted, her voice hard and imperious, "in my vision, she disappeared right before my eyes. She returned, much later, disheveled and angry. When she came to me, she told me she'd been to see Daris Antonius, and she wanted to know how that was possible. How she could've traveled such a distance without being aware of ever leaving. And in such a short amount of time."

At the baffled looks they all shot at her, the woman smiled like a cat that ate a very fat canary.

"I don't believe you," Rydon barked at the woman. She laughed, dancing a finger in front of Rydon's face.

"I cannot tell you how often I hear that," she sang, then waved her hand dismissively. "It matters not. It is one of her powers," she added, her tone cool even as she looked at Rydon knowingly. "She's never manifested it before. My vision showed me our conversation, and the one that comes after her return, so I know it was her first time. She's very close to her majority. I wonder what other powers will surface."

This last was said in such a way Croak sensed she already knew the answer.

Rydon must've as well because he stepped closer to the woman.

"What..." he shook his head, scrubbing a hand down his mouth and beard. "What kind of power is that?"

The blonde shrugged. "All the Olympians have the power to disappear and reappear elsewhere in an instant. But I have never seen it, obviously. It is only because of my visions I know that's what happened to her tonight."

"When will she be back?" Croak asked, his teeth chattering.

"I don't know," the woman replied, vapor puffing as she exhaled. She shrugged. "I can't tell time from my visions. But I was still inside the gambling den when she found me. Although, not many people were around. My best guess is morning. What morning, though... I'm not sure."

Rydon swore.

CHAPTER 18

Daris rode beside Hermes as they crossed into Pyrgos. He was still coming to terms with being Terena's eudaemon. As they rode, he recalled all those little moments that now made sense. How Terena's blood healed his wound after General Peleon had stabbed him in the eye. Daris scoffed when he thought of Melanos, staring at him and calling him 'eudaemon' when Terena had Bethana's fangs in her arm. At the time, he'd allowed Rydon to push him aside, despite the overwhelming urge to give her his own blood.

Cursing under his breath, Daris shook his head. He should've asked Melanos about it. The god clearly had known their connection. Hells, *Daris* had known. He'd dreamed of the woman all his life, and yet he allowed the circumstances to sway him.

He wondered if Terena knew. And if she did not, what would she do when she found out?

"Look how they cheer for you, lord!"

Daris was jarred from his thoughts by the shouts of the crowd as Hermes waved royally at them. The god did not fear that word would spread of his large army advancing on Emperor Solon. In fact, everywhere they went, he had his men travel to nearby towns and villages, spreading the news.

"Are you not worried he'll send his armies ahead of your arrival in Metilai?" Daris had asked, sitting across from the god in a tavern little better than a hovel. Hermes had laughed as if the question was ridiculous. He'd looked so at home in the shabby environment, Daris wondered if the stories of the gods being greedy landlords, hoarding riches they collected from the temples in their names, had any merit. Looking at Hermes surrounded by the humblest of people, Daris doubted it. More likely, the priests held onto those riches, their fat bellies getting fatter while they preached to the poor.

By the time they reached the border near Tursk, the mayor of the wealthy town of Pera opened his arms and his home to the god, who graciously accepted the mayor's beautiful manor for their accommodations.

Hermes stood in the dining hall with his closest men, including Daris and his Liodari. The rest of the army built an encampment outside of the city, swelling the taverns and inns with business unlike any they'd seen in years.

Raising a crystal goblet filled with ruby red wine, Hermes smirked at them.

"It's good to be king," he murmured, shattering the expectant silence and the men roared their approval.

Daris took his seat at the god's right hand. He'd been reluctant to sit there while his men sat further down the table, but Hermes had been insistent and Daris did not argue.

As servants set heaping plates of food before them, the men tore into the bounty. Dried figs, fat pigs surrounded by roasted vegetables and fruits, cheeses of every available variety and wine, so much wine, lay before them in an excess Daris had only ever seen on the high days in Sparta. He supposed this was a special occasion. How often had anyone the opportunity to dine with a god?

"I've sent Soros ahead with a host to find Terena in Calla," Hermes said, startling Daris out of his thoughts. Captain Soros was the only one of his officers Hermes had deigned to introduce back when he and the god had first spoken. The god seemed to favor the captain, and Daris had wondered if it meant he was the most cunning of his men.

Looking over at Hermes, who popped a dried fig into his mouth, Daris speared a piece of meat. "With news of Sonah?"

"Aye," the god said in a low voice. Daris leaned closer. "I don't want her thinking I lied to her and sent her on a fool's errand."

Daris chewed slowly, thinking. "I have men searching for Sonah," he said at length, glancing up at Hermes. "But there hasn't been any news."

"She'll pop up sooner or later," Hermes said with a shrug. "She's one of the reasons why I've been spreading word of our progress through the provinces. If she's anywhere near civilization, she'll hear of it and come to us."

Daris grunted. "Good. If we can find her and bring her to Terena—"

"She'll be more willing to forgive you?"

Daris had years of training to control his emotions, and yet his hand jerked at the god's response, his fork clanging against his water glass.

"You think I do not know of your betrayal?" Hermes purred, his voice like silk, though Daris heard the sharp edge to it. "I've spoken at length with my niece about you," he added when Daris remained silent.

"I did not betray her," Daris replied, his tone short. "I did not kill her prince."

"I know," Hermes said, surprising Daris.

He gawped at the god, who winked at him. "You know?"

"Aye," Hermes scoffed. "I know the crown prince lives."

Daris turned his head so he could better see the god. "Did you tell Terena?"

Hermes made another snorty scoffing sound as he waved his fork at Daris. "Of course not."

Fuming, Daris set his cutlery down beside his plate and glared at the god.

"Why not?"

Hermes shrugged. "Adversity reveals character." He wiped his mouth with his napkin and leaned back in his seat, grinning at Daris. "You, my new friend, are about to find out if she truly loves you."

Daris pushed at the oversized metal handle on the heavy wooden door to the rooms he'd been provided for the night. Walking straight through to the bedchamber, he frowned at the large four-poster bed with thick fur blankets and pillows. After removing his armor and sword, he untucked his tunic.

With a sigh, he walked back into the dining area where he spied doors leading to a balcony. Opening the doors, a brisk wind greeted him and he immediately felt the tension ease from his shoulders. Daris hung his head, his grip tight on the stone balustrade, and looked out over the village.

A sound behind him made him stiffen. Daris looked over his shoulder and saw a shadow move toward the bedchamber. His sword was on the bed and he smothered a curse before stepping quietly back into the room and over to the bedchamber. He stopped in the doorway when he saw his sword was no longer on the bed.

Daris took one step before a blade at his throat stopped him.

Awareness tickled up his spine and he knew without looking who was there with him.

Terena stepped out of the shadows, her face impassive as she held his sword steady.

"Ren," he said. It was the only thing he could think of right then as a slew of feelings threatened to overwhelm him. He'd dreaded and longed for this moment for so long, and now it was here he could not think of the right thing to say.

Terena lowered the sword slowly, her eyes locked on his. He saw the emotions mirrored in her gaze and something else, a haze he speculated came from a night spent drinking.

As if reading his thoughts, Terena dropped her eyes and tilted her head. Stepping away, she regarded him, assessing. He tracked her but did not make a move. He wanted her to decide.

"Are you real?"

Daris's eye widened as she paced before him.

"Aye, Ren. Are you?"

She pursed her lips, and the movement made him want to embrace her, ready to wipe the worry and uncertainty from her face with his passion. Instead, he stood rooted, waiting.

"I think so," she said at last, still pacing. She looked like a caged animal, waiting for someone to tear apart. "I was... I was in Ermanel, with," she looked around, confused. "Where is this? Where am I?"

Daris wiped a hand over his mouth and the movement made her stiffen. "We're in Pera. In Pyrgos. Hermes is—"

"Hermes!"

Daris jolted with the force of her exclamation. Her face turned thunderous.

"He's here? Where?" Terena lurched forward, and he instinctively reached for her arm. The contact sent a jolt of awareness like lightning through his body. Terena's eyes flew to his, the shock registering on her face as well.

For a lifetime they stood still, eyes locked. He wished he was eloquent, gifted with the ability to say what he was feeling.

His sword was lax at her side, but he didn't care. He had to touch her.

He couldn't fight it anymore.

Daris reached out, cupping the back of her neck, and pulled her to him. For a moment she seemed to melt, as hungry for him as he was for her.

"No!"

She wrenched away, breathing heavily. Terena's lip curled as she lifted his sword.

He dropped his hands, watching as she took another step back, her eyes narrowed.

"I don't know what's going on," she said, shaking her head, "but this can't be real."

"Aye," Daris replied. "And yet, if I'm dreaming, you wouldn't have pulled away."

She laughed harshly. "What if it's *my* dream?"

"You would've killed me by now."

Her eyes widened and she grinned ruefully before turning away.

The silence stretched as he watched her, the war going on inside her head evident in the myriad expressions chasing each other across her face.

"Did you do it?"

Daris stiffened. He knew what she meant, but he waited for her to look at him. When she did, he took a step closer.

"I did not."

Her face twitched and her beautiful hazel eyes swam with tears. Blinking them away, she inhaled raggedly.

"You swear?"

He did not respond straight away. Taking several steps closer, Daris's breath became shallow when she did not stop him.

"On my life," he whispered.

The sword clanged onto the flagstone at their feet and they came together desperately. Her hands in his hair drew a groan from him and he kissed her hungrily.

His pulse pounded in his ears as his lips drank her in. Daris slanted his mouth over hers, savoring her panting breaths. He moved closer, crushing her body against his, and it was as if a dam burst.

Her hands were everywhere. She tugged at his tunic. Daris pulled back to yank it over his head before lunging back in as if she was air, his salvation. His lips crashed against hers as his hands ripped at the leather corset she wore. Fabric tore, and he pulled her against him.

"Daris," she moaned when he finally got her tunic off. Her breasts were bound and he snarled, tugging at the ends to loosen the fabric. When it was off, a violence he only felt in the heat of battle threaded through him and down into his belly as he drank her in.

He pushed her onto the bed. Daris was on her before she could do more than lean forward. Terena's arms wound around his back as he found her lips once more. When his mouth trailed down her neck, her frantic fingers tugged at the laces of his breeches, her hand sliding inside. He closed his eyes and groaned.

Daris wanted her so badly, she'd become an obsession. Even his alliance with Hermes was only to gain a closer foothold to this incredible woman panting and writhing beneath him.

Daris ripped the top few buttons from her breeches, her hot breath against his neck making him feral. She lifted her hips so he could pull her pants down, dragging them off her legs and chucking them across the room. He turned back, shoving his breeches down. Grabbing her hips, Daris pulled her toward him and thrust deep inside her.

Terena cried out, arching her head against the bed, her hips lifting to meet his. Her legs wrapped around his waist and Daris gripped her hip with one hand as he cupped the fullness of her breast with the other, bringing the hardened nipple to his mouth. Her sharp intake of breath and muttering his name was his reward. She moved her hands to his head, her fingers tightening in his scalp almost to the point of pain, but he was mindless to it. Pleasure and the knowledge Terena was in his arms at last made him senseless.

Her cries sharpened, her breathing quickened, and she met his thrusts with equally furious ones of her own. As the stirrings of his completion focused down his spine, Terena moved.

Flipping them until she was astride him, she planted her hands on his chest and rolled her hips, the dragging motion making him see stars. She threw her head back and moaned as he lifted his shaking hands to her thighs.

Daris breathed through his nose to control the orgasm so close to ripping through him. When he looked up at her, she was staring down at him, that hooded gaze he loved so much sending him over the edge. His hold on her hips tightened, and he knew she'd have bruises there come morning. That only made him come harder. She followed him over the edge a moment later, her head thrown back as she screamed his name to the heavens.

Daris gasped for breath as they rode out their pleasure together. Pulling her down onto his chest, his lips found hers in a slow, luxurious kiss that made heat slide to his groin and his cock twitch.

She must have felt it, if the throaty chuckle was anything to go by. She sighed and lifted off him, moving to fit her body against his side. Terena kissed him once more before moving her head to the crook of his neck, shifting her body to nuzzle closer. He tightened his arms around her, running one hand up and down her silky back in lazy strokes while he recovered.

Daris sighed against her head, turning slightly to kiss her hair. She grumbled against the movements as he tugged one edge of the bedding to cover them. Sighing contentedly, Terena mumbled something before settling once more.

As he succumbed to the heady aftermath of their lovemaking, Daris smiled for the first time in months.

Seconds turned into minutes, the sounds of their breaths calming. Daris tightened his hold and closed his eye.

"I love you," he whispered.

But she was already asleep.

CHAPTER 19

PERA, PYRGOS

Terena woke with a start. She was nestled against something warm and hard. Her hand rested on a muscled forearm and for a panicked second she thought she'd foolishly bedded one of the drunkards at the gambling den the night before.

What the fuck was in that sweet the seer had given her?

Then she remembered Daris, and she stiffened. Turning her head slightly, she felt his warm breath fan her neck, and she shivered.

What the fuck?

She moved her head back to better view his profile.

Aye. It was, indeed, Daris.

Carefully, Terena lifted Daris's arm and slid away. As she inched closer to the edge of the bed, he mumbled something and she froze. Long seconds passed before she felt safe enough to move, slithering out of the bed. Turning, she looked down at his face shrouded in shadows in the bedchamber's gloom.

How had this happened? One minute she was in the gambling den with the blonde witch, Cassandra; the next she was in a strange room and Daris's sword was on a large bed. After grabbing it, she'd heard someone coming toward her. Finding Daris on the other side of the blade was not something she'd been prepared for.

How long had she thought of their reunion, what she'd say to him? What he might say to her? She was still very wounded over his betrayal, but a part of her could not stop thinking about him. Her traitorous heart would soften and make her relive memories of him before everything turned sour. Her hunger for him had not abated, obviously. But she hadn't thought she'd jump right back into bed with him before hearing him attempt to explain away his involvement with Lerek's murder.

What the fuck was wrong with her?

Terena moved on silent feet to the doorway where a scattering of clothes lay cold and forgotten. She picked up her breeches and tunic, frowning at the missing buttons on her pants before glancing at the bed. How the fuck was she supposed to get back to Ermanel now? Would Croak even still be there? Did Rydon know what would happen—

"Will you not even say goodbye?"

Terena went rigid, hands on the flaps of her pants. Without turning around she answered, "I didn't wish to wake you."

"Coward."

Heat flashed through her body. Turning slowly, she glared at him. He was sitting with his back against the headboard, one knee lifted beneath the covers, his arm propped on it. She was glad of the shadows, for they hid her body's response to him as he watched her.

"I need to go," she mumbled, gripping the front of her breeches closed. She swore under her breath when she couldn't find her hair tie. She let out an impatient huff. "The others will wonder where I've gone."

"They do not know you're here?"

"One does," Terena laughed.

"What's that?"

"Nothing."

Terena reached down to grab her sword belt when Daris's fingers closed around her wrist.

"Don't go," he whispered.

Terena looked up, his ruined eye uncovered, the scarred brow scrunching with his other brow.

"Stay with me," he added.

"This was a one-time thing," she muttered, yanking her wrist out of his hand. She rose, ducking her chin as she put on her belt. "It will not happen again."

"Really?" He scoffed. "I have no say in it?"

"No, you don't! I'm an idiot when it comes to you. Gods, Daris! You took my sister! Why would you do that?"

"How else was I supposed to get you to come back? To listen to me!"

"So you kidnap a defenseless young woman?"

"You know I'd never let anything happen to her."

"I don't believe a word coming out of your mouth. You've lied to me before, Daris." Terena snapped, tossing a look at him over her shoulder.

Hands balled at her sides, she looked around the room. How was she supposed to get back? Cassandra didn't tell her anything about what this was. Did it have anything to do with whatever that candy was she'd so cleverly sneaked into her mouth with that kiss?

Daris grabbed her hand, making her fumble back into him.

"Stay. I will tell you everything." Daris's voice was gruff and rumbled through her back as he lifted their twined fingers over her head to pull her back into his chest.

"I don't have time."

Terena pulled her hand from his, pushing on his arm until it fell away. She took a few steps from him.

"I didn't kill him, Ren. On my honor as a Liodari. As a Spartan. I did not kill Prince Lerek."

An all-too-familiar stab of guilt hit her belly, but it wasn't as painful as it had been in the past. Frowning, Terena turned to look at him.

"I have to go."

She had no idea how she was to return to the others, but one thing was certain; she could not stay and listen to him. Not now.

"Did you hear me?"

Terena threw up her arms. "I don't have time for this! I don't have time for you. We'll talk another—"

Daris took a couple steps closer, his face deceptively calm. "You don't have time for me? So, you come here, we make love, but you don't have time to listen to me? About the reason you fought with me? Stabbed me? Oh, aye," he laughed, his lips twisted sardonically when her eyes widened. "Did you not notice the new scar?" Daris patted his left hip. A jagged line started below his ribs to right above his hip bone, pink and puckered. It looked new.

Terena grew sheepish before recollecting herself.

"Be glad you're immortal."

Daris laughed bitterly. "Very nice. What happened to the woman who came in earlier and couldn't wait to be in my arms?"

Terena pressed her lips together, shooting him a glare. Her eyes caught on something and she bent over, grabbing his discarded breeches and tossing them at him. He caught them and put them on.

"A momentary lapse in common sense," Terena fumed, stalking past him. His hand shot out, grabbing her neck. Terena let out a squeak as he shoved her against the wall, his body so close she squirmed to put some distance between them. Anything to get away from his heat and the dangerous gleam in his eye.

His nostrils flared, and Terena swallowed hard. Daris's hand was warm and strong with only the slightest pressure on her throat. She knew if she wanted, she could move away.

But she didn't.

Terena hated herself for that.

"Get your fucking hand off me."

"Oh no, my love," he purred, his hot breath rousing the butterflies in her belly. "You're going to stay right here until we've finished our conversation."

"Daris," she said in warning, her gaze locked with his.

"I've waited months to see you. I am not fucking letting you go until you hear me out."

"And then you'll let me go."

One corner of Daris's mouth curled up. The way his face could change from strong, courageous leader to seductive, possessive lover made her insides melt.

Terena desperately fought to recall why she hated this man.

"I won't let you go," he whispered, his gaze falling to her lips. "Ever again. You are mine."

"I am not yours."

He let his hand fall from her throat, his fingers glancing off her skin in the softest of caresses. The pad of one finger rested where her pulse hammered her skin.

Terena's heart rolled over. Blood heated and moved slowly beneath her skin and she felt the languorous pull of his body, adjusting her limbs to fit within the embrace of his powerful frame.

"I think your body disagrees with you," Daris murmured, leaning closer until his lips were on her ear.

No! Do not give in!

Terena listened to her head this time. Desperate to get away from him and have a serious conversation with her traitorous body, Terena willed herself to think of Croak. Of Rydon. Gabriol and Orry. All of them waiting for her.

Slipping a dagger out of her belt, she held it at his back. Right at his kidney. With a cruel tilt of her lips, she sighed.

"Think again, *my love*."

Before she could stab him, Terena stumbled, no longer in Daris's darkened bedchamber.

DARIS FELL FORWARD INTO THE WALL.

Growling as he rubbed at his sore forehead, he swore in Greek.

Then blinked.

She was gone.

Baffled, Daris stepped back, his disbelieving gaze taking in the space in front of him as if Ren might somehow reappear from the shadows.

A muffled banging reached him from the other room. Daris stalked to the nightstand where he'd set his eyepatch. Before he could pick it up, Hermes stormed in, his face various shades of red as his gaze darted around the empty bedchamber.

"Where is she?" Hermes roared, his eyes on fire as he strode through the room, lifting Daris's discarded clothes and tossing them down again.

Daris wiped his hand down his face. He grabbed his eyepatch and fitted it over his ruined eye before rising and grabbing the tunic Hermes had thrown. Daris looked at him warily before pulling it over his head. The god stalked across the large bedchamber, cursing under his breath.

"Who are you looking for?"

"My niece," Hermes hissed a few inches from Daris's face.

Daris's spine stiffened, and he narrowed his good eye. "She's not here."

"I can see that, *Eudaemon!*" Hermes spat, jerking his head around as if he'd conjure her from thin air. Turning his furious gaze back to Daris he said, "Where did she go?"

"I don't know," Daris answered, raking a hand through his hair. At Hermes's scowl, he raised his hands in supplication. "I didn't know—"

"When did she get here? What did she say?"

Daris, surprised by the god's ferocity, blinked at him in shock. "Lord—"

"Don't—!" Hermes closed his eyes and held up a hand to Daris as if trying to control himself. Still with his eyes closed, his fingers folded until he held up only his forefinger. "I want to know exactly when she came to you. What was said? Did she say where she is?"

Daris gaped at the god. A second later he composed himself, crossing his arms at his chest. "I don't know how it's possible. No one informed us she was here—"

"That's because she wasn't," Hermes closed his eyes again, once more visibly calming himself before he continued. "She used her powers. She ported here."

Daris's eye widened. "What? What's that mean?" He strode to Hermes's side, facing the god when he turned away, his hand lifted to his chin. "What's that mean, Hermes?"

"Tell me what was said."

Daris sighed. "She... seemed confused. Wanted to know if I was real. Where I was."

Hermes flapped his hand. "And? Did she tell you where she was?"

Daris eyed the god for a few seconds, debating.

As if sensing his indecision, Hermes's lips curled into a sneer.

"Do not think to deceive me, Daris. You will not like my response."

"That's not my intention," Daris bit out, walking a fine line between angering one god and protecting another. Hermes's reaction to Ren's visit made his hackles rise and his battle instincts kicked in.

Flexing his right hand, Daris said, "But I want to know why her being here would anger you so."

Hermes canted his head. "Where. Is. She?"

Daris felt the color rise in his neck and muttered, "She's in Ermanel."

Hermes clapped him on his shoulder before pivoting toward the doors. He called back over his shoulder. "Come! We ride for Ermanel!"

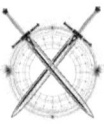

CORVO, ERMANEL

Terena gasped, grabbing hold of her chest as she blinked away the bright light that nearly blinded her. Hand lifting to shield her eyes, she yelped when her pants fell to her hips. She hastily grabbed them to hold them in place. Squinting, Terena barely saw the buildings along the quiet street.

Her heart in her throat, she shivered in her meager clothing as she turned in a circle, finding herself standing outside of a building in a rundown part of Corvo, Ermanel. Daris and his warmth were long gone.

Stopping in front of a familiar building, Terena recalled it was where they'd gone last night to find the seer. Running her hands up and down her arms, Terena took a step toward the building when the doors opened. Surrounded by the dark, the slightly unkempt blonde witch, Cassandra, emerged. Hands still on the doors, her tattooed lips stretched in a slow grin.

"You're back," she said in a throaty voice.

"Did you do that to me?" Terena snapped, taking a huge step toward the woman.

Cassandra threw back her head and laughed. "No, goddess. *You* did that. But I did see it in my vision before you walked into my gambling den last night. Come," she stepped back, gesturing with a languid wave toward the interior. "Your friends await."

Terena stood rooted in place for a moment before striding after the blonde woman. Her hips swished in a way that made Terena scowl, as if she was purposely mocking her.

Cassandra whistled and Croak thundered forward out of a darkened back corner, his eyes blinking owlishly at the blonde. When he turned his gaze and spotted Terena, his mouth dropped open and he reached for her, grabbing her up and swinging her before she could react. He set her back down, and she saw a tear escape his eye before he ducked his head.

"Hey," she said soothingly, cupping his face in her hands. She twisted her head to meet his glazed eyes. "Croak, I'm all right. I'm fine."

He shook his head and swallowed. Someone thumped her on the back and she swung around, only to find herself wrapped up in another fierce embrace, this time the arms like iron bands and filled with more muscle than Croak would see in his lifetime.

"Where the fuck did you go?" Gabriol asked gruffly, releasing his hold. Rydon ambled behind him, reaching out to pull her close, and kissed the top of her head. Terena felt the heat rise in her face and chest, warmed by the love she felt for these three.

"You won't believe me if I told you," she laughed, her voice shaky as she looked at each of them. Vassori came up behind her and laid a hand on her shoulder, moving past her to stand beside Gabriol.

Terena's gaze swung to Cassandra, who stood idly by, arms crossed in front of her with her finger lazily twirling a lock of her hair as she watched them.

"Cassandra said you ported somewhere," Croak said, his voice stronger now as he frowned down at her. "I didn't know you could do that."

Terena scoffed. "That makes two of us, Croak." She narrowed her eyes at Cassandra. "But you did."

The woman shrugged with a coy smile. "I saw it. Long before I met you."

Terena waved a hand at her. "I think it's time for you to tell us all you know."

Cassandra laughed. "All I know? Hardly. But I will tell you what you need to know."

Rydon grunted. "Today, witch."

Cassandra clicked her tongue, wagging a finger at him. "Alas, Eudaemon, I am no witch. More's the pity. But I can see the future."

"Will I end up married to a gorgeous woman?" Croak asked. "What am I talking about? Of course I will."

"Are you a god? Do you—" Gabriol butted in.

"How are you not dead?" Rydon added. "How has the emperor—"

"Stop!" Terena yelled with a slash of her hand. Turning back to the blonde, she asked, "How is it you can see the future? Are you like the oracle? A child of Apollo?"

The woman laughed as she turned away, those fucking hips swishing and setting the small bells on her girdle tinkling.

With a wink over her shoulder, she replied, "I was Apollo's lover."

CHAPTER 20

IBROS

Sonah jolted awake. Looking around in a panic, she lifted her hands to rub the sleep from her eyes.

It was the darkest part of night. The fire had died out long ago, and she shifted, narrowing her eyes to see through the void. As her eyes adjusted, she could just make out the sleeping bodies of the soldiers.

Moving as slow as a snail, Sonah rose, wincing when she placed one of her hands on the ground for leverage, the bindings still cuffed to her wrists disturbing the wounds there. She tugged them off, her eyes still on the sleeping soldiers.

When one of the soldiers moved to his back, Sonah froze, her body positioned awkwardly. Still, she remained motionless until the man was resettled. Exhaling, she straightened and moved onto her toes, tiptoeing away from the tree they'd set her against and away from the Rivermen.

Sonah stalled for a moment, debating going back to gather some supplies, then shook her head against the idea. The longer she remained, the more she risked getting caught.

And she had no wish to see what they would do to her if they caught her escaping.

Without further delay, Sonah quickened her steps until she was swallowed by the dense trees.

An owl hooted, nearly causing Sonah to scream and her soul to jump out of her skin. Clutching her chest, Sonah's gaze darted around. The quiet settled once more and Sonah turned, intent on putting as much distance between herself and those brigands, when she heard a low growl.

Sonah froze. Everything in the forest stilled and fell silent. She held her breath, listening. Long seconds passed and Sonah let out her breath, puffing out thin white trails into the frigid air and took another step.

The growl came again, this time from behind her.

Closer.

Sonah stumbled as she turned. She had no weapon and could not see through the thick darkness. Only shadows moved as she took another backward step, her foot crunching on the frosted leaves beneath her.

She winced when the low growl sounded again, longer this time and much closer.

Sonah stopped moving. Holding up a shaking hand, she whispered, "Who's there?"

Her eyes widened and she brought her hand to her chest as a pair of emerald eyes shown out of the dark. The animal was large; the eyes would reach her navel, she was certain. Its pale fangs were slick with saliva.

Sonah shook all over, her heart racing beneath her palm as she swallowed. Another few steps and she could see the animal was a wolf. Its snout was black, but there were patches of white along its front legs. In the gloom of the forest, there was no way to tell for sure but, of course, what color the wolf was certainly wasn't the issue at the moment.

"Good... wolfy," she whispered as the animal padded closer.

It stared at her for a few more agonizing seconds, then dropped its head and nuzzled her boots. Sonah clutched her throat, standing still and stiff as the wolf nosed over her britches. She yelped when it stuck its snout in her crotch.

"Sir! That's very inappropriate! We just met."

As if it understood, the wolf raised its head, staring at her through those beautiful green eyes and huffed. It backed up a few paces and Sonah loosed a chuckle.

"Thank you," she said with a sigh. "It was lovely to meet you, but I have places to be. Please don't eat me."

She waited another second after she'd finished speaking to see if the wolf would do anything. When it stood there gazing back at her, she backed up a step. It didn't move or growl again, so she moved another step and another.

Sonah smiled and turned.

The wolf let out a low growl.

"Come on," Sonah said, her voice shaking. "I thought we were friends now. I can't stay here. Please let me leave."

Feeling ridiculous for having a conversation with an animal, Sonah looked around, but of course, no one was about. If she didn't hurry, she was sure someone would wake—or worse, that blasted Riverman might come back from wherever he'd fucked off to. If he found her missing, Sonah knew he'd chase after her.

"Please?" Sonah looked into the wolf's emerald eyes and turned slowly. As she walked, the wolf fell into step beside her. She glanced down at him, but kept walking, her steps more assured the longer she walked without the wolf pouncing on her.

In fact, he seemed to walk *with* her. Sonah cast surreptitious glances at him as she walked faster and faster. Sure enough, he remained at her side, loping along without a snarl or growl in her direction.

When they made it to a clearing, Sonah turned, looking around. She had no idea where they were and, therefore, which direction to take.

"Which way?" she asked aloud, chewing on her lip in thought.

The wolf huffed and Sonah started, her head snapping around to him. He looked at her, then turned his head to the left, staring off at something in the distance. Sonah frowned and made to go in the opposite direction when the wolf growled.

Sonah rubbed at her arms, shaking beneath the borrowed cloak that was too thin for this weather. Looking down at the wolf, she frowned. "What?"

He looked at her for a second and then turned his head again to the left. When she didn't react, he started to walk in that direction. He turned and looked at her again, then turned and padded off once more.

"I mean... I guess that way's as good as any," she mumbled as she set off after her new friend.

Sonah wasn't sure how long they walked before their surroundings became lighter. She'd spent the hours talking to her new friend, telling him all about Ren and Croak and Rydon, of Gabriol and Orry. She'd even told him of Daris and the Liodari. When she'd spoken of Jason, the wolf had growled, and Sonah had clamped her lips shut.

Lifting her eyes, Sonah grinned at the blues, pinks and oranges of dawn breaking.

"Look at that," she said to her companion. "Dawn's here. It'll be easier—"

Sonah blinked, slowing as she turned every which way. The wolf was gone. When did that happen?

"Not only am I talking to an animal," she grumbled as she started to stomp away, "but now I'm talking to myself."

Irritated the animal had disappeared without so much as a growl to let her know, Sonah trudged on, her eyes scanning the horizon. The first pangs of hunger started to gnaw at her belly and she grimaced.

Sonah cursed under her breath thinking of how long she'd most likely have to walk until she reached civilization. She had no money, either. How was she going—

Stopping abruptly, Sonah squinted, hoping her vision wasn't playing tricks on her. In the distance she barely made out the tops of several buildings. Huffing a laugh, Sonah started jogging toward what could only be a village. Her side ached, and she slowed, pushing her hand into the spot below her ribs where it cramped. Sonah whimpered, thinking on the last time she'd had anything to drink. Hopefully, someone in that village would take pity on her and give her water, at least.

A low rumbling sounded behind her and Sonah glanced back, then did a double take. A dark cloud seemed to be heading right for her. Sonah quickened her steps until she was running, moving out of the path of the darkness coming toward her.

The rumbling resolved into hooves beating the ground as horses galloped into sight and Sonah was glad she'd moved to the side as five riders bore down on the village. Sonah quickly pulled up her hood, turning and hunching her shoulders.

The horses slowed, the whines of the animals protesting the sudden momentum change and Sonah winced as she heard a rider shout. The horses drew closer and Sonah cursed the gods for her ill luck.

Still walking with her head down and her cloak pulled tight around her hunched frame, Sonah did not look up when the first rider circled her.

The rider called out something in a foreign language and Sonah scowled. It sounded like Greek. *Fuck! Have the Liodari found me already?*

Worried the riders were Spartans sent to retrieve her, Sonah bolted, the cold air snatching the breath from her lungs and the hood from her head, the stitch in her side screaming at her. Black spots formed at the corners of her eyes, and Sonah let out an angry shout as she felt her body about to give out.

Before she hit the ground, something banded around her waist and she was lifted. Her head lolled back and the grip on her tightened as she looked up into the grinning face of her captor.

"Fane??"

CHAPTER 21

THURIA, IBROS

"Thought you'd get rid of me that easily?"

Sonah scowled up at Fane, who grinned at her like a fiend. Struggling against his hold, Sonah slapped at his arm.

"I wish! You're about as easy to get rid of as lice," she grumbled.

Fane threw his head back and laughed. As she twisted to get into a more comfortable position, Fane slowed his mount and set Sonah down when they'd stopped. Horse hooves sounded behind her and Sonah turned to see one of the men was the soldier from Messene with Fane at the inn. Two more soldiers pulled up near them.

When Sonah made to turn back to Fane, another rider came into view and Sonah's heart stopped.

Shrieking, she ran for the big man who dismounted much more gracefully than she would've imagined for a man his size and leaped into his arms.

Melanos laughed as his powerful arms wrapped around her and swept her up in a spin that left her breathless. She squeezed him tight, tears springing to sting her nose and eyes. She blinked rapidly to clear them.

The god they'd rescued from the cave outside of Thuria a few months ago grinned down at her, his face the most welcome she'd seen in ages.

"What are you doing here? I saw you when we were attacked, but I thought it a hallucination!" Sonah asked him breathlessly, squeezing his arms as he loosened his hold on her. She felt Fane come up beside them, but paid him no mind. She had eyes only for the god whose presence put her immediately at ease.

"I heard there was a beautiful woman in need of rescuing from Rivermen," he said in his deep, rough baritone.

Sonah grinned up at him like a crazy person. "Well, this beautiful woman thanks you for the thought, but I freed myself."

"Of course you did, clever girl," he said with a smile and tweaked her nose.

"Were you followed?" Fane asked, swiveling to look around. "Did anyone see you escape?"

"No," Sonah laughed, stepping out of Melanos's arms and turning to her would-be rescuer. "No, I left while they slept."

"While they slept?" Fane asked, scowling as he turned around again. When he looked back at Sonah, he asked, "So you've been walking for hours? Alone?"

"Aye," Sonah said with a shrug. "Well, mostly. I befriended a wolf and he followed me up until a short time ago."

"A wolf?" Melanos exchanged a look with Fane over Sonah's head and she sighed. Of course they thought her insane. What normal person makes friends with a wolf?

"Aye, a wolf," Sonah mumbled. Holding up a hand, she added, "He was very well mannered. And he kept me company without eating me, so..."

"You escaped Heylisian soldiers—nay, not just Heylisian soldiers but the worst soldiers: Rivermen. And you befriended a wolf while making your own way to Thuria—"

"Wait, this is Thuria?" Sonah asked, looking around. The soldiers behind her chuckled as Fane covered his mouth with his hand.

"Aye, little one," Melanos laughed, "this is Thuria. And unlike

Fane here, I fully believe you capable of besting Rivermen, escaping on your own and then befriending a wolf. You are a daughter of Ares, after all. No fear."

Sonah cocked her head. "Well, fear wouldn't have helped me in that situation. Besides, I had to do it on my own after this one let me be captured."

Fane's mouth dropped open and he stuttered objections while the others ribbed him mercilessly. Sonah grinned at his discomfort.

"Enough," Melanos called out, putting a huge arm around Sonah's shoulders. "You must be starving. Let us find some food and water for our goddess. Then we can head north to find your sister."

"Wait," Sonah said and they stopped to look at her. "One of the Rivermen said Ibros is now Heylisian territory. Is that true?"

The men glanced at one another before Fane spoke.

"I have not heard it officially, but there are Heylisian soldiers everywhere. Spartan soldiers as well. We've had word from our officers that the Heylisians escorted Duke Ovenno on his way to Sparta. Although, they believe it was a ruse to explain their presence."

Sonah chewed on her lip. "What if they're in the city? What if—"

"They are not," Melanos said in a tone that made her relax. "This is my city. We've already dispatched one squad nearby."

Mounting their horses, Sonah settled as they neared the city a short time later. She was grateful for the small inn Melanos led them to and pictured the warm bed awaiting within. She was even more grateful for the food being set before them, her stomach growling so loud Sonah put her hands to her belly to quiet the sounds.

"You said earlier you had heard from your officers," Sonah said, to Fane as he passed her a goblet of wine. "What news did they share?"

Fane smacked his lips after taking a drink. "That your sister was heading to Ovenno."

"Oh, thank the gods! Wait, why Ovenno?"

"The message did not say, although I wonder if she'd heard you were going back there with Duke Ovenno. You know, before you decided to leave on your own." Fane arched an eyebrow at Sonah.

"Perfect," Sonah mumbled. "If I'd known Terena would be there I wouldn't have left in the first place. I knew she'd come for me, but I thought she'd go to Sparta. I was so afraid of leaving with the duke, and since King Altos would not help me, I helped myself. That's when I left with Prince Lerek."

Fane's head whipped around to her so fast his ale sloshed over his hand. "What? What do mean? Prince Lerek is dead!"

"No," Sonah sighed. "He was in Arestia Castle, a guest of the king's. Long story, the prince wanted to fake his death, but it didn't go to plan. Now his twin is dead and everyone thinks Prince Lerek is really Prince Isher."

"And how is Sparta involved?" Melanos asked, his voice a low growl as he cast a narrowed gaze at Fane and the Spartan soldiers sitting with them.

"All I know is, we were sent to Metilai to rescue the firstborns," Fane said, holding up a hand placatingly. "When we arrived, Daris— Commander Antonius—went with his second to Prince Lerek's rooms. Something about repaying a debt. Next thing we knew, the commander and Jason returned and all hells broke loose. The prince was dead, and we had to abort our mission. We hid in an old apartment outside the palace for days. I recall the commander being very agitated. He would leave and come back without telling us anything. We heard someone was arrested for the prince's murder and was to be executed a few days later."

"Aye," Sonah laughed mirthlessly. After she took a drink of her wine, she grimaced. "They arrested me and Terena. *We* were the ones to be executed."

Fane nodded, hanging his head as he stared at his tankard. The other Spartans looked from him to Sonah to Melanos. By the looks on their faces, she knew this was the first time they were hearing any of this. The Liodari was an elite branch of the Spartan military, and these soldiers were not privy to the missions the Liodari carried out.

"Aye, Sonah. I know that now. At the time, however, you were a nameless, faceless assassin."

"But I wasn't," she said, narrowing her eyes. "We were tortured, and scared, and about to be murdered ourselves."

"We knew nothing of that at the time," Fane said, exasperated. He reached out a hand, laying it on the scarred table close enough to her fingers to barely touch. "I wish we had. It makes sense now why the commander was so angry those days. He kept cursing Prince Lerek. I still don't know what went wrong. We were there to get the firstborns and Prince Lerek out, but we needed a distraction. Someone was to slip a sedative into Prince Isher's drink and change his clothes to make him look like his twin. The sedative only feigned death, though, so while everyone was preoccupied with the crown prince's demise, the funeral would provide a way for us to escape with the real Prince Lerek and the firstborns."

"So the plan was to have Prince Isher buried alive?" Sonah glared at Fane.

"No, of course not. The effects would've worn off before that ever happened. We needed the distraction to buy us enough time to stage our rescue.

"We were to wait until the day of the funeral to enter the palace grounds, where the firstborns and Prince Lerek would meet us and we'd escape undetected.

"It was genius, really, and the sort of thing the Liodari excel in. None of us had any doubts until we received word that the crown prince was murdered. The commander changed our plan so he could rescue you and Terena before the execution. Commander Antonius took a few men with him while the rest of us were to proceed with the original aim of getting to the firstborns. I don't know what went wrong, but obviously, you escaped without his help."

"Aye," Sonah whispered, lost in the memory.

The table was silent for a long time before Sonah sat back and glared again at Fane.

"Why did you say Daris killed Prince Lerek?"

Fane blanched. "What? When? I never said that!"

"Aye," Sonah nodded, jabbing a finger at him. "You did. I heard you. That night we all went drinking before everything went to shit! I heard you and Jason and Michael talking. You didn't know I was there, but I heard you. You said Daris was cold for killing Terena's lover."

Fane's face turned ashen, and his mouth fell open. For painfully long seconds, he said nothing. "Gods. You... heard that? That was *you?*"

"Aye," Sonah confirmed, waving her hand. "Do not deflect, please. Why did you say that? He clearly didn't, and yet you said that and then I went and told Ren. And everything just... fell apart."

Fane scrubbed his hand down his face, looking haggard and much older than his years. He stared at the table long enough for the silence to become uncomfortable. Sonah flicked a glance at the other soldiers, noting their eyes were pointedly on their tankards. Only Melanos stared back at Fane, his features cold.

"We knew he'd gone to the prince's rooms, but we didn't know why. Only what he'd said, something about a debt." Fane shrugged and sighed. "Commander Antonius handpicked all of us for that mission. Before we even left Sparta he swore us to secrecy. After we learned of the prince's death, the commander told us no one outside our group was ever to know anything we'd done. I assumed it was a confirmation of his crime."

"Where did you go after you got the firstborns out?" Melanos asked in his gruff voice. Sonah was grateful for his interjection because she was feeling so ill. Fane's revelations matched so much of what Lerek had shared. But she still felt guilt over her part in it.

The part that had blown up in her face.

"Aurora," Fane answered. "The commander had an understanding with Duke Aurora, who took responsibility for the firstborns. When we arrived, the commander lost his shit on the duke.

We didn't hear much, but what we did led us to believe the commander blamed Duke Aurora for the mess. I'd never seen a royal so terrified before. Michael thought the commander might actually kill the duke but, despite his fury, Commander Antonius didn't so much as touch the man.

"We were supposed to stay the night, but the commander wanted to leave right after he had it out with the duke. We delivered the firstborns and left. One of them rode back with us to Sparta."

Sonah snorted. "Aye. Prince Lerek."

Fane shook his head and grunted. "I did not know it was him, Sonah. Commander Antonius kept him away from the rest of us and brought him his meals personally. We were fine with that because he cried most of the trip. It was unsettling. Now I understand why.

"And I apologize for saying anything about the commander and the prince that night with you nearby. I am more sorry than you know. Believe me, I wish I'd kept my damned mouth shut."

Sonah followed Melanos to the horses. She had slept most of the day after they'd eaten and only rose when Fane came to her door to ask if she wanted to join them for dinner. They'd agreed to head north to Ovenno and Sonah had barely slept after that, nervous energy making for a fitful night.

"Did you ever find Bethana?" Sonah asked. When she'd last seen Melanos, he'd told them he'd be heading back toward the caves where Daris and Terena had found the nymph in her serpent form. Poseidon had cursed them both more than a thousand years ago, and while Melanos was freed from his curse, Sonah had often wondered if he'd been able to break his beloved's curse.

Melanos gave her a sad smile. "I did not. I searched every cave near the falls, even taking the path through the falls as your sister did. To no avail."

Sonah paused, and Melanos turned to look at her with a frown.

"We're nearby," she said softly, gazing at him. "And it's on the way."

Fane walked up at that moment. "What's this?"

Sonah motioned to Melanos. "He never found his love, Bethana. I was about to suggest we find her. Together."

Fane began shaking his head and Sonah grabbed hold of his arm. "It's on the way. And we don't really know where Ren is right now. But we do know where Bethana is, roughly. We should do this. For Melanos."

The look on Melanos's face when Sonah turned to him almost broke her heart. He looked so hopeful but tried to hide it with a nonchalant shrug. "If the others don't mind."

"Melanos!" Sonah cried out in exasperation. "You're a god! I'm a god! By my math, we outnumber these... three."

The edge of Fane's mouth quirked up. "Aye. That's impressive math. Look," he stood with arms akimbo, smiling at Melanos. "I'm fine either way. I just wanted to ensure she was all right. Now that she is, I'm good to go wherever."

"Fane, what of our—" One of Fane's friends started to speak.

Fane cut him off. "At the end of this, it is my hope you'll journey with us to Commander Antonius." He looked between Melanos and Sonah. "When Sonah was captured, I sent word to Sparta. I've yet to hear back, but our soldiers here shared news of Terena's whereabouts and rumors of a vast army coming from the north. I don't know if your sister journeys with the northern king, but at least we know she's close."

Sonah glanced over at the three warriors behind Fane. King Altos was more than likely looking for her, and Fane had just sent him a boon. Nothing to do for it now but find her sister and then Daris.

But first...

"Then it's settled," she said in a firm voice. "We go in search of Bethana." With a quick nod of her head, she walked purposefully toward the horse Melanos had procured for her and whispered to the mare, "Please be my friend?"

CHAPTER 22

CORVO, ERMANEL

Rydon stared at the blonde witch. He stood in front of the couch she'd settled on when they'd all filed back inside. She'd groaned loudly when she'd sat, her arms stretched over the back of the plush velvet couch, regarding them all with a grin.

Terena sat on the couch, her body shifted to face the witch. Ren's clothes were rumpled and—were the buttons on her breeches missing? Beside her, the witch smiled as she settled a hand on Ren's knee. Croak had elected to stand at Rydon's side, mimicking his stance as was his way, eyeing Rydon out of the corner of his eyes before adjusting his arms in a similar fashion.

Gabriol pushed his way between them, shoving Croak aside as he leaned into Rydon. "Did you know?"

Rydon flicked an annoyed glance at his friend. "And not tell you? No."

Gabriol grunted, folding his arms.

"How are you Apollo's lover?" Terena asked, her face pinched as her eyes roamed over the blonde's face. "Apollo and the rest of the Olympians have been gone for over a thousand years."

The woman gave a dismissive tilt of her head, the fingers of her left hand lifting slightly off the seat back. "And yet..."

"How? And how did you know where to find Daris?"

"Daris?" Croak called out, his eyes wide as he shot Rydon a look. Rydon scowled and ran a hand down his beard.

Pressing her lips together, the woman, Cassandra, didn't bother to look at Croak before answering Terena. "I didn't know where to find him. *You* did."

Terena slapped the seat cushion. "How?"

Cassandra shrugged. With a coy smile, she answered, "I saw you port for the first time. I knew it would be with me. I knew we'd have this conversation here now." She shrugged again and leaned forward, clasping her hands around her knees as she tipped her head toward Terena. "Perhaps your heart knew and took you there."

Terena stood so fast, she startled the witch. Even Croak stepped back, catching on Gabriol's foot and earning himself a slap to his shoulder that had him stumbling away.

Rydon sat on the edge of the table in front of the couch. "What do you mean, witch? Speak plain."

"You keep calling me that," Cassandra said slowly with a *tsk*. "But I do not have their powers. I am a seer. As I was in Troy. A priestess to Apollo."

"And where the fuck is Troy?" Croak asked with an exasperated sigh. He'd taken the seat Terena had vacated, flopping down beside Cassandra with his legs stretched out.

"You have other things to worry about," she drawled, looking past Rydon.

He looked over his shoulder and saw Terena, her shoulders hunched and arms across her middle as if she was ill. Rydon went to her side, his hand on her shoulder.

"What is it?"

"He knows you were there," Cassandra called out, drawing his attention back to her.

"Who are you talking about, woman?" Rydon asked, his voice harsher than he'd intended. She was a walking paradox, and he was sick of her riddles.

"Hermes."

Terena's head shot up. Rydon glanced between her and the blonde, worried at Terena's sudden pallor.

"How?" she whispered.

"He felt your presence."

Terena strode past Rydon, her face contorted. "How did I know where to find Daris? Is it because he's my eudaemon?"

Cassandra blinked. Her eyes widened slightly, shifting between Terena and Rydon. Something passed over her clear green gaze that Rydon couldn't name. He felt uneasy, all of this god shit coming at them too fast to decipher.

"Is it because he's a eudaemon?" Terena repeated, snapping her fingers in front of Cassandra.

The woman turned to her, the look gone from her face. "If you like."

Terena cursed and turned away.

"How do they sense each other? I am Sonah's guardian, and I've not been able to sense her," Rydon snarled.

"Maybe it's because I'm getting closer to my nameday," Terena mused.

Cassandra laughed in surprise. She looked at Terena with a wide-eyed smile, incredulous.

"Darling, you *know* why. Think."

Rydon smashed his fist into the table, scattering used glasses and plates onto the floor. The crash startled the blonde and her eyes whipped to Rydon.

"Stop playing. Speak plain!"

"What do you know?" Terena asked, as if she dreaded the

answer. Rydon looked back at her, feeling a sick sense of dread himself as he waited for the seer to respond.

Cassandra's smile widened.

"Cassandra, please," Terena said softly.

Rydon felt something flip unpleasantly in his gut at the look on Cassandra's face when she turned to him. "Gods are clever, and Hermes most of all."

"What did he do?" Rydon asked, even though a part of him already suspected.

Cassandra confirmed it with a look before she turned to Terena. "Daris isn't just your eudaemon."

"He's her lover," Croak snorted, crossing his arms. At the looks Terena and Gabriol shot him, he shrugged. "What? Not anymore, though. Lying bastard."

"What else is he?" Terena asked, the words rough. Rydon took in the way her face had lost color and her right eye twitched. His gut twisted painfully as he waited for Cassandra to speak.

"Come now, goddess," Cassandra crooned as she leaned forward, her arms on her knees. "You already know. Deep down inside? You knew in each of the last circles."

Terena brought a hand up to her mouth, her hand shaking as she looked at the witch in horror.

"We are bound. He's my soulmate."

"Soulmate?" Croak snorted, looking between Terena and Cassandra. "How the fuck did you come up with that? Are you still drugged?"

"Soulmates are not real," Gabriol scoffed, his large arms crossed at his chest. "They are the stuff of fairytales, stories for young girls and old maids."

"They are real," Cassandra replied, a hard edge to her voice as she glanced at Gabriol.

"The Fates bound you together," Cassandra confirmed.

Terena barely heard the woman through the keening noise inside her head. She felt ill and elated, ready to jump out of her skin while wanting to run as far from this conversation as possible. There was no rational thought beyond the need to be near Daris, to see him, to touch him, and yet her mind balked at the idea of them being bound. Daris had no choice but to love her. Because the Fates had decided for him.

It wasn't real.

That thought made her go ice cold, her body shivering so much she was relieved to feel Rydon's warmth as he moved closer to her side, his face screwed up with concern.

"Why?" Terena asked after a quiet steeped in tension. "Why would they do that?"

Cassandra sighed and tilted her head back, closing her eyes. Terena's nerves were screaming at her and she wanted to launch herself at the woman.

"I do not know," the seer replied at last, the words doing nothing to ease the chaos of Terena's thoughts right then. "Perhaps it is tied to your destiny. Or his destiny is as great as your own. But that is the answer to your question. You ported to him because your soul knows where his soul is. Always. At any given time. You will always find him. And he will always find you."

"That's some fairytale shit right there. I can't wait to tell Sonah!" Croak muttered.

"It's rare," Cassandra said absently. "And it almost always never ends well."

"What's that mean?"

Cassandra's lips turned down before dropping her gaze.

"So she can just port to wherever Daris is?" Croak looked at

Terena with a raised eyebrow. "That's not a very helpful power, sis. I hope you at least stabbed him when you saw him."

"You are simple, boy," Cassandra laughed. "They keep you around for your looks or your sword?"

"What do you mean?"

"Your looks, then."

"I—"

"Do other gods portal? Port? Is that what it's called?" Rydon asked.

Terena flashed him a grateful look. So many questions to ask, questions Hermes should've answered and didn't. If this stranger could help her with more than just finding the amulet, Terena needed to trust her with how ignorant she was about being a god.

The woman didn't seem to have any alliance to Hermes, that was clear, and if she was Apollo's lover, he must've been the one to banish her here. And yet, if he was able to banish her to Elysium, why couldn't the other Olympians come back without Terena's help?

"Aye. All the gods port," Cassandra replied. "At least, the Olympians. Did you come here looking for lessons in how to be a god, or are you finally going to ask me the question you actually came to have answered?"

"You're a piece of work," Gabriol grumbled.

"Let's not forget," Cassandra said with a shrug, "you sought *me* out." Looking at Terena she said, "I know you're looking for the Amulet of Kaïra. I will tell you where to find it. But first, you must take me with you to Metilai."

Croak burst into laughter and Gabriol swore. Terena tensed but did not look away from the woman.

"We're collecting tourists now?" Rydon asked Terena, his lips pressed tight enough to whiten the corners.

"We should charge extra for that, Ren," Croak chimed in with a grin.

The doors burst open and all of their heads swiveled around.

Vassori strode in, a grinning Orry behind her with Migela sauntering in last.

"Right on time," Cassandra murmured. When Terena glanced at her, the woman winked.

"What's happened?" Gabriol asked, closing the distance between them. Vassori handed him a crumpled missive. Orry trudged to Croak's side, his eyes shining.

"A message from my brother," Vassori said, her expression turning guarded when she spotted Cassandra lounging on the couch.

Rydon waved a dismissive hand. "You may speak freely. I have a feeling the witch—my apologies, Cassandra—will be traveling with us."

Vassori frowned at him, then shook her head. "He's on his way here, to us, in Ermanel. He's just crossed the border from Elis. He wants us to wait for him."

"Wait for him? Why?"

"Says he has a surprise for you."

"It must be Sonah!" Terena threw herself at Vassori, wrapping her arms around the woman's neck. Vassori laughed, hugging Terena back.

As they all gathered closer, Terena spared a glance at Cassandra. The woman had risen from the couch, her hands pressing down on her skirts as she rounded the table to reach their happy circle. The bells at her waist sang as she moved.

"I suppose you'll say you saw this as well?"

Cassandra's cunning smile was verification enough for Terena.

"So what happens next?"

"Obviously, we're waiting for Xoran," Croak shouted, pumping both arms in the air as he walked toward the doors with a whoop.

As they all filed in after him, Cassandra looped her arm through Terena's and sighed.

"Do you know what the surprise is? Is it Sonah?"

Cassandra's smile turned wicked. "I know what the surprise is," she demurred. "And I cannot wait for you to see it."

CHAPTER 23

IBROS

They had ridden most of the day until they neared the border to Elis.

As dusk fell, the waning sun took all the warmth with it, and Sonah found herself shivering uncontrollably until Fane had taken pity on her and called a halt for the day. Now, Sonah huddled closer to the heat from the small fire Melanos had built.

"Are you not warm enough yet, little one?" Melanos asked in his deep baritone. Sonah glanced at him and shrugged one shoulder.

When her teeth stopped clattering she sighed. "I've spent much of this past year on the road with my friends and yet I've not spent a winter outside of the White Palace. I long for the warmth of my bedchamber."

"This is no normal winter," Melanos said. "Although I do not feel it as you do, it is still unpleasant. And unusual."

"There was a catastrophic event in the north," Fane said as he chewed on a twig. "Almost two years past. It buried the north in ice and snow. Affected the rest of the continent in various ways we've had to adapt to. Some of us had never seen snow before."

"What is this event?" Melanos inquired, settling back against his saddle.

Fane shrugged and shifted onto an elbow as he gazed at the fire. "I'm not sure. The scholars have varying opinions. Stories range from the wrath of the Titans to cosmic realignments."

Melanos grunted. Sonah watched him out of the corner of her eye as he frowned down at his thick hands. They toyed with the edges of his cloak.

"What is it?" Sonah asked softly.

Melanos glanced at her, surprise in his eyes before shrugging it away. "'Tis nothing."

"Your face suggests otherwise."

The god's lip curled up. In the months since she'd last seen him, he'd allowed his ashen beard to thicken, and she wondered if it was in response to the cold.

"I do not know of any cosmic realignments from my time, but I do remember the gods affecting the weather similarly."

"Oh?"

Melanos looked up at Triodos, one of Fane's Spartan brothers, who watched him with an intensity that made Sonah scoot closer to the god.

"Aye. I've seen arguments that have kept Helios from riding his chariot across the sky, forcing weeks of darkness on the rest of us all because of a spat. I've seen that wretch, Poseidon, fly into a rage and take out his frustrations on the coastal towns of what was once Sierras, a beautiful island in the Gulf of Heroes. Eventually, the entire island was buried beneath the waves."

"Oh, aye!" Yianni, another Spartan soldier in their group, spoke up excitedly. "I've heard sailors speak of ruins beneath the waves while they patrolled the gulf!"

"If Terena were here," Sonah sighed, "she'd be able to tell us all about it."

Melanos laughed and nudged her shoulder with his big hand. "We don't need your sister for that, little one. I was there when it happened."

For the next hour, Melanos regaled the group with stories of the gods. Sonah looked around at their small group and saw them listening with rapt attention. She too, listened in fascination, but she also longed for her sister and their friends. Loneliness pressed in on her and tears stung her eyes.

Sighing, she settled onto her side and pulled her thick cloak around her while the men talked on. A few minutes later, she felt something heavy drop over her and her eyes slid open to see Melanos had draped his cloak atop hers.

Too tired to protest, she closed her eyes once more.

The sound of rushing water made Sonah's heart speed up as they neared the falls where only a few short months ago, Terena and her friends had found Bethana's lair.

"Do you think we'll find her?"

Before Melanos could answer her, Fane shouted back at them. Yanni waved his arms, both men grinning at them.

Sonah jogged beside Melanos's long-legged stride and when they reached the others, Fane pointed to the left. "We found an entrance!"

Following behind Melanos, Sonah rubbed her arms with her gloved hands and huffed her way to the dark cave that swallowed the others.

Inside, it was colder still, and dark enough to make her squint against the change. She heard Fane murmuring to the Spartans as she closed in. When her eyes adjusted, Melanos was making his way further inside, into a narrow corridor.

Sonah followed the others at a much slower pace. If any of them ran into the serpent, they'd deal with her long before Sonah was in sight.

Digging beneath her cloak and leather jacket, she grasped her dagger and unsheathed it from the belt. If she was the last line of defense, gods help them all.

Sonah froze as a long, low hiss sounded in the cavern, bouncing off the wet stone walls around them. She moved closer to Fane, who held out his hand for her without looking back. Tucked into his side, she felt slightly safer as her eyes darted around the dim cave.

"Bethana!" Melanos's deep bellow made Sonah jump. She clutched at Fane's bicep with her free hand.

Silence and the roar of water was the only response to his summons. They stood there, frozen, at the edge of a large pool of water, the glassy surface reflecting the stalactites from above. Sonah swore she might faint from the anticipation.

"Bethana! It is I, Melanos!"

Sonah shuddered and tightened her grip on Fane.

Hissing sounded behind them and Sonah whipped her head around, eyes wild. Fane shoved her behind him as he spun, holding his sword ready.

"Melanos."

The voice was otherworldly, sinking into Sonah like a stone and making her stomach drop. She shook from head to toe, pushing closer to Fane.

The water rippled and the serpent emerged, multifaceted green scales shifting as water sluiced off the magnificent creature. Sonah's mouth dropped open and her heart stopped.

Melanos strode to stand in front of their small group, his large frame blocking out her view of Bethana. Fane took several steps back, pulling Sonah as well.

Peeking over his arm, she watched as the serpent lowered her head, her forked tongue flicking out as she regarded the god who was once her lover.

"Bethana," Melanos said, his voice making tears spring to Sonah's eyes. She squeezed Fane's arm, her lips trembling as she watched Melanos drop to his knees before the former nymph.

Sonah felt Fane stiffen beneath her fingers and she dared a look up at him to see he, too, gawped at the prostrated god.

"Centuries I've waited for you to come," Bethana hissed, slithering closer to Melanos who knelt before her with his head bowed. "Centuries in which I lost so much of myself."

"I know."

Sonah's heart ached for the god who humbled himself now for the woman he loved. They all watched the scene and Sonah felt the need to turn away.

She tugged at Fane's arm and when he looked down at her with a frown, she motioned with her head. His brow furrowed, glancing back at the god and his nymph before he gave her a curt nod.

Stepping slowly so as not to draw the serpent's attention, they edged back far enough away to hide in the shadows of the corridor they'd come from.

"I was cursed too, my love," Melanos was saying and Sonah craned her neck to see beyond Fane. "I could not leave the cave that wretch put me in. But not a day has gone by that I did not think of you."

"The daughter of Ares said you were in a cave not far from here," Bethana hissed, her head lowering to Melanos's eye level.

"Aye, my love. And yet it was still too far."

The serpent regarded him in silence for a long moment. Sonah squirmed to move around Fane so she could get a better look. Her foot caught on someone's boot and she stumbled. Fane's hand snaked out and grasped her wrist, but not before the tumble of loose stones broke the silence.

Bethana's head snapped up and her tongue flicked out as she hissed long, low and mean. Everyone froze. Fane's hand was a vice on her wrist.

Melanos lifted his head as Bethana moved around him, her focus on the interlopers.

"I smell her," the serpent hissed, narrowing her slit eyes. "Come out, baby Ares."

Fane's grip tightened and Sonah winced. He shook his head slightly at her.

"It is not—"

"Do not lie!" Bethana swung her head around before her attention was back on them. "It is her. I can smell her. The taint of Ares is all over her."

"She is the younger daughter," Melanos said in a soothing tone, his hands out to placate the serpent. "Both of these young gods are not like their father. They are unlike any of the Olympians—"

"You dare defend them to *me*?" Bethana's voice sharpened and Sonah felt her pulse thud in her eardrums.

"I am not defending them," Melanos muttered, his hands splayed as he rose slowly. He was almost as tall as Bethana. "They broke my curse. I thought, perhaps, they could break yours too."

"Where is the other?"

Sonah's heart stuttered as Bethana continued to watch them in the dark. Although Sonah felt certain the shadows hid them, she was less certain Bethana's eyesight was as bad as hers.

"I don't know," Melanos said, his voice hardening. "But Sonah is here, and she wants to help us. Help you."

Seconds passed in which the serpent continued to regard them, the unnatural tilt of her head and the way her tongue flicked in and out not reassuring Sonah at all.

But Sonah trusted Melanos and the others to help her if needed.

And so she edged around Fane, snapping her wrist out of his grip, and stumbled forward into the cave.

She jerked back when Fane grasped her cloak, momentarily choking, before she twisted sharply and his hold slackened. Taking a few tentative steps forward, Sonah shot her gaze between Melanos's scowling visage and Bethana's eerie eyes.

"He's right," Sonah said, proud her voice only had the slightest of tremors. She swallowed and held her hands out like Melanos. "I told Melanos I wanted to help you and that is why I'm here. Although, I don't know how."

The serpent watched her through eyes that made Sonah shiver and drop her gaze. She began to fidget with her hands. Catching herself, Sonah tucked her hands beneath the folds of her cloak and cast Melanos a beseeching look.

The giant god smiled reassuringly at her. "I have found that, when all else fails, do what your heart tells you. You want to help Bethana break the curse? Listen to your heart."

Sonah chewed on her lip as she thought on Melanos's words. She heard the Spartans speaking softly to one another, and she glanced over at Fane, who watched her with intensity; Sonah felt heat climb up her throat, threatening to choke her.

Behind her, Sonah felt Melanos move closer, the heat from his body enveloping her, soothing her, and her shoulders loosened. With a sigh, she lifted her head and asked Bethana, "May I touch you?"

Fane inhaled sharply, and she was certain he was about to object, but Sonah took a step toward Bethana, determined. "I... I must touch you, I think. I—"

"You may," the serpent hissed.

"Sonah—"

"Let her be," Melanos said, his tone rife with warning.

Fane bristled, but as Sonah crept closer, she glanced at him with reassurance.

Sonah knew the serpent was big but this close, she was massive. Shuddering, Sonah couldn't help but think of Croak's account of how Terena had gotten the fangs for King Altos.

She hoped she wasn't going to be another victim of Bethana's rage.

Tentatively, Sonah held out her hand. Pressing it against the serpent's scales, she willed herself not to shudder at the textured surface. She swallowed, grateful Bethana did not strike her. Stepping closer, she pressed her hand firmly on the scales and closed her eyes.

Nothing happened. Sonah frowned. As the seconds passed, she became frustrated, ready to pull away.

Then she felt it.

Warmth stole over her body, rising from her belly, through her arms and down her hands. She tingled all over, as if ants raced over her skin.

Sonah squeezed her eyes tighter, tilting her head as she braced against the rush of heat threatening to consume her.

Gasps sounded behind her, and she heard Melanos swear softly.

Words she did not know filtered in and out of her thoughts. Sonah opened her mouth and whispered these words. This unknown language was as much a part of her as her skin, her hair, her breath. The words sounded all around her, the air vibrating with energy she could feel pulsing within and without, swirling around her as if seeking to be closer to her.

Sonah's eyes snapped open, the last of the words echoing in her brain for a long moment after she'd spoken them.

Her heart in her throat, Sonah's eyes widened as she stared.

"Gods save us," Fane uttered.

Melanos stood beside her now, his presence large and solid and yet she felt him shaking. Sonah, too, wasn't sure if what she saw was real.

The most beautiful woman she'd ever seen, with hair like spun gold, almost a foot taller than Sonah, stood before them. Her iridescent skin gleamed from the water, sparkling as she moved. She had a figure most men would covet, a thin blue robe clinging to her generous curves. Watching them through large brown eyes sparkling with gold, she lifted a tremulous hand to her face, her long fingers falling off her pale cheek as her gaze found Melanos.

With a cry, she launched herself at the god, who wrapped her up in his thick arms. Sonah felt tears track down her face.

A hand slipped into hers, tugging her back and she looked up to see Fane, who looked at her with awe in his brown eyes.

"You," Melanos said, lifting his head, pulling back only enough to turn to Sonah, eyes bright with unshed tears. "You are a wonder."

Sonah's chin quivered at the emotion she saw in the god's expression, and she gave him a watery smile. Bethana had her head buried in Melanos's neck and Sonah looked up at Fane, motioning with her head to move away and give them some privacy.

The others followed them out, everyone lost in their own thoughts. For Sonah's part, she marveled she even had the power to do something so... miraculous. She'd never done anything remotely like that, and began to wonder if there were other facets to her powers she could tap into.

As they stepped outside the cave, waiting for Melanos and Bethana to emerge, Sonah became aware of everyone staring at her.

"What?"

Fane shook his head. "What you did, Sonah." He let out a hysterical chuckle. "It was incredible. Did you know you could do that?"

Scrunching her nose, Sonah lifted a shoulder. "I just did what Melanos told me to do. It felt right. In here." Sonah tapped her fingers against her chest, over her heart.

"Do you think he'll come with us now?" Yianni asked, his dark brown eyes thoughtful as he turned to Fane. "Do you think he'll pledge himself to Sonah now she's freed Bethana from the curse?"

"I don't want him to pledge himself to me," Sonah said firmly, aghast. She shook her head, slashing her arm out as she spoke. "If he comes with us, it will be of his own accord and not because of a debt. And certainly not because of a pledge. He and Bethana more than earned their freedom. I will not be the one to enslave them again."

"I am glad to hear you say so," Melanos said in his booming voice, startling them. He gripped Bethana's hand in his as they strode closer. "But even I know when a debt is owed, whether you wish it or not. I will join you, little one. Wherever your path takes you."

CHAPTER 24

ERMANEL

"Our little family's getting bigger."

Terena looked up and grunted a greeting as Rydon sat down beside her.

"Vassori is growing on me," Terena said. Then she motioned with her chin to Cassandra, who sat leaning against Croak as they laughed about something on the other side of the campfire. "But Cassandra is still an enigma. There are moments I feel she could be a friend. And others..." She shrugged.

"Aye," Rydon sighed, stretching out his legs. "The woman confounds me as well."

They'd eaten dinner earlier and were now enjoying the fire as darkness settled around them. Orry was curled up on his side with his head in Migela's lap. The assassin stroked his hair as she stared into the fire, and beside them Croak lounged against his saddle. Vassori was conversing with Gabriol, their heads close together.

"We're not safe here," Terena said in a low voice, her eyes fixed on the fire. "Xoran better show himself soon."

"We'll be safe when he gets here. Ermanel is still part of the empire."

"You all may be," Terena grumbled, settling her arms on her knees. "They'll know who I am straight away. Croak, too."

"They're still with Heylisia?" Gabriol asked, looking over at them from his seat beside Vassori.

"Aye," Vas said. "Xoran learned of Emperor Solon's agreement to a betrothal between his newborn daughter and the duke's son."

"What?" Terena choked on her ale. "Serephina's given birth? When was she even pregnant?"

Migela signed, a look of confusion on her face.

"Serephina is the emperor's second wife," Orry explained.

"And mother to the heir, whose new baby sister is now engaged to a man twenty-three years her senior," Vassori responded with a snort. "Xoran told me she was pregnant right after the firstborns escaped. When the emperor had him searching for you and your sister."

"How *did* they escape? Did we ever figure that out?" Croak asked, the last words stretched as he yawned. Cassandra was curled up beside him with her eyes closed and a smile on her lips.

Vas looked around at the others. "What, you don't know?" She scoffed at the blank looks they gave her. Terena raised an eyebrow, and the tracker shrugged. "Your man got them out."

"What man?" Rydon scowled at Vas.

"Wait, Daris?" Croak asked, sitting upright. His eyes darted to Terena. "Did you know?"

Terena felt the heat rise in her throat, almost choking her. "When would I know, Croak? You think I'd keep something like that from you?"

Croak shrugged and leaned back down, propping his weight on his right elbow as he observed her. "Dunno. Pillow talk confessions you didn't want to share? Wouldn't blame you. Made an ass of you."

"That's enough," Rydon growled as Gabriol tossed a dried fig at Croak's head.

"What? She's over him, anyway. Right, Ren?"

Terena fumed silently. Thankfully, Gabriol asked Vassori about the other provinces, leading to talk of military strategy Terena tuned out.

All she could think about was Daris.

Another betrayal. Using Lerek's murder to help the firstborns escape. How could she not have put that together? Of course, Daris killing Lerek made sense now, as did his meeting with Duke Aurora just a month before that. He'd denied it that night she ported to his bedchamber. And a part of her—her traitorous heart—had believed it.

Terena recalled the first time she'd seen Daris. In Aurora. They must have been discussing plans for getting the firstborns out.

And Lerek was the diversion they needed to make their plans work.

Rydon shot up, startling her. Opening her mouth to ask him what was wrong, she saw Gabriol rise and unsheathe his sword. Rydon, too, had his weapons out. Vassori yanked Croak to his feet before crossing to stand beside the mercenaries. Terena rose, and Migela pushed Orry down near Cassandra before crouching in a defensive stance with her daggers ready.

"If we were Heylisian soldiers, you'd be dead."

Rydon glared at Captain Soros as he strolled into their camp. Behind him, several of Hermes's soldiers flanked him, hands on the hilts of their swords as they swaggered closer.

Putting away her swords, Terena lashed out at the captain. "Are you lost? Where's your master?"

"We are the advance party. Hermes is on his way."

"Wonderful," Croak grumbled as he dusted himself off. "So why are you here?"

"Looking for you lot."

"Well, I'm not sitting around waiting for him, if that's what you're here to tell me," Terena said, crossing her arms.

"And where are you going that you cannot wait for Lord Hermes?"

Terena snorted. "Not that it's any of your business, but I am following Sonah's trail. You can stay behind and tell *Lord Hermes* if you wish. Come dawn, we're gone."

More soldiers poured into the small clearing until it was crowded. Soros began shouting orders to his men and soon they were occupied with setting up tents and disturbing their peace. Orry sat beside Croak grumbling as they waited for Soros's men to settle.

The captain joined them a long time later, sitting next to Vassori as he warmed his hands at their fire. After Terena introduced Soros to Cassandra, the captain turned a calculating stare at Vassori. The tracker stared back in silence. Rydon spoke before Terena could ask Soros what that was all about.

"How long before he arrives?"

With a shrug, Soros twisted his lips, the scar on his upper lip making his mouth look wider. "Days."

"You know," Orry said, clearing his throat as everyone's attention turned to him. "I've been translating some texts in my research into the shroud and several mention cyphers and their amulets. One in particular is interesting as it allows the cypher to—"

"Breach!"

The distant shout reached them even as the roar of soldiers pouring out from the woods to their left made Terena and the others bolt up from their seats, unsheathing weapons as they looked around. The clashing of metal on metal tore through their encampment.

Soros took off, and the others were a moment behind him, swords drawn. Croak stopped to grab Orry by the cloak. Cassandra struggled to run and Croak dropped back to assist her.

Terena fell back to join them when the first arrows shot past.

"Fuck!"

"Run!" Terena roared at Croak and shoved him away.

She felt the slowing of time until it seemed to have stopped. The only sound was her breath. She exhaled and a flash of red edged her vision.

Her body was consumed by fire, crackling across her skin until she no longer felt tethered to reality. She spun, swords connecting with the nearest soldier. After hacking off his arm, she turned toward her next target. Her movements were effortless; her speed in relation to the soldiers she felled defying space and time. The power of her bloodlust took over and she grew more powerful, more savage, the longer she fought.

The pulsing within her ears and the red haze dissipated abruptly and she fell forward onto her knees. Her eyes felt heavy as she looked up at the others. Her brow furrowed as Vassori swam in and out of focus, rubbing something at her chest as her lips moved in a litany Terena could not hear.

She tried to rise, but a wave of dizziness so sharp consumed her and made her rock sideways.

"Terena!" Rydon caught her under her arms.

"What the fuck happened? Is she hit?" Gabriol yelled as he caught up, sliding to his knees at her side.

"There she is!" The shout from a nearby Heylisian soldier signaled the end of their reprieve. More soldiers poured out of the woods ahead of them.

"Run! Run!" Gabriol shouted.

"I need to talk to your sister!" Orry cried out as he ran to catch up to Croak.

"Oh, you think *now*'s a good time?" Croak snapped.

The clash of steel and the soldiers' roaring surrounded them. Rydon lifted Terena roughly, moving them far from the fray. Terena opened her eyes to see Orry, Cassandra and Croak huddled near the riverbank with Migela. The assassin stared back at them wide-eyed before turning and signed something at Croak and Orry.

"What's happening?" she asked, her voice faint. Rydon didn't answer. Water splashed up, and Terena opened her eyes.

A group of Heylisian soldiers were running toward them and

gaining. Her eyes widened as one of them lifted a bow, an arrow trained on her and Rydon. Terena cried out and jerked hard enough to make Rydon lose his balance. He fell, and they rolled together.

Crawling, she made to stand just as wolves attacked Captain Soros and his men from all sides. Her eyes finally registered the large wolf racing toward her and she stumbled back. At the last moment, Rydon hacked at its shoulder with his sword. Croak shouted from somewhere behind them and she turned, her head heavy, watching her brother fight off two soldiers.

Rydon grabbed her arm and yanked her behind him as more wolves came at them.

"Loose!"

Rydon and Terena ducked reflexively as a volley of arrows rained down around them. The wolves closest to them fell over dead or ran off, their whines and yelps fading as they disappeared back into the woods.

Terena turned to see Soros with some of his archers getting ready to release more arrows. Rydon yanked her back and they ran. Croak came forward to cover them, snarling as another Heylisian soldier fought his way through Soros's men. Vassori pushed a dead soldier off of her and Migela helped her up just as Gabriol roared at them to move.

"Stay with her," Rydon shouted at Croak, then turned back to the fighting with Gabriol at his side.

"What's wrong with you?" Croak yelled in her face, half dragging her into the shelter of a tree whose hollow was large enough to shield her. Cassandra dropped down beside Terena and held her hand, smoothing away the hair plastered to her brow. Orry bent down next to her, his lips trembling as his eyes searched her face.

"This is what I was trying to tell her," Orry snapped at Croak. "Something's drained her powers. There must be a cypher nearby!"

"Do not kill him!"

Rydon's head snapped up as Soros ran toward him and Gabriol.

They had just struck down the last wolf when Rydon saw a young man crawling along the ground. He clutched at his arm, and from the way he held it, Rydon could see it was broken. An amulet glowed faintly at his chest, the amber light hidden when he turned to look desperately for an ally.

Soros caught up and yanked the man up by his collar. The man let out a yelp, his legs kicking out ineffectively.

"You know him?"

"I know his kind," Soros spat, shoving the man but not letting go. He dragged him to the nearest tree and pushed him so his back cracked against the bark. The man was young, a few years older than Terena, perhaps, and the wild look in his eyes betrayed his fear. He pressed his lips tightly together and cradled his arm.

"Where the fuck did the wolves come from?" Gabriol gasped, wiping his sword on his breeches. "Solon's got animals fighting for him now?"

"This piece of shit is a cypher," Soros said again, his arm at the man's throat. The man's grey eyes widened as his gaze darted between Soros and the others. "What's your power, boy? How do you control the wolves?"

"He what?" Rydon asked.

"Answer me!" Soros screamed in the man's face.

The man flinched, his sweat-soaked black hair dripping down the side of his neck as he closed his eyes. Soros's men surrounded them, leaning in to get a better look at the cypher.

"He can't speak with your arm at his throat," Rydon barked.

A rustling behind him made Rydon turn his head, and he saw the men parting to let someone through. Terena pushed her way to the front with the rest of their friends close behind her.

"Are you all right?" Rydon asked, at her side in two strides as he lightly gripped her elbow. She nodded, her eyes heavy as she blinked up at him.

"I'm fine," she whispered.

"What happened? Where'd the wolves come from?" Croak asked, looking between Rydon and Soros at the young man held against the tree.

Soros kneed the cypher viciously in the gut. He fell, and the captain called out for some rope.

"Caught ourselves a fucking cypher," Soros said, flashing a crazed smile at Terena. "And a good one, too. He can call on wolves. Let's find out what other animals he can control."

The captain tied the man's wrist, and the cypher cried out when Soros yanked his broken arm back to tie the other.

Terena moved forward, her steps halting.

"That's not necessary. His arm's already broken. Secure it to his chest until we get to camp. He's not going anywhere," she said, one hand out as if to stop Soros. "Tie the rope to his good hand and hold it if it makes you feel better."

Soros shot her a disgruntled look but did as she said. Terena crouched down in front of the cypher. Rydon watched them closely as Terena and the young man stared at one another. Something flashed in the cypher's eyes like recognition.

After an endless moment, Terena reached out and the cypher flinched. Looking into his eyes, her fingers cupped the amulet at his chest. She looked down at it for a long time, then back at the young man.

"Artemis has blessed you," she said, and a hush fell through the group.

The cypher stared back at her, fear and frustration warring across his youthful face.

Terena regarded him for so long, Rydon opened his mouth to say something. Tearing the amulet from the cypher's neck, Terena watched when he cried out as if she'd punched him in the belly. His face crumpled, and he screwed his eyes shut tight, sobbing, and hung his head.

Terena rose slowly to her feet and Rydon moved closer, worried she might still be weakened.

As she looked down at the cypher, Terena tied the amulet around her neck and tucked the stone beneath her tunic. The amber glow faded until the jewel was an ordinary orange color.

Looking around the small clearing at everyone gathered, Terena leveled a look at Soros. "He comes with us. And no one is to touch him until Hermes catches up."

CHAPTER 25

ERMANEL

Lerek sat on the ground, the grass spiky from the winter frost. He swore under his breath as he brushed some twigs off his breeches. Settling once more, he pulled his legs up to rest his arms on his knees and gazed out at the silent stream, his mind unsettled after a day filled with revelations.

He knew Sonah had been hiding something when he'd questioned her, but he'd no idea it was anything like what the Imperial Guard had shared. When Captain Xoran had caught up to them, Lerek had questioned him, too. The news was the same; Terena was a god. And according to Xoran, in love with the Liodari commander.

That Terena had hidden her true nature from him rankled. And he'd thought of the many times over the years he'd reasoned away things that now made sense. How fast she moved. Her strength. Her fighting skills that had nothing to do with her father, the previous Captain of the Imperial Guard.

What bothered him the most, though, and what kept him from sleep, was her relationship with Daris Antonius.

Lerek sighed and lay back, hands clasped at his stomach as he gazed up at the sky between the swaying branches high above. Many times he'd sat companionably with the Commander of the Liodari and thought him a good man, a strong leader. They'd formed a relationship of sorts over the months he'd been in Sparta, and Lerek had even looked forward to the times they'd sit together playing Tavli and talking about everything.

But they'd only spoken of Terena once.

Lerek recalled that evening, when Daris had dined with Lerek in his rooms shortly after their arrival in Sparta. It had been Daris who'd asked about her. Lerek had dismissed it as idle curiosity about the woman who was to be executed the day the Liodari had spirited him and the firstborns out of the White Palace.

Not wanting to share the depths of his feelings for Terena with the Liodari commander, Lerek had denied their relationship. He'd even pretended ignorance about knowing Ren as anything other than his father's Royal Tracker. Daris had stared back at him long and hard, but made no comment. Soon after, they'd moved on to another topic.

Now he wished he'd said more, had claimed her then and there. Perhaps then Daris would've stayed away from her.

Lerek closed his eyes, willing away the image of Daris with Terena that immediately dominated his mind. He vowed to find her. Soon.

Something cracked behind him, and Lerek opened his eyes, frowning.

A shadow moved over him.

"Well met, prince."

Lerek gasped a second before something hit him in the head, and he was out cold.

THE CYPHER SAT ON THE GROUND IN TERENA'S TENT, HIS BROKEN ARM BOUND to his chest. His head hung down, the long black strands of his hair hiding his face from her.

"You are not Heylisian."

The man twitched, but otherwise gave no response.

Sighing, Terena rose and ventured closer. Rydon moved back to allow her room as she crouched before the cypher.

"What's your name?"

Nothing.

"This is going to go a whole lot better for you if you cooperate," Terena said with a glance behind her at Rydon's scowling visage. "You've no friends here, but if you speak with me, I promise to release you."

The man stared back at her, his dark grey eyes red-rimmed. Still, he said nothing.

"How is it you ended up in Emperor Solon's army? Conscripted?"

The man blinked.

"Barra des oté Osta?"

Terena looked back at Rydon in surprise. "You speak Ostan?"

Rydon flicked a glance at her. Turning his gaze back to the cypher, he repeated his question.

"Sa," the man said at last, his voice so soft, Terena leaned closer.

Rydon settled onto one knee beside her. "Eken barra ó?"

The cypher shifted, pressing his lips together as he flashed Terena a look. After a moment, he began to speak, his words low, guttural and fast. Her eyes swung back and forth between the two, watching Rydon as he responded, asking more questions. The man's head moved animatedly as he spoke, his eyes shifting to Terena every once in a while, motioning to her with his chin.

"Ask him if he can drain someone's powers. Someone like me."

Rydon again spoke to the cypher in Ostan. The man shook his head and laughed, launching into another rush of foreign words.

When he stopped, Rydon ran a hand down his beard and turned to Terena, his face grim.

"He says that's not the amulet's power. As you said, the one he carried was from Artemis, allowing him to control wolves."

"Did they have another cypher in their group?"

After another exchange with the young man, Rydon shook his head. "No, he was the only one. He was in Metilai looking for someone. A prince from Osta. He's been missing for years, and the queen of their kingdom sent many before him to find this missing prince. General Peleon's soldiers caught him while looking for amulets like the one he wore. But he claims the amulet isn't his."

Terena searched the man's face as he watched her. "How? We were told no one outside the bloodline it was gifted to can use the amulets."

"Aye," Rydon said as he rubbed his jaw. "He claims his queen used blood magic to force the amulet to answer to him. She's done this many times. He doesn't know how it works, just that she's done it before and she'll do it again until she finds whoever this missing prince is."

"Fucking hells." Terena's pulse ratcheted, and she looked at Rydon with alarm. "If she can do that, what's to stop Solon from doing the same? Find Soros and—"

"Lady Terena?"

Terena frowned at the voice coming from outside her tent. "Aye?"

The man stepped inside, his gaze shifting from her to the cypher and back again. "Captain wants to see you."

Before she could respond, he turned and ducked out of the tent.

Terena looked back at Rydon, who scratched his chin.

"Want me to come?"

She sighed, slapping her hands on her thighs before rising. "No, I'm good. See if you can get anything else out of him."

Terena made it to the captain's tent, where one of his men pulled back the flap to allow her entry. She saw Soros sitting behind his field desk, feet propped up on a bucket he'd overturned. He looked at her knowingly, spinning a dagger on his desk. A small smile danced on his handsome face beneath his unkempt beard.

"Well?"

Soros looked down at the dagger he was playing with, the smile turning coy. "I have a gift for you."

Terena arched an eyebrow. "A gift? What?"

The captain looked up at her, a gleam in his eye. She sighed again, turning to leave. He dropped his feet to the ground, swiping up the dagger as he leaned forward in his seat and called out to the soldier outside.

"Bring him in, Torinos."

A few seconds later, Torinos, along with another man she knew only as Scar, came into the tent, holding up a man with a black hood over his head. The man's hands were bound at his back and his clothes were filthy. Dried blood caked the neck of his tunic, which was torn in several places.

Soros waved his men away and the prisoner fell to one knee as Torinos and Scar let him go and quit the tent.

Terena looked from the prisoner to Soros who was now as giddy as a child on his nameday.

At Terena's look, Soros rose, tucking the dagger into the sheath at his waist and went over to the grimy man, yanking him back to his feet.

Eyes locked on Terena's, Soros lifted the hood from the prisoner.

The blood drained from Terena's face.

For a fleeting moment, she thought the world rocked beneath her.

"Isher," she breathed.

Isher, gagged and bound, stared at her wide eyed. Then he took a step toward her. Soros kicked the back of Isher's knee and the prince crashed to the ground.

"What the fuck?" Terena whispered, her horrified gaze flying to Soros. "Where—"

"One of my scouts found him. Never thought a routine scouting would yield the Captain of the Imperial Guard's campsite, let alone a prize such as this."

Terena stared at the prince. He must've been the surprise Xoran had mentioned in his message to them. A flash of anger choked her. She was disappointed it wasn't Sonah. Isher wasn't the surprise she'd wanted.

Soros kicked Isher in the back, and the prince fell onto his face. He squirmed, maneuvering to regain his position on his knees as he turned hateful eyes to the captain.

Terena couldn't tear her eyes away from him.

"He'd wandered away from Xoran's camp," Soros continued, crossing his arms over his chest as he moved to stand at Terena's side. "What shall we do with him?"

"Leave," Terena whispered.

Soros hesitated, and Terena felt his gaze searching her face, but she dared not look away from Isher. "I thought—"

"Leave," Terena said, turning at last to face the captain. Whatever he saw on her face made him throw his hands up in compliance. She turned back to Isher when Soros left.

The silence was thick, pressing in on all sides until all she could hear was a deafening roar in her ears. Isher didn't take his eyes off her.

He started speaking, his words garbled behind the gag, and he shook his head. Bringing up his right leg, he planted his foot and rose unsteadily. The prince breathed heavily, watching her, eyes filled with fury. But there was wonder there, too.

And then his face softened, and he gazed at her with—

Terena cursed and moved, striding forward to yank him around. She grabbed hold of one of his wrists and unsheathed her dagger. Moving the blade to cut the bindings, she spotted the bracelet on his wrist.

Terena froze.

Exhaling raggedly, she grabbed a fistful of his tunic and spun him to face her, dagger raised to his face as she yanked the gag from his mouth. Taking two steps back, she sneered at him.

"You fucking worthless dog," she said softly, an edge to her voice she saw gave him pause. "That bangle you wear was a gift I gave Lerek. Is it not enough he's dead? You need to *become* him?"

Isher closed his eyes and when he opened them once more, she saw something she hadn't seen in a very long time.

Dread flashed through her.

"After everything we are to each other, it saddens me you think I'm my brother."

Terena's mind screamed at her until she thought she might faint. Taking another step back, she shook her head.

The prince lifted his chin and smiled. The way Lerek used to smile at her.

"Say it," he whispered.

Terena shook her head again.

He took a step closer and stopped. "Say it."

Her lips parted and her heart thundered behind her ribs. She felt as if the world had stopped turning.

Swallowing, Terena took another step back. But she could not escape what was in front of her eyes. What her heart knew before her mind did.

"Lerek."

Lerek stared at Terena, drinking in everything about her, from her disheveled sable hair to the mud-crusted boots as she paced in front of him. She was more beautiful than he remembered. Harder, too. Her face seemed thinner, and her hazel eyes had an almost manic glint to them, although maybe it was shock at seeing him alive.

"How?"

Lerek blinked out of his reverie to focus on her question. "How? That is a very convoluted story."

"Try anyway," Terena bit out, twin spots of color pinking her cheeks.

He sighed. "Might I have some water? Your men stole me away from camp some time ago and I am parched."

Terena's beautiful eyes narrowed. "Swallow your spit."

"Not going to make this easy, are you?"

Terena laughed, the sound snapping out at him like a slap, and he flinched back.

"No, *Lerek*. I don't think I will." She walked to him, stopping within inches of him. "Start talking."

Lerek straightened. This was a very different Terena from the one he'd known his whole life. The one who had befriended him when most children were scared to say anything to the crown prince.

The one who stole his heart and was the reason he'd come up with the most foolish idea that had brought them to this place right now.

Pursing his lips, Lerek shifted and dropped his gaze. "My father would never let me marry you," he started. When he looked back at her, she'd flinched back, staring at him in horror. "I asked him for permission before you and I ever... I was in love with you—*am* in love with you—long before you returned my feelings. I went to my father, but he refused me. He already had someone in mind. The sister of King Yorgos of Lasteika. The alliance would bring him one step closer to pulling Pyrgos into his empire. So, I put a plan in motion to switch places with Isher. When the convoy to meet the new northern king left, Isher was to travel with them. As me."

Terena looked baffled. All the color had drained from her face.

He took a step forward and his chest squeezed when she jerked back. Lerek held up a hand. "It wasn't supposed to happen the way it did. In my mind, my father wouldn't know what happened until well after you and I married. That's why I asked you to stay in Aurora, do you remember? That's where I was going to meet you once Isher left with the convoy."

Still looking at him as if she didn't know him, Terena did not reply.

Lerek continued. "Someone betrayed me. I don't know who, but I promise you, Terena, I will find them and I will—"

"How was Daris involved?"

Lerek stilled. His eyes narrowed as he watched her. "Daris?"

Terena pursed her lips and waved a hand at him. "Commander Daris Antonius of Sparta. How did he figure into your plan?"

Rubbing absently at his wrists, Lerek shifted. His voice cold, he said, "You are overly familiar with the Liodari commander, I think."

The flood of color rising in her face made his blood boil.

"You're in no position to judge," she snapped, her chest rising and falling rapidly.

"I'm not judging, Ren," Lerek retorted. "I just can't help but think your mourning period was brief for all you claimed to have felt for me."

Terena rushed toward him, and for a flash of a moment, he was frightened of what he might've unknowingly unleashed.

Grabbing his tunic in both fists, she brought her face within inches of his and whispered, "Your ridiculous plan put me and Sonah in your dungeons." She pushed him away and rubbed a hand over her face. "We were to be *executed* for a crime we didn't commit and when asked about Sparta's involvement, your first thought is of how I didn't properly mourn you? Are you *fucking* kidding me?"

Looking desperately around the tent, Terena made to move past him, but he grabbed hold of her arm.

"I'm sorry!"

The words felt inadequate, and he searched for something more. "I never meant for you to get arrested. I tried to talk to you that night when you found us, but you... I am sorry, Ren. I am so fucking sorry. I cannot say it enough."

"And Sonah?" Terena asked as she jerked her arm out of his grip. "Did you not think of her?"

He hung his head. "She was always meant to travel with Isher. I knew it was a possibility she might figure it out before he even reached the north, but I also knew she loved him and would keep our confidence. I swear, Ren, on Gaia and all the old gods, I never thought this would happen. And when it did, I begged Daris Antonius to leave me in Aurora with the firstborns. But he had orders from his king to bring me to Sparta."

Swallowing, Lerek took a step forward, wincing as Terena held up a hand with a warning glare. He sighed. "I allowed the commander to convince me it was for my own good. That someone plotted against me at the White Palace, and until I knew who, the only way to keep me alive was to stay away from Metilai. You have to understand, I thought I could use Sparta to form an alliance with me. If I could get King Altos to agree, I could go back to Metilai and force my father to—"

"Force your father?" Terena laughed, her eyes dark with disbelief. "Your plan may have been naive, Lerek, but I never took you for stupid. How exactly are you going to force your father to do anything? You hatched an ill-conceived scheme and got your brother killed! And it almost cost me and Sonah our lives as well, all because you could not *force* your father to do anything!"

Heat flooded Lerek's face and neck. Lips pinched, he took a moment before answering. Terena was entitled to her anger, but gods was he tired of everyone treating him like a silly child.

"My father will do as I say because I have a feeling I know who was behind my attempted assassination and Isher's murder. I can leverage that to stave off war and bring some order back to the continent."

"Oh, brilliant!" Terena clapped slowly. Lerek's face burned hotter. "Pray, who do you suspect?"

"Never mind that now," Lerek grunted with a slice of his hand. "I know I'm in no position to ask, but would you grant me a favor? Return me to my camp and come with me to Metilai. Your friends, your warriors, are welcome to join us."

Terena's face darkened, her eyes calculating as she canted her head.

"I forgot how arrogant you are," she said softly, the words punching into his chest like a hammer. "What part of 'your father tried to fucking kill me' was lost on you? Gods above and below. Your false death has—"

Terena stopped abruptly, which was fortunate because Lerek could feel his birthright ready to rear its ugly head with sharp words he would not filter. Her expression flashed from stunned to unreadable, and he was left unsettled. Lerek watched her in silence as her gaze dropped, shielding her from his probing curiosity.

"I..." she swallowed and took a step back. "Soros!"

Lerek jerked back, hands up as two large men came through the tent flap. Lerek backed away. The man who'd captured him watched him with a hungry, feral glee while the other man grabbed him.

"Soros, tie him up and put him in my tent. And have Rydon bring the cypher here."

Lerek opened his mouth to protest, but his captor's lips curled back as he snatched Lerek's wrist and wrenched his arm back hard enough to make Lerek gasp.

"Take him away. Now."

"Ren, please! What—"

His captor yanked his arm, eliciting a grunt of pain from Lerek as he dragged him out of the tent. Lerek dug in his feet, protesting and shouting for Terena.

Before the soldier holding him pulled him away from the tent, he heard Terena say something about a prophecy.

"There's no need for—"

"Nighty night," the brute holding him said, bringing the hilt of his sword to Lerek's temple.

CHAPTER 26

ELIS

Sonah crouched on the riverbank, slurping the water from her cupped hands. Grateful for this one moment of respite, she glanced over her shoulder when one of the men's laughter burst loud enough to carry to her from their little camp.

Crunching sounded behind her and Sonah turned, expecting to find one of their group. Instead, the wolf she'd befriended after escaping the Rivermen stood staring at her through beautiful emerald eyes.

Easing down so her knees rested on the damp riverbank, Sonah tucked her heels beneath her and smiled at her friend.

"Hello," she whispered, not wanting to frighten him away. Then she quirked a brow at her own ridiculousness. Scare him away, indeed! Smothering a smile, Sonah leaned forward. "I wondered where you'd gone."

The wolf ambled closer, stopping a couple of feet away. Sonah set her hands on her thighs and sighed. "Well. I'm glad you found me. My friends found me as well! Most of them, anyway. I hope to find my sister, soon."

Scrunching her face, she bit her lip as she regarded him for a moment.

"Would you come with me? She's in Ovenno."

The wolf opened its mouth and panted softly, its eyes never leaving her face. After a moment, it took two steps closer.

Sonah beamed. "I'm going to take that as a yes." Without thinking, she reached forward, intending to pet him, when she realized what she was doing and froze. Pulling her hand back slightly, she asked, "May I touch you?"

The wolf cocked its head and waited. Sonah pulled her chin up and shrugged. *And I'll take* that *as a yes.*

Tentatively, she put her hand near his shoulder, pushing down slowly until her fingers prickled on his pelt. Smiling, Sonah pushed her fingers through the soft fur. The wolf turned his head to her, startling her. He pushed his snout against her arm. Sonah grinned and ran her fingers back through his coat, repeating the motion several more times. She whispered nonsense to him, telling him how he would be her best friend. Well. Besides Terena.

"Do not move."

Sonah jerked up at the voice. The wolf turned its head, growling low and deep as it moved slowly to face the newcomer.

Melanos stood there, a spear in his right hand leveled at the wolf. Sonah's pulse exploded in her ears and she lurched upright, hands outstretched as she stared wide-eyed at the god.

"No! Please!"

"Move away, little one."

"No! This is my friend! My wolf, Melanos."

"Is that what you are, lycanthropo? A friend?"

The wolf continued to growl as he prowled closer to Melanos.

"I beg you," Sonah gasped, taking several halting steps forward until she stood next to the brindle wolf. "I beg you, Melanos. Do not harm him. He has done none to me."

Melanos continued to scowl at the wolf whose hackles stood on end. It lowered its shoulders.

"Please!"

"You've not told her, lycanthropo?"

"Who are you talking to? Who is 'Lycanthropo'?"

"Your wolf is no wolf, little one," Melanos said softly. "Shift. Now."

This last was said to the wolf, Melanos's anger ratcheting to a dangerous point.

Feeling faint, every hair on Sonah's body stood on end and fire raced down her body. Her mouth opened and, in an otherworldly voice, spoke to the wolf.

"Do as he says, my friend."

Melanos's head jerked to her, his mouth dropping open. Sonah gasped and put a hand to her mouth.

What just happened?

A moment later, the wolf began to rise, its body twisting, reshaping, pulling and pushing in a grotesque dance until a man crouched where the wolf once stood. His naked body was hunched over and his dark brown hair shielded his eyes.

Stunned, Sonah gaped at him, then snapped her gaze to Melanos.

The silence dragged until it pressed on her chest and she opened her mouth to suck in a breath. It seemed to break the moment, as Melanos took a step toward them. Tilting his chin in the slightest of acknowledgement, the man lifted his green eyes to Sonah.

She was now certain she would faint.

"*You?*"

THE RIVERMAN WHO'D CAPTURED SONAH looked down at her, green eyes narrowed, before dropping his gaze once more. He stood before her stiff, hands clenched at his sides, and Sonah blushed to the tips of her toes when she realized she'd been staring at his nakedness.

Slapping a hand over her eyes, Sonah unclasped the buckle at her throat and thrust the garment at him. She sighed gratefully when she felt the weight of it leave her hand and turned around.

"Why are you here? What could you possibly have hoped to gain? You must know my friends outnumber you. Were you mocking me? I called you my friend! I thought you were my friend."

Sonah's mouth snapped shut after vomiting every thought in her head, the heat of her embarrassment deepening as she thought of her quiet conversations with the wolf. How this man must've laughed himself sick at her foolish mutterings.

When the silence stretched to the point she could no longer bear it, Sonah pivoted, relieved to see the warrior's form covered partially with her much-too-small cloak. His bare legs stood rooted, the muscles bunching as he shifted his weight and Sonah cursed herself for looking.

Lifting her eyes to his, arching an eyebrow as she waited for his response, she saw Melanos move closer to her from the corner of her eye.

The Riverman tilted his head ever so slightly in the god's direction but looked at her finally.

"I didn't mean to deceive you," he started, then pursed his lips as if rethinking his words. After a moment, he returned her gaze. "At first it was to ensure your safety after you left the camp and then—"

"My safety!" Sonah scoffed, glancing at Melanos whose thunderous expression would have leveled a lesser man. As it was, the Riverman's attention was solely on her. "*You* were the one who kidnapped me! My safety seemed the least of your concerns when you took me from my friend!"

"I hadn't planned it," the man snarled, his nostrils flaring. "I thought you were one of their victims at first."

"Victims?"

"Explain," Melanos growled.

The Riverman opened his mouth, glancing at Melanos. Pursing his lips, he took a step forward, meeting the sharp end of Melanos's spear.

Sonah gasped, her head snapping around to Melanos. "What are you doing?"

"I'm ensuring he stays where he is, lest he find himself without a cock."

Sonah colored again. "I don't think that was his intention," she sputtered.

The Riverman cast Melanos a venomous look. "The men we were following are known in the area as smugglers. They steal children, women," he spat, turning his glittering eyes to Sonah. "We'd set a trap for them and you stumbled into it."

"I didn't—I mean, I wouldn't—" Sonah mumbled, shifting her gaze between the two. If her face became any hotter, her head would surely explode.

"You did," the man insisted. "And I thought I was protecting you. Until we made camp and Hector—one of my brothers—recognized you. He told our captain you were the Royal Taster. Sonah Yahn. After that, your fate was sealed."

"And yet," Melanos said in an ominous tone, still with his spear at the man's neck, "you did nothing to stop her escape. Why?"

"Did Pytho send you?" Sonah asked, her eyes searching his face for answers. "She said to find the green-robed man and he'd lead me to the Rivermen. Have you spoken with her?"

"I do not know anyone by that name. As I said, I didn't know you'd be there."

"Why did you allow her to escape?" Melanos snapped.

The man squirmed, his feet shifting on the cold ground beneath him.

"Melanos," Sonah said, her voice firm for the first time since this confrontation began. "Might we continue this conversation closer to the campfire? Perhaps get... what's your name?"

"Leander," the Riverman answered.

Sonah lifted a hand. "Leander, right. I remember now. Well, I suggest we get Leander some clothes and food and hear him out."

Without waiting for Melanos's agreement, Sonah stomped past both males and made her way back to their campsite.

A few seconds later, she heard the Riverman's padding footsteps behind her, followed by Melanos's much heavier tread.

The others looked up when they neared. Fane jumped to his feet, grabbing his sword and yanking it from its scabbard. Color blossomed in his cheeks, staring in disbelief at the newcomer.

"Stand down," Sonah said, silently patting herself on the back for how imperious she sounded. "He is with us now."

"That's yet to be determined, little one," Melanos barked, but not unkindly.

Which is why she softened her tone when she replied. "He is with us because I say he is, Melanos."

Sighing, she motioned for Yianni to make room in their circle for Leander to sit and bade Fane to get him some clothes.

When she took her seat beside him, she looked up at Melanos with a quirked brow. "And I'll thank you to refer to me by my name. 'Little one' demeans me."

"Aye, goddess," Melanos grumbled, and she twisted her lips in a rueful smile to match his own.

When she looked away, she caught Bethana staring back at her. After a moment, the woman winked.

The Riverman, startled, looked over at her. His expression turned wary, and he glanced at the others around the circle. "Goddess?"

"Aye," Fane snapped as he threw a bundle of clothes at Leander. "You kidnapped the daughter of Ares. Now talk your way out of that, you worthless maggot."

VILLADELLE, TURSK

Fane had argued against staying in Elis on their way north to Ovenno. Leander had agreed, about the only thing the two men had in common. He'd shared what he knew of troop movements in Elis and Ermanel, suggesting they instead cross into Pyrgos and travel through the independent provinces to reach Ovenno.

A week later, they reached Tursk as the sun kissed the horizon.

Sonah was desperate for a soft, warm bed to sleep in.

And a bath. Gods knew she needed it.

So, she convinced the others to stop in Villadelle for the night. They'd arrived in the late afternoon, and Sonah had immediately requested a bath.

Flopping onto her bed, Sonah closed her eyes and waited for the bathwater to be brought up. Smiling, Sonah recalled Melanos walking into the room with a tub, looking for all the world as if the bulky basin seemed to weigh no more than a bucket.

A knock sounded at her door and she sprang up, excited at the prospect of her relaxing bath. Yanking open the door, Sonah blinked stupidly at the beautiful woman on the other side of the door.

"Bethana," she said after staring at the nymph. Stepping aside, Sonah gestured for the woman to come in. "I was expecting my bath water."

Sonah closed the door and turned to face Bethana. The nymph stood with her delicate hands clasped in front of her, a shy smile on her face. Her golden hair was plaited in a thick braid falling to her waist. Despite riding as much as the rest of them, the woman seemed refreshed and without the mud-speckled clothes Sonah still wore.

She tugged self-consciously on her own filthy locks that had long since come undone from her braid.

"Aye, I came to offer assistance with your bath, if you'd like," the woman said in a soft, lyrical voice.

"Uhm," Sonah scrunched her chin. "I... thank you, lady, but I do not need help. Though I appreciate the offer."

Bethana smiled, the enchanting expression making Sonah even more aware of how feral she must look to this woman. Bethana's iridescent skin flashed teal and blue as she moved within the small room.

"I know you used to be at court, so must be unaccustomed to such a simple life," Bethana gestured to the sparse bedroom. Sonah glanced over her shoulder at the thin blankets on her bed and the lone armoire that had seen better days.

She shrugged. "Aye, but I've adjusted since... you know. Everything."

Bethana nodded. "Of course. But as the daughter of Ares, I cannot sit by without at least offering my services. As a water nymph, I can make your ablutions more pleasant."

"Ah, right." Sonah nodded. "I'd forgotten. While that sounds lovely, I do not wish to put you to work. Just the act of bathing will be such a treasure I fear I might never emerge once inside."

Bethana laughed. "It is up to you, of course. At the very least, I have a bath oil I've prepared for you. It should ease your aches from riding."

The nymph held out a small jar filled with what looked like honey.

"When did you have time to make this?" Sonah asked even as she held out her hand for the jar.

Bethana winked. "Oh, I have my ways."

After Sonah thanked her again, Bethana turned back to the door. "If you change your mind about my assisting you, please let me know. I—"

Another knock sounded just as Bethana opened the door. Leander, the Riverman, stood on the other side, hands laden with buckets of steaming water.

Bethana gave Sonah a knowing smile before she inclined her head and moved aside for Leander to enter. Sonah fanned her face, turning toward the bed so Leander would not see how flustered she was of a sudden.

"I didn't mean to interrupt," he muttered as he poured the contents into the waiting tub. The Spartan soldiers came in as well, their heads studiously locked on their chore before they hustled out of the room.

When Sonah turned around, she noted with a startled squeak she and Leander were alone, Bethana and the others nowhere in sight.

"Lady," Leander said in a raspy voice. "Do you... desire anything else?"

Sonah's eyes almost popped out of her head.

In a voice more shrill than she intended, she sputtered, "Aye! I desire your departure at once!"

He chuckled and turned to leave. Sonah grabbed a boot she'd discarded near the foot of her bed earlier and chucked it at the door as he closed it.

His deep, throaty laughter on the other side faded long before her heartbeat settled back into its normal rhythm.

CHAPTER 27

ERMANEL

Rydon had been surprised to see the Heylisian prince when Soros's man arrived with the gagged and bound royal, but when the soldier informed him he was to bring the cypher to the captain's tent on Ren's orders, he spared no further thought on the man.

Terena's face was sickly pale, lips parted and trembling as her eyes raced to every corner of Soros's tent. Settling the cypher on the ground against the captain's cot, Rydon drifted closer to Ren and waited for her to acknowledge him.

She lifted both hands, covering her face before she shook her head once and dropped her hands. Her eyes looked at him owlishly.

"False death betrays love."

Rydon frowned, tilting his head and waited for her to continue.

A moment passed in silence, then another, the seconds sliding past as he waited for her to go on. If she expected him to understand her meaning from that sentence, he could not think why.

"The prophecy," she added, hands splayed. "The prophecy Pytho told me. Those are the first words: false death betrays love. Lerek's death was false! He didn't die, Rydon. Isher did."

Rydon's eyes widened to the point he feared they might drop out of his skull. "What are you saying? That wasn't Prince Isher?"

"No," she whispered, shaking her head. "That was Lerek. A scout found him. Lerek was traveling with Xoran. *That* was Xoran's surprise! And according to Lerek, the only ones who knew who he really was before Xoran found him were the Spartans."

Rydon's lip curled into a sneer. "That lying bastard—"

"Aye," Terena said in a voice filled with disdain. "I've a mind to head straight to King Altos and bash his head in."

"I meant Daris Antonius."

Terena's gaze dropped away as she scowled. "Him, too, I suppose. Although he might be forgiven since he was following orders."

"Here we go," Rydon muttered, raking a hand through his hair. He turned away from her, pacing the limited space with hands on his hips.

"Believe me, I'm still angry at the commander." Terena reached out and wrapped her fingers around his arm, squeezing gently. "But he is as much a pawn as the rest of us when it comes to the games of sovereigns."

"Aye, that is true, although *you* are no pawn. You never were. From now on, if they take advantage of you, it'll be because you allow it. You have the knowledge of who you are now to aid you in putting down your foes. With Hermes and Sonah, when we find her, we'll be unstoppable."

"I'm worried," Terena said, before chewing at her nail. She wagged a finger a moment later. "Now we know Lerek isn't dead, it must mean he's the part of the prophecy about false death. Don't you see, Rydon? He betrayed me, he betrayed our love, letting me think he was murdered. It has to be what Pytho meant."

"What's the rest of it? Do you recall?"

Terena made a face, her features darkening as she thought. "Aye.

That it would forge Athena's Weapon. I don't know what that means. Hermes told me *I* was Athena's Weapon."

"Could mean that because of Lerek's death and your arrest, you decided to fight back? Become her weapon in truth?"

"No." Terena shook her head, popping her finger back in her mouth to nibble at the nail. "No, she said false death betrays love, and *then* Athena's Weapon is forged. So that means..."

Rydon crossed his arms, waiting.

"Fuck!"

Terena's outburst didn't surprise him. She was wound up so tight before Lerek's return from the dead, he worried she might be close to her breaking point. Her eyes raced back and forth and the nervous way she chewed on her nail—gods, was that blood at the corner of her mouth now? Had she chewed so far down the quick she'd drawn blood? And she didn't seem to notice either, which made Rydon nervous for her.

"Terena," Rydon dropped his voice to a low murmur, leaning forward to force her to meet his gaze. "You will not solve it in your current state. And what is your plan for the prince?"

"He stays with us."

"Why?" Rydon spread his arms. "What's that gain us except another target on our backs? Xoran will have to tell the emperor who took his son, and we'll have all of Heylisia converge on us!"

Terena remained silent, her eyes on the ground. Rydon released a rough exhale, rubbing his hand up and down his face before waving it at her.

"What about him?" Rydon added, motioning to the cypher sitting on the ground. "Why did you have me bring him here?"

As if seeing the man for the first time, Terena started, her eyes widening. After a beat of silence, she turned to Rydon. "Ask him what powers the other cyphers Solon has in his ranks can wield."

Rydon crouched down next to the cypher and spoke to him in Ostan. The man regarded her in silence before turning back to

Rydon. He spoke fast, pausing every once in a while as he thought. When he was finished, Rydon's expression turned pensive.

"He says he's only seen three in his time with the Heylisians. One moved small objects with his mind, while another manipulated fire. Both of them men much older than him.

"The last was a woman whose power was the same as you had mentioned before. She can drain someone's energy, not power. And he's only ever seen her do it on other Heylisian soldiers. She left their company a few months ago and he hasn't seen her since. Shortly after, he was assigned to the group that attacked us."

"Curious," Terena said as she stared at the cypher, his steady gaze locked on her, too. "Take him to the edge of the camp and release him. Tell him to go home. To Osta. And never return."

Rydon grunted his assent. He thought for a moment. "You should have Vas send a message to Xoran. About the prince. You can give him back after we've found the amulet. If you don't, Xoran will retaliate, Ren. He'll have to. He cannot let this pass; he needs to save face with his men. Not to mention the emperor."

"I'm not worried about that."

Rydon waited. When she didn't continue, he grunted. "Fine. Then what?"

"Remember what Cassandra said?"

Rydon groaned. "The witch said many things. To what do you refer?"

"She said she wanted to go to Metilai. We never told her where we planned on going and yet she knew. I know you don't believe her visions, but I do. We need to go. First thing in the morning. Would you do me a favor and tell Soros I'm staying in here tonight?"

"Aye. I can do that. But we cannot go to Metilai alone." Rydon shifted his weight and grimaced. "Ren, we should wait for Hermes. He'll be here any day now. And what about Sonah?"

"I'll have Cassandra find her. She's a seer, after all. Fuck, should've thought of that sooner."

"And if she cannot? Or worse, sends us on a wild goose chase? You cannot trust what she says, Ren. She's manipulative—"

"I think there's more to her. Do you really believe she'd withhold that information from me? She knows what I'd do to her if anything happened to Sonah because she didn't warn me."

"I think it's a bad idea. I think it's a bad idea to go to Metilai, too. We should wait for Hermes."

"The emperor owes me answers, Rydon."

"Ren, no."

"Aye. We're going back to the White Palace."

While Soros had his men break down camp, Terena had sought out Vassori with a message for Xoran and bade her ride to his camp.

"I'll meet you in Metilai," Terena had told her, clasping the tracker's arm as Vassori nodded.

Striding toward where Cassandra and Rydon were, Terena called out to the seer.

"Have you had any visions of Sonah?"

Cassandra's gaze shuttered. Fidgeting with her skirts, she glanced down. "Aye."

Terena puffed out a breath. "Really? Where is she? Do you know? Is it clear from your visions?"

Cassandra waggled her head. "She's safe. I do not know who she is with, but they are friends. I cannot tell where she is right now, though. I don't have a sense of time with my visions. I see a very large man, blond, with a beard. And... a woman. Her skin is... different. I see a wolf but... he's a man?"

"No riddles, please, Cassandra." Terena groaned. "She's safe though?"

"Aye?"

"Do you see me with her? In your visions."

"Aye. We're all together. And Vassori is with us, so maybe it's Metilai."

"You cannot tell?"

"I'm not familiar with the surroundings." Cassandra looked at the ground, her lips pursed. "I see a tall blond man sitting on a throne. Different from the one before. And Sonah is with him. I see you but you're wearing a uniform—"

"The only throne that makes sense is Metilai. But the blond man isn't Solon. The emperor has dark hair." Terena looked down, thinking. "And the amulet. Do you know where it is?"

Cassandra lifted her chin. "I do not, but I last saw it in Ravos. At Sydney Hall. And it was in my vision of—"

"We have a problem."

Terena turned as Rydon strode toward them, a deep scowl on his face.

"What now?"

"When I let the cypher go, he told me General Peleon was sending an army north to Ravos. The cypher said that's where he and the others were headed when they ran into us."

"Why?"

Rydon wiped a hand down his beard. "Duke Ravos claims to have Sonah Yahn."

"Impossible. And isn't he dead?"

Rydon shook his head. "The new Duke Ravos."

The blood drained from Terena's face. Her eye twitched, and she squeezed them shut, pressing her fingers into her eyeballs. "Galen," Terena muttered. "Why the fuck did we not hear of this sooner?"

Rydon shook his head. Turning, he bellowed for Captain Soros.

Terena's attention drifted to Soros as he and two of his men brought a bound and gagged Lerek toward them. Lerek's eyes spit fire as he struggled against his captors.

"Where do you want him?" Soros asked as the men shoved Lerek forward. The prince stumbled, and it took every ounce of Terena's willpower to stay mounted as he fell to his knees.

Once upon a time, she would've skinned the men for their treatment of him.

Lerek glared at their group, sneering as best he could around the cloth in his mouth.

"I questioned the cypher," Rydon said, hands on his hips. "He said Duke Ravos claims to have the Royal Taster."

Soros shrugged, looking between Terena and Rydon.

"Sonah," Terena snapped. "The Royal Taster is my sister, Sonah."

"Fuck," Soros said, his head falling back.

"Aye. And General Peleon marches north with an army to claim her."

As Soros processed this information, Terena looked away, her face neutral.

"Croak!"

"What?" Croak called out. He walked Cerberus closer to her.

Terena sighed. "Lerek rides with you."

"What? No!"

One of Soros's men grabbed Lerek under one arm and lifted him as if he weighed no more than a child. As they strode toward Cerberus, Croak dismounted, stalking toward Terena with a disgruntled look.

"He's not riding with me, Ren! I have no desire to be a target for a random Heylisian squad should they happen by! No offense, Lerek."

Terena ignored him as she mounted Nyx.

"Mount up. I'll have them bind you two together."

"For fuck's sake, Ren, that's insulting!"

"I don't care if he's insulted."

"I meant it's insulting to me!" Croak put his hands on Ren's knee, his eyes wide as he pleaded with her. "You take him! He's *your* lover."

"He is not," Terena said. Lerek narrowed his eyes at her.

"Fuck!" Croak kicked at the ground, sending rocks and bracken scattering. The horses shifted, and a chorus of protests and curses made him glare back at the others.

Without another word, he waited while Soros helped Lerek mount. Croak sprang up onto Cerberus in front of Lerek, his face bright red as he mumbled beneath his breath, barely waiting for the men to bind them together before turning Cerberus and riding off.

Captain Soros arched a brow at her. "Where's the cypher?"

"I let him go."

"What?" Soros stared at her, incredulous.

"I still have the amulet. We don't need him."

"He was the one who could use it!"

Terena shook her head as she walked. Soros followed.

"You know I have to let Hermes know, right?"

She shrugged. "Tell him."

The captain groaned and wiped a hand down his face. "We should wait for him."

"No. You can stay and wait if you want. But my sister is in Ravos. So I must go."

"With an army marching north?" Soros scoffed, looking over at Rydon for help. "Do *you* think that's a good idea?"

"No," Rydon said. "But if we can get to Sonah before the army gets her first, I'm willing to try."

Terena smiled gratefully at Rydon. Flashing the captain an irritated look, she swatted his arm and walked past him.

"I wasn't asking, Captain. We ride for Ravos."

DARIS RODE BESIDE HERMES WHEN THEY MET UP WITH TWO OF CAPTAIN Soros's men. They dismounted, each falling to a knee, their heads bent to the ground as they muttered their greetings to the god.

"Where's Soros?"

"He left us behind to find you, Lord Hermes," one of the men, a mercenary by the name of Scar, said as he lifted his scarred face, his thick beard bisected by a nasty gash running the length of his cheek down to his clavicle. "We were attacked by Heylisian soldiers who had a cypher with them. When questioned, the cypher said Sonah Yahn was in Ravos and he and the soldiers who'd attacked were on their way there when they ran into us. An army is on its way north to Ravos from Metilai as we speak."

"Where is Terena now?"

"They are on their way to Ravos, lord. Captain Soros also wanted us to tell you we found Prince Lerek."

Hermes glanced at Daris before turning back to the soldier. "And where is the prince now?"

"They took him with them."

Heat sizzled across Daris's skin. His jaw tightened but allowed no other outward sign at the news Ren traveled with her former lover.

"How long ago?"

"Two days."

"Where in Ravos?"

"The capital, lord. They are headed for Colinas."

Daris looked at Hermes finally, unsurprised the god stared back at him. A long moment passed as they locked gazes before Hermes pulled on his reins, turning his mount.

"Then we go to Colinas."

An hour later, a hawk circled overhead in lazy passes before swooping low to land on Elias's outstretched arm. The Liodari pulled his horse aside, and Daris and the rest of his men followed suit while Hermes's soldiers rode past.

As Daris waited, Elias plucked the rolled-up missive from the hawk's leg and handed it to Jason. Lifting his arm, Elias launched the bird into the air.

Jason read in silence. Lifting his head, he looked around for Daris.

"From Captain Athanasi. You won't believe this," Jason shook his head. "Sonah's been found. She's in Villadelle. With Fane, of all people."

Daris tore the parchment from Jason's fingers and read the message before handing it back to him.

"Captain Soros's man just informed us that they have reason to believe Sonah is in Ravos. Terena and the others are on their way to Colinas to get her."

Jason frowned. "That's not possible."

"Aye," Daris said. "An army is also heading north to Ravos from Metilai. It's a trap."

"For what?"

"Terena," Daris spat. He thought for a moment then looked back at Jason. "I want you, Trojus, and Elias to stay behind. Write back and tell Fane to meet you here. Then join us in Ravos."

"At once."

"Jason."

His lieutenant turned back, waiting.

Daris leaned over as he glanced ahead. He couldn't see Hermes around the circle of men separating them, the others pulling farther and farther away as the Liodari remained by Daris's side.

"Say nothing to Hermes or his men. And if they ever ask you about the contents of the missive, tell them it was King Altos needing us back in Sparta, but that I sent you back without me. I'll tell him I stayed behind to see Terena."

"But if she's riding into a trap—"

"I don't trust Hermes to continue traveling to her aide if he hears Sonah is safe nearby," Daris said, glaring at Jason. "You get Sonah, and I'll make sure we get to Terena in time to help her."

"Aye, Commander."

Daris galloped to the front of their column until he was alongside Hermes. The god didn't bother looking at him, lifting a hand instead as if to tell him to proceed with his message.

"King Altos needs us to return to Sparta. Heylisian incursions at the border. I've instructed my men to return without me."

Hermes's profile was impassive. Daris rode beside him in silence for a minute, but the god did not reply.

Pursing his lips to hide his annoyance, Daris made to drop back when Hermes spoke.

"Why?"

Daris furrowed his brow. "My lord?"

"Why are you staying behind?"

"Terena."

Daris watched the god's profile, seeing the corner of his mouth tug up.

"Of course."

"I would've stayed regardless," Daris said. "I wish to find Sonah, as well."

Hermes was silent for a long time after, and Daris turned his thoughts to Terena. He hoped he could get some time with her alone. There was no telling what Prince Lerek had told her about Sparta's involvement with his... departure from the White Palace. Daris did not think for a moment their night in Pera meant she'd forgiven him for his lie of omission.

And he'd be damned if he'd let the prince find his way back into her arms.

CHAPTER 28

TURSK

Sonah groaned for the millionth time since they'd set out. She didn't think she'd ever get used to riding a horse. Maybe she wasn't built for it. Were gods even supposed to ride horses? Not for the first time, she wondered what their world was like when the gods ruled.

She glanced to her right, where Melanos rode with Bethana wrapped in his embrace. Sonah sighed wistfully as she took in the way the nymph's head lay against Melanos's chest, eyes closed and a small smile on her lips. Here was a woman who'd been cursed to live as a serpent for a millennium, and yet she seemed more comfortable in the saddle than Sonah.

And Sonah had spent much of the past year in one.

Sighing again, she shifted her gaze to Leander. He had a strong profile, emerald eyes narrowed and lips pinched in concentration.

The Spartans were still cautious around Leander, but Melanos seemed to have warmed to him. She'd worried she'd made a mistake including Leander in their numbers, but he'd proven himself useful, especially with his hunting skills.

As if sensing her attention, Leander glanced over at her, smug when he caught Sonah staring. Heat burst over her face and she turned away, cursing the man under her breath when he chuckled.

A hawk circled above, and Sonah lifted her chin, shielding her gaze against the late day's sun, the bright rays filtering through the trees in a blinding brilliance of power. The hawk let out a keening cry and dipped, flying dangerously close to their horses, and she startled, her fingers fisting tight on the reins until her mount danced beneath her.

"You'll make her rear if you keep clutching the reins like that," Leander said softly beside her. Sonah gasped, her head whipping in his direction, and the horse responded by edging closer to his mount. He reached out, steadying her, and Sonah shivered as his earthy scent invaded her senses.

Gods, he smells good.

He looked up at her sharply and Sonah froze. Had she spoken aloud?

"Are you all right?"

Sonah nodded several times, then realized how ridiculous she must seem. But his voice had dropped, and the huskiness made her belly flip.

"Aye," she breathed. Big mistake. Inhaling more of his intoxicating scent caused a tiny stream of drool to escape her mouth.

Gods, please open up the ground beneath me and swallow me whole!

Leander's lips quirked up. "Lady?"

"Aye?"

"Is everything—"

"What's it say?" Melanos called out, jarring Sonah out of her stupor.

She jerked away from Leander and looked ahead to where Fane sat, his arm extended, the hawk she'd seen now perched on his forearm. Leaning over to Melanos on his other side, Fane handed him something.

Sonah watched Melanos's face as he read whatever Fane had

handed him. Melanos lifted his head, a scowl on his handsome face. He turned to look at her.

"The commander is with Hermes."

"Who?" Fane asked.

"He's the Messenger God, an Olympian," Melanos said in a gruff voice.

"But one of the better Olympians," Bethana added. "He was always kind to me."

Sonah frowned. "Another god? How? And what's he doing with Daris?"

"I don't know," Melanos muttered, rubbing his hand across his beard.

"Is Terena with them?" Sonah asked excitedly, straightening in her saddle.

"No," Melanos grunted. "She's in Ravos now."

"Ravos, why?"

"He does not say," Melanos grunted. "But the commander is still in Ermanel. Looks to be a few days ahead of us. His man, Jason, will stay behind to meet up with us."

Sonah swallowed, darting a glance at Leander, who watched her through narrowed eyes. Pressing her hands to her hot cheeks, Sonah ducked her head. She was acting foolishly. Jason hadn't bothered to visit her while she'd been at Arestia Castle. So why should she care whether or not the Liodari was now waiting for them?

Sonah lifted her eyes to find Leander still staring at her. Blood of the gods! Why did she feel so awkward all of a sudden?

"Well, then... let's start heading east," Sonah said, flicking the reins and trotting off.

"Wrong way," Fane called out.

Sonah's face flamed as she wheeled her mount around and followed after the others.

ERMANEL

At night, Leander transformed into his wolf form to hunt for their dinner, which was convenient and about the only good thing she had to say for his company. Otherwise, she was on edge. And always too warm.

He'd sit too close, or lean in too close, or breathe too close. It was annoying.

She'd objected once when he'd returned with a brace of haddon, leporids with ears larger than Leander's hands, their thick feet dragging on the ground as he held them at his side. He'd dumped them in front of a grinning Melanos. The god had gotten to work skinning the animals while Leander dropped onto a log beside Sonah. His breath stank, and she'd told him so, which did nothing to the man's ego. Instead, he'd thrown his head back and laughed.

"Aye, it usually does after I go hunting."

Sonah wasn't pacified. "Well then, don't sit so close to me!"

Leander had flashed her a wicked grin. "Well then, stop being so beautiful, and I will."

Sonah groaned, recalling how hot she'd gotten at his words, even now pressing a hand to her overheated skin. Which was ridiculous because it'd been raining all morning and she was soaked and freezing.

"Everything all right back there?"

Sonah glanced at Melanos's back and twisted her lips. She opened her mouth to retort when something whistled through the air.

"Cover!"

Leander's roar made her ears ring and Sonah cried out when her horse reared back. Fane and the Spartans wheeled their mounts around until they encircled her. Shouts came at them from all sides, and Sonah's breath caught. They were quickly overrun; Fane was knocked from his horse while soldiers attacked the Spartans, her protection gone.

Melanos bellowed something she couldn't understand. Swinging around, Sonah saw Bethana running toward her. Sonah's horse bucked and she lost her grip on the reins. The horse's movements made her slip. With a cry, she fell awkwardly from its back.

The ground rushed up to meet her. She grunted as pain lanced up her arm and hip. Hands pulled at her, and she looked up to see Bethana screaming at her, her beautiful face contorted. At last, Sonah shook herself out of her stupor and scrambled to stand.

Sonah screeched when someone tore her away from Bethana, grabbing her braid and yanking hard. She slammed back onto the wet ground.

Fighting for air, Sonah scrabbled on the slick grass when a soldier forced her back down, pinning her with his much larger and heavily armored body. Myriad shouts and cries filled the clearing, but Sonah saw nothing but stars, the pain in her scalp almost unbearable. She struggled to breathe as he crushed her ribs with his thighs.

Turning her head, she looked up into the hate-filled eyes of the soldier, his wet and muddied uniform the white and gold of Heylisia but with the eagle emblem of Ovenno stamped on his breastplate.

That thought registered a second before the man raised his hand, his sword aimed at her heart.

Sonah's eyes widened, and she opened her mouth to scream as the blade came down. The look of confusion on the man's face when it bounced off her gave her a chance to recover. Sonah jammed her knee into his groin and rolled away as he tipped over.

Swallowing against the painful tightening of her throat, Sonah slipped in the mud and bit her tongue, her elbow smacking the ground. As she rose, blood dripped from her mouth and she blinked at the carnage around them. Looking up, she saw Bethana, a vortex of water funneled around the soldiers near her, sweeping them up and cutting off their cries.

Someone shouted her name, and Sonah looked up to see Leander's terrified expression, his face contorted as he fought, motioning at something behind her.

Sonah turned as Duke Ovenno came through a crowd of soldiers fighting Melanos and the Spartans. The duke's face was speckled with blood and dirt, snarling at her as he advanced.

"Finally," Duke Ovenno seethed, his nostrils flaring as he stalked her. Backing away, Sonah looked around for help. Melanos and Leander were locked in their own battles with Bethana, Fane and the Spartans nowhere in sight.

"I've had to trek across this fucking continent to find you. Because of you, I've been humiliated and threatened by Emperor Solon, my daughter held captive in his court, and my wife threatened with beheading! But I will redeem myself when I deliver you to him."

Sonah gaped at the duke, whose face was twisted and blotched with a red so deep she thought he might be possessed by the demons of the underworld.

"I will not go easily," Sonah said, cursing her shaky voice as she backed away.

"Oh, you think this will be easy? You are an ignorant child, always have been. I knew Altos would do something to stop me from bringing you back. He insisted he didn't know you'd gone, but I know it was all part of his plan. So I had my own men searching for you. I've been onto you since Ibros."

Sonah swallowed. "If that were true, you'd plenty of chances to capture me."

"I would've if it weren't for the fucking wolves." Ovenno stopped and held out his arms, his sword catching the sunlight. The smile on his thin lips made Sonah shiver. "They seem to have abandoned you at last."

He sprang forward, taking Sonah by surprise. His hand clamped around her wrist and, with the back of his sword hand, struck her across the face.

Sonah stumbled and would've fallen if not for the duke's hold on her. Stars burst behind her eyes and her cheek flared with heat. Blood pooled in her mouth from where her teeth bit into her cheek and she gagged.

Duke Ovenno dragged her away, shouting orders at his men as they continued to fight off Melanos and the others. Sonah's face throbbed, and tears flowed freely as she trudged behind him, senseless.

When she regained her faculties, Sonah screamed, swinging her free arm, clawing at the duke's hand, her nails sinking in deep. The gouges were long and jagged, and she smiled like a maniac when he roared, letting her go.

Sonah fell with a grunt. Scrambling to her feet, she slipped and crawled along the ground, panting as she tried to scream, hoping the power would be strong enough to level every man there.

It didn't work. Her scream was only a scream and she whimpered as she staggered toward Leander.

Duke Ovenno caught up easily, grabbing her scalp and yanking her back. Sonah cried out when her butt hit the ground, the collision sending razor-sharp pain shooting up her spine. The duke rounded to her front, glaring down at her. Sonah's pulse hammered in her ears so she could not hear whatever he was shouting at her, spittle forming at the corners of his lips. She could do nothing but stare up at him, terrified.

Before she could register the sword in his hand, he raised it and stabbed it toward her belly.

As before with the other soldier, the sword bounced back, and Duke Ovenno grunted in surprise. Sonah snatched her dagger from its sheath and sprang to her feet. The duke tried stepping back, but Sonah screamed and swung her arm, slamming the blade into the base of his neck.

Duke Ovenno's eyes widened, blinking twice as he brought his hand to his neck to clutch at the wound.

Sonah watched in horrified awe as blood poured through the duke's fingers. Her breath swirled in the air as he dropped to his knees, dead at her feet.

"You should eat, Sonah," Bethana said softly, pushing the bowl of stew a few inches closer to Sonah.

They sat inside a tavern after riding away from Duke Ovenno's ambush. They'd lost Triodos in the fight, and Fane had taken turns with Leventis and Yianni leading his horse with his body draped across the animal's back.

Sonah had been numb, staring vacantly at the horizon while leaving her mount to navigate behind the others. Hours later, Melanos had called a halt when they spotted a small village, and they found their way to the tavern for food and rest.

The place was loud, with laughter punching through the conversations around them, making Sonah hunch further into herself. The others remained quiet and she was thankful for it.

"Maybe she just needs some air," Melanos murmured, pulling Bethana's seat closer to his side. Sonah lifted her eyes, watching as the nymph laid her head on the god's shoulder, her eyes trained on Sonah.

"That's a good idea," Sonah mumbled. Pushing her chair out, she made to stand when Leander rose beside her.

"Let her be," Bethana said. Sonah did not look at Leander to see if he'd listen, but she hoped he would.

She wanted to be alone.

After Melanos and the others dispatched the rest of Duke Oven-no's men, Bethana had helped Sonah to her feet, although she recalled little after the nymph dragged her away from the duke's body. Sonah didn't know how long they'd ridden before she'd vomited on her cloak and tunic, her body shaking and her hands unable to hold the reins.

It wasn't until much later at the inn while she was in the bath with Bethana stroking a washcloth across her back that she broke down and cried.

The air outside the tavern felt wonderful after the stifling heat within. Sighing, Sonah went to the railing, placing her hands on the worn wood and tilted her head up. Closing her eyes, she savored the bite of the winter air.

The building had been built at the edge of a cliff with the back of the tavern overlooking the valley below. She imagined the view during the day must be magnificent. The night, however, cloaked everything in black with only the stars and the full moon breaking up the void.

After several deep breaths, she opened her eyes and stared at the star-studded sky, idly picking out constellations, her mind blessedly blank despite the day's events.

The smell of smoke reached her, the aroma of bossena leaves tantalizing, and she turned, scanning her surroundings. Stiffening when she spied the dark figure of someone over her right shoulder, Sonah turned back as if she cared not a wit she was not alone. Whoever it was also decided not to break the silence.

Long moments stretched before Sonah turned back to the shad-owed figure.

"May I have one?" she asked, motioning with her hand.

The figure did not respond.

Frowning, Sonah asked again, this time in Greek, her words stilted. She knew the language—albeit poorly, and only so much as to appease her matron. Lady Maranou loved to wax on about how a lady should know all the languages of the continent, even though

Sonah reminded the woman the lessons were useless for someone who never ventured outside of Metilai.

The stranger remained silent.

"I can pay you," Sonah said, reverting back to the common tongue. Fumbling through her pockets until she found some coins, Sonah held them out to the person hidden in the shadows.

When that failed to get a response as well, she sighed and stuffed the coins back in her pocket as she turned away.

Not very friendly in these parts, she decided as she closed her eyes.

Rustling behind her made Sonah snap her eyes open. She turned to see the figure lean forward before a long, lean arm reached out through the folds of a cloak, slender fingers holding a cheroot. Sonah's eyes widened, and she lifted her gaze from the smoke to the man whose dark gaze was steadily watching her.

A moment passed before Sonah reached out, her fingers brushing his as she took the offering and nodded in thanks.

The man stood and took a step forward. Sonah tensed. A scratch sounded, and the smell of sulfur hit her nostrils as he held out a small flame, the fire highlighting his sharp features. Dropping her gaze, Sonah leaned forward, unsure of how to light the cheroot as she'd never had one before.

"Put it between your lips and breathe in as I light it," his rough voice commanded softly, the sound like the soft scrape of fingernails across her nape.

Sonah shivered, her hand shaking slightly as she lifted the cheroot to her lips. He brought the firelight closer, and she closed her eyes as she breathed the smoke deep into her lungs.

The man stepped back into the shadows. A second later, Sonah coughed, her throat spasming against the harsh smoke, tightening and making her eyes water. She coughed more, heat rising to her cheeks at the man's soft chuckle.

A long time passed before Sonah's breathing returned to normal, and she calmed enough to take a long, steadying breath as she wiped at the tears trailing down her face.

"First time?"

Sonah flicked a glance at him before dropping her gaze to the cheroot.

"Aye."

Silence stretched, filling the space between them and Sonah was about to turn away when he spoke again.

"Are you all right?"

Heat rose once more beneath her skin at the sound of his velvety voice. Nodding, she whispered, "Aye."

Turning back to the railing, Sonah looked out over the valley, hidden beneath night's embrace. The quiet settled around them, the occasional chirp of an adderton bird in the distance the only interruption.

After a while, Sonah sighed and hung her head. In a low voice she said, "I killed someone today."

He did not respond, and she wondered if she'd even spoken her thoughts aloud. Glancing over her shoulder, she caught his regard as he brought his cheroot to his lips and the small ember at the tip dispelled the shadows over his glittering eyes.

"That was also a first for me," she added.

He chuckled, the sound rumbling over her pleasantly.

A long time passed before he shifted, the sound of his movements making her stiffen.

"Did they deserve it?"

Blinking, Sonah considered for a moment before she gave an abrupt nod. Dropping her gaze to her feet as she toed the dirt beneath her boot, she whispered, "Aye."

He said nothing as he stared back at her, the silence stretching as he took another drag on his cheroot. He shifted closer, leaning his large frame against the worn wood of the tavern.

"Doesn't make it easier," he said in that sinful voice.

She lifted her startled gaze to his. From where she stood, with him still mostly in shadows, Sonah could not see the color of the glittering eyes that seemed to look into her soul.

Sonah turned away, lifting her cheroot for another drag, this time a much smaller one. Settling her hands on the cool railing, she looked back up at the stars.

The silence this time was too thick for her to feel comfortable, so she glanced back at him and asked, "Have you taken a life?"

A beat of silence and then he answered. "Aye."

Sonah twisted to look at him, narrowing her gaze. "Many?"

Seconds ticked by before he grunted. "Aye."

Fear and a strange curiosity compelled Sonah to turn fully, her eyes searching through the darkness for what she could see of his features.

"Are you a soldier?"

When the man failed to answer, she dropped her gaze and turned away, self-conscious as if she'd crossed a line.

Unsure of what to do or say, Sonah decided the best course of action was to leave the man to his peace. She lurched forward, intent on returning to the relative safety of the tavern and her companions.

His voice cut through her as she moved past him, his words slicing into her soul.

"Ovenno was always going to die by your hand. It was his fate."

Cold flashed through her, followed by a heat so searing it scorched a path from her chest down to her belly.

Pulse pounding in her eardrums, Sonah froze, her eyes locked on her fingers gripping the door handle as the heat of his gaze burned her.

"What does that mean?"

The man leaned closer and Sonah flinched back, her eyes wide as she caught his gaze. She could have sworn she saw silver race over the irises. He took another long drag of his cheroot, letting the smoke curl out of his mouth in a very suggestive manner, even to someone as inexperienced as Sonah.

"I know all about death."

Nothing about this conversation was normal, Sonah decided, chiding herself for instigating in the first place. She was sorely out of her depth with this man, and she felt like a child for the first time in years, the events of the last year and her still fresh first kill notwithstanding.

"Sonah."

At the sound of her name, Sonah started, her eyes widening as they locked onto the man, still embraced by the shadows.

"When you get to Lethe, stay there until your eudaemon comes for you. Otherwise, I'll have to kill a god, and I'd rather not."

Not only did this stranger know who she was, but he knew about eudaemons. How could he know so much?

Wrangling her fear, Sonah stepped closer to the stranger, intent on getting answers.

Light from the moon made him visible at last, and she swallowed against the harsh beauty of his face. He was viciously handsome, his features rugged as if cut from granite, his eyes not black but a pewter grey sparkling like jewels.

Before she could speak, the man's eyes widened a fraction of a second before they narrowed and his hand snapped out, gripping her chin.

"Até?"

Startled, Sonah pushed him away, his hand falling from her face as a river roared in her head and her heart thrashed.

Dread slid icy fingers down her spine, and she bolted, snatching open the door of the tavern and hustling inside.

As she made her way back to her friends, Sonah cursed herself for being too cowardly to even find out who the man was.

When she finally settled her head upon the thin pillow in her room many hours later, Sonah's last thought before sleep overtook her was she knew without a doubt she'd see the man again.

CHAPTER 29

RAVOS

Cerberus threw a shoe shortly after they passed into Ravos. Terena was in a mood, having spent the last few days attempting to ignore Lerek, who continued trying to speak with her whenever they'd stopped to rest.

Every time Rydon pulled down the prince's gag to eat, he'd call out for her, or Croak. It had gotten to the point she ate away from the others in her tent.

Captain Soros had just updated her on Hermes's progress across Ermanel when Croak came running in, the tent flap flying back as he entered with a dramatic sigh and stricken mien.

"We cannot continue! I must find a farrier!"

Terena exchanged a look with Soros who cocked his head and immediately quit the tent. Alone with her brother, Terena sighed and flopped down onto her bedroll.

"Where in hells do you think we'll find a farrier?"

"Lethe is close," Croak said as he wrung his hands. "Have Soros send someone—"

Terena was about to protest when a thought struck her. Sitting up, she stared at Croak before bouncing to her feet.

"You know what? *You* should go. And take Orry with you!"

Croak's face twisted. "What? Why? No, that's not—"

"Aye!" Terena said, nodding. She put her hands on Croak's shoulders. "In fact, go now. I'll come back for you when we've finished in Colinas."

Croak continued to stare at her as if she'd grown a third eye. "No! I'm coming with you!"

Terena shook her head. "I'd feel better if you and Orry were somewhere safe. It's bad enough we're in Ravos where any moment Solon's soldiers might find us. At least if you're in Lethe Monastery while we're searching for this amulet, I don't have to worry about you both."

"Terena?"

Terena grinned when she heard Rydon call out. Squeezing Croak's shoulders, she moved past him and out of the tent where Rydon stood waiting.

He pulled up when he saw Croak coming out from behind her. "What's going on?"

"Cerberus needs a farrier. So Croak and Orry will go to Lethe and wait for us there while his horse is cared for. I'll have Migela go with them."

She turned back to Croak. "Tell Migela I want her to go with you. Or better yet, have Orry tell her."

Croak made strange noises in protest, but did not contradict her. He stabbed a hand through his hair and left without another word.

Rydon watched as he left before turning back to Terena.

"A scout returned with news of a large host coming this way from Heylisia. The cypher wasn't lying. Soros's men captured one of their scouting party. Said they are heading to Colinas to claim the Royal Taster. That she's wanted for treason and the murder of Prince Isher."

"Fuck!" Terena fumed. "They know about Lerek. But how the fuck did they get their hands on Sonah?"

Soros came bounding toward them, his chest heaving as if he'd run the entire way.

"I've already sent a message to Hermes," Soros said without preamble, folding his armored arms across his chest. "I said we'd wait until he catches up before we march on Colinas."

"How many times do I have to say it? I'm not waiting," Terena said as if he suggested she cut off her arm. "You wait and catch up to us when you can. I'm going after my sister."

"No, Ren," Rydon snapped with a slash of his hand. "We are not splitting up any more of our forces. You cannot go into the city without the captain and his men."

"They must've heard about Hermes's army by now," Terena's voice was plaintive and she swallowed to calm herself. "Surely, they won't risk the battle just to get their hands on Sonah!"

"Maybe that's why they sent such a large force." Soros snapped.

"All the more reason for us to wait," Rydon added.

"And if they take her before we get there, they'll have leverage!"

"What if it's a trap?"

"I don't care!" Terena's patience was wearing thin. "I'm going to get my sister!"

"Send another hawk to Hermes and have him meet us in Colinas," Rydon ordered Soros. "Hopefully, we can stall until they get there."

"Whatever makes you feel better," Terena said, throwing out her arms. "But I am going after my sister."

CROAK CHASED AFTER RYDON. BY THE RIGID SET OF HIS SHOULDERS AND THE way his hands fisted at his sides, Croak knew it wasn't a great time to seek out the mercenary, and yet he rarely paid heed to the voice in his head screaming common sense.

"Rydon—"

"No."

"But—"

"No."

"You didn't even—"

"Croak," Rydon snapped, rounding on Croak fast enough to make him leap back. He thrust his forefinger in the air between them, his face pale around his auburn beard. "Your sister has decided against listening to reason and I am—once again—having to run into certain death with her because she has a problem with logic."

Croak threw up his hands in surrender, his eyes wide. "Listen, I hear you. She's always been like that and it's worse now for some reason. I blame Daris. And Lerek, I guess. For starting it all. But you won't die, old man. You're Eudaemon. And since you're Sonah's guardian, you'll have nothing to worry about for at least four years. You're a mercenary and immortal. Be *me* for a second! She's sending me to a monastery! Me!"

"Aye," Rydon grunted as he turned to stride away. "For your safety. Would that she thought of her own as much as she does yours."

"Well then, convince her to remain behind! If we all stay at Lethe, we can wait for Hermes to show up. Hopefully, Sonah, too."

"Sonah's in there!" Rydon cried, whipping around as he shot an arm out behind him. Croak stumbled back against the man's ire. Gods, Rydon was scary just being... Rydon. Now, he looked like his head might explode. A vein ticked furiously at his temple, and the way his nostrils flared, Croak expected smoke to curl out any moment.

Blinking up at the enraged mercenary, Croak could only gawp. "What? What do you mean, she's in there? In where?"

"She's in Colinas, you fool," Rydon growled before turning away. "Where've you been that you do not know she's the reason we're here?" His strides were long enough Croak jogged to keep up. Soldiers cleared a path as he neared.

"How? When did she pass us? I don't get it."

Rydon stopped and stabbed a hand through his hair, dislodging more strands from the bun at his nape. Croak didn't consider him a handsome man, but the way he looked now reminded Croak of the feral agrius, the half-bear half-men who fought for the Titans in the Immortals War.

It was not a good look.

"I think Xoran played us."

"No surprise there," Croak said, shaking his head sagely. "I told you he was a snake."

"Aye, but your sister seems to think we can trust him."

"Once again proving her faith in humanity is a deep flaw. How do we rid her of it?"

Rydon snapped around, his eyes bulging and Croak's hand flew up to guard against his wrath.

"Find Migela and tell her she is to accompany you and the cleric to Lethe. We will come for you when we've got Sonah. Do you understand?"

"Why does Cassandra get to stay with you? If she stays, I—"

Rydon rounded on him. "Say you understand."

Croak's chest puffed out. He opened his mouth to argue but when Rydon's eyes blazed brighter Croak thought better of it and instead inclined his head.

"I understand."

"Good. Now get the fuck out of here."

CHAPTER 30

RAVOS

After the strange conversation with the even stranger man outside the tavern, Sonah told the others of Lethe Monastery and her connection to the monks there, persuading them it was a better option than chasing blindly after the Liodari.

"They are waiting for us," Fane had argued. "We'll most likely run into them before we reach the monastery."

"All the better, then," Sonah had said with a shrug. "But we ride for Lethe."

Leander, for the second time in their travels, sided with Fane. "You're basing this all on the word of a complete stranger? It could be a trap."

"He knew things," Sonah had replied. "And we'll be safe at Lethe. I know the abbot and monks there. They'd never do anything to harm me."

"Except give you away to a nobleman to use in his games with the emperor!"

"He did that out of love! He thought he was giving me a chance at a good life! How could he know the man was so vile?" Sonah had yelled. She'd looking around at the others as they'd watched her in silence.

"We go to Lethe. And if Jason—if the Liodari find us on our way, they are welcome to journey with us."

"The commander is your eudaemon," Melanos had said, leaning across the table. "You'll be safe with him. We cannot have something like what happened with the duke happen again."

"The commander is not my eudamon," Sonah had replied. She'd then told them of her conversation with the oracle. Melanos had exclaimed, thumping the table hard enough to make their tankards topple. He'd gone on to say how he'd had a feeling Daris was Ren's eudaemon when he'd first met him, but had not pressed the matter because of Ren's condition at the time.

"I'll be safe with the monks until Rydon can come for me," Sonah had added. "And since he's with Ren, she'll come for me, too."

"Are you certain of this, little—Sonah," Melanos had asked, his gaze tender.

Sonah had only nodded, keeping her eyes shielded from Leander. He'd seemed angry with her, his jaw clenched and eyes narrowed the few times he'd deigned to look at her. For the life of her, Sonah could not figure out why the man was upset. She thought she'd acquitted herself admirably during their skirmish, considering her lack of fighting skills.

Sonah had gone to bed shortly after, no longer interested in arguing over their destination. In the morning, they set out in silence.

Now, Sonah's gaze shifted to her surroundings as they walked their horses, giving them a rest from the constant galloping, for which she was grateful. They'd barely crossed the border into Ravos and still no sign of Jason or the Liodari. Fane and the Spartans had ridden off earlier in the day to search for them, promising to meet them in Lethe whether or not they were successful.

"Lethe is another hour this way," Sonah said, gesturing with her right hand.

"South?"

"All right."

"No, I'm asking. Lethe is another hour south?" Leander asked, his voice rough. Sonah glanced over at him. His expression was stony, his eyes looking past her.

Frowning, she shrugged. "If south is that way, then aye, we go south."

"You don't know which way south is?" Leander sneered.

"Careful," Melanos muttered, his eyes flashing.

"No, I don't know which way south is, Leander," Sonah sighed. She refused to be baited by the Riverman just because he was in a foul mood. "But I know where Obsidian Bay is because I know this area. And because I know this area *and* I know where Obsidian Bay is—to my right—I know the monastery is also," she paused, raising a brow at him, goading him. "Where? Ah, yes. To my *right*."

Pulling the reins so her horse would move in the direction she meant for them to follow, she hid her blooming smile when she heard Bethana's tinkling laughter at her back.

"Forgive me for being concerned for your wellbeing," Leander snapped, crowding her with his horse so she was forced to look over at him. His expression was thunderous but there was also fear there which made her snap her mouth shut against the shrill retort she almost unleashed.

"You need not worry so much," she said instead, proud of how calm she sounded. "Need I remind you I've now survived two kidnappings and two attempted murders? Also, I'm a god, so..."

"But you are not immortal!" Leander spat. "I couldn't get to you fast enough to prevent those men from almost killing you! You should be dead—"

"Aye!" Sonah shouted, pulling her mare to stop. She glared at Leander, who gave as good as he got. Jabbing a finger at him, Sonah said, "I should be! But I'm not! Maybe the Fates intervened on my behalf, I don't know, but whatever happened to stay those murderous fiends, I am not dead!"

"The goddess is right," Bethana said as Melanos drew close. "The Fates did intervene."

"What?" Leander and Sonah said at the same time.

"I know she's vulnerable without her eudaemon," the nymph said, her beautiful smile mesmerizing. "So I made her an oil imbued with protection spells to make her invulnerable. This way, whenever she bathes with it, no one can harm her."

Melanos's deep chuckle broke Sonah from her stupor.

"What?"

"When?"

Bethana reached out, her cool fingertips glancing off Sonah's cheek. "You saved me, goddess. A nymph every other god ignored when Poseidon cast his curse on me. Not one of them came to our aide. Except you. And your sister. Melanos was right. We owe you a debt. In this small way, I serve."

The sting of tears made Sonah blink rapidly and duck her head. *Don't cry, don't cry. You're strong. Don't cry.*

Her emotions under control again, Sonah lifted her head and smiled at Bethana.

Big mistake.

Sonah sobbed at the look on the woman's face, the compassion wrenching the tears from her eyes.

"You're not just a nymph to me." Wiping the snot traveling quickly to her lips she said with a shudder, "You're the best friend a girl could ever ask for."

LETHE MONASTERY, RAVOS

"Riders at the gate, Abbot Malis!"

Croak sprang up from the couch in the abbot's office. They'd arrived the day before and Orry had immediately sought out the abbot so he could scribble his nonsense and read his boring books.

Startled upon hearing the monk's shout, Orry cried out and tossed the book he'd been reading into the air. He scrambled after it as Croak rushed toward the door. Croak knocked into him, and Orry fell onto his ass.

"We don't have time for you to play!" Croak yelled at his friend, grabbing his sword belt from where it hung on a peg beside the door.

Abbot Malis wrung his hands as he ran after Croak, his mincing steps hindered by his robes.

Migela came flying around the corner and collided with Croak.

"Fuck!" he squeaked, shaking away the stars from his eyes. His nose throbbed, and he glared at the assassin, who was rubbing her forehead. "Watch where you're going!"

Croak rubbed at his aching nose and brushed past Migela, tearing a path through the courtyard and up to the wall walk. Peering over the wall, he blinked at the sight before him. He let out a shout, waving his arms and laughing.

"Sonah!"

His new sister looked up at the sound of his voice, a smile stretching across her face. She stood in her stirrups, almost falling off her mount as she waved back frantically.

Croak moved back and ran down the steps to the courtyard, passing a flustered Orry who pivoted to follow. A small procession followed on their heels as Croak yanked open the door and ran to the gates, startling the monks peering out through the hatch at the riders.

The door barely widened enough for him to slip through before Croak was racing out, his arms spread wide as he tore down the wooden bridge to where Sonah was dismounting.

She was barely on the ground before Croak swooped her up in his arms, spinning her once in a crushing embrace before setting her back down. The girl laughed, her voice cracking as she shook. Croak blinked, his smile fading as he pulled back to see tears tracking down her face. He frowned at the fading bruises near her mouth.

"Hey, hey," Croak crooned, crooking his finger to lift her chin. Her beautiful green and brown eyes swam with tears, and she swallowed as another sob racked her body. She tucked her head into his neck, snot and tears soaking the collars of his tunic and jacket.

He tightened his hold on her, closing his eyes against the rush of feelings overwhelming him.

They stood like that for several moments before the sound of labored breathing behind him made Croak stiffen. Turning to glance over his shoulder, his lips quirked up on one side when he caught Orry's beaming face, the apples of his cheeks stained red as he panted from exertion.

Sonah pulled away to see the newcomer and another sob tore through her as Orry bounded forward, wrapping his thick arms around both of them.

Croak lasted five seconds before he had to pull away from the stench of Orry's armpits.

"Enough of that," Croak grumbled, wiping at a tear. He sniffled. "You stink something awful, Orry. I daresay even the monks have provisions for a bath. You should definitely avail yourself of one."

Sonah giggled, darting forward to give Croak a quick hug before she planted a wet kiss to Orry's plump cheek. If possible, the cleric reddened further and Croak cackled.

"Oh, I'm so glad to see you," Sonah said, her voice still shaking. She swallowed and motioned behind her at the rest of her party. "I know you'll remember Melanos. And this—"

"Melanos!" Croak shrieked, already launching himself at the giant god. When he pulled away, the god grinned down at him, slapping a large hand across Croak's chest, sending him stumbling a few steps back into Orry and Sonah.

"Gods, it's good to see you too, Melanos. And grateful Sonah wasn't traveling without protection."

"From what we've seen," Melanos said with a wink at Sonah over Croak's shoulder, "the little one—I mean, Sonah—can protect herself."

Croak laughed uncertainly, seeing the look passing between him and Sonah. Before he could ask what the god meant, his gaze was caught by the stunning woman dismounting behind him. Croak's mouth dropped open, and he stared at the vision slowly walking toward him.

Straightening his spine, he plastered a look of haughty indifference on his face and crossed his arms. The woman stopped beside Melanos and wrapped her long, beautiful fingers in the crook of Melanos's elbow.

"And who might this be?" Croak asked in a voice one octave lower than his normal tone. He heard Orry snicker behind him. Sonah came to his side, her smile radiant.

"This is Bethana," Melanos said, looking down at the gorgeous blonde with a smile that would melt all of the north. The woman beamed up at him, a glow about her making her appear ethereal.

Croak gaped at them. "Beth—*the* Bethana?" Shaking his head, he speared a hand through his hair. "Gods you look... you look... very different from what Ren described."

The woman smiled at him indulgently. "I hope so."

Croak stared at her long enough for it to become awkward. Even Melanos shoving him lightly on the shoulder didn't shake him out of his ensnared gaze until Orry dropped his arm across Croak's shoulders.

"Bethana," Orry began, his voice taking on an ingratiating, reverent tone he used whenever he was about to kiss someone's ass. "The naiad who fell in love with a god and was punished by Poseidon to life as a serpent."

The awe in his voice made Croak worry his friend would drop to his knees at any moment to kiss the poor nymph's feet.

"I've read your story countless times in the old texts we have—well, they are at the White Palace with High Cleric Christos but—my lady, you are a legend, as are you, Lord Melanos, and it is an honor to meet you both."

Croak rolled his eyes. "This is Ormano Peredor, our friend. If you ever want to be bored to tears or you just cannot sleep, call on Orry to regale you with tales from his studies as a cleric. That'll do the trick."

Sonah laughed and squeezed his waist, looking around him as she grinned at Orry's flushed face.

"And who are you?"

Croak eyeballed the man standing beside Sonah's horse, taking in the stranger's mud-splattered cloak and dirty clothes. His brown hair was unkempt, and his emerald eyes narrowed against Croak's scrutiny. He stood with his legs spread apart, his arrogance radiating off him like Orry's stench: constant and powerful. His lip curled as the man shifted his gaze to Sonah.

"Leander."

Croak lifted an eyebrow and looked from the man to Sonah. She ducked her head. He looked to Melanos. The god shrugged.

"That's a story you should hear from your sister," Melanos grumbled.

Melanos led Bethana past them, heading across the bridge to enter the monastery. Orry, too, followed in their wake but Croak continued to assess the stranger.

Even beneath the layers of clothes, Croak could tell the man was powerfully built. He had a stubbled beard and the look of anyone who'd ridden hard without resting, much like Sonah and Melanos. Bethana seemed to be the only one unaffected by the road. Croak doubted the woman could ever look less than beautiful.

Well. Except when she was a serpent.

"Stare any longer," the man growled, his voice dropping low as he ambled toward Croak and Sonah, "and I'll rip out your eyeballs and feed them to you."

Croak blinked, affronted, and glanced at Sonah when he felt her stiffen. Looking back at the stranger, he scowled. "Go fuck yourself."

Without waiting for a response, Croak turned Sonah and walked back inside the monastery.

CHAPTER 31

COLINAS, RAVOS

Terena climbed to the top of the hill overlooking the city of Colinas in the valley below.

Crouching, she narrowed her eyes against the sunrise. She heard the soft crunch of snow behind her seconds before Rydon bent down at her side. Gabriol came up on her other side.

The gates to the city were closed, with more soldiers than usual posted on the city walls.

"Nothing but Heylisian uniforms in sight," Rydon mumbled, running his hand down his beard.

"We need to scout the perimeter, see if there's a way inside," Gabriol said.

Rydon grunted. "Let's go take a look."

"Gabe," Terena said as she laid a hand on the mercenary's forearm. He turned to her with a frown. She motioned behind them as she stared back into Gabriol's blue eyes.

Gabriol glanced over at Rydon before nodding. He pushed back onto his feet and strode away. Terena looked back over the city.

"What are you planning?"

Terena did not respond right away as she took in the soldiers above the closed city gates.

"Ren."

Sighing, Terena motioned with her head. "Do you think it strange Cassandra swears this is where she saw the amulet last, and now we find out Duke Ravos has Sonah?"

"Don't forget the army coming our way from Heylisia."

"Hard to do," she laughed, flashing him a grin. "Normally, I'd let you and Gabriol sneak inside. Find a way to get to Sonah while I sit out here and antagonize the shit out of these soldiers."

Rydon snorted. "Normally? Really?"

Sighing, Terena got to her feet and turned to face Rydon, clapping her hands on his shoulders, her fingers digging into the fur pelt over his cloak. "Do me a favor. Have Soros put five of his best men around Cassandra. I want her well away from any of the fighting before I go down there."

Rydon nodded. "All right." He rose but stopped when Ren spoke again.

"I think I'll flex some of my powers this time. Show them we're not fucking around."

Rydon groaned. "Can I convince you otherwise? Gabe and I can sneak inside and grab Sonah before the duke knows she's missing. We'll get the amulet too. I swear."

"Oh, I'm not worried about the amulet just now. I'm here for Sonah. Besides, I have something better in mind," Terena said with a smile.

She turned as Lerek, hands bound and a gag in his mouth, stopped several feet away with Gabriol's large hand wrapped around his arm.

"Bring him."

Terena stared up at the plain stone walls surrounding the city. The gates were closed, and the path leading up to it empty.

Helmed soldiers armed with spears, shields, arrows and spikes stared down at them. No one moved in the eerie dawn, and for a moment, Terena imagined they were just another fortification. Statues created to terrify rather than real men.

It mattered not.

Today, Terena was the one that would terrify.

"Lord Galen," Terena called up, her eyes scanning the line of soldiers for the duke. "Step forward."

Rydon's mount nickered at her side. Nyx stamped a hoof. On her left, Lerek grumbled something she couldn't hear.

Terena waited, but the duke didn't present himself.

"What now?" Rydon muttered.

Ignoring him, Terena shifted in her saddle and sighed. "Lord Galen! Do not make me wait. Come now."

Still, no movement from the city walls.

Terena frowned, then leaned forward to look past Rydon to where Captain Soros sat astride his warhorse. Terena gave the man a tight nod, and the captain leered in response.

Holding out his hand, one of his men strode forward with a spear. Handing it up to the captain, Soros hefted it for a moment before cocking his arm back and thrusting it up and forward.

Terena watched with a slight sneer as the spear slammed into the throat of a soldier. A roar sounded behind her as the man fell from the wall walk and, for the first time that morning, the soldiers atop the walls moved.

Terena flashed Soros a grin and he sketched a bow.

Hermes's captain was not a god like them, but he was not mortal, either. Whenever she'd asked Hermes about him and the cadre of criminals he surrounded himself with, the god became dismissive. She admitted she didn't care enough to pry further; just grateful he was on their side.

More movement drew her attention back to the city walls as soldiers separated to let a heavily armored man through.

"You bitch!" The man screamed down at her. "How dare—"

"Is that you, Galen?"

The man paused, then shouted back, "No, I am not. I—"

Terena again looked at Soros, who had another spear in his hand. She'd turned back to the large man who'd screamed down at her when the spear caught him in the side of his throat, along with two others who were regrettably standing nearby.

"I can do this all day, Galen," Terena yelled up. "Show yourself. Better yet, bring me Sonah Yahn. That's all I want. I will leave without further bloodshed if you bring her out."

Movement along the wall to her left caught Terena's eye. A tall man of slender build came forward, one gauntleted hand on the wall ledge. Terena narrowed her eyes, waiting. After a moment, the man took off his helm, his thinning wheat-colored hair standing on end as he scowled down at her.

"I will not open the gates for you, you traitorous bitch," the man screamed out. "You are here without provocation or invitation. If you do not leave now—"

"I have Crown Prince Lerek," Terena called out, her frustration at how long this had dragged on showing in the shrill tone of her voice. She closed her eyes for a second, then looked back up at the new duke. "So it's an even trade. Sonah Yahn for the prince."

"Crown Prince Lerek is dead!"

"And yet here he sits. Now where is my sister?"

"Who is your sister?"

"If you do not know by now that Sonah Yahn is my sister, then you are stupider than you look. Bring me Sonah Yahn. Now!"

"I am a duke, you insolent baggage! I am now Duke Ravos! And I will not—"

"Luca," Soros barked out. "Shall I?"

"No," Terena grumbled, shaking her head. "No. Unfortunately, I need him still. At least until he BRINGS ME MY FUCKING SISTER!" This last was screamed up at the new Duke Ravos as Terena shot up in her stirrups.

The ground trembled beneath them.

Laughter sounded behind her from Hermes's men as she sat back down. Terena caught Gabriol's smug smile.

"Listen to what I'm trying to fucking tell you!" the duke roared at her. "I do not have Sonah Yahn! I don't give a fuck about Sonah; never even gave her a moment's thought except to laugh at how pathetic she was. Especially not since the day she was hauled away to be executed!"

"I know you have her, Galen. Send her down and I won't kill you. Promise."

There was a shuffling of bodies as the duke moved back. Rydon shifted, moving his mount closer to Terena.

"I don't like this."

"They won't try anything," Terena said, her eyes trained on the battlements. "Not with Lerek at my side."

Galen, Duke Ravos, stepped back into view. Leaning his arms on the stone wall, he quipped, "Sit tight, Luca. She'll be along shortly."

He moved back, his grating laughter drifting down to them as he moved behind the cover of his men. When he again pushed to the front, he crossed his arms, smiling wolfishly at them.

"You're not actually buying this shit," Soros hissed, surprising Terena when he stopped at her side.

"You heard the scout," Gabriol said. "She's here."

"And yet, any sane man with a god at his doorstep would've brought her out by now." Soros replied with a sneer.

"Lord Galen—!"

"I'm the duke now, you brat! You will address me properly or I will finish what the emperor clearly failed to do!"

"Oh my gods, this man!" Rydon sighed.

Terena grinned at him. Turning back to the apoplectic duke, Terena cupped her hands around her mouth and yelled, "I don't fucking care what you call yourself these days, you overblown shit! You have five minutes to bring my sister to me."

Terena didn't wait for the man's response. She turned Nyx and looked over at Captain Soros. "Pull your men back to that ridge there," she said and nodded over the man's shoulder. "I don't want our men in range of their archers if this buffoon is stupider than he's already shown himself to be."

"What are you planning?" Rydon asked.

Terena leaned toward Lerek and yanked his gag down. She turned to Gabriol. "Take Lerek. I want you all next to Soros when Ravos's men come out."

"What?" Lerek scoffed, complaining, while Rydon and Gabriol voiced their concerns.

"Terena—"

"No! You can't—"

"Listen!" Terena hissed. They all shut their mouths. "I want him to get cocky. I want him to make a mistake and he'll do so if you are all well away from me. I'm going to make his men come out and attack me."

"You're going to do what?" Gabriol scoffed.

"Ren, if you do that, at least let me—"

"No," she said, shaking her head at Rydon. "I have a bad feeling Xoran fucked us. I think he told Solon everything and this is a trap. I don't think Sonah's here. Duke Ravos would've flaunted her in front of me by now if she was."

"Then let's just fucking leave," Rydon said.

"Let me speak to him," Lerek pleaded, moving his mount closer. Rydon growled, intercepting him with his larger stallion. He frowned at the mercenary before turning to Terena. "Please, Ren. He is a friend. He'll listen to me."

"Please, do as I asked. Stay close to Cassandra. And don't move from that ridge. I don't care how bad it looks. Do not. Agreed?"

"At least let me stay with you," Rydon growled, edging his horse closer.

"No," Terena said, her tone harsh.

Rydon stared at her a few seconds more before following after Soros, Gabriol and Lerek.

When she was alone, Terena looked up at the battlements. The duke was nowhere in sight.

Holding out her left hand, Terena curled her fingers and called up to the men above in a voice not her own, fueled by the power raging in her blood. "Open the gates for me. I am alone. Come for me. Now."

Terena had only ever used this power once while training with Hermes back in Olympia. It had come out of nowhere, surprising her and making Hermes laugh and clap with glee. The power of compulsion was from her mother, he'd said. Once it manifested, he'd had her practice with it until it came to her easily, without her needing to even think about it.

As her powers ignited, the light beneath her skin no longer shown white. A dark red light glowed, racing through her veins as the compulsion worked its way through the men standing above her. Her vision turned red.

The grating of the portcullis sounded as it raised and Terena tensed. She dismounted slowly, slapping Nyx's rump. The horse trotted off after Rydon and the others.

Terena shivered beneath her cloak, the soft wolf fur tickling her cheeks as anticipation fired in her veins. Her fingers flexed.

The gates yawned open and men with swords waited impatiently to rush her. Terena widened her stance and shook out her hands.

A moment later, the soldiers roared as they ran toward her.

She heard Rydon bellow at her and Lerek shout something that was swallowed up by the men stampeding her way.

Time stopped.

Red flashed behind her eyes. Fiery red light pulsed beneath her skin along her veins. Heat slid down her fingers as she fanned them out.

Terena took a breath.

She expected the Twins, her short swords, to appear. But when time resumed in a sudden snap, Terena's fingers flicked forward.

A pulse rushed out, the ground beneath her quaking. Dirt and snow flew as an invisible force rumbled forth, the ground tearing in a massive wave, crashing into the soldiers.

After the deafening roar of the shockwave, the dust cloud dissipated in a quiet patter like raindrops falling. Nothing remained of the soldiers.

Nothing but ash.

The sudden silence following the quake was so absolute, Terena swore she could hear the flap of the pennant atop the tallest spire of Sydney Hall off in the distance.

She felt peaceful, her breath expelling evenly. Even her mind was quiet for once.

A choked cry from above her on the wall made Terena snap her eyes up. Duke Ravos's face was so stricken his chin wobbled. His jaw slackened as he stared in pure terror down at her.

"Abomination," he said, his voice cracking on the word. Even as low as it was spoken, it carried on the wind to her, settling into her bones.

Long seconds passed before Terena smiled.

"No, Galen. I am retribution."

Rydon had lived thirty years in this world. Because of his profession, much of that was violent, especially with the power shifts and greed of royals.

And he'd seen things he had thought lost to this world for a millennia.

But he had never seen anything like this.

"What the fuck just happened?" Lerek breathed.

"She's becoming who she was always meant to be," Cassandra said.

Lerek snorted. "A monster?"

Rydon opened his mouth to curse the fool but Cassandra spoke first.

"That's what you see?"

Lerek looked at her in disgust. "Was this necessary?" He waved at Ren as she walked slowly toward them, her head bent so Rydon could not see her face. "The Terena I knew would never have done this!"

"The Terena you knew had to hide who she was in order to fit into your world," Cassandra rebuked gently. "Your father's done worse and yet you do not call him monster."

"My father's never—"

"Your father locked her up in your dungeons. Your father wanted to kill her because of who she is." Rydon snapped. "Do not compare her to your father ever again."

Lerek glared, but did not reply. Rydon tensed when he felt Cassandra lean her head on his back. She squeezed her arms and he exhaled, closing his eyes.

Someone began clapping. Rydon opened his eyes to see Soros, a wide grin on his face, clapping as Terena drew close. It was picked up by a few others, and Terena smiled.

Mounting Nyx, she looked at Rydon and Cassandra, then Gabriol. She frowned uncertainly at Lerek's expression.

"What?"

"Are you fucking kidding?" Gabriol said, spreading his arms.

"I told you I had a plan."

"Aye!" Rydon snarked. "I thought maiming. Perhaps a few deaths. Maybe. A tiny bit of what we saw in Olympia before we left?" He shrugged. "I get it. You need the practice. But this?" Rydon ran both hands through his hair as he looked over Terena's shoulder at the decimation she'd made of Ravos's soldiers. "No, Ren. I did not think *this* was the plan."

"And when the fuck did you learn to do that? *How* did you do that?" Gabriol asked.

"I didn't know I could, honestly," Terena said, and for the first time, Rydon glimpsed the woman he'd met on the day of her execution. Uncertain. Vulnerable. Scared. "My plan was to use the Twins like I did before we left Olympia."

Terena turned Nyx and rode away from the city walls. After a long moment, Rydon and the others fell in beside her. Captain Soros whistled, and soon his men were riding away, likely back to their camp.

"Did anything different happen that made you change your mind?" Rydon asked, mostly curious. He was also cataloging the changes to her abilities as she neared her nameday. Hermes had warned them unique powers would manifest the closer she came to her majority and powers all gods had would grow stronger and more consistent.

"There was no thought, Rydon," Terena said, her voice almost sad, and he thanked Gaia for it. Lately, her demeanor was colder, her patience shorter. He feared what she was becoming and yet he knew her ascension was inevitable.

"It was... the same as walking. The same as breathing," Ren said, lifting her face to his.

Rydon frowned as he watched her. Her expression was strange. She seemed troubled.

But excited, too.

A cold mask slipped over her face and she shrugged. "It was them or us."

CHAPTER 32

RAVOS

"Commander."

Daris looked up to see Aslan, one of the assassins Hermes liked to keep close to him, his dark face half hidden beneath the black mask covering the lower half of his face. His dark brown eyes were barely visible beneath his thick black brows. A large group of soldiers followed in his wake. He wheeled his mount around until he walked his horse at Daris's side.

"Scouts came back with word of the Heylisian army heading toward Colinas. And another report from the city, lord. Lady Luca is there with Captain Soros and they are outnumbered. Lord Hermes wants you to take a hundred men and ride out quickly to their aid, as our vanguard."

Daris nodded and Aslan pulled away, galloping back to his place at Hermes's side.

"It seems the emperor is also set on finding Terena," Daris called out, a hard edge to his voice as he looked over his men. "We ride to defend her. Hermes and his men will follow, but we are the only thing stopping our friends from slaughter."

Daris unsheathed his sword, stabbing it into the air as he cried out. "Honor in life! Glory in death!"

The others roared. Daris leaned over his stallion and took off.

LETHE MONASTERY, RAVOS

Croak stumbled out of bed, his head throbbing. The world swam as he held his arms out to steady himself. The pounding in his head was fucking unbearable.

"Croak!"

Sluggishly, Croak turned to the door, his lips drawn down. "Hello?"

The door banged. Croak groaned, the sound splitting his head open.

"Stop that," he mumbled as he took a slow step toward the door. If he didn't get there fast enough, he worried Orry might make that ungodsly racket again, and this time Croak wasn't certain he'd hold in whatever was still left in his belly.

Unfortunately, Orry slammed his hand into the door three more times. By the time Croak reached it and pulled it open to glare at his friend, he'd soiled the front of his already filthy tunic.

"How the fuck are you still asleep?" Orry squeaked in an annoyingly high voice. Gods, could he not see the pain he was inflicting?

"Are not all sane people asleep at this hour?"

"No, Croak," Orry snorted. "Everyone's awake and about to sit for the noon meal. And guess what? Hermes has arrived."

Croak's heart skipped a beat and he swallowed against the bile rising in his throat. "What? Hermes? Here?"

"Aye, so get your ass ready, and—no, never mind that. You need a bath and a shave because you are disgusting. But best you make yourself as presentable as you can and try to stay out of Hermes's line of... smell."

Croak bared his teeth at Orry, who stepped back with a hand over his nose.

When Croak finally emerged, he was wearing a clean—well, cleaner—tunic and had done a poor but acceptable job of brushing his hair. The shave would need to wait, but splashing cold water on his face had helped to revive him enough to finish his ablutions as quickly as possible. Hermes was an asshole, but he was still a god. Croak didn't want to think what he'd do to him if Croak took much longer.

"Ah, if it isn't the useless appendage Terena calls 'brother'," Hermes's voice boomed when Croak arrived in the refectory.

The tables were set out in rows, with one of them moved to the front of the room facing out. Hermes, of course, sat in the middle, surrounded by his sycophants, the bloodthirsty criminals all leering at Croak. The chatter grated on his frayed nerves and the sudden outbursts of laughter made him wince.

"I would've arrived sooner but," Croak shrugged. "I don't give a fuck."

The monks seated at the tables on either side of him gasped as Croak passed them on his way to Hermes's table.

He spread his arms and shrugged at the god. Croak was paying for last night's overindulgence, but he'd be damned if he'd let Hermes belittle him in front of everyone. The god could strike him dead, but Croak still had his pride.

Reaching the front of the room, Croak looked around for Sonah. As he searched, his eye landed on Melanos, whose face resembled dark clouds before a storm. Bethana sat next to him at the table to the left of the abbot.

Croak wondered why they weren't seated with Hermes.

"Croak."

Spinning around, Croak's eyes widened, and he smiled at Sonah, who stopped at his side with a radiant smile.

"Isn't it fantastic?" Sonah added breathlessly. "Hermes is going to Ravos and he wants us to join him. He's taking me to Terena! I'm so excited, I cannot wait to see her!"

Croak arched an eyebrow as he took a seat beside Sonah. Across from him, Migela gave a shake of her head and scowled at him.

"How did you even know we were here?" Croak asked as he reached for the bread.

Hermes smiled at Croak as one does at a dumb child. "Not that I owe you an explanation, boy, but I'm feeling generous today."

Croak snorted.

"I felt the presence of a god," Hermes continued, ignoring Croak's facial expressions as he looked over at Sonah. "Imagine my surprise when I found not one, but two gods."

"Your powers never cease to amaze," Croak mumbled, eyeing the serving dishes with barely concealed nausea.

"We leave within the hour."

Croak turned to Sonah with a quizzical look. "I thought you said we had to stay here. To wait for Rydon, here."

Sonah glanced at Hermes over Melanos's shoulder. Leaning in to speak quietly to Croak, she said, "Aye, but do you not think this is better? Why should we separate yet again if he can take us to him and Terena?"

"The stranger said you should wait here for your eudaemon," Melanos said, his low voice husky. Sonah dropped her gaze.

"Right. And don't forget the reason Ren sent us here in the first place. To keep us safe. I'm certain she wouldn't want you there," Croak added before pinching his lips.

He recalled Sonah telling him of the strange man she'd met after she'd killed Duke Ovenno. Once he'd gotten over the shock of that little detail, Croak had listened while she'd recounted her conversation with the man who'd known who she was and whom she'd killed. And the warning he'd had for her about remaining at Lethe.

Leander chose that moment to loom over them. Croak glanced up and frowned. "What?"

Leander glared down at him. "You're in my seat," he growled.

Croak's brows hit his hairline. He scoffed. Winking at Sonah, he slid down the bench, making room for Leander. Croak leaned back to speak around him. "Oh, I cannot wait to see Jason again."

Sonah's cheeks colored prettily as she dug into her food.

"If he's going off to fight," Melanos said when Leander had settled, "we should remain here, Sonah. There's a reason you met that man that night. There's a reason for his warning. The Fates must've sent him."

Sonah grumbled something around a mouthful of food.

"You should all stay here," Croak said. "I'll take Orry and go with them. She'll believe me over Hermes that you're actually here. If he goes alone, Terena might go gallivanting off somewhere else."

"Aye," Melanos said with a nod. "That's a better idea."

"What's a better idea?" Orry asked as he happily crunched on a carrot. "I couldn't hear."

"You and I are going into battle," Croak said as he lifted a goblet to his lips. Taking a sip, he groaned and set the goblet down with a shudder.

"What?"

"It's water," he grumbled.

"Aye," Sonah said. "You do *not* need any more ale."

"Hey," Orry said, rapping his knuckles on the table, catching everyone's attention. "What were you saying?"

Croak sighed. "You and I are going with Hermes to Colinas."

"What? Why?"

"So we can tell Ren Sonah's here."

"But Hermes will do that, I'm sure."

"She won't believe him."

"What are we going to do there?" Orry whined. "You know I am of no use in a fight."

"Don't worry," Croak said as he forked some eggs. "There won't be any fighting."

Melanos and Leander chuckled as Orry gaped at him.

"Are you insane? Why do you think he's heading there?"

Croak looked from Melanos to Orry, nonplussed. "Uh, what part of 'Terena's there' is confusing?"

Orry snorted. "The part where we are riding right into a battle between your sister and Heylisia!" Orry leaned closer and hissed, "Commander Antonius and his men are on their way to help but Terena is facing an army from Metilai! It sounds like they've set a trap for her! You and I should stay away. Far away. Here, in fact. We should stay here."

Croak looked from Orry to Melanos. He even looked at Leander, who arched an eyebrow at him as if Croak was about as smart as a newborn kitten.

"How do you know this? Where have I been? Have I been asleep longer than I realized?"

Melanos laughed. "Hermes arrived about an hour before you woke. He gave us a shortened account of what he and the others have been up to. The cleric speaks true. You'll be riding into battle. As you said."

"I was joking."

"Joke or not," Orry scoffed, "we should not be going anywhere near Ravos. What's wrong with staying put? Hermes is already upset I'm even here! He told Ren I was to stay in Olympia. Besides, I have scrolls that need translating. I promised to figure out the secret of the shroud. Not to mention helping Ren find that amulet."

"She's got Cassandra for that, you idiot," Croak snapped. He put his hands to his head and groaned. Today was not the day to be hungover.

"Croak!"

At Hermes's bellow, Croak winced, letting out a pained whine. He closed his eyes and lips, willing the nausea to settle.

"Aye, my Overlord?"

"We're leaving."

"You said an hour," Croak whined.

"And you need to help the men prepare."

For the love of all that's... gods!

"Lord," Croak said and swallowed. "Aye. Fine. But it's only me and Orry coming with you."

Croak kicked Orry under the table when his friend opened his mouth to protest.

Hermes came to stand behind Melanos. As if the god felt him, Melanos straightened in his seat, and, if possible, seemed to grow three feet taller.

"You do not wish to join us, God of Heroes?"

Croak felt Leander stiffen at his side. Melanos's face turned dark and Bethana dropped her chin.

"What's going on?"

Orry gasped, and when Croak looked over at him, his friend had his hand cupped over his mouth, his eyes wide like a child witnessing his first solstice parade.

"Of course," Orry breathed, his gaze turning reverent as he stared at Melanos.

"I will stay here and ensure Sonah Yahn's safety," Melanos gritted out. His hand was clenched on the table and Bethana put her much smaller one over his white knuckles.

"Of course," Hermes muttered. He bent closer as if to speak privately in the god's ear, he instead added in a loud voice that carried through the room, "I remember how you fled the battle in Thuria. I wonder if you've told your nymph you're the reason she was cursed. As punishment for your cowardice."

Melanos shot up from the table, knocking over plates and spilling water as the monks scrambled to save what they could. Hermes jumped back with a laugh.

Croak watched the gods as they faced off, Melanos's bulky form twice the size of Hermes. In a battle between the two, Croak would still bet on Hermes because the fucker fought dirty.

"Calm down," Hermes said after one of the most tense moments of Croak's young life. Hermes had the gall to clap Melanos on the shoulder before turning away. "I was only kidding."

The look on Hermes's face belied his words. Melanos fumed as he dropped his gaze to the floor. Croak wasn't sure what to think about any of this shit. Clearly, there was more to Melanos than they knew.

And bad blood between him and Hermes.

"I wish Melanos and Bethana to remain behind with me," Sonah said, quickly jumping to her feet. Croak was surprised at Leander's hand coming out to rest on her forearm.

What the fuck was going on between these two? She hadn't been gone long enough to form any real attachment to this man—and a Riverman, to boot!—so what the fuck was going on?

Croak reminded himself to have a conversation with her and Terena when they returned.

"You're coming with us," Hermes said.

Croak rose from his seat slowly, motioning to Orry to do the same. His friend stared at him a beat before he grudgingly rose as well.

"No, I am not," Sonah said, steel edging her voice, "And you will inform my sister I am here and await her arrival."

Croak froze. Holy fucks. He should've warned Sonah about Hermes. To be fair, he'd thought they'd have more time and honestly, that was clearly Terena's domain. Because she's a god.

Swinging his eyes to Hermes, Croak felt his heart wither at the cruel smile wreathing his face.

"Child," Hermes started in a syrupy voice that fooled no one, "I did not ask."

"Hermes," Croak interjected as soon as Sonah opened her mouth again. "Let's leave her here. She won't be able to help; she doesn't have powers. I'll be useless too, thinking about her out there. You know Ren won't be any help either once she finds out her sister is there."

"She's a lot more powerful than she should be at her age. I can feel it," Hermes said, eyeballing Sonah like he was sizing up a lamb for slaughter. "Powerful enough to break not one curse but two. What else can you do, I wonder?"

"It matters not because she's still mortal," Melanos seethed, rising to his full height, which placed him only inches taller than Hermes.

"And so I will remain here and await my eudaemon and my sister," Sonah added.

Hermes stared at Sonah as if he wanted to gouge her eyes out. Croak wiped sweat from his brow as he waited. The glare Sonah was sending Hermes's way was not helping.

"All right then!" Croak said with a clap of his hands. "Let's... all right, Hermes, we—Orry and I—will come with you and then... Sonah, you just wait here. That's a good girl."

Sonah swatted his hand away when he patted her head, and Croak slouched behind Leander.

He plowed into Orry, who was clutching some papers to his chest. Scowling at his friend, Croak looked over his shoulder at the gods glaring daggers at one another.

"Gods save us from... gods," he muttered as he followed Orry out of the refectory.

CHAPTER 33

COLINAS, RAVOS

"Y ou've... changed since I last saw you."

Terena pulled up short when Lerek spoke, her beautiful eyes widening, reminding him of the many times he would gaze into them in the past, wishing those moments would last forever.

Pulling himself up straighter in the saddle, he looked away.

No. She was not the same person he'd fallen in love with. This woman, this god, was someone else entirely.

If he was being honest, a part of him resented her for it. And yet, another part loved her. Ached for her.

"Aye," she answered softly, narrowing her eyes. "But I'm also still me."

Lerek scoffed, shaking his head. "I think perhaps the seer is right. You are who you were always meant to be. You just hid it better."

Folding her arms, Ren gave him an arch look. "Funny. I was thinking maybe the trauma of you dying and me being accused and almost executed for your murder made that part of me come out. It's been a fun year."

Lerek's eyes widened. "I get that you're still angry with me. I really do. But that's no excuse for this."

Ren stared at him for a moment and he shifted beneath her regard.

"Do not make the mistake of thinking any of this has to do with you," she said at last, her voice barely above a whisper. She walked closer until she had to crane her neck to look at him. "That time has passed. I've moved on."

"Oh, I've heard," Lerek replied, hating himself for the jealousy in his voice. He was careful to keep his face neutral but there was no denying the edge in his words.

Terena's face hardened and Lerek cursed himself some more. What was wrong with him? She was a god, aye, but he was still in love with her. He should be doing everything he could to win her back. And yet a small part of him couldn't forgive her for hiding her divinity from him.

And then, of course, there was Daris Antonius.

"Whatever you've heard makes no difference to me."

Lerek opened his mouth but she'd already moved away, her gait stiff as she passed a disdainful Soros. The captain of this ragtag group swaggered over to him with a quick glance over his shoulder at Terena's retreating form.

"I don't see you getting back into her breeches anytime soon, princeling," Captain Soros said, and those close enough to hear sniggered at his words. Lerek felt the color blooming on his face as he glared down at the captain.

He turned his mount away, but one look at the line of soldiers nearby and Lerek stifled a groan. There wasn't a friendly face in the bunch. Croak and Orry had been his last hope, but Ren had sent them away to gods knew where. Lerek could only hope that—

"Captain!"

Lerek turned to the man jumping smoothly from his horse as he strode toward Captain Soros. Terena changed course to intercept the man.

"What news?"

"The army approaches, lady," the man panted, his eyes swinging between his captain and Ren. "Looks to be five thousand strong."

Terena's lip curled, and she took off running, grabbing the man named Rydon by the arm as she leaned in to speak with him.

Lerek's heart pounded as he looked over his shoulder, wondering how far out his father's army was.

He knew Xoran would've sent a message to the emperor once he'd been taken, but he hadn't anticipated this response.

As if he'd known exactly what Lerek was thinking, Captain Soros grabbed him by the cloak and yanked him off the horse. Lerek cried out when he landed, pain shooting up his back and legs. His hands were still bound so he couldn't use them to break his fall and now he shifted awkwardly to sit upright, only to be grabbed by the back of his collar.

"Take him and put him at the center of your ranks," Ren cried out, pointing at them as Lerek was dragged away, his feet scrambling to keep up with his upper body. Everywhere he looked, the men were moving into battle formations, and Lerek tried desperately to see beyond them to the city.

He began shouting, his voice hoarse as he screamed for Galen's men, but the gates were shut after Ren's destruction. Lerek prepared to call out again when something was stuffed into his mouth. His eyes flew wide and he jerked violently against the soldier's hold, to no avail.

When he was surrounded, Soros broke through to stand in front of him. The man's scarred lip twisted and he tapped his finger against his chin.

"I don't think you'll want to be awake for this," the man muttered. Before Lerek could protest, the man lifted his hand and struck him with the pommel of his sword.

"Let's see you get out of this, you bitch!"

Terena didn't bother replying to Ravos's taunts. His screeching grated on her nerves. Despite the emperor's army at their heels, Terena was preoccupied by the brief conversation she'd had with Lerek.

It unnerved her how he'd behaved toward her. Granted, he'd never actually seen her use her powers before. Being a god was also a topic they hadn't broached earlier.

Walking with Rydon as he offered advice on their next move, Terena glanced over at Soros. Ignoring the fact Rydon was still speaking, the captain offered his own input.

Terena nodded as if she'd heard both men, but Lerek's words kept creeping back into the forefront of her mind, insidious poison making her forget the task at hand.

"Everyone ready?" Soros shouted and the men behind them roared.

Terena blinked, frozen. What were they doing? What—

"Over here!" Rydon grabbed her, and she sighed as everyone mounted their horses. A moment later she was astride Nyx, pulling on the reins to follow Rydon.

Shouts behind her rumbled to a roar, and Terena spun.

"They're here!" Soros shouted, raising his sword high as he called out last minute orders and the men lifted their shields in a wall. Lances and swords lowered in defensive positions, and Terena glanced behind her to see their archers on the ridge.

"Ready?"

Terena looked at Rydon. Although her heart had sped up, her blood tingled at the battle to come. Excitement made her skin prickle.

"Oh, I'm ready," she said with a wink at the merc.

"Try to keep up."

She tossed her head back, laughing as she splayed her hands. The Twins formed, the runes etched on the blades lighting with the red glow of her power and she felt the bloodlust of her sire turning to fire within her chest.

Solon's army appeared on the horizon, and she felt the anticipation build in her veins. As they neared, their war cries crescendoed, the earth shaking from the approaching horde.

At the last moment, Terena jumped from Nyx's back, slapping her rump. As the horse reared and galloped away, Terena took off running, a primal scream ripping from deep within her, her left arm raised to the sky as she charged.

"The God of War is with us! Victory is ours!"

At Terena's words, Captain Soros and his men roared as she raced to the front of their lines. Out of her periphery, she saw Rydon and Gabriol charging with their weapons raised, their mouths wide; they, too, bellowed for blood.

She did not stop running. Screaming as the Heylisians drew within striking distance, Terena leaped impossibly high before slamming onto the soldiers in front of her. Her arms swept out and let her short swords have their first taste of Heylisian blood. Her vision blurred red for a moment before it cleared, everything focused more keenly than she'd ever seen in her life. Like a woman possessed, she snarled as she hacked at everyone within her reach. Blood roared in her ears, and Terena danced through the mess of soldiers, their cries music to her ears.

In the thick of Heylisian soldiers, she lost sight of Rydon and Gabriol but she did not fear for them. She had no fear at all, only the driving force of her bloodlust, insatiable no matter how many she slaughtered.

More.

More.

More.

Terena grinned as she caught the terrified expression of a soldier a moment before she carved his head from his shoulders. Spinning, the Twins easily sliced through the bodies around her like hot steel through butter. Never had her blood sang with such vitality before and she was drunk with the power thrumming in her veins.

And then she saw him.

A vicious growl rumbled up her throat from the bowels of the underworld when she spotted General Peleon, his helm gone and his dark hair plastered to his head with sweat and blood. He fought behind two of his men, thrusting one in front of one of Soros's men, who caught the blow meant for the slimy bastard.

Terena laughed as she took off running. Her breath caught when Peleon locked onto her. A look of surprise flashed across his face at how close she'd gotten. Then the coward turned tail and ran.

Someone grabbed her from behind, and Terena lifted and swung her sword reflexively, blinking in confusion when Rydon swore and ducked away.

"It's Daris!" Rydon shouted in her face more than once until she nodded dumbly. "Daris and the Liodari are here!"

Cries sounded all around as Soros's men fought with renewed ferocity, their sorely outnumbered ranks bolstered by the oncoming Liodari and Hermes's men.

Terena's eyes were wild as she looked where the others were pointing, swords raised in the air as more and more of their soldiers roared at Daris's arrival.

Her breath hitched when she caught sight of him, spellbound as Daris leaped from his mount.

Rydon shouted in her ear, yanking on her arm. She stumbled away as he drove his sword into the belly of her would-be attacker. Shaking off the stupor, Terena rejoined the fighting, spinning and weaving her way through the mass of Heylisians pressing in around her.

"Do not let them take him!"

Terena swung around at the sound of Soros's bellow and saw a group of Heylisian soldiers surrounding Lerek. Duke Ravos and his men had emptied onto the battlefield during the fighting, and now besieged Soros and his men. The captain's men fell under the might of the Heylisians around them and she watched in futile frustration as Lerek was pulled away. She ran toward them, her legs stiff and her gait halting as if she fought with herself about what she was doing.

Fire raged beneath her skin, and a flash of red blinded her momentarily. Terena gasped when her vision cleared. Looking down, she saw her hands ringed with red fire, crackling like lighting. When she held her hands out, white smoke pooled in her palms around the hilts of the Twins. She stared down at her hands, uncomprehending.

Someone shouted in front of her and Terena glanced up in time to see a Heylisian soldier rushing at her. The soldier screamed as he raised a wicked looking sword with a hooked end like a scythe. Terena blocked his killing blow. Fire raged through her at the contact. Red lighting crackled along the swords, startling the warrior and he stumbled back.

Lashing out with both hands, she cut the soldier's head from his body, turning away before it fell to the ground, her eyes on her next victim.

Terena's body was on fire from within, her heartbeat racing at an unnatural speed as she burst forward, her mind focused on destroying the men in front of her. The Twins spun faster than light, and Terena barely registered the contact with whatever body parts she struck.

She spared a glance at Lerek over the shoulder of the man she was fighting, his face white as he gawked back at her. The men around him pulled him away, finally getting him mounted and moving away from the carnage.

Terena cried out as he disappeared, her movements a blur as the red light at the edges of her eyes tunneled her vision until she no longer thought of the prince.

Bodies eddied away from her and she caught sight of Daris surrounded and outnumbered.

Her heart stopped when he went down.

CHAPTER 34

COLINAS, RAVOS

Terena ran through the battlefield, shoving people out of her way or pausing long enough to slice into a soldier who had the audacity to step in front of her.

She watched the spot where Daris had been fighting, silently urging him to appear, her lips moving in silent prayers to the Fates. Her breath fogged out in front of her and panic squeezed her lungs.

A roar from her right had her snapping her gaze around, and she spotted Hermes thundering toward the soldiers fighting on the far side of the field. Shouts and cheers rang out from Soros's men and the fighting took on a fevered pitch. Her breath hitched and she slowed, her eyes caught on another warrior who roared as he chopped his way through the Heylisians behind Hermes.

Melanos?!

The god looked much as he had when she'd last seen him after she and Sonah had gotten him out of his cave. He wielded an axe in his hands and a monstrous expression as he swung up and into the chest of a doomed soldier.

As Melanos made his way through the battlefield, the soldiers with him and Hermes fought viciously, terrifying the Heylisians. They screamed and began to fall back. A moment later a horn sounded their retreat. Those still able to run did not need further urging.

Terena made her way slowly through the mess as the chaos of the Heylisian retreat momentarily made her lose sight of Melanos. She spotted Hermes once more, his lips pulled back in a ferocious grin as he cut through the Heylisian soldiers easily.

She was about to turn away when her breath caught. Daris came out from behind him, slamming his sword into a soldier who'd almost succeeded in catching Hermes in the back.

Terena ran.

As if the Fates were finally helping, a path cleared before her, and she tore across the blood and body littered ground, her eyes locked on Daris.

Victorious shouts sounded all around her as the last of the emperor's warriors left the battlefield. Hermes turned, grabbing Daris in a crushing embrace before turning to lift his sword, his own shouts drowned out by the men around him. Terena slowed, her heart still racing, and took several deep breaths.

At that moment, Daris turned, his grin fading as he caught sight of her.

Time slowed. Terena heard nothing but the exhale she released. She sprinted forward, watching as Daris stabbed his sword in the ground and ran.

He caught her as she flew into his arms, her lips crushing his as he spun her, his arms like vices at her back.

Nothing mattered to her but him. He devoured her and she let him, his mouth slanting over hers, his tongue delving deep and she clutched his face, hungry for more. His hand cradled the back of her neck and she locked her ankles at his waist, his grip on her scalp painful, but still she pressed closer.

Terena couldn't think beyond how complete she felt in that moment. It was the same as when she'd seen him that night weeks ago after she first ported. She was still angry with him for lying about Lerek, but that was a problem for when she was ready to let sanity rule her thoughts. Right now, all she wanted was him.

Daris tore his lips away, his beautiful blue eye searching her face. The heat of his breath fanned her cheeks and she felt wetness there. He cupped her jaw, his thumb wiping at the tears spilling unchecked as she gazed back at him.

"Glad we made it in time," Daris said, breathless, a smile playing on his lips.

Terena swallowed, her teeth chattering as her chin trembled. "Daris."

He slammed his lips back on hers, the long kiss almost painful, snatching her breath. Her fingers dug into his arm and she panicked at the lack of air in her lungs before he pulled back and dropped his forehead to hers.

"I missed you, Ren. So fucking much."

Daris didn't give her a chance to respond before he kissed her again, and Terena was grateful for it. Her head spun as heat tore through her body.

"I guess she missed you, too."

The laughter that followed broke through the haze of Terena's lust. She pulled back, savoring the desire on Daris's face before glancing around at the audience they'd drawn.

She dropped her feet to the ground, still holding on to Daris. His hands fell to her waist, tightening his grip, and stared at her as if he could not look away. Terena flushed as she looked around at the leering soldiers, her eyes landing on Hermes, who scowled.

"You've got some explaining to do," she ground out, her fury at the god burning through her desire.

"Well, if you can tear yourself away from the commander long enough for a conversation—"

Terena sprang forward, ready to launch herself at the god, but Daris's arm froze her in place. Hermes's smirk darkened as he arched an eyebrow at her before turning to stalk away. Some of his men followed, others dispersing as Daris shouted out orders.

Terena stepped out of his arms, but he kept one hand on her hip. A shout caught her attention, and she turned, grinning as Melanos came up to her, grabbing her away from Daris as they spun, hugging and laughing.

After setting her down, Terena took a deep breath, wiping her hands down the leather of her breeches. Opening her mouth to launch a thousand questions at the god, she caught movement at her periphery and turned to see Rydon jogging over, Gabriol and Migela at his side.

"Croak's here, too. They came with Hermes." The mercenary said as he and the others hugged her in turn.

"Where?" Terena asked, her eyes searching behind them. Rydon and Gabriol exchanged greetings with Daris and Melanos. "Is he all right?"

"He's fine," Gabriol grunted, jabbing a thumb behind him. "He's at the tree line with Orry and Cassandra."

"Why are they here? How—"

"Hermes made us come," Melanos said with a scowl. "We were at Lethe, with Sonah—"

"Sonah!" Terena cried, grabbing Melanos's arms. "You found her?"

"Aye," Melanos said wryly. "She found us. And more besides. We've much to catch up on."

"Is she here? Did you bring her?"

Melanos shook his head. "No, she stayed behind and awaits you. With my Bethana."

Furrowing her brow, Terena tilted her head. "Bethana?"

"As I said, we've much to catch up on."

Rydon lifted an eyebrow at her, motioning to Daris with a tilt of his head. She felt the heat creep up her neck once more and she scowled.

"Come," Daris said, slipping his hand into hers and tugged her to follow. "Hermes is heading into the city."

"Wait," Terena said, digging in her heels. Daris turned to her impatiently. "I left Nyx across the field," she added with a scoff. "Let me go—"

"Rydon," Daris called over her shoulder. "Have someone—"

"Oh, no," Terena huffed a laugh. "No, I'll be riding on my own."

Daris gave her a look she was sure he used to intimidate his enemies, but she refused to be cowed. She might be in love with him, despite everything, but he still owed her an explanation. For a lot of things.

The last thing she was going to do, now that she'd gotten her fear and desperation to see him out of the way, was ride off into the sunset with him on his horse.

By the set of his jaw, she could see he wanted to argue but raked a hand through his mud-splattered hair and gave her a curt nod.

"I'll meet you there," Daris said before turning to stalk away.

Terena watched him for a few moments. When she turned back to her friends, she made a face at Rydon who chuckled at her.

"I thought you were going to tear his clothes off right then and there."

"If he hadn't been wearing his battle armor, she might have," Gabriol snorted.

Terena shoved him and he laughed.

"Glad Hermes decided to show. For a minute there, I thought he'd only sent Daris and a handful of his men." Rydon snarked after they found their mounts where Croak, Migela and Orry waited.

Terena hugged her brother, then turned and embraced Orry.

"Daris is here?" Croak asked, his brows in his hairline.

"Aye," Rydon said with a sly grin as he mounted. "And it looks like he's been forgiven."

"Just because Lerek's still alive doesn't mean Daris isn't still an asshole," Croak grumbled.

A headache began to form at her temples, and Terena growled low as she mounted Nyx.

"He's not forgiven," Terena snapped. The others laughed and she cursed at them. "It was a momentary lapse in judgment. He's not getting off that easy, believe me."

THE RIDE THROUGH COLINAS WAS EERY. THE STREETS WERE EMPTIED AND the City Watch nonexistent. As they neared Sydney Hall, Hermes's soldiers were already setting up their encampment, surrounding the castle gates and taking up the area beyond to the main entrance of the structure.

Rydon raised his arm in greeting when he spotted Vassori standing near the entrance to the castle with Cassandra. He dismounted, glancing at Ren, whose face was wreathed in smiles to see the women again. Migela jogged ahead of her and embraced the seer as Ren walked up.

"What are you doing here?" Ren asked Vassori. "We were to meet in Metilai."

"Aye," Vassori said with a grimace. "But after finding my brother, he told me of the emperor's trap for you in Ravos. I came as fast as I could."

"I need to speak with you," Cassandra said to Ren, laying a hand on her arm to draw her attention.

Ren looked at the woman and nodded. "All right." Turning to Rydon she motioned with her chin. "Can you find us some tents? Have Croak and Orry help you put them up." Turning back to Vassori she said, "We'll speak more later."

"No, Rydon, please stay." The seer said as she reached out her arm toward him.

He frowned but came closer. Over his shoulder, he gave Gabriol Ren's instructions and his friend set off in search of Croak and Orry.

Migela signed something to Cassandra and the woman shook her head, telling her she needed to speak with Rydon and Ren privately. Migela gave her a tight-lipped smile before striding away after Gabriol with Vassori behind her.

Folding his arms, Rydon shrugged at the seer. "What's going on?"

The woman bit her lip, and the instant stab of desire made Rydon grunt in dismay. He shifted his stance wider, hoping he seemed unbothered. The last thing he needed was this woman knowing she had any power over him.

"Do you recall our conversation back in Corvo, about the commander?" she asked Ren in a loud whisper. Rydon expelled a frustrated breath as he stepped closer to hear her better. Terena bent closer as well, frowning.

"Be specific."

Cassandra flapped her hands impatiently. "About being soulmates."

"Aye." Ren replied with a groan.

"Are you sure I should be here for this?" Rydon was uncomfortable already with the direction this conversation was taking.

Cassandra ignored him. "I've seen the commander's death. In Metilai after you become immortal. I didn't realize it was Metilai because I've never been, but when I heard about the Heylisian army coming here, I thought perhaps the future changed and it would no longer come to pass."

"Wait, what?"

"I'm getting a headache," Rydon grumbled.

"What did you see?"

The seer shook her head. "His death. In battle. And I still see it. I'm worried there might not be a way to change the outcome. What if the Fates mean for him to die? What if that's been his fate all along?"

"You saw this before and said nothing?"

Cassandra jerked back, affronted. "I thought we were going to Metilai! Then you received word of your sister here and the army coming for her, so I thought that the Fates had intervened twofold!"

Rydon shifted his gaze to Terena, whose ashen face and trembling lips told him how she'd received this news. "I don't understand a word of what she's saying, but we'll find a way to save him, Ren," he said, more to give her hope than any genuine conviction he felt on the matter. He still had no clue why he was in on this conversation.

Cassandra exhaled raggedly, reaching out to grip Terena's hands. "That's just it," she hissed. "I don't believe there is. I think... I think this is why you are soulmates. Do you know what happens when one soulmate dies? The surviving soulmate is fractured. They become twisted, their soul blackens and they become monsters. I think Daris's death is what the Fates had in mind all along. I think what that will do to you is tied to your destiny."

"How can that be?" Ren's voice cracked.

"The amulet is here," the seer went on, her eyes shifting between Ren and Rydon. "In Sydney Hall. Surely, that's why we received word that Sonah and the army were here! That the Fates wanted you to find it before going to Metilai. But I was wrong. His fate has not changed."

This was a fucking lot, and Rydon could see how well Ren was taking this. Her body trembled and her mouth was doing that thing where she tried to speak but no words came.

"Are you mad?" Rydon snarled. "Why the fuck would you bring this to her now?"

"Would the Fates be this cruel?" Ren whispered in shock.

Cassandra nodded. "Oh, aye. And worse."

Terena turned her head and stared off into the distance as Rydon glared at the seer. She pinched her lips and straightened her shoulders.

"But I have a thought," she said as the silence stretched.

Like a drowning man thrown a lifeline, Terena wrenched her head around, her eyes narrowing on the seer.

"I think," Cassandra said, wetting her lips. "I think if you... break the bond, or make *him* break the bond..."

Ren reared back, staring at the seer as if she'd turned into a gorgon.

"How the fuck is that going to help us?" Rydon snarled, dropping his head so his nose was an inch from Cassandra's face. "We don't know how to do that. She's a week out from her nameday. There's no time for us to go on another fucking adventure to figure out how to sever their bond!"

"We... don't have to. We're already on the adventure."

"What's that mean?" Terena asked.

"Do you know what the Amulet of Kaïra *is*? What it does?"

Ren stared back at her with a blank look as Rydon growled at Cassandra.

The seer groaned loudly, wiping a hand over her brow. "It corrupts the minds of men. The cypher who wields it breaks into the mind of their victim and twists whatever desire they focus on. So if the victim is ambitious, wanting to better his lot in life, he might... I don't know, try to kill the olive oil vendor and take over his business. Or assassinate a king if he desires a position of power."

"None of that makes sense. How does that break the soulmate bond?" Rydon asked with an edge to his voice, betraying his fear. The amulet sounded diabolical, and he thought they might be better off leaving it alone.

It was Cassandra's turn to growl at Rydon, her lip curling back in a way that made her look seductive instead of angry.

Turning back to Ren, Cassandra held up a hand. "Before I go on, you must promise to hear me out before you—"

"Say it already!"

"If," she cast a quick glance at Rydon before turning back to Terena. "When we find the amulet, we can get the cypher to use it and—"

"We don't have a fucking cypher to use it." Rydon seethed. He swallowed, taking a moment to compose himself. "And in case you haven't noticed, we don't have the amulet."

Cassandra ignored him, focused on Terena. "You need to get the cypher to use it on Daris. Before that though, you need to make him *want* to break the bond."

"He doesn't even *know* about the bond," Ren said, her voice small.

When Rydon looked over at her, her face was still pale and she seemed haunted. He took hold of her hand and squeezed it.

"You need to tell him. And then make it seem like it's the worst thing ever for you two."

"What? Why?"

"Because when the cypher gets into his head, she can amplify his desire to break the bond. It'll make him do something... stupid... that should break it."

"Should?" Rydon snapped.

"Theoretically."

"The cypher's a woman? You've seen her?" Ren asked.

"Yes to both."

"What will it make him do?"

Cassandra opened her mouth to reply, her eyes shifting between them. Taking a step back, she held out her hands.

"You have to remember, you are bound by the Fates, so it has to be something significant. Something... unforgivable. So, theoretically, that's how we break the bond. But we need to control the situation so—"

"Unforgivable?"

"And that will break it?"

Cassandra waggled her head. "Theoretically."

"What about in reality?"

"I don't know!" Cassandra sniped with a stamp of her foot. "We're dealing with the Fates here, and I'm trying to walk a very fine line between saving her soulmate and getting us all hunted by the Furies!"

"What?" Rydon gasped, lurching forward. "What about the Furies?"

"Never mind them. If this works, they won't bother with him. Or us."

"But they might? If he breaks the bond, the Furies will kill him?"

"I don't think so," Cassandra whined, her eyes darting between the two. "If he's under the influence of a power beyond his control, like the amulet, they might not retaliate."

"Fucking gods," Rydon groused, stabbing his hands into his hair and turning away from the seer.

"So, none of this is anything you know with certainty," Ren bit out, her face blotched as she glared at Cassandra. "You're asking me to trust that this will work without any guarantee."

"If you've a better idea, goddess, I am all ears!"

"Talk to Hermes, Ren," Rydon cautioned, watching as the wheels spun inside that head of hers. "Don't do anything rash. He knows way more about this stuff than we do."

"But can we trust him?" Terena pondered, her eyes on the ground.

"I don't know him," Cassandra replied. "But I know the Olympians as a whole are not trustworthy. He's not called the trickster god for nothing. If you confide in him, he might twist the situation to suit his needs."

"But isn't that why I found him?" Ren asked, throwing out her arms. "I have to believe the Fates led me to him for help! If I do this, won't they punish us? I'm drowning, here, Cassandra!"

"Your destiny is too big for them to punish you."

Ren took a deep, shaky breath and dropped her head back. A long, tense silence stretched as they watched Terena wrestle with all the seer had shared.

"So, I have to get him to think I don't love him."

Rydon's chest swelled and he clenched his jaw tight to stave off the sting of tears the sorrow in her words evoked in him. Gods, why the fuck can't they leave this poor woman alone?

"Do whatever you need to. However you need to. Once that's done, the cypher can do her thing and then..."

When she didn't continue, Rydon frowned. "And then?"

"Remember, this is just an idea, all right?" Cassandra pleaded, backing away another step. "So, theoretically, if he's under the cypher's power, maybe, if everything goes to plan, he might... try to kill Sonah."

"What?" Ren gasped.

"Are you *fucking* insane?" Rydon roared. Both of them bounded toward the seer, who squeaked as she took a few running steps away.

"It was just a thought!" Looking at Rydon, Cassandra waved her hand at him. "And he won't do it anyway, because *you'll* be there to stop him! You'll take the killing blow instead, and, because you're her guardian you'll be fine!"

"By the *fucking* gods, woman," Rydon raged.

"Well, do you have a better idea?" Cassandra hissed, lunging forward like an angry little dog, baring her teeth at him. "The whole point is to get him to do something unforgivable! If he tries to kill Sonah, I'm fairly certain that counts! You'll save Sonah because you'll be right there; the bond will break once he does that. We save both Sonah and the commander with this plan. See?"

"How the fuck did you come up with something so convoluted—"

"Will it work?"

Rydon's head whipped around as he stared at her in horror. "You're not considering this!"

"Have you seen this?" Ren asked, her eyes on Cassandra. "In a vision?"

"No," Cassandra said mournfully, shaking her head. "But I saw the cypher wearing the amulet. Right after I saw Daris fall in battle."

"So where is she? And how are we supposed to convince this stranger to go along with this scheme?"

"Uhm…"

"Speak, woman!" Rydon swore he saw red whenever this woman was around. His head was about to explode from the amount of blood pounding in his skull.

"Again, this is only what I saw in the vision. But good news, we do find the amulet. You know, because, uh… the woman is wearing it. In the vision. She'll definitely do it for you."

"Why?"

"Who's the woman?" Ren asked. "Do we know her?" Her shoulders slumped as she gazed at Cassandra.

The seer gave her a wan smile, and she let out a hesitant chuckle.

"Aye. You know her well. It's Sonah."

CHAPTER 35

COLINAS, RAVOS

"May I speak with you?" Terena clenched and unclenched her fists as she stood before Hermes.

He was in the dining hall of the castle, laughing and conversing with his cohorts. As she approached, Hermes took one look at her face and dismissed his men.

"What ails you?"

Terena frowned. "Huh?"

"You look like you drank spoiled milk. What's wrong?"

Searching for a good place to start, Terena let the silence stretch as she discarded thought after thought.

Hermes rapped on the table, snapping her out of her head.

"What is it?"

Sighing, Terena settled her arm on the table, her finger idly tracking the grain of the wood. "Is there any reason... I could not use... an amulet, like the cyphers do, but Sonah could?"

Hermes frowned. "No."

"I could use it, too?"

The god shook his head. "No. And neither could Sonah. But," he shrugged and took a sip of his drink. "You don't need to. You have powers of your own. And she does as well."

"So, you've never heard of a god... using an amulet with powers from another god?"

"No."

"And it's not possible?"

"No."

Terena's mind whirled. Cassandra had seemed so certain of the vision she'd seen.

According to the seer, there was a party or celebration of some sort and when someone called out to Sonah, she'd turned around. The emerald at her chest glowed so brightly it had blinded Cassandra and she'd broken from her trance, but she was adamant it was Sonah with the amulet.

"What's troubling you?"

Terena lifted her eyes to Hermes, who watched her with concern. A part of her desperately wanted to share this burden with him. He was a god thousands of years old. He would know what to do. And yet, a part of her kept her from telling him about it.

Instead, she gave Hermes a tight smile, ready to lie and tell him nothing was wrong. Everything about Cassandra's ridiculous plan was flawed but, if she was right and it worked, they would save Daris. But what if Daris still died? Soulmate bond or not, he'd still be mortal. Terena feared what his death would do to her.

Rubbing at her forehead, she made to stand when a thought struck her.

"How did you make Rydon immortal?"

Hermes blinked. He gazed at her long enough for the ever-present silver in his eyes to snake around his eyes twice. "Why?"

"Is... can I do that? Can I make someone immortal?"

Hermes shook his head. "No."

"But you can."

His face shuttered. Long seconds passed, and she worried he

would not respond. Her knee bounced as she waited, unwilling to drop his gaze.

"You know I can," he said softly.

Terena exhaled as her pulse ratcheted up. "Do you... would you do it for me? As a favor?"

Hermes's eyes turned calculating. "Croak?"

Tears sprang to Terena's eyes, and she breathed heavily through her nose to stop them from falling. "No. No... not Croak. Although, maybe."

Hermes grabbed his knife and speared a piece of lamb, chewing on it as he continued to regard her. "Daris?"

"Aye."

"Why?"

"Will you do it for me?" Terena whispered, hating how her voice broke over the words. She couldn't recall ever being this vulnerable in front of the god, and she feared he would see her as weak. Or worse.

Mortal.

Gods, how she hated... all of this. Hated how she felt about Daris, hated that his love for her would bring about his death. But most of all, she hated being a plaything for the Fates.

Hermes leaned back in his seat, crossing his arms as he watched her. Terena schooled her features, hardening her eyes as she stared back at him.

"What will you do for me?"

"Really?"

His lower jaw moved from side to side as he made her wait.

"No. Not really." He stood abruptly, stretching with a loud groan. Turning to face her, a beautiful smile brightened his face. "You're my niece. Of course I'll do it for you."

Relief so profound flooded through her she let out a sob, overwhelmed by her feelings. Putting her hand to her chest, she gave him a tremulous smile as she stood.

"Thank you, Hermes. Thank you."

Impulsively, she reached out and hugged him. Grinning at how stiff he became, she pulled away.

Turning to leave, Terena raised a finger and turned back to face the god, who stood with his brow furrowed as he stared at the ground.

"Oh, and Hermes," she said, snapping his attention back to her. "Say nothing to Daris about this coming from me. Please?"

Hermes smiled back and bowed his head. "My lips are sealed."

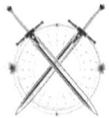

As dusk fell into deepest night and the only sounds were the low murmurs of the few soldiers still sitting around the fading campfires, Terena sighed and turned to search out her tent.

Her nerves were shot from the events of the day. The way Cassandra and Rydon looked at her every time she caught their eyes worsened her mood. They were waiting for her to have the conversation with Daris about their bond and she was putting it off. Dread was a wonderful co-conspirator in procrastination.

Terena gasped, her hand flying up to her mouth as Daris's large frame blocked the dim light from the fires, his face shrouded in shadows.

"You startled me," she mumbled, thankful for the dark and how it hid the rising color in her face.

"You've been avoiding me," he said after a silence lasting several heartbeats, which she counted.

Her hands shook and her pulse raced. This moment was inevitable, and yet, coward that she was when it came to this man, her mind fought for ways to get out of it.

Daris edged closer, his body stiff. He seemed angry, and she wondered how he'd react to what she was about to tell him.

"You're not denying it," Daris said, his gravelly voice scratching beneath her skin like the most sensual of claws.

She swallowed, crossing her arms over her chest.

"I have been, aye."

He took a step closer and her heart skipped its next beat, faltering in her chest before speeding up to twice its normal pace.

"Why."

Not a question. Terena licked her dry lips and opened her mouth to reply but nothing came out.

He stepped closer.

"You come to my rooms in Pera," he said, that low timbre turning her blood to honey. Another step closer and his mouth was inches from hers. "And you leave me wanting you more than ever."

"It wasn't real," she whispered, heart thundering so loud she could not hear herself.

"Is that what you've been telling yourself?"

He shifted his stance and she took a step back, wincing at the hurt she saw on his face before he hid it behind the shadows once more.

"Daris—"

"Something's changed."

"Aye."

"What."

She sighed, bringing her hands up. Those ineffectual appendages flapped as if that was all the answer he needed and she knew he deserved more.

Ducking her head, she shook it once before meeting his gaze. Severing the bond would destroy her. Destroy them. And yet, if there was a chance she could save him by doing so, she would do it.

"It's not real, Daris," she said softly, her voice cracking on his name.

He shifted again, lifting the brow of his ruined eye as he waited for her to continue.

"You and I," she laughed or sobbed; she did not know. Tears

stung her eyes and once more she thanked the night for shrouding her pain. "You and I are not real, Daris."

"The fuck we're not," he all but snarled at her, his vehemence so sharp she felt a stab of fear.

"You—" she shook her head again and placed a trembling hand to his chest, finding the thick corded muscles beneath his tunic rather than the boiled leather and bronze breastplate he'd worn earlier. Her body reacted immediately, a bolt of desire so sharp and loaded it arced down her chest to settle low in her belly.

Terena pulled back her hand and shook her head again. He must think her a moron with all the head shaking. "You and I were... for whatever reason, you and I are... bound. We are soulmates. Bound together by the Fates."

To his credit, Daris only narrowed his good eye at the revelation. Then a look of awe filled his face, his expression lightening with wonder as he gazed back at her. His shoulders slumped a bit and he straightened. She caught the slow exhale escaping his trembling lips.

"In truth?" Daris whispered. The way he said it made her heart cramp.

"Aye," she replied in a voice strengthened by the conviction she was doing the right thing. The only thing she could do to save him. To save herself.

"So you see, none of this is real."

Daris canted his head and stared at her, waiting. When she did not reply, he grunted, "How so?"

Looking at him as if he'd asked her which way the sun sets, Terena scoffed and lifted her head to the star-studded sky. She angrily swiped at a tear audacious enough to defy her will.

"You don't know? You have to ask?" She huffed a laugh. "You don't love me, Daris. You don't." When he opened his mouth to object, she cut him off with a swipe of her hand. "You think you do, and it feels like it to you; it feels real. But it's not. *They* made you feel this. They bound us together, and the feelings you have are only there because the Fates made it so."

Daris stared at her for so long she started to shiver. Whether from the cold seeping beneath her cloak or the way he regarded her so steadily, she could not say.

"You think what you feel is love, but it's really just a... a manifestation of the bond they placed on you, on us."

"You think I don't love you," he said, his voice unnaturally pleasant.

"I think you *think* you love me," she demurred, ducking her head. She could not hold his stare.

"I *know* I love you," he countered.

She laughed and even to her ears it was false and forced and she started to panic. Why was she fucking this up so much?

"I'm telling you, you don't. You do, because you have no choice. You never did. That's what this is; you don't love me because you chose me, Daris," she said and hated the way she sounded so desperate, but she needed him to believe it. For both their sakes. "Don't you want to find someone who—"

"I *did* find someone," he growled, taking a deliberate step closer, crowding her.

"You—"

"I found *you* and I fell in love with you, and you have the fucking nerve to stand there and tell me what I feel for you isn't real? After everything—" he shook his head, looking back at her with his heart in his eye and his hand at his chest. "You think what I feel, here," he thumped his chest hard enough for her to wince. "You think it's not real? That I don't *really* fucking love you?"

Terena shook her head, which was the exact wrong thing to do.

His face changed, a mask so dark, so filled with violence, it did not belong to him. Daris was a warrior, aye. Through and through. Yet whenever there was battle, whenever he'd had to fight, he'd never been this.

Terena's temper flared to match his wrath.

How dare he? she thought as she stared him down. Did he not realize how difficult this was for her as well?

"I know you believe it, Daris," she fumed, no longer willing to back up as he neared, his chest pressed against hers aggressively. "But it is only an enchantment. Magic. The Fates. Before you were even born, our bond was decided. You had no choice—"

"I don't need a fucking choice!"

His shout reverberated throughout her body, drawing a deep shudder as she willed her heart to stop responding to him. Her chest throbbed with the pain of not being with him, of saying these words to him, of denying the very thing that made her heart soar.

"I do!" Terena screamed back at him, her chest heaving against the pain, against the torment of saying things denying their bond. She took a step back. Nearby, soldiers stopped to stare at them.

Daris stilled at her words, blinking his good eye as he stared at her for endless moments after her words stopped echoing between them.

The expression on his face was as if she'd plunged her hand into his chest and yanked out his still-beating heart. He looked at her as if she'd betrayed him; she feared that, aye, she might have.

Hardening herself against the expression that threatened to break her, she squared her shoulders and stepped back.

"Believe me," she said, hoping to placate him. "I do not take pleasure in your pain. It is my pain, too. But I won't—I can't—believe it's real unless *we* make the choice. Without the bond. Without the Fates pushing us toward each other."

"Do you love me?"

Gods. Terena closed her eyes against the agony his words speared through her, cutting more cleanly than the sharpest of blades.

"Of course I love you, Daris," Terena whispered, finally looking at him. "That's my point."

"Your point?"

"Aye," she breathed, putting out her hand. When she realized she'd meant to touch him again, she pulled it back sharply, holding it to her chest as if burned. "I love you. I love you so much I ache when

I'm not near you. I dream of you. I am formless without you. But is that me? Or is that the bond?"

"That is *love!*" Daris bellowed, his arms stretched out.

"It is the bond!"

"Why does it matter?" Daris's question was so plaintive, tears sprang once more to her eyes and she ruthlessly blinked them back.

"I want the choice," Terena begged. "I want to choose you. And I want you to choose me. I want to have found you because I—" Terena pounded her chest—"cannot live without you."

"I truly do not understand," Daris said with a frustrated swipe of his hand through his short hair. "I love you. I don't care why. You are... *everything* to me."

"Daris—"

"You want me to defy the Fates? Is that it? You want me to spit in the faces of the gods and tell them I do not want this gift—"

He stopped to scoff, and the way he swallowed, Terena was certain he was holding back tears of his own.

Daris straightened and looked down at her with defiance. "I will not. I will not be the one to tell the Fates I do not want this... this treasure they have seen fit to give me. I fucking love you. And you want me to tell the gods I do not want the bond they have given us, to love each other, to be everything to each other and for each other, because what, you didn't get to choose? You are choosing right now!"

He shook his head at her, his face a mix of love and hate so powerful she gasped and stepped back.

"No," he whispered, tilting his head as he watched her. "Do it if you must. But I will not be the one to break this bond. I've been given a gift more valuable than any god has ever given a human, a gift I will spend the rest of my life doing my best to earn, to be worthy of: you. There's no power strong enough to make me willingly break this bond with you. I don't want to. Ever."

"Not even for me?"

Daris's face crumpled for an instant. It was gone so quick she thought she'd imagined it, and yet the answering stab to her heart at his hurt made her knees buckle. She reached out to steady herself, but he stepped away, looking at her as if she was a monster.

Perhaps she was.

"Is this because of the prince?" Daris asked a long time later, his voice barely above a whisper, and yet they shouted through her brain like the bells at solstice. "Is... do you still love Prince Lerek?"

"What?"

"I know you've seen him," Daris said, his voice a mix of desperation and defiance. "I don't know what he told you, Ren. But I did not betray you. I kept the truth from you, aye. I gave my word to my king no one was to know he was alive. I know it was wrong and I am sorry I kept it from you. Don't ruin us because of some misplaced guilt you have that you moved on!" His lips parted and he looked at her, lost. "Unless... you haven't."

Terena lifted a hand to her chest. It physically felt like her heart was cracking into a thousand pieces inside her ribcage.

"This is about *us*," she gritted out, her throat tight. A part of her wanted to throw her arms around him and tell him to forget everything she'd said.

Then Cassandra's face flashed in her mind, and the consequences of not doing this filled her with dread.

"Do you think," she said when she felt she could speak without crying, "do you think if we didn't have this bond, you'd still love me?"

"Without doubt," he snarled.

She nodded. "Then why won't you let me have this? If you've no doubt, why do you fight me?"

"He doubts *you*."

Daris's head jerked up, instinctively putting his body in front of Terena as Hermes came into the clearing. Behind him, Daris heard Terena sigh and step to his side but Daris didn't take his gaze off Hermes.

"That's it, isn't it?" Hermes asked, leisurely strolling to a stop a few feet away, arms crossed at his chest. He lifted one hand to his lips, then pointed at both of them.

"He doesn't believe you'd choose him, too."

"Hermes—" Terena huffed, taking a step toward him.

"Incidentally," Hermes said as he paced away, a smile tugging at the corner of his mouth. "I agree with him."

"No one asked you," she grumbled.

Daris did not respond. He stared back at the god, a riot of emotions warring inside him. He did not trust himself to speak.

"Believe me when I say, dear niece, your little tantrum about 'choosing' and 'oh, is this real?'" Hermes laughed when they startled at how his voice had morphed into hers. "—is pointless. If you go against the Fates to sever the bond, you risk incurring more than their wrath. The Furies will hunt you down for the affront, and then where will you be? Not in love with a fine warrior sent to help you with your destiny and certainly not fulfilling the prophecy."

Daris knew the god was not helping him out of the goodness of his heart.

He wanted something. And yet Daris could not think of what it could be.

"Thank you so much for your sage counsel, Hermes," Terena said insincerely as she fluttered her lashes at him. A second later, her face darkened and she glared at him.

"But stay the fuck out of our business."

Daris lurched forward to grab her as she stomped off but Hermes stayed him, a hand pressed to his chest.

"Don't mind her," Hermes purred. "She's just wrestling with the fact her free will has strings."

"What does that mean?"

"I didn't realize they bonded you," Hermes huffed, ignoring Daris's question. He moved to block Daris's view of Terena's retreat. "Complicates things a little but..."

The god clapped his hands, startling Daris. "I have a solution to this little drama, if you're interested."

Daris flashed a frustrated look at Hermes as he tried to step around him. The god moved, blocking his attempt.

"I can make you immortal."

Daris started. "What?"

Hermes splayed his hands. "Terena just asked you to prove your love for her. And she told you how. Soulmate bonds are not easily broken. And definitely not if you're mortal."

"I'm not—"

"Right now, aye. You're not mortal. But in another week or so..."

Daris's stomach dropped. He watched the calculating smile bloom on Hermes's face.

"You know how to break the bond?"

Hermes tried to hide the triumph flashing in his eyes but Daris caught it before the god ducked his head.

Moving away, he sighed loudly as if this conversation was bothersome and not one of the most important of Daris's life.

"As I said, you'll need to be immortal for it to work, but aye. I know of a way to break such bonds."

Daris knew the god too well by now to know he wouldn't offer such a gift without something in return.

"What do you want?"

Hermes smiled in a way that made Daris regret asking.

"I want *you,* Daris. I want your allegiance. Your sword."

Daris stood rooted as Hermes stepped closer, bending so his words growled in Daris's ear and the words made his heart quake.

"I want your soul."

CHAPTER 36

COLINAS, RAVOS

"We're going to Lethe now, right?"

Croak strode after Terena when she moved past him, throwing back the tent flap with a little more force than was necessary. His arm snapped out to stop it front slapping him in the face as he followed her inside.

Terena ignored him while packing up her things.

"All right, good. I'll take that as a yes. When do we leave?"

Terena swore under her breath. He waited while she sat there, presumably thinking.

"I need to do one thing first," she mumbled. Tying up her bedroll she glanced at him over her shoulder. "We'll go right after, I promise."

Croak crossed his arms and exhaled. Loudly.

"Fine, but I don't know how happy she'll be to hear that you, once again, put someone else ahead of her."

Terena shot to her feet. Croak took a step back, bracing himself for her rage. His shoulders fell when she turned away, gathering her clothes and shoving them into a rucksack.

"It's not a someone, Croak. Cassandra's been badgering me about that stupid amulet and I just want to find it and get it over with already."

"Ah," Croak said as he watched her finish. "I didn't think you were still looking for it since, you know, we found Sonah."

"Well, I am," Ren snapped. She moved past him out of the tent and instructed one of Soros's men to have it torn down.

"Or better yet," she said as she turned back suddenly, making Croak falter as he, too, paused. "Let the men know there's an empty tent in case anyone is without."

Not waiting for a response, she strode off, with Croak hot on her steps.

"Orry was saying something about the amulet," Croak panted as he kept pace with his sister.

"Right," Terena snapped her fingers. "Good. Go get ready to depart and tell Orry as well. I'll find Rydon and the others. And where the fuck is Cassandra?"

"The beauteous witch was with some of the soldiers, telling fortunes."

"She's not a witch," Ren muttered. "She's a seer."

"Whatever."

"Where?"

"Huh?"

"Where was she?"

"Oh," Croak spun, looking at his surroundings. When he caught sight of the three tents near the fire pit to his left, he pointed. "Just past those tents there; turn left. You can't miss her."

Terena nodded and strode away.

Croak watched her and sighed. Turning around, he glanced at the soldiers nearby and began walking in a random direction. As he strolled through the encampment looking for Orry, a hand grabbed hold of his arm.

"Croak," Vassori said, standing close enough to kiss him which, if he was honest, wouldn't be the worst thing. "I need you to do something for me."

Croak sighed and patted her hand where it still clutched at his arm. "Fine. You can kiss me if you want, but I am warning you, one won't be enough. I've been told by many women that my kisses are addictive."

Vas rolled her eyes and groaned. She tugged at him, pulling them away from the soldiers into a secluded spot at the edge of the camp.

"Ah, even better. Prying eyes and all."

Ignoring his comment, Vassori glanced around. "Xoran wanted me to tell Ren he was taking Prince Lerek back to Metilai. During the battle. He didn't want her thinking he'd betrayed her, but couldn't see a way around it. With the way things are right now, he won't be able to search for Sonah."

"He doesn't have to," Croak said as he crossed his arms. "We found her."

Vassori blinked. "You have?"

"Aye. She's at Lethe Monastery. We're going to go get her now. Well, after Ren finds the amulet. Which is somewhere inside Sydney Hall."

Vassori opened her mouth, a thoughtful expression on her face. Croak edged closer. "Anything else, my ravishing tracker?"

"Aye."

Croak frowned at the strange expression on her face. Before he could comment, she continued.

"Tell Terena that Xoran's offered to be her eyes and ears within the palace. And that he hasn't betrayed her, despite having come here and taken the prince."

"Why not tell her yourself?"

Vas stomped her foot. Adorable.

"I can't be the one telling her my brother isn't a traitor just because he took the crown prince! She'll think I've betrayed her as well and kill me. You need to tell her. She won't hurt you."

"I'm sorry, but hurting me is exactly what my sister would do. It's practically written in the sibling handbook. You should know this, having a brother of your own. And she's a god, so I'm ninety percent positive she might hurt me fatally."

"Please, Croak."

Croak dropped his head and closed his eyes. "You should go and get ready to leave. We're meeting at Sydney Hall. I need to find Orry."

"All right but, you'll tell her?"

Croak twisted his lips. "I'll tell her for a kiss."

"How about a punch to the throat?"

"I will go tell her now."

Terena was pacing near the entrance to Sydney Hall when Croak called out for her. She turned and watched as he jogged over with Orry trundling along after him.

"I forgot to tell you something earlier."

Terena rested her hands at her hips as she watched her brother. He pulled at the collar of his cloak, his gaze everywhere but on her. She folded her arms, twisting her lips as two spots of bright red blotched his cheeks.

"I, I... I saw... I saw Xoran, earlier."

Terena stilled. Her smile dropped.

"Go on."

Croak shifted his gaze to his feet and toed the ground with his scuffed boot. "So, he said to tell you he was taking Lerek with him, but it didn't mean he was betraying you. He said he had to, because it would look weird if he didn't. I agree, personally."

Terena closed the distance between them and Croak lifted his chin as if expecting a blow.

"Seems kind of an important detail you... forgot to tell me. You seeing him, and all." Terena said in a deceptively soft tone.

Croak shuddered and held up his hands. "In my defense, there was a *lot* going on. I only remembered because I saw Vassori and you know," Croak snapped his fingers as he smiled wanly at his sister. "It came back to me. I thought it was something you should know, so..."

Terena opened her mouth, and after a beat, nodded. "Weird he wouldn't say that to Vas, though. After all, they came here together."

"So weird."

"Huh."

"And," Croak's voice strangled on a chuckle and cleared his throat. "And, he'll be your eyes and ears inside the White Palace in exchange for you finding the amulet. Which we're doing anyway, so, win-win."

Terena furrowed her brows. "Vassori!"

Croak winced and took a step away as Terena looked around. Vassori came bounding up, breathless, as she looked between Croak and Terena.

"Aye?"

"I need you to ride for Metilai. Find a way to speak with your brother. Tell him I accept his terms and I've sent you as our intermediary. When we're done here and I have Sonah, we're going to Metilai and I want you to update me on everything he's heard or seen. Understand?"

Vas exhaled and nodded. She glanced at Croak who was still looking down at his feet. Terena frowned.

"There's an apothecary south of the palace, near the road leading to the army barracks. You can't miss it. The man's a friend. You can trust him. Give me a week and I'll meet you there."

"Aye, Ren," she mumbled and turned away. She cast a last look at Croak who nodded at her.

"Cassandra!"

Terena grinned when Croak winced for the second time. The seer stood near Rydon and she could tell by the set of his shoulders and the scowl on his face Cassandra was baiting him. Cassandra had told her she liked the big mercenary and teased him whenever she could, but the dumb oaf didn't seem to understand her overtures. Perhaps he needed a more obvious sign.

"Stop flirting with Rydon! I need you a moment."

Laughter rose around them as Cassandra grinned and whirled away from Rydon, swishing her hips in a decidedly exaggerated fashion. Rydon's eyes were riveted on her movements.

"Yes, oh goddess divine?"

Terena twisted her lips. "Tell me again where the amulet is?"

Cassandra's smile fell as her expression turned serious. "It should be in the duke's chambers, inside Sydney Hall. It was there the last time I saw it. In a drawer by the bed. My vision confirmed it's there."

"You were in Duke Ravos's bedchambers?" Croak scoffed.

Cassandra gave him a nasty smile. "The previous duke's, aye."

"Oh gods," Croak said as he put his hand to his mouth and stared as her as if she'd sprouted horns. "Old Duke Ravos? That guy was missing the whole front bottom row of his teeth! And he had a mole the size of the continent on his neck which I'm fairly certain was a twin he'd eaten in the womb. You were sleeping with that guy?"

Terena threw her head back and laughed, even as the seer punched Croak in the arm. He flinched back and whined about it as she yelled at him. Vassori turned to greet Migela, who strolled up and grinned, watching with arms akimbo.

"I didn't mean the old, old duke! You do know Lord Galen is the new duke, aye? I slept with *his* father. *That* duke."

Croak waggled his eyebrows. "Oh, that duke was ravishing. Too bad Emperor Solon had his face melted off."

Cassandra's face grew thunderous and Terena reached out to pull Croak away. Clearly, her brother lacked the survival instincts every other human was born with.

"Enough," Terena said, looking between the two. "So, you were with the former Duke Ravos and saw it in his bedchamber?"

"Aye."

"Great. Galen hasn't been the duke long enough to have changed the furnishings so we'll start there."

"What if Lord Hermes has already claimed the rooms? Should we tell him the amulet—"

"No," Terena shouted, then clamped her mouth shut as she looked around. She held out a hand to Cassandra, who'd been startled by her outburst. Leaning closer, Terena whispered, "I do not want him knowing about it. Not yet. I've told the others to keep quiet about it as well. I'll tell him myself when I'm ready."

Cassandra gave her a dubious look but nodded her assent, regardless.

"And what do we tell him when he sees all of us running around the castle?" Croak asked, still rubbing his arm where Cassandra had punched him.

"That we decided we're staying at Sydney Hall as well."

DARIS WAITED FOR HERMES TO FINISH SPEAKING WITH HIS MEN BEFORE approaching. As the others left to do the god's bidding, Daris looked around to ensure their privacy.

"You look like you could use a friend."

Daris swung his gaze back to Hermes. The god smothered a smile as if he already knew what Daris wanted to discuss.

"May I have word?"

"Aye, of course," Hermes said as he stretched his arms wide. "Come."

He turned and strolled to a table on the left side of the room. The main hall looked as if it had been used to feed the soldiers, because the room was a mess. Dishes still had food on them, as if they'd been interrupted. There were chairs knocked over and water carafes still full in the middle of the trestle tables.

Daris licked his lips. His pulse raced and the way his throat clogged up, he should've taken more time with this idea. And yet, the longer he waited, the greater the chance he might lose her forever.

Bracing himself, Daris pushed away his hesitation and said, "I will swear an oath to you, Hermes. In return, you make me immortal and tell me how to break the soulmate bond."

Daris caught the quick twitch of Hermes's lips before the mask fell over his face, obscuring his emotions.

He was about to open his mouth to speak when someone shuffled into the hall, calling out to Hermes about Terena wanting access to a bedchamber.

"Fine!" Hermes shouted back, the lethal look on his face catching the messenger by surprise. Daris did not recognize the man, assuming him to be someone on Duke Ravos's household staff. The man stumbled back, his mouth opening and closing like a trout out of water. "Tell her she can take the duchess's rooms."

"We don't—"

"Then whatever fucking room is best! Get out!"

Hermes closed his eyes, the fury melting away from his face as if by magic. Daris watched him as he regrouped.

"Great. Swear your oath to me to me now, and I'll make you immortal."

"And tell me how to break the bond."

"No," Hermes said in a low voice.

The strange silver liquid in his eyes swam across his irises, darkening the blue so they looked more like the deepest depths of the ocean.

"I thought—"

"I'll need a little more than your oath," Hermes said in a conversational tone that did not fool Daris. He waited for the god to continue. When he didn't, Daris sighed and asked what more he wanted.

"I, too, have had time to think since our last conversation. To be made immortal," Hermes feigned a shiver and it was all Daris could do to stop himself from rolling his eye. "It is no small thing. In the old days, we'd all have to meet atop Mount Olympus and discuss it in a forum where other gods would have their say. Then we'd all vote—"

"But you made Rydon immortal."

"The Fates marked him as Eudaemon. I was just the messenger."

"So this is not something you can do alone?" Daris scrubbed a hand over the lower part of his face. He swore inwardly. If this was not something Hermes could do, he'd have to find another way.

"That's not what I said," Hermes said, interrupting Daris's thoughts. He looked over at the god with a frown, waiting.

"I can do it alone," he said with a shrug. "But you won't even know it's done because you're still Eudaemon. At least for another what... week. But this is one of those situations where I'll need to give you the gift first, because you won't be able to do what I need you to do without it."

"A dangerous task, then," Daris said with a curt nod. "I will do it."

Hermes laughed, incredulous. "You don't even know what it is yet."

Daris thought about this for a moment. "Does it involve me killing anyone Terena cares about?"

Hermes scowled. "No."

"Betraying her?"

"No."

"Then it doesn't matter."

"You should rethink—"

"Will you do it or not?"

The slow way Hermes smiled made Daris want to scratch his skin. He pushed aside the screaming inside his head warning him this was not a smart move.

As a Spartan, especially as the leader of the Liodari, Daris prided himself on always listening to that voice.

Prudence.

And yet, equally loud, was his heart shouting at him this was the only way to hold on to her.

"I will, Commander. Whenever you're ready."

Squaring his shoulders, Daris settled his hands atop the pommel of his sword.

"I am ready."

CHAPTER 37

COLINAS, RAVOS

The room was as gaudy and overdone as Terena had expected. She'd known the previous Duke Ravos all her life and the vain, materialistic duke was definitely a 'more is more' person. He'd only deigned to speak to her because of her position within the emperor's court. But if you were not of noble blood, you were nothing.

As she searched through the duke's personal chambers, Terena groaned at the amount of stupid shit one man can accumulate.

"Half this stuff is junk," Croak said as he sniffed at something before setting it back down.

Terena laughed at the look of disgust on his face as he glanced around the room.

Cassandra was busy running her hands along a nightstand crusted with emeralds and rubies. It looked like it belonged in the throne room of one of the gandanas, the rulers of old Osta before the fall of the Olympians.

"Did you find something?"

Cassandra shook her head. Hands on her hips, she scowled at the nightstand as if it offended her. "No. When he showed it to me... well, he brought it from another room but hours later, he put it inside this drawer. But it's not there. I thought perhaps there might be a false bottom or something but really, the man was not that clever."

Croak snorted as he tossed another pillow onto the floor. Jumping on the bed, he sighed and stretched out, crossing his arms to cradle the back of his head. "Other than his face, why'd you sleep with him?"

"Croak!"

Orry giggled, exchanging a look with Migela as the mute assassin covered her mouth.

"He's not wrong," Cassandra muttered as she crouched to look beneath the nightstand. Giving up after a minute she pushed a lock of her blonde hair away from her face. "I don't think it's here."

"We've not been looking long," Terena said as she wandered around the perimeter of the room. Pausing in front of a group of vases, she picked up the smallest one, no bigger than her hand, and turned it over.

"Oh, Lady Terena, this wasn't the room I... that is to say, this is the duke's room. I told the other woman to inform you when she was in here earlier, but perhaps she did not relay our conversation. You see, Lord Hermes will be sleeping in here."

Everyone looked over at the newcomer. The man was small, with a thick head of sandy hair that was artfully messy. Like many Heylisians, he wore his hair long to his shoulders, and was clean shaven, although Terena wondered if it was because he might not be able to grow a beard. Terena had forgotten his name.

"Of course he will," Croak said with a chortle while he lounged on the bed.

"Perhaps I can find you another room if the former duchess's rooms—"

"No need," Terena said as she rose from where she'd been looking. "I'm not staying here."

"Who are you again?"

The man colored at Croak's question, earning a chuckle from Cassandra.

"I am Miltos, steward to Duke Ravos."

"Be a dear," Cassandra said as the man wrung his hands. "Have someone bring up a hot bath for Lady Luca. She'll need rose and seneca oils for the water, and if you do not have seneca, lavender will do."

Terena opened her mouth to say she wasn't planning on staying long enough for a bath but one pointed look from Cassandra and she shut her mouth and turned away.

The man, Miltos, shifted his brown eyes between the seer and the others, his hands twisting painfully in front of his long casta, a voluminous robe made of raw silk. It was much too long on him and the front of it was wrinkled, thanks to his constant tugging.

"I will see to it immediately," he said after a long pause while the others went back to ransacking the rooms. It took him a moment longer to leave. As he retreated, Croak threw a pillow after him, to Cassandra's amusement.

A loud roar from somewhere down below echoed up to them. Terena jerked upright, looking around as she narrowed her eyes in concentration. She rubbed at her chest, frowning. The ache was back. She'd had a few blessed hours without it, but it returned with a vengeance of a sudden.

"What the fuck was that?"

Terena flapped a hand at Croak as another roar sounded, fainter this time.

"What's going on?" Cassandra whispered.

"It sounds like someone dying," Orry mumbled.

Terena prowled to the door, her heart palpitating. She leaned out and looked up and down the corridor.

"Maybe it's coming from outside," she said. Terena opened one of the mullioned windows and leaned out.

"No," Cassandra said as she sat back on her heels. Her hands were planted on her thighs, twisting to look up at Terena. "I think it was coming from beneath us."

"Inside the castle?"

Cassandra shrugged. "Somewhere beneath us."

"Helpful as always," Croak groaned, shifting his arms so one of them was now across his eyes. "Have you ladies found it yet? If not, I think I'll break in this bed. How about it, Cas?"

"It's 'Cassandra' to you, and I wouldn't sleep with you if it was the only way to save your sister by doing it." She held out her hand to Terena. "Sorry, Ren."

Terena and Migela exchanged a grin.

"We're wasting our time," Croak muttered.

"He's right," Cassandra sighed as she got to her feet. She cringed and put her hand to her back. "It's not here."

"Fine. Then we leave for Metilai."

"No!" Croak cried out as he shot up from the bed. He stared at Terena with his mouth open. "We get Sonah first!"

"Right," she said. "That first."

Terena held up a hand when it looked as if Cassandra might object. She motioned to the seer with her head and when the woman drew closer, Terena lowered her head and whispered in her ear. "I spoke with Daris. I think I convinced him to break the bond."

Cassandra reared back with a gasp but Terena pulled her back. "Shh! And, because you weren't very reassuring about its success, I asked Hermes to make Daris immortal."

The seer's mouth formed an O.

"Secrets, secrets, are no fun," Croak called out, tossing a pillow their way. "Secrets always hurt someone."

"Child," Orry snorted.

Cassandra crossed her arms, a perplexed look on her face. "Good. Good. That should help. He should be fine now, although I'm not..." She shook her head and stared down at the floor.

"When I concentrate on the commander now, I see nothing but black. That's never happened before."

Terena gripped Cassandra's arm. A low ringing buzzed in her left ear, but she shook her head to clear it. Didn't work. Migela prowled closer, her gaze swiveling between them.

"What could it mean?"

Cassandra cupped her face in her hands and groaned. When she pulled her hands away, she blinked owlishly at Terena. "I don't know. I don't understand. First, my vision about the amulet was wrong, and now this. I'll try again tonight to see if perhaps it's just me. Sometimes when I get fatigued my visions are fuzzy."

"But you just said you've never had this happen to you before. Where you see only black."

"Should we find the commander?" Orry asked. "Just in case?"

"Ugh, no," Croak said with his arm across his face. "If you ladies go hunting for him, he'll get an even bigger head."

"Shut up," Terena groused as she tossed one of the discarded pillows at his face. When he grunted at the contact, she strode out of the room, still rubbing at her chest.

"Let's go."

"Did you hear that noise?"

Rydon caught up with Ren as she descended into the main hall, the others following close behind. Except for Croak. That boy sauntered down the stairs like the wastrels he'd seen in the courts of Decu, his homeland. Those useless twits thought everything started when they arrived, so there was no reason to rush.

"What?"

Rydon matched Terena's determined stride. "The inhuman bellow that sounded earlier?"

"Aye, we heard it," Cassandra said, puffing along behind them. "Do you know what it was?"

"No, I—"

"We didn't find the amulet," Ren interrupted. "We're leaving for Lethe to get Sonah."

"Fantastic," Rydon said as he smacked his fist into his left hand. "Gabriol is still upstairs. I'll go get him and meet you outside."

"No. Wait." Turning, Terena snapped her fingers a few times as she called out Croak's name. "Croak, go get Gabriol. And where is Orry? If he's still upstairs with Migela, bring them with you."

"Right." Croak pivoted and went up the steps just as leisurely as he'd come down them.

"Faster than that, Croak!"

Croak waved his hand over his shoulder without bothering to turn around.

"Where are you going?"

Rydon, Cassandra and Terena stopped dead in their tracks when Hermes and his cadre stormed in. Terena dropped her head back and let out a loud groan.

Spreading her arms she turned to Hermes.

"Lethe."

"Not yet."

"What? Why? I'm going to get Sonah."

Hermes moved aside and Rydon's eyes caught sight of Daris. The commander's bloodshot gaze was fixed at a point over their heads, his face ashen.

Rydon swiveled his head between Daris and Terena. Terena did not look at the commander, either.

Something felt off.

"Send her eudaemon," Hermes said as he turned to walk away.

Terena scoffed and stalked after him. His men flanked him, moving closer to Terena as she stopped in front of the god.

Tipping her head back, she glared at Hermes.

"Well, that's convenient, because he's going as well."

"Daris," Hermes said with a flick of his fingers. Daris moved to his side, his face impassive.

What the fuck was going on with him?

"Go to Lethe with Rydon and bring my niece."

Daris nodded and turned without a glance at Terena.

"What?" Terena opened her mouth as she jerked forward. "You're not—"

"Terena!"

The ground shook when Hermes bellowed her name. Rydon's hand moved to his sword.

This was not good.

Terena's face darkened. When she turned back to Hermes, Rydon's eyes darted between the two. She was unrecognizable. The expression on her face was one he hadn't seen before but did not portend anything good.

"You raise your voice to me like I am a witless child but that cannot be. Because I am not witless, nor am I a child."

Hermes puffed up, the swirling silver liquid in his eyes zinging back and forth like it was possessed.

"You *are* a child, niece. I have lived for millennia. And you *are* witless, if you think you can leave without my permission. Remind me again which circle we're in? Ah, yes, the eighth and final circle. If you fail this time, it's not just you that's fucked."

The cavernous hall became sweltering. Terena's eyes were bright, glowing red, and her hands shook.

Rydon gripped his sword, his eyes wild as he took in everyone's positions.

"What's going on?"

Rydon cursed, swinging around to see Croak coming down the stairs with Gabriol, Orry and Migela. Gabriol immediately unsheathed his sword and Migela did the same with her daggers. The portly cleric clutched some books to his chest with one hand as he frantically batted his hand at Croak to pull him back.

"What's going on," Hermes said in a booming voice, "is your sister is about to learn a very valuable lesson."

Closing the distance, Hermes held out his hand. A metallic sound rang out as his caduceus formed.

Terena snarled, and Rydon's eyes almost popped out of his head when she held out her hands and the Twins materialized. The runes etched on the blades activated and red light pulsed up and down the blades once. Gone was the white light he'd seen several times when she'd used them.

"Put away your swords, niece," Hermes whispered.

Rydon edged closer. Hermes's men did the same.

"Hermes, what the fuck?" Rydon whispered.

The god shook his head, a look of confusion on his face before it melted away into a thunderous expression.

"Put away your staff, *uncle*."

"I will not ask again."

Terena laughed unpleasantly. "You seem to think you have power over me. I may not know as much about being a god, but I *am* one. Nor am I as strong as you, but I am a daughter of Ares. I'm supposed to be here. This is *my* story, old man. Not yours."

There was a brief moment where Rydon thought his heart stopped.

No one moved. Even Croak's gasp was cut off.

Before anyone snapped out of their shock, Hermes backhanded Terena with his caduceus.

Daris roared and leaped at the god, his arm pulled back, aiming his sword at Hermes's neck.

But the sword stopped inches from his skin, and Daris dropped to the ground as if hitting an invisible force.

Two of Hermes's assassins charged at him, hauling Daris up by his arms and holding him captive between them. Even that wasn't enough to break Rydon from the sheer shock immobilizing him.

The god looked horrified for a brief moment, staring at his

caduceus as if he'd never seen it before. The look was gone so fast, Rydon thought his eyes played tricks on him.

Hermes spared a glance at Daris, snarling something Rydon could not hear past the thundering in his ears.

Terena, on the ground, stared up at the god as if seeing him for the first time.

Taking advantage of everyone's stupor, Hermes grabbed Terena by the top of her head, his fingers clamping tight enough to make her wince and cry out. Rydon bolted toward her. One of Hermes's men had a dagger to his throat before he moved two feet.

Hermes crouched, bringing his face within inches of Terena. Croak was shouting like a madman, and when Rydon twisted to look at him, he saw Gabriol and Migela on the ground with more of Hermes's criminals surrounding them.

The fat cleric whimpered on his knees, the books he'd been holding scattered on the floor. Croak was ashen, looking at his sister with wide, haunted eyes as another one of Hermes's undesirables held him by the scruff.

"You think you're indispensable?" Hermes seethed. "I still have your sister. The heir! You forget, *niece*, I am eternal. And you are still fucking MORTAL!"

He raised his hand to strike her again. Gabriol and Croak shouted and Rydon cried out to Terena as the world went black.

CHAPTER 38

Croak dropped to the ground as soon as the asshole holding him let go. Blinking against the void, Croak crawled forward, stretching out a hand to keep him from bumping into anyone else.

Especially Hermes.

Croak had no idea what had just happened, except Hermes had hit his sister and no one had done a thing to stop him.

Someone stepped on his hand and Croak slapped his other hand over his mouth to hold his scream in. There was shuffling and Croak sat up in a crouch. This same darkness reminded him of when they'd first met Vassori. And in Agraboda, when he'd found the Shroud of Faybhen.

Magi had attacked after everything went dark.

Croak stood slowly, his arms outstretched. He heard a low growl and some of the men cried out.

Screams erupted from all sides. Croak dropped back down, covering his head as a body fell over him. He hoped he was going in the direction of the stairs where Orry had been but then he doubled back when his hands slid in something wet on the stone.

Croak sat up when he heard Rydon cry out Terena's name. He shuffled as fast as he could on his knees, keeping his hands up to guard his head. Terena answered and Croak whipped his head in the direction of her voice.

"Ren!"

"Croak!" Her panicked voice sounded like it was coming from everywhere. "Croak, stay where you are. I—"

Her voice cut off abruptly and Croak swore under his breath. Gathering his courage, he sprang up and ran full speed. He smacked into something solid and grunted as he stumbled back. A voice whispered, overlapping and echoing, the sound building with unintelligible words and the howl of dogs.

Dogs?

Croak rubbed at his face and shook his head to clear it. "Ren! Ren where are you?"

Something bubbled in his belly. Croak laid a hand over it. "I know, buddy. We'll get food soon. After this fucking family drama is over with."

As he stepped again, the bubbles became more intense and Croak paused, frowning. His insides fizzed and the sensation was so foreign, Croak smacked his stomach a few times to make it calm down.

Light came back, or rather, the world came back and Croak was no longer in Sydney Hall. He was outside in a courtyard near the stables. Gasping, Croak swung his head and body around, his panting breath squeaking on the inhales.

"What the fuck? What the *fuck?*"

A moment later, Rydon materialized, followed by Gabriol, crouched down low and holding onto a blubbering Orry. They all exchanged a look before Rydon surged forward, his clunky steps looking like the first steps of a baby learning to walk.

"Ren!"

As his voice died away, Ren rounded a corner with stumbling steps. Breathing raggedly, she sobbed when she saw them and ran. Croak and Rydon shot forward to meet her. Throwing her arms around Croak, Terena cried into his neck. He choked back his own sobs as he tightened his arms around her.

"Terena!"

They all startled as Cassandra came careening around the side of the stables with Migela.

The assassin pushed Croak aside and hugged Terena.

Cassandra came up to the women and enfolded them as best she could but she was not as tall as them.

"What the hells happened in there?" Croak asked, swallowing hard and asking again when his voice cracked.

Melanos thundered toward them on his horse, his eyes wild as he leaped off and stalked toward them. Arms out he yelled, "What's happened? The—"

"We need to go! Now!" Cassandra said, pulling Terena toward the stables.

"Wait," Ren said and pushed the seer away. She ran to Rydon with Melanos hot on her heels. "I need you to go to Lethe. Please go. Go get Sonah and meet us in Metilai."

"I'm going with you," Melanos said, his narrowed eyes on Rydon. "Bethana's there with Sonah."

"No!" Croak cried out. "Ren, no! We can't keep fucking splitting up! We need to stay together. Please!"

"It'll be the first place he looks!" Ren shouted, and Croak hung his head, his fingers threaded atop his hair. "Even if they follow him there, it's much easier for Rydon and Sonah to get away than if we were all there. From what just happened, I don't think Hermes will get over my mouthing off to him anytime soon. No, we need to separate to save everyone. Meet us in Metilai. At the—"

"Wait!" Orry's eyes darted around as he found himself the center of attention. His cheeks turned ruddy and he swallowed as he turned to Terena. "If my rooms remained untouched since my departure, it would be the safest place to meet up."

"And if someone else is staying there now?" Croak snorted.

"We're wasting time!" Rydon cried out with a slash of his hand. "Meet us at the Boar's Head Inn on Chivanos. It's a mile or so from the White Palace. The innkeep's a friend."

"Done."

They all scrambled to leave. Croak had never saddled Cerberus faster in his life. He growled when Orry couldn't get his saddle fitted and pushed his friend aside so he could finish the job. Mounted and ready to go, Croak looked back as Rydon started down the path.

"Rydon!" Terena called out, her face streaked with dirt and tears. She wiped at the blood crusted on her nostrils and gave him a wan smile.

"Thank you."

"Thank me when we're all together again," the mercenary said. He nodded at all of them and turned, heading for Lethe Monastery and Sonah.

DARIS STUMBLED FORWARD. THE MEN HAD RELEASED HIM WHEN ALL THE light disappeared, leaving them surrounded by a black void. As soon as he was free, he swung his blade behind him, grinning when he hit someone. He moved away, about to call out for Terena when he heard Croak calling for her.

Swinging around, Daris swore under his breath. He couldn't see a thing, not even his hand in front of him. All around, the room had descended into chaos with men crying out and screams echoing. There were growls and barking coming from all sides, as if a pack of dogs had been let loose in the hall.

He kept his sword up and moved his left hand in an arc. Terena called out to her brother and Daris moved toward her voice. Her voice cut off and his heart stopped.

What just happened? Was Ren hurt?

Before he spiraled further, the dark dissipated and the survivors swung their heads around, looking at each other and at the carnage.

Daris took a halting step forward, his head swiveling wildly when he realized Terena was gone. Hermes let out a roar that shook the ground.

"Where is she? Find her!"

Hermes grabbed a sword from the ground near one of the bodies of his men and ran for the doors. Daris was still trying to figure out what had happened. He took note of the other missing people.

Terena's friends were gone, too.

Daris ran after Hermes. He was still lethargic after Hermes had failed to make him immortal, but he shook it off. Shuddering, he recalled the pain as Hermes's power raced through his flesh. Yet, nothing happened. He felt no different, despite the agony that had seized his organs.

The god had been frustrated, eventually saying it must not have worked because Daris was still eudaemon. Daris didn't know how Hermes had known it hadn't worked. The god had ranted about his powers being weakened. He'd mumbled something about not being himself, of something twisting his thoughts and the fact that he couldn't make Daris's immortality permanent enraged Hermes further.

There was no time to worry about the god's wrath. The look in Hermes's eyes when he'd left the hall just now made Daris run faster.

"Terena!"

Hermes's bellow made the ground tremble even more so outside than when he'd done it earlier. Soldiers, servants, courtiers all scrambled away from Hermes, their cries trailing Daris as he ran to catch up to him.

"The horses are gone, lord."

Daris looked over at the man who'd spoken, seeing the thin little man who'd introduced himself earlier as the steward. He couldn't recall the man's name, but Daris wanted to skewer him for giving Hermes any information endangering Terena further.

"Fuck!" Hermes turned, his eyes landing on Daris. He still had his sword out, and he tightened his hold as the god stalked over. Grabbing the collar of Daris's tunic, Hermes brought Daris uncomfortably close.

"Don't ever do that again. You are mine now."

"It didn't work on me, remember?" Daris spat. "And don't you ever fucking hit her again. God or not, I will come for you."

"Come for me," Hermes sneered, shoving his face nose to nose. "But remember I'm your only chance of breaking your soul bond. Good luck trying to find someone else to help you. It may not have worked now, but only because you're still eudaemon. Once that is done, I will honor my end of the bargain, Commander. I fully expect you to honor yours." He thrust Daris away. "Gather your men. We ride for Lethe. Soros!"

The captain came bounding forward, his lips compressed as he nodded.

"Have Scar stay here to hold Colinas. Give him as many men as he needs. Take the rest to Metilai."

Soros thumped his chest and departed.

"Where did those dogs come from? What happened in there?" Daris asked, striding after Hermes.

"Nothing I cannot work around," Hermes fumed, his aquamarine eyes an inhuman hue with the silver in them swirling around.

"Why don't you port there? If Terena can do it, I assume you can as well."

Hermes screamed and Daris widened his stance, ready for the inevitable quake.

Nothing happened.

"I cannot! She—she *bound* me!"

Daris knew there were many aspects of Terena's powers he had yet to discover. Gods, there were aspects *she* had yet to discover, but he suspected she wasn't strong enough yet to bind Hermes.

Unwilling to antagonize him further, Daris remained silent as Hermes raged. When his men left to do his bidding, Hermes turned and Daris gawped at the change in his expression. The god looked confused, frightened.

Catching Daris's eye, Hermes looked at him, his face white. "I don't know what's happening. I'd never hurt her. I don't—I don't understand..."

A soldier approached, drawing the god's attention.

More of his men arrived and Daris frowned as he watched Hermes speaking. It was as if his brief confusion never happened. The god's fury returned, barking orders at his soldiers as if he hadn't just confessed his remorse and horror over hitting Terena.

While Hermes was occupied, Daris marched toward the stables. Someone had already saddled his horse. Frowning, Daris looked around as Jason, Elias and Trojus rode up with Fane and another Spartan.

"Fane," Daris grunted as the soldier dismounted, his hand to his heart.

"Commander," Fane said with his head bowed.

Daris thumped the former Liodari on the chest. "I'm glad you found us."

"Aye," Fane said with a grim smile. "And not a moment too soon."

"Indeed. We must ride for Lethe Monastery."

"Aye," Jason said with a grin. "I figured we'd be going after her so we readied the horses."

Daris slapped the side of Jason's leg as he passed, thanking him.

As they set off for the monastery, Daris hoped Terena had gone elsewhere.

LETHE MONASTERY, RAVOS

Rydon thanked the monk, Talian, as he and Melanos passed him and entered the small antechamber of Lethe Monastery.

"Lady Sonah and Lady Bethana are in—"

"Let me guess," Rydon said over his shoulder, smiling grimly at Talian as they walked. "In the courtyard?"

Talian smiled, his craggy face brightening as he bowed and turned back, leaving Rydon and Melanos to continue on through the large corridor dividing into three smaller ones. The one on Rydon's left led to the dormitory and Abbot Malis's office, while the one to the right led to prayer rooms, classrooms and other rooms Rydon hadn't bothered to visit.

They continued straight, reaching an arched wooden door with iron rivets and a simple latch handle opening into the courtyard.

Surprised to see many of the monks out and about so late in the day, Rydon's lips curved in a knowing smile as soon as he spotted the likely source of their continued enjoyment of the outdoors. Sonah sat on a stone bench next to Daniel, a beautiful blonde woman beside her, speaking with sweeping arm gestures and animated expressions as the small group of monks sat enraptured by whatever tales she was spinning.

"I knew I'd find you here."

Sonah did a double take when she spotted Rydon and Melanos. Jumping up with a gasp, she flew to Rydon, bouncing up and into his arms as she rested her nose in the crook of his neck. Rydon grinned and spun her once, her squeal of delight causing his cheeks to hurt with how wide he smiled.

"How are you here? No one heard you coming! Is Ren with you?"

"It's just us, Sonah. And we need to leave as quickly as possible." Before he let her go, Rydon squeezed her hard one last time. He glanced at the woman embracing Melanos. After a quick introduction that left Rydon reeling, he recovered as he took in Sonah's radiant smile. "Come. Get your things and—"

"We can't!" Sonah said. She gripped Rydon's forearms and looked over his shoulder. "I'm not alone! You'll never guess what happened to me on the road."

"It's a good thing we have time on our way to Metilai. I definitely need to hear your story, Sonah."

"Wait, what?" Sonah darted forward to grip Rydon's arm. "Why Metilai? Where's Ren?"

"I'll tell you on the way," Rydon said. "Hermes is on his way here and will take you if we do not leave now."

"Bethana and I will meet you at the gates in five."

"Aye, good."

"There's something else," Sonah said as she chewed on a fingernail. "I—"

"Riders at the gate!"

Rydon looked at the man who'd come running with the news.

"Fuck!"

CHAPTER 39

LETHE MONASTERY, RAVOS

"Riders at the gate!"

Sonah jumped as Talian rushed through the courtyard, hands flailing as he hollered the news, presumably to Abbot Malis who stood nearby.

"Can you tell who they are from their colors?"

Talian glanced at Sonah and Rydon before answering the abbot. "Spartans."

Sonah swung around to Rydon. "Spartans?"

"Aye, lady." Talian folded his hands beneath his robes. "But—"

"Fuck," Rydon said as he scrubbed at his face. When he turned to Sonah, his face was an unpleasant red and his eyes flashed. "It's Daris."

"Daris? Daris Antonius? How? What—"

"I've already let him in, lord," Talian interrupted, his harried gaze shifting between all of them. "He'll be here any moment."

"Listen," Rydon said as he tugged on Sonah's hand sharply. "He must be alone, but he's still here for you. Play along and at the earliest opportunity, get yourself to the back exit. You remember where, aye?"

"Aye."

Rydon gave her a brief nod before he ran out of the courtyard with Melanos. Bethana moved closer to Sonah and took hold of her hand.

Sonah pasted on her best smile (she didn't have one) as the door opened and Daris walked through. Spotting her immediately, he flashed a quick smile before his face turned grim. As he neared, his usual stoic mask was firmly in place.

"Daris!"

Daris inclined his head as he stopped a few feet away. He muttered his greetings and gave a deep, formal bow to the abbot.

"It is a pleasure, Abbot."

Abbot Malis smiled warmly at Daris. "You are always welcome, son, as long as you mean no harm to anyone under my protection."

Daris had the good grace to duck his head as he smiled. "I assure you, I am not here with ill intentions. Just a warning, for the lady."

"What warning?"

Daris's eye widened as he looked at Bethana. His brow furrowed as he glanced at Sonah.

Sonah colored. Gesturing to the nymph, she said in a voice reminiscent of a screeching cat, "Daris, this is Bethana."

"Lady," Daris murmured after a long pause.

"I've heard much about you, Commander," Bethana said in her soft, musical voice.

"All good, I hope."

Bethana grinned at Sonah, whose blush took over her whole body. "Of course. If it was otherwise, I wouldn't have believed it. I had the measure of you when we first met."

Daris hesitated, his good eye flicking to Abbot Malis before he turned to look at Sonah. Suppressing a shiver at the black leather patch over his destroyed right eye, Sonah dropped her gaze to his grimy boots.

"May I speak with you? Alone."

The plea in his voice, soft and raspy though it was, made Sonah glance at Bethana, who tightened her grip. Glancing at her, the nymph winked and dropped her hand. She followed the abbot out of the courtyard.

Sonah turned back to the commander. There were a thousand other things she wished to do in that moment, but nowhere on her list was speaking with Daris Antonius after the disastrous way they'd left things the last time she'd seen him.

When they were alone, Sonah fiddled with the hem of her corset, looping her fingers around the strings until she wound them so tight around her forefinger it cut off all sensation.

"Are you still not speaking with me?"

Sonah's gaze snapped up and for a moment words eluded her. What could she say? 'I'm sorry for being so drunk I eavesdropped on a conversation I had no business spreading and ruined your relationship with my sister' seemed appropriate but also very lacking.

"Daris," she started, swallowing past the huge lump of regret in her throat. "I am so sorry." She took a step closer, holding out her hands, palms up. "Really. I can't say it enough. As soon as Ren comes, I'll tell her what an idiot—"

"She's not here?"

The note of suspicion in his voice made her pause. Sonah scrunched her face. "I... no? I thought she'd be coming with you. I told Croak to let her know I'm here. He said he'd tell her himself and when you all were done with the fighting stuff, he'd bring her back. Are they not with you?"

Daris stifled whatever comment he was about to make and turned his head away. Sonah waited. Turning back, Daris brought a hand to his mouth as he considered.

"No. They are not. We had a—Ren had a... disagreement with Hermes. But I don't see how even that would keep her away. I know how much she's missed you."

"Really?" Sonah brightened. "So... you two... talked? Is everything all right between you again?"

Daris scowled and turned his head away. "We did speak, aye. But, no. There's been a... complication."

"Complication?" Sonah frowned. Crossing her arms, she waited for Daris to say more. When it became apparent he wouldn't, Sonah reached out, laying a hand on his chest. "What do you mean, Daris? What's happened?"

"You must be Commander Daris Antonius."

Sonah groaned, clamping her mouth tight as she closed her eyes and counted to five. When she opened them, Leander stood beside her, his muscled arms crossed at his chest. He wore a sleeveless tunic, much as he'd done while they traveled, claiming his blood ran hot because of the whole shifter thing.

"Leander—"

"Aye, I am. And you are...?" Daris asked, his scratchy voice pleasant as he smiled over at Leander. Sonah rolled her eyes when she caught the wink he sent her.

"Daris, this is Leander." She frowned and turned to Leander whose chest looked about three sizes bigger than it had earlier. "I forgot to ask if you have a last name? Sorry, that's weird."

"I am Leander of Gadanar."

"A little far from Osta, aren't you?"

Sonah's head swung back and forth between the two men as they spoke.

Leander shrugged. "It's been many years since I've been."

"What brings you to these parts?"

Raising his chin a notch, Leander narrowed his green eyes. "Found my way into the company of this beautiful lady. What brings *you* to these parts?"

Sonah wanted to melt into the ground. What was he doing? Whatever would possess him to speak like this to the Commander of the Liodari? *The* Liodari!

Thankfully, when Sonah lifted her hotter-than-the-sun red face to Daris, she caught the faint smile on his face.

"I've also found my way to this beautiful lady." Again with the wink to Sonah, which Leander must've caught because he moved closer to her.

"He's my sister's eudeamon," Sonah grumbled, taking a step away.

"Really?"

Sonah nodded.

"Croak told you?"

Looking back at Daris, Sonah nodded. "No, Pytho did. Long story. But Croak said he and the others went looking for a tracker in Ovenno on Hermes's orders and then they found Cassandra in Ermanel, and she's the one that told them, although I haven't met —""Sonah!"

Sonah barely registered the large body that all but tackled her. Solid arms banded around her and lifted her off the ground. Sonah squeaked as Jason swung her around before setting her back on the ground. Her cheeks flamed when he leaned down and kissed her cheek with a loud smack.

Now would be a fantastic time for her to manifest a divine power like invisibility. Between Daris's amused expression, Jason's grinning, beautiful face she'd definitely missed these past months, and Leander's thunderous mien, Sonah felt certain that somewhere in the realm the Fates were laughing.

Stepping back so Jason had more room, Daris grinned at Sonah's red face. The man standing over her shoulder like an enraged gargoyle looked at his lieutenant with murder in his eyes. Fane came up just then and her face lit up momentarily when she spotted him.

After she'd embraced him and the Spartan soldiers who'd ridden with him, Sonah turned back to Jason and blushed.

"Where've you been?" Jason asked, his eyes sparkling as he searched Sonah's face. "We've been all over the continent looking for you! Why'd you leave in the first place?"

Daris could tell by the stunned look on Sonah's face she had no idea what question to answer or who to speak to. The man beside her, Leander, puffed out his chest as if that alone would deter Jason. But Jason had eyes only for Sonah. Daris worried his lieutenant was still enamored of the little goddess.

"We don't have time for that." Daris moved closer to Sonah. With a wary glance at her protector, Leander, Daris frowned. "Hermes is on his way. You need to leave. Now. Tell Bethana—"

"What a coincidence!" Sonah inhaled and smiled genuinely for the first time since he'd arrived. The act she was putting on earlier disappeared and she seemed herself once more. She leaned closer and whisper shouted, "Rydon said the same thing!"

"Rydon's here? Is he alone?"

"Aye. Well, no. He came with Melanos. But he said we needed to hurry because Hermes was on his way here to take me with him. I'm not sure where, he didn't say. But where is Ren?"

"All right," Daris said with a quick look around. The monks had vacated the courtyard, the sun having sunk beyond the roofline, casting their surroundings in long shadows. "Go with him. Don't tell me where. Just go, and I'll tell Hermes you were already gone when we arrived."

"Wait, I'll go with you," Jason said as he flashed her a grin.

"No," Daris said with a shake of his head as Leander too made to protest. "If you leave, how do I explain where you are when Hermes asks? He'll be slower moving with his army but, make no mistake, Hermes will be here soon and you need to be gone."

"Melanos!"

Daris cringed at Sonah's shout. He glanced up in time to see the curled-lip look Leander shot Jason who looked back uncertainly. He was relieved they wouldn't be traveling together.

The god must've been around the corner because he came

bounding into the courtyard with the nymph running behind him. Bethana looked alarmed, but calmed when she saw Sonah was unharmed.

"We need to leave! Daris came to warn us, too."

"Come with us," Melanos said, his expression solemn as he clapped Daris on the shoulder.

"I cannot," he said with a sad smile. Turning to Sonah, he impulsively reached out and hugged her. He turned his head to her ear and whispered, "Tell Ren I'm sorry. And I'll do as she asked."

"What?"

Daris didn't respond as he pulled away and kissed the top of Sonah's head. He closed his eye for a moment before moving back.

"I—"

"Riders! Riders, lord!"

Daniel burst into the courtyard, screaming and flailing his arms as he made his way to them.

"Fuck!"

Everyone turned around as Rydon came running at them, his hand around Sonah's arm before Daris could even open his mouth.

"You traitor," Rydon seethed, eyes spitting fire at Daris. "You brought him right to us."

"I came to warn her," Daris said. "If you take off now, we can stall him."

"There's no time," Leander snarled, yanking Sonah away from Rydon. "Who the fuck are you?"

Rydon glanced at Leander, nonplussed to see him amongst their group.

"Leave your things," Melanos said as he made his way toward the rear exit of the courtyard. Daris frowned.

"Hermes comes!"

"Where are you going?"

"Fuck! We're out of time. Sonah, stay at my side," Rydon said loudly.

"What the fuck is going on?" Jason asked with a sidelong glance at the huffing Leander standing next to him. The young man looked as if he were about to go on a killing spree.

"We were fine until you lot showed up."

Jason scowled at Leander. "Who *are* you?"

"He's the Riverman who kidnapped Sonah," Fane said with a grin.

CHAPTER 40

LETHE MONASTERY, RAVOS

Hermes eyed them all, pacing before them as if deep in thought. Sonah shivered and edged closer to Rydon. Leander was on her right, his solid frame doing nothing to allay the fear coursing through her as she watched the god's thunderous face.

"You have ten minutes to gather your belongings," he said after a very long silence.

Sonah did not move. She glanced at Rydon, who reached over and squeezed her hand.

"Where are we going?" Daris asked. He stood in front of them off to Rydon's left, his stance wide as he regarded Hermes with a calm expression.

Out of all of them, Daris was the only one not bothered by Hermes's tantrums. So far since his arrival, he'd almost pierced Sonah's eardrums twice.

"Metilai," the warrior beside Hermes replied, his voice too loud in the tense quiet. He turned to address Hermes. "I heard her and the seer woman she has with her speaking about their destination."

Sonah caught the scowl Daris hid as he turned and walked back into line with her, Rydon and Leander. He turned to face the god again as he gripped the collar of his breastplate.

"Let me go ahead with my men," he said in a bored tone. "I'll take Rydon and Sonah with us. If we run into her before she gets to Metilai, we can convince her to return with us once she sees Sonah."

Sonah grimaced, shooting a glare at Daris even as Rydon squeezed her hand to the point of pain.

"Why would I want her to return? That's where I want her. In Metilai. Do you not see?" A smile slowly stretched across his face. "You will go ahead," Hermes said with a negligent wave, "but Sonah stays by my side. Take Rydon with you."

"What will you do?" Daris asked, again in a tone that made it seem as if he didn't care either way what the answer would be.

Hermes smiled and it made Sonah's belly flip. Bile climbed up her throat to choke her as she watched the unpleasant way his lips curled.

"I'll be right behind you, marching on the city with my army to destroy everything Emperor Solon built."

Sonah bent over and vomited.

RYDON SWORE AS SONAH BENT OVER, DRY HEAVING AFTER SHE VOIDED everything—barely any food, really. Before he could move to help, Leander had his arm around her waist. The man glared up at Hermes and Rydon moved in front of them to hide his ire from the mercurial god.

"Lord," Rydon said aloud, calling over his shoulder at Hermes. "I beg a few hours rest before we leave. The lady is obviously unwell and cannot go anywhere as she is."

Hermes eyed Sonah, his expression a mix of dismay and disgust. "Clean her up as best you can and then go."

"Lord—"

"Eudaemon," Hermes said in a soft voice that never boded well, "if I have to repeat myself, I think I'll just stab you for the fun of it." He shrugged. "I know you won't die, but it might make me feel better."

Rydon ducked his head, checking his fury behind three deep breaths. "Aye, lord. We will leave anon."

"Good." Hermes turned away, but as Leander rose with Sonah still hunched over and panting softly, he turned to them with a raised finger.

"You." Pointing his finger at Leander, Hermes frowned. "Are you the Riverman who took my niece?"

Leander glowered at the god and Rydon stilled. He gripped Sonah around her bicep while Leander continued to hold her about the waist.

"I am her protector," Leander bit out.

"Oh, but... she already has one of those."

The way Hermes was speaking so casually to Leander made Rydon's neck hairs stand on end.

He tried to shuffle them back, positioning himself in front of Sonah in an effort to further hide Leander from the god's notice, but it was no use. Leander was too stupid to know when to keep his mouth shut and Hermes's ego was too fragile—especially after Terena's defiance—to know when he's being goaded.

Daris moved in a leisurely fashion, stopping in front of their trio as he faced Hermes. Rydon had seen him pull his sword on Hermes when the god had struck Ren, but even he knew he'd only get one mercy from Hermes.

"He's a child, lord," Daris said with a weary sigh. "Enamored of the goddess is all. Let him take care of Sonah and then we'll be on our way."

"Stand."

Daris closed his eye and glanced at Rydon over his shoulder. Unsure what the commander was trying to communicate, but knowing whatever it was, the situation with Hermes was about to get very violent.

Rydon swung his head around to the monks still seated quietly at the trestle tables, their heads together or unabashedly staring at the performance Hermes was subjecting them to. He feared for their safety and wished he'd thought to get them all out of the monastery when Hermes first arrived.

"I said, stand." Hermes's words were clipped, his voice razor sharp as he turned to glare at Leander. To the young man's credit, he stood to his full height, several inches taller than Rydon. He kept his arm around Sonah, but his hand had fallen to the small of her back. Sonah sighed and leaned heavily against Rydon.

Hermes stepped forward, his gaze riveted, watching Leander with such intensity, Rydon brought his hand to his dagger.

Stopping inches away, the god narrowed his unnatural eyes, the silver fluid racing around his irises like a frenzied rat tail.

"You're a shifter," Hermes mused.

"Aye."

"What's a shifter doing in Heylisia's military? Don't they kill your kind?"

"Aye."

Hermes lifted a brow.

Leander sneered. "I went to Metilai with my mother when I was a boy."

Hermes waved his hand lazily for Leander to say more.

"I joined the military when I turned twenty and was assigned to the Rivermen. 21st Regiment."

"You're a...," Hermes paused and sniffed at the air before scrunching his nose in thought. "A wolf."

"Aye."

"How were you not caught?"

"I shift at will."

"Yes," Hermes sighed and looked up at the high ceiling. "I know what shifters are. But something about your story..."

He strolled closer to Leander, stopping within a foot. "...is off."

Rydon's grip on his dagger was painful. The exit to the spring behind the olive grove was right behind him. If Hermes did something, Rydon could easily escape with Sonah.

"You see, I know the royal family in Osta. In fact, they must be the oldest family still in power from when we ruled this realm."

Sonah twisted her head up at Leander, who was as still as stone. His face was just as stoic as he stared hard at Hermes. Rydon feared the god would lose his temper at any moment with this kid. He burned to pull him back or step in, but he moved closer to Sonah instead. If this shifter wanted to stay in their company, protecting Sonah, Rydon had to see if he deserved to.

"I... made a mistake with my niece," Hermes said casually.

Rydon blinked. He felt Sonah flinch, the tension in her frame about to snap.

"It was very out of character. I don't know what is happening but I feel... different lately. Regardless, I have been taken to task so let's move on, shall we?" Hermes added, this time through gritted teeth.

"Lord?"

"I'm feeling magnanimous," Hermes said with a flourish of his hands, ignoring Leander's question. "I was shown mercy, so I will, in turn, show you mercy."

Leander's frown deepened. He flicked a glance at Rydon, who was staring so hard at Leander, it was a wonder the shifter didn't have a burn mark on his cheek. "Mercy, lord?"

"Yes!" The god clapped his hands together and kept them pressed to his lips as he stared at Leander. The shifter kept his stance wide and his body loose, despite his clenched fists.

"You see, normally, I would've killed you as soon as you lied about your mother." Shrugging, Hermes paced away. "But as I said, I was shown mercy today. So, you're welcome."

Leander hesitated. "I... don't understand."

"He's calling you a liar," Rydon snapped. Gods, the boy wasn't bright. Exchanging a look with Sonah, Rydon returned his gaze to Leander. "Speak true, or he'll kill you."

"I have," Leander said with a withering glance back at Rydon.

"You said your mother brought you to Metilai," Hermes purred.

"I did not."

Hermes's response was to crook his eyebrow.

Still, Leander remained silent.

"You try me, boy. By the time you went to Metilai, your mother was long dead."

Leander's face drained of color. Rydon caught the slight twitch of his head, the only sign he gave of his surprise.

"Do you deny it, then? That you lied when you said your mother brought you to Metilai?"

"I did not say that. I never said she brought me."

"Gods," Rydon said before he could stop himself. He braced, waiting for Hermes to rebuke him. Sonah's brow was sweaty. A drop tracked down the side of her face, and he cursed Leander again. It wouldn't be a bad thing if Sonah threw up again. At least then they'd have an excuse to end whatever the fuck this was.

Instead, the god cocked his head as he prodded Leander with his silence.

"I do not know how you know of my mother," Leander started, glancing quickly at Sonah before dropping his gaze to his feet. "But aye, she died before I left for Metilai. I brought my mother's ashes with me when I left Osta. I wasn't going to let that—" Leander cut himself off with a shake of his head. For the first time since Rydon had met him, Leander looked as young as Croak.

The shifter lifted his gaze to Hermes, his posture straight, but not with challenge. To Rydon, he seemed resolved.

"I returned to the land of my father. For a new start. I found purpose in Heylisia. Where my legacy wouldn't follow me. And now I have an even greater purpose." Turning his head, he looked down at Sonah, who gazed back up at him.

"I have made vows to protect her," Leander continued, his voice overly loud in the thick silence of the dining room. "Ones I cannot break. Nor do I wish to."

Rydon watched the interaction between the god and the shifter. He didn't know either well enough to know what they'd do next, but whatever happened, he was ready to spirit Sonah away. He'd throw her over his shoulder if he had to. Rydon knew Daris would assist as best he could, although he worried there was something going on between him and Hermes that wouldn't allow him to hurt the god.

Not for the first time, Rydon wondered how the two had met in the first place.

"Sonah." Hermes looked over at her. Rydon tensed. "Do you vouch for this man?"

"What? Yes? Aye." Sonah frowned and looked between the two. "Aye."

Hermes nodded. He crooked his finger and after a moment's hesitation, Leander followed. The two huddled together. Hermes was whispering something to Leander no one was close enough to hear.

"Be ready to run," Rydon said near Sonah's ear. "Back exit. Melanos and Bethana are already out there."

Sonah nodded.

"Daris. Go fetch Melanos. I don't know why he thinks I do not know he's here." Hermes turned and grinned at everyone in the room. "And that, my dear gentlemen and, of course, my beautiful niece, is the end of tonight's entertainment. But keep an ear out for our next production. I call it, 'The Fall of a Small Man'."

Hermes grinned and clapped his hands before abruptly striding down the center aisle between the tables. Rydon watched him walk away with a few of his men trailing behind.

"What the fuck was all that about?" Daris asked as he came over. Rydon shrugged.

He turned back to Sonah, offering his arm for her to take. As soon as she did, she pitched forward and emptied her stomach.

Sonah paced her room. It may have been a cowardly move on her part, but she did not wish to watch Hermes swan about as if he was the king of the realm. She'd decided during his conversation with Leander that she did not like the god.

A knock sounded at her door. Before Sonah could call out, the door creaked open and she gasped as Bethana snuck inside.

"Wha—"

"Shh," the nymph cautioned, bringing a finger to her lips as she closed the door. Moving quickly, she grasped Sonah's hands. "We have a plan to sneak you out."

"But I can't leave!" Sonah whispered loudly, growling when Bethana shushed her again. "What about Leander? Hermes is acting crazy enough to actually kill him!"

Bethana waved her hand as if it was a ludicrous thought. "He won't. Hermes won't do anything that will push you further away. You and your sister are too important. Listen to me. Rydon is waiting by the spring near the olive grove. Melanos and I spoke and he's going to stay behind with Hermes. I will come with you."

Sonah shook her head even though she wanted to do exactly as Bethana was saying. "I don't know..."

Bethana gripped her hands harder. "Would you rather stay here with Hermes or would you rather go to your sister?"

"What about the others? What about Daris? And Leander! He's—"

"Hermes has your wolf by the short hairs," Bethana sniped and Sonah scrunched her face in confusion. What did that even mean?

"Hermes is trying to control your sister by holding on to you," the nymph continued. She dropped Sonah's hands and strode past her, gathering Sonah's meager belongings.

Before long, Bethana had gathered everything into a bag and shoved it in Sonah's arms. "We need to leave here while Melanos and the commander are distracting Hermes. They will be fine here. Neither of them can die, so I doubt Hermes will exert himself too much in trying."

"He could still hurt them," Sonah mumbled as she followed after Bethana on wooden legs. The nymph opened the door and, after peeking out into the corridor, motioned for Sonah to follow.

They snuck down the hall and the steps leading behind the refectory through the courtyard. Sonah glanced behind her. Before she could turn her head back around, she smacked into Bethana.

"Ow!"

Rubbing at her nose, she glanced up to find the nymph frozen in place, staring up with her mouth opened.

"And where are you two little mice scurrying off to?"

Daris's mood could not sour further. He stood in the wide courtyard beside Melanos, his hand on the pommel of his sword in a hold so tight his hand cramped. Trying to regulate his breathing, he stared out at Sonah's dawning horror.

"You know," Hermes went on with a wag of his finger as he gave Sonah a fiendish grin. "If I didn't know any better, I'd think you were trying to get away from me. But that can't be!"

Hermes spread his arms and looked around at his men, all of

whom were grinning or chuckling at the women as they huddled close together. Bethana tried to move in front of Sonah but the little goddess was having none of it.

"Aye, I was trying to get out of here," Sonah called out, her voice shaking but loud as she lifted her chin. Glaring at the god, she fisted her hands at her sides. "I'm going to find my sister. And you will do nothing to stop me."

A few of the men made sounds of amusement as Hermes's grin turned feral. His eyes darkened. "Oh, little mouse. I think you under-estimate what I will do."

Daris shifted and glanced at Jason. His lieutenant was staring at Sonah with impotent rage. They all knew what was about to happen and none of them could do a thing about it.

Hermes glared at Sonah for a few charged seconds before the young shifter was brought forth. Bloodied and barely able to stand, he was dragged before Hermes by two of his men.

Sonah's face lost all color and she darted forward, screeching Leander's name. Bethana grabbed her arm and held her back as Sonah raged at Hermes, tears streaming as she yelled unintelligible words at the god.

"You did this," Hermes said, his eyes wide as he held up his hands. "I had a feeling you and your friends were planning some-thing foolish and, since I can't kill your eudaemon, the poor shifter drew the short straw."

Sonah glanced over at Jason before looking away quickly. Daris exhaled, grateful Sonah at least had the sense not to bring any scru-tiny on someone else she cared for.

Snatching her arm out of Bethana's grip, Sonah swiped at the tears on her cheeks and set her lips in a sneer. "You are an unbeliev-able coward."

A few gasps sounded around them that were quickly stifled as Hermes's face turned red. But the goddess did not back down.

"No wonder you lost the war."

Dead silence greeted her words which fell heavily in the air around them. Daris's heart thudded wildly, his chest full of pride at the young woman's bravery.

"Watch yourself," Hermes snarled, edging closer to the wolf shifter on the ground. He bent and snatched at Leander's hair and lifted the man's face to Sonah. "Or I will kill him right now."

"What will you use as leverage then, I wonder," Sonah spat, her eyes manic as she glared back at Hermes. She didn't spare a glance at the shifter.

Hermes did not respond and a moment later, Sonah's smile turned wicked.

"You know," Sonah said in a soft voice, although still loud in the stunned silence. "I thought you'd be more powerful. You're a god, thousands of years old and yet... you're threatening me with the death of this boy."

Daris dared a glance at Melanos, who was grinning at Sonah.

Hermes did not reply, but his face betrayed him. Daris looked between the two and noticed a flash of panic before it disappeared from Hermes's face, so fast Daris must've imagined it.

Sonah took a step closer. "You're the only Olympian in this realm," Sonah continued, narrowing her eyes. "You've been here awhile, I think. But chose to stay in the north until Terena found you."

Still, Hermes said nothing, fuming in silence as he glared back at Sonah.

"Even now that you've found us..." She cocked her head, shifting her eyes to the ground. When she looked back up at the god, she frowned. "You're not as powerful as you were before, are you?"

Daris noted the subtle shift in the air around them as Hermes's soldiers looked at one another. Hermes looked as if his eyes were about to burst from his head. Melanos's grin widened.

"That's it, isn't it?" Sonah asked in a voice more thoughtful than inquiring. "You can't use your powers, not like before, am I right?"

"You are killing him with every word out of your mouth, Sonah," Hermes growled.

"Aye," she said, her eyes turning sad. "I believe you. I don't want you to hurt him, so you have me. For now."

Sonah sighed, and for a moment looked older than her years as she glanced behind her at Bethana. When she turned back, her eyes found Daris, and she gave him a tight smile.

"But the others are to leave to help Terena in Metilai," she added.

"No," Hermes ground out, his grip tightening on the shifter.

"Do you know how negotiations work?" Sonah sneered, stepping closer to the god. "At the very least, let Leander go."

Hermes dropped his hold on the shifter, who fell over onto his hands. Sonah moved to his side with a glare at the god.

"I will never forget this," Sonah whispered up at him, and Daris wasn't sure if it was gratitude for Hermes releasing Leander or a promise of retribution to come.

CHAPTER 41

METILAI

The fanfare with which Lerek was greeted upon his return rivaled that of royal weddings. As he'd passed through the gates of the White Palace, a shower of white rose petals rained down on him, catching on his borrowed cloak and on his lap as he gazed up to the stairs where his father stood.

He frowned when he noticed it was not his mother, Empress Adanna, at his side, but rather his second wife, Serephina. Her son, Lerek's half brother, was shifting from foot to foot at her side, trying to grab her hand. Lerek opened his mouth when he caught sight of the bundle in her arms. Serephina watched his progression with a neutral expression.

Lerek dismounted when he reached the courtyard, the crowd roaring at his back. He pulled the edges of the wool cloak around his chest as a strong breeze shook him.

"I wouldn't believe it until I saw you for myself," his father, Emperor Solon, said, his voice shaking. He reached out with trembling hands to grip Lerek by his shoulders. A second later, his father pulled him roughly into an embrace that threatened to choke Lerek.

Thumping his father on the back before pulling away, Lerek's smile did not reach his eyes. His father's eyes were glassy with unshed tears. Lerek couldn't recall ever seeing his father this emotional.

"It is you," he whispered, and pulled him in for another quick embrace. Lerek closed his eyes and allowed it, but stepped away before his father was ready to release him. He glanced at Serephina, then the baby snuggled close to her chest. When he caught her eye again, Serephina tightened her grip on the bundle, giving him her signature nasty glare. He inclined his head as he put his hand over his heart.

"It is, father," he said curtly as he moved past the emperor toward the castle doors. The Imperial Guard posted near the doors stepped aside as he strode forward.

His father hurried to catch up but Lerek didn't slow his steps. He continued beyond the grand entry to the back, where the large circular staircase would take him to the gallery leading to the royal residences.

He was tired and hungry and cold. The pomp and other useless celebrations marking his return would have to wait.

"We need to talk, son," his father called out at his back, the heels of his boots clacking along the marble. Lerek spared him a look over his shoulder and frowned when he saw his uncle, General Peleon, at his father's side.

"We will, Emperor," Lerek responded, his tone short. He didn't miss how his father had called him 'son' in front of the retinue following in their wake. Lerek could count on one hand the amount of times his father had addressed him as such.

"But I am tired after a long journey and wish to rest first," he added, his only concession a brief smile before turning down the corridor leading to his rooms.

Lerek's steps faltered as he neared the double doors, recalling the last time he'd strode through them. He'd been excited to see his twin brother, Isher, after months apart.

Excited to enact the plans he'd made to marry Terena and leave Isher behind to stand as his double. How naive and selfish to think of himself over his own brother.

And now Isher was gone.

"Prince Lerek! A moment, please."

Lerek glanced over his shoulder at his father's steward, Salorus, huffing his way toward him, his face red and sweaty. "What is it?"

"Your Highness," he panted, closing his eyes a moment as he fought for air. "My apologies, but your rooms are... at the other end of the hall. Please, follow me."

Lerek frowned as he turned to the steward. The man had a wan smile on his face as he motioned for Lerek to follow.

Glancing at Xoran, he arched an eyebrow. The Captain of the Imperial Guard came stalking to his side, his face and garments as dirty as Lerek's.

The man had found him in the midst of all the chaos in Colinas. As Lerek looked over at Terena fighting like a demon—well, like her father, Ares—the Heylisian soldiers with Xoran had surrounded him, ensuring his safe escape from the fighting. Before Lerek could protest, or at the very least speak with Terena one last time, Xoran had him astride a horse and they were tearing away from the battle-field and the city.

"I know where my rooms, are, Salorus. And they are this—"

"I apologize for the confusion, Your Highness, but your father... that is to say, when you were—oh bother." The man groaned and wiped his forehead. "Your brother, Prince Adonis, is the crown prince. After—after your death..."

Lerek blanched. His eyes darted to Xoran who gave him a quick nod. Growling, Lerek stalked toward the steward, waving his hand. "Fine. Where are my new quarters?"

"This way, Your Highness," the man mumbled as he quickened his steps, his robes fluttering at his feet. Salorus turned right and walked toward a set of double doors near the end. Lerek snorted and shook his head.

Of course.

Not only had Adonis taken over his title and his rooms, but now Lerek had to make do with his much smaller accommodations.

Dismissing the steward with a snap of his fingers, Lerek stalked inside.

"Xoran!"

"Aye, Prince," Xoran muttered. He looked dead on his feet, but stood straight and tall as he focused on a spot over Lerek's shoulder.

"I want a word with you," Lerek said as he strode through the antechamber into the dining area. The clack of Xoran's boot heels told Lerek the soldier followed; but, of course he would.

Lerek quickly divested himself of his cloak and tunic, tossing both on the ground as he made his way to the bathing chamber. There were servants galore to prepare his bath, but Lerek wanted this time alone with Xoran before his father and the others thought it acceptable to intrude.

"You're working with Terena, are you not?"

Xoran, to his credit, did not betray his thoughts. His face remained carefully blank as he shifted his narrowed brown eyes to Lerek.

"Highness?"

"Don't," Lerek said, holding up a hand. He turned away, hands on his hips. When he looked over at Xoran, the man had his eyes trained once again at a spot beyond Lerek.

"I know you're working with her. Do not lie to me. And so the next question becomes: why am I not confronting you in front of my father?"

Lerek was impressed with Xoran's stoicism. Of course, the man would have learned to keep his thoughts and feelings in check around a mercurial egomaniac like Emperor Solon.

"Fine," Lerek muttered, waving a hand. "This is not a trap. I need your help. I am not trying to trick you in any way. If I wanted you executed as a traitor, I could've spoken with my father and you'd already be in the dungeons. Listen for a moment, and consider what

I am about to propose, and I swear I will let you leave with your secret intact. Agreed?"

Xoran stared at him with eyes barely dilated, unnerving in their cool regard.

Lerek sighed. "I'll take that as assent. Look, my father is up to something. He's been up to something before I... well, before. I know you know this, but I suspect it has something to do with his obsessive hatred of the gods."

Lerek stabbed a hand through his hair, grunting and wincing as his fingers stuck on some matted locks. "This is where you come in. I need two things from you. First, send a message to Ren, asking her—no, demanding her—to come to Metilai. I wish to receive her in private. While you're awaiting her response, stay as close as possible to my father without rousing suspicion. I want to know everything he's doing. Who he speaks with—especially if he's meeting with anyone from the cleric's guild. Any conversation he has with High Cleric Christos, I want to know about it."

Lerek stared at Xoran, waiting for the man to say something. When he didn't, Lerek turned and swiped the stack of towels sitting on a stool near the tub.

"Fuck! Why can't anyone just fucking listen to me? Am I that big of a joke? Look at stupid fucking Prince Lerek, everyone! No brains, no balls, and—and..." Lerek kicked at the towels now littering the marble floor with such viciousness, one flew up and hit Xoran in the legs.

"And no fucking brother! Because I came up with the most ridiculous plan in the history of planning and got my twin killed!"

Lerek dropped onto the edge of the tub, cradling his head in his shaking hands. His heart thrashed in his chest, and for a horrible moment, Lerek's eyes and nose stung from holding back tears.

Quiet settled around him and he closed his eyes, swallowing past the lump in his throat.

The shuffling sound of hesitant steps made him jerk his head up. He frowned as Xoran opened and closed his mouth several times.

"Go ahead," Lerek said with a sigh. Dropping his head back, he closed his eyes. His lips wobbled when he tried to smile. "Say whatever you wish to say. Whatever it is will not be worse than what I've already said."

A shadow caught his eye when he brought his head back upright and he opened his eyes to see Xoran's dark eyes watching him with something resembling cautious optimism.

Lerek knew that look. He'd seen it many times in the mirror right before his father tore him down for whatever grand idea he'd come up with that his father had laughed at.

"What, Xoran?"

Xoran's scarred hand lifted to rest over the pommel of his sword. He inclined his head.

"I will do as you ask."

Someone was living in Orry's old room.

"I told you!" Croak hissed, smacking Orry in the back of the head. As his friend grumbled and hit back, Croak looked up at the feeble light from the second-story window.

"Fine. You were right."

"No, no." Croak tsked and wagged his finger at Orry. "Say it the way I told you."

Orry dropped his head back and groaned. Croak whisper shouted for him to be quiet.

With his fingers digging into his eyeballs, Orry swore. "You were right, oh handsome one. There is no smarter or," Orry swallowed, "virile man alive, and I should've known better than to contradict someone of your superior intellect."

"Better."

"Now what?"

"Let's head to the apothecary. Ren should be there by now."

"Fine. But we should—"

"What have we here, boys?"

Croak froze. Low chuckles and the sound of metal clanging came from behind them. Turning slowly, both Croak and Orry looked wide-eyed at the trio of guards leering at them. One had his sword out, idly tapping the blade against the side of his leg as he grinned maliciously at them.

"Sorry, Your... Watchfulness," Croak said with a smile. "We are weary travelers who seem to have gotten lost. We'll just go and find our big group of very large and dangerous friends and leave you to your... City Watching."

Croak tugged on Orry's sleeve and made to leave when one of the guards shoved him in the shoulder. Stumbling back, Croak sighed and closed his eyes for a beat.

"Not until you tell me what you're doing here. This is the clerics' residences."

"Oh!" Croak said, slapping his forehead as he looked at Orry in feigned shock. "You told me this was the brothel with the contortionist from Boha!" Turning to the three guards, Croak put a hand to his heart and graced them with a sheepish smile. "Sorry, boys— guards!—apologies. My friend obviously doesn't know the difference between a whorehouse and a cleric's asshole. Excuse us."

"I wish I could," said the one with his sword out. His apologetic smile was about as genuine as the shroud they'd given Duke Aurora all those months ago. "But you see, we've been looking for Ormano Peredor," he brought up his sword to point at Orry. Like an idiot, Orry raised his hands and squeaked. "So if he's Ormano Peredor, the cleric, then you must be..."

Before Croak could protest, his hands were grabbed by a guard who'd surreptitiously snuck up behind him. He'd been so worried about what Orry would do, he hadn't seen the guard at all until it was too late.

"I don't know who this 'Ormano Peredor' is," Croak called out as the guard bound his hands. Another did the same to Orry who looked at him in terror. "If you knew us at all, you'd laugh at the idea that I'd ever be friends with a cleric."

Orry's expression became mulish, and Croak closed his eyes as he bit off a curse.

"Is that right?" The leader of this little group of assholes tapped his lip as if in thought. "Then why is this fat fuck wearing the robes of a cleric?"

"Hey!" Croak shouted, bursting forward, his face heating and his heart pounding murderously. "Only I get to call him fat, you fucking waste of sperm!"

"Croak!"

Croak shut his eyes again as the guards broke out in surprised laughter.

"Croak? As in Croak Luca?" The ringleader cackled like a loon. "Oh, this is a good day, boys."

As they pushed Croak and Orry out of the alley, their laughter rang in Croak's ears, making his blood boil.

Orry nudged him and smiled wanly at him. "Sorry, Croak."

Croak shook his head. "Not yet, Orry. But I have a feeling we're going to be."

Terena walked out of the Boar's Head Inn with Gabriol, Cassandra, and Migela, heading for the apothecary.

When Croak was four, he'd fallen into a patch of rattleberries and almost died. Her mother had a basic knowledge of medicinal herbs but nothing that would save her son. Lorence, their father, had taken Croak to an apothecary named Neokles, on the advice of Empress

Adanna. She used the apothecary's services, despite his being a disgraced cleric.

After saving Croak's life, he'd become a regular fixture at family meals, teaching her mother more about herbs, to the point she became his assistant.

"I'm worried about Croak and Orry," Terena grumbled as they walked. "They should've been back here by now."

"Must have stopped at a brothel on the way," Gabriol snorted.

"If they're not at the inn by the time we return from the apothecary, we'll go looking."

They'd been in Metilai close to a week now, and they were finally to meet up with Vassori.

The tiny shop was wedged between a cobbler and an abandoned tea room. It was in a less populated part of the city, which suited them perfectly.

As soon as they walked inside, Terena closed her eyes and breathed in the scents of the cozy shop. Thyme, elerian, lavender, summer wart and rosemary were the ones she could pick out as they walked to the small counter. It was filled with canisters of different herbs and balms, little vials of red, blue, green, dark purple, and clear liquids, some stoppered with corks and others with melted wax over the cork. Terena knew from experience the waxed vials held poisons.

"Ah! Come to rob me blind, have you? Go on, then, take what you want. Too old to bother."

Terena grinned at the feeble voice as Neokles walked out of the doorway to his sparse bedroom in the back. He walked with a very pronounced hunch, the knotty cane he held thudding with every other step. When he saw who had entered, he managed a wicked smile.

"Well, well. So this is what I have to do to get you to come out and see old Neokles, eh? Agree to let the Captain of the Imperial Guard have a secret meeting in my shop?"

Terena shot a wink at Gabriol who stood with his thumbs tucked into his belt as he smiled at the old man.

Kissing him on his balding head, Terena went on Neokles's other side and tucked her hand into the crook of his elbow.

"I would've come sooner, old man, if I'd known how much you've missed me."

"Of course, I missed you. Haven't seen you in at least a year."

"I've been... busy."

"Aye, busy." He turned to her when they reached the counter and he'd sat on the little stool behind it with a groan. "I suspect you've had to be careful, considering the emperor tried to kill you once already."

"More than once," Gabriol said.

"Right," Neokles sighed.

"So." Terena crossed her arms. "You said Xoran wanted to hold a meeting here. I think we're the ones he's meeting with, if it is for today. We came to meet with his sister, actually."

"Didn't mention a sister. Said he'd be here at ten bells."

"So we have an hour to kill," Migela signed as she leaned against the bookshelves to the left of the door.

"I'll go look for the boys," Gabriol said as he walked to the door. "I'll either come back this way or meet you at the inn."

"Thanks, Gabe," Terena called out as he closed the door behind him.

"You have a book by Circe, the priestess," Cassandra commented, looking down at the tome in her hands. Flipping it over, she squinted to read the text. It looked to be bound in red leather with faded black lettering on the front.

"That is not just any book," Neokles said. His face became animated as he smiled at Cassandra. "You are holding Circe's grimoire."

"You're joking," Cassandra said sharply as she swung her head around to regard the herbalist.

"Not when it comes to witches," the old man said with a wink.

"Do you know what this means?" Cassandra asked Terena. She

shrugged as she watched the seer turn the book over and hug it to her chest.

"It's a book of her spells, incantations, creating amulets—"

"And how to *find* amulets." She stepped closer to Terena, turning the book in her hand as she motioned with it. "This book will help us find the Amulet of Kaïra."

"The Amulet of Kaïra," Neokles said in a voice filled with horror. "No, you must not! No!"

He made to stand, groaning the entire way up. Terena went to his side to help him, but he waved her away as he glowered at Cassandra.

"Give me that!"

Cassandra pulled the book away, holding it up high behind her. "We need this to find the amulet! The emperor is looking for it, too, and I think you'll agree, Terena finding it is the lesser of two evils."

"The gods hid it for a reason!" Neokles hissed as he reached up to try to take it from her. Instead, Terena reached around him and plucked the book from Cassandra's hand.

"And yet the key to finding it sits in your dusty old shop?"

Flipping through it, Terena glanced up at him. "Why do you have this? I would've thought you, a good citizen of the empire, would've handed this over to the clerics or the City Watch to have it burned."

"I would never! That book was a gift from—"

Terena glanced up at Neokles when he stopped speaking. Curiously, Cassandra chuckled as the old man stared down at the wood floor with a bemused expression.

"What is it?"

"What?" The old man looked up at her, befuddled.

"You were saying something." Terena held the book up. "You said this was a gift from...?"

"Aye. That was a gift from—"

Again, Neokles stopped abruptly. Terena frowned and glanced at Cassandra. The seer stared at the old man with a knowing smile.

"Are you going to tell me the secret, too?"

Startled, Cassandra swung her gaze to Terena. "What?"

Terena narrowed her eyes, using the book to point at Cassandra and Neokles, who seemed very interested in his nails.

"You two are hiding something. What's going on?"

Cassandra shook her head and Neokles held his hands up as if he was not to blame.

"She told me I shouldn't say."

"Who?"

Neokles opened his mouth to answer when the door burst open. Gabriol took two steps inside, his eyes wide and his braided locks disheveled.

Terena straightened as he caught her eye. Before he could speak, Xoran and Vassori came in behind him.

"We've got trouble," Gabriol said, his expression cold.

"Your brother has been arrested," Xoran nodded. "He and the cleric were just brought before the emperor."

CHAPTER 42

METILAI

X oran smuggled them inside the palace with Lerek's help. Terena was surprised to learn Lerek had approached Xoran to spy on his father, making keeping the captain's promise to Terena easy.

Her mind barely registered the fact when Xoran first arrived at Neokles's shop. Terena's thoughts were instead occupied with the news of her brother's and Orry's arrests.

Pacing the small pantry, Terena grumbled an apology when she accidentally stepped on Vassori, who grabbed onto Ren's arm so she wouldn't trip. The room was stuffy but much larger than many of the rooms they'd stayed in over the past year.

"We're sitting ducks," Gabriol snapped, cracking his neck. He leaned against a wall to the right of the door.

Terena sighed and planted herself beside him. Across from her, Cassandra huddled close to Migela, who was signing something to the seer. Terena frowned when she caught the end of their conversation.

"No," Terena said with a shake of her head. "You're staying here,

or somewhere safer where only Xoran or Lerek know where you are."
She turned her attention to Cassandra. "If you can try to... do whatever you do to see where the amulet is, do it now. If it doesn't work
or we're interrupted, wait until Xoran takes you somewhere safer.
And you," she pointed a finger at Migela, who stared back at her
with a nod. "I want you to stay at her side. Do not leave and do not
let her leave. Anywhere you go, she goes. When we're out of here,
we'll find the amulet and use to it help us against Hermes if he tries
anything."

"I doubt he'll try to hurt you again," Vassori said. "But he will use
whatever means necessary to get you on his side once more."

"That's never going to happen," Terena mumbled, pushing away
from the shelves at her back.

"It will," Vassori said with a sympathetic smile. "It's inevitable.
You'll need him. For what's to come."

Terena looked at the tracker. She'd told Vassori what happened
before leaving Ravos. Vassori hadn't seemed surprised Hermes had
hit her, nor about what happened after, which the tracker called his
'punishment'. Terena had disregarded it at the time, but wondered if
the tracker knew more than she was letting on.

"You know," Terena said as she crossed her arms. "This isn't the
first time you've said some cryptic shit. If you're going to stay part of
this team, Vas, you need to start talking. Why was Hermes looking
for you in the first place?"

Vassori's gaze darkened. "I am a cypher."

Gabriol pushed away from the wall to face her. "We know that
already."

"What did you mean about Hermes being punished? Who
punished him? What did he do? And how do you know what's to
come? Are you also a seer like this one?" Terena nodded over in
Cassandra's direction but her eyes remained locked on Vassori.

Vas shrugged. "I am no seer. But I am bound to someone.
Someone like you. But more powerful. Much more. I cannot say
more or I'll be censored. But I know who punished Hermes and I

know why. Someday, I'll be free to say more, but I am not now. Trust me when I say, it is all for you. You are all that matters right now."

Terena smirked. "Me? What about Sonah?"

"Her time will come."

"And in the meantime?"

Vas opened her mouth to answer when two quick knocks sounded on the door. Gabriol straightened. Two more quick knocks after a pause and the door opened enough to allow Xoran to squeeze in.

"What news?" Terena asked before Xoran closed the door. The man looked at them all, his usual cocky sneer and insults gone as he studied Terena. His hair was unusually disheveled and his hand shook as he brought it up to his mouth.

"It's not good." His gaze drifted over all of them before he nodded at Terena. "Lerek asked me to bring you to his chambers. You are to wear this."

He produced a long black cloak and bronze helm in the style of the City Watch. Terena took the items from him, handing the helm to Gabriol while she fastened the cloak.

"What about Gabriol? Or Vas?"

Xoran shook his head. He exchanged a look with his sister Terena couldn't decipher.

"Lerek said only you. I've found a place for your friends to lie low until we've a plan in place."

"No," Terena said. "Take these two there now. I'll find more of these for your sister and Gabe."

"You don't understand," Xoran hissed as he took a step toward her. His momentum was halted as Gabriol slammed his hand on Xoran's chest.

The captain gave Terena and Gabriol an exasperated look. "I'm trying to help you, Luca. We can hide *you*, but any more and we're inviting trouble. The city is crawling with soldiers right now. The emperor is hosting a special feast two nights from now and the royals have already started arriving. He's even extended a truce to the Dukes Aurora and Tursk.

"Your decisive win at Colinas has already reached the ears of the visiting royals and dignitaries. The emperor and General Peleon are getting hammered with questions about their safety with you and Hermes running around. Stories have already reached Emperor Solon about the army at your back. His response was to triple the guard within the palace and Sergeant Ironia has recruited two hundred more men into the City Watch since I've arrived back in Metilai."

He sighed and held up a hand when Terena was about to respond. "Lerek has something planned, but he only wants to speak with you. Vas and Gabriol need to stay. For now."

"Fuck that!" Vassori said at the same time Terena voiced her objection.

"I'm not leaving them behind! Vas and Gabe come with or I am razing this place to the fucking ground right now."

Xoran clamped his mouth shut and glared at his sister. After a moment of tension so thick Terena wanted to scream, Xoran nodded curtly and opened the door.

"You two stay here," he whispered to Migela and Cassandra. Xoran looked at his sister and motioned with his head. She followed him out of the room, with Gabriol at her heels.

Before leaving the room, Terena turned to Migela. "Wait for Xoran. I'll find you when I can."

Cassandra impulsively reached out, grabbing Terena's hand before she could leave.

Her face was pale, and she chewed on her bottom lip as she raised fearful eyes to Terena.

"Do not kill the emperor," Cassandra said hurriedly. "Whatever happens. I've seen it, Ren. Do not kill him. He'll provoke you. Don't fall for it."

Terena frowned. "I'm only going to see Lerek. I don't plan on killing Solon."

Cass's chin quivered and her eyes turned blurry. "He doesn't know what he'll unleash. He thinks he's clever, but he's not the one in control. Save your wrath, Ren. Do not kill him."

Terena stopped herself from rolling her eyes when she caught the desperation in the seer's expression.

"Have you seen something?"

Cassandra loosed a shaky sigh.

"I've seen it all, Ren. Gods help us."

THE LONGER HE WAITED, THE MORE LEREK HATED HIS IDEA. AND HONESTLY, after the disastrous way his idea to run off and marry Terena had turned out, he worried this might be another one of those outcomes.

Lerek strode for the door, ready to find Xoran and call a halt to everything, when a single loud thump of the door sounded.

Xoran called out to enter and Lerek rushed forward, grabbing the handle and swinging the door wide.

"Quick," Lerek muttered as he stepped aside. He nodded as Xoran passed, his eyes immediately moving to the vision behind him. It took him a moment to realize she was not alone. One of the mercenaries from the camp and another woman came in with her. Terena closed the door behind her and smiled grimly at Lerek.

The mercenary, a large beast of a man with long ashen hair braided in the style of the Roisons, glared over at him as he crossed his thick arms. The steel blue of his eyes promised pain and punishment, neither of which suited Lerek.

"These aren't your rooms," Ren said, looking around the antechamber. "What happened? Solon gave them away already?"

"You've heard?" Lerek scoffed as he shifted his attention back to his love.

"Heard what?"

"About my brother? Adonis, my half-brother."

Terena frowned and the way her nose scrunched made his heart stutter. He looked away.

"What about him?"

"Father had him officially announced as his successor. Only a month ago, but... He occupies the crown prince's chambers now."

"You're the crown prince," Terena said with a tilt of her head. Her hair flopped down her shoulder to swing gently. The way the light caught—

"Lerek?"

"What? Aye, I am, but not technically. Father arranged for a feast on Helios, two days from now, to reinstate me as crown prince and heir to the throne. He's invited the royals and other dignitaries, including several from beyond the Black Sea."

"Congratulations."

"Highness," Xoran stepped in, looking between Lerek and Terena. "I must return to get her friends safely secured. I'll meet you in the throne room."

Before he left, Xoran turned back. "There's an empty guest chamber in the Diamond Tower. One floor above the main gallery. It hasn't been assigned to anyone arriving for the feast, so I'll take your friends there. Do you know—"

"I know this castle like the back of my hand," Ren said before he finished speaking. She never moved her eyes away from Lerek while she spoke, but looked at Xoran when she finished.

Ren and Xoran exchanged a look. Lerek's brows drew down as his captain closed the door softly behind him.

Turning to Ren, Lerek opened his mouth only to find she'd wandered further into the rooms, moving into the small dining room with its elegantly appointed crystal centerpieces and gleaming cherry Desseron chairs. One of those chairs could feed the orphanage of St. Adonis for a year.

No matter how many times Lerek complained about the excess, his father turned a blind and surly eye.

And this was only the youngest prince's former rooms.

"It feels strange being back."

Lerek jolted at Terena's words. She'd spoken softly, running her hand along the backs of the chairs. The other two remained in the antechamber.

Turning, Terena strolled into the main room, the plush seating strategically set. A large fire crackled in the hearth off to the right.

"Aye," Lerek answered, clasping his hands behind his back as he followed her into the other room.

He watched as she gazed around at the furnishings and art on the walls. Pausing to look at a marble bust of his father, she tossed a wink at him over her shoulder.

"Was your father elated? His favorite son back from the dead."

"Don't..." Lerek shook his head. "Don't say that."

"What?" Terena quirked an eyebrow at him as her lips parted. "He wasn't happy to see you?"

"Of course he was," Lerek grumbled, mirroring her movements. He stopped when she did, crossing his arms over his chest.

"How's my brother?"

Lerek stiffened. He knew Ren well enough to know when her voice went all soft and sweet, it wasn't a good thing.

"He's in the dungeons still. I'm working on something to get him out but I wanted to tell you about it first. Because I need you to play a part."

"Distraction?"

"Aye."

Terena stared back at him before moving away, her eyes roving about the room once more. Casually, she glanced at him over her shoulder.

Lerek cleared his throat. "As I said, my father is hosting the succession dinner in two days' time. I need you to blend in with the City Watch—don't worry, I'll have Xoran supply you with the rest of

THE HEIR OF WAR RISES

the uniform—and then make your surprise appearance. You'll confront my father, keeping him and his Guard busy while I slip out and free your brother."

"And Orry."

Lerek hesitated.

Shit. He'd known she was going to bring it up, but still he'd shoved it away, hoping she'd just agree to the plan and they could deal with their friend later.

Swallowing, Lerek lifted his head. "High Cleric Christos has Orry."

When Ren's head swiveled around, he held up his hands to forestall her. "Look. It happened before I even heard about it. Christos went directly to my father and Orry was transferred within an hour."

"Transferred? Transferred where?"

"He's at Thanoras House."

Lerek waited for her reaction. Thanoras House was the cleric college, where acolytes and scholars go to become clerics or priests. Orry matriculated at the House years ago and Lerek hoped it would assuage her anger, at least.

"He has plans for him," Terena said under her breath, but he caught it as she neared him.

"Aye, knowing Christos, of course he does. But at least he's safe."

Ren gave him a doubtful glance before turning away.

"So. I go in and, all by my lonesome, I distract your father with all the royals and dignitaries in attendance."

"Not to mention the Imperial Guard and City Watch."

Lerek frowned as he shot a glance at the behemoth mercenary. The blank stare the man looked back at him with made Lerek shudder.

"Aye, thank you Gabe."

"Something tells me you won't have a problem with them," Lerek muttered.

The woman snorted and Ren flashed her a grin.

"Orry is still a problem." Ren shook her head as she looked at the ground in thought. "We'll just have to get him out after I deal with your father."

"Ren," Lerek started, then cleared his throat. "I know this isn't the time—"

"No," Ren said as she pivoted. "It's not. Get me the uniform and I'll do it. I'll be the distraction. Work with Xoran on the details of your end. But they include Vassori and Gabriol," she said with a wave of her hand at her friends.

Taken aback by how short she was with him, Lerek simply stared back at her. When she tilted her head expectantly, all he could do was nod.

"Good," she chirped, striding past him to the door.

"And, Lerek?"

Lerek looked over at her. She seemed like a stranger to him. Pain stabbed through his chest, as if his heart was shriveling. It was all he could do not to bring his hand up to rub the hurt away.

"Get him out alive. If anything happens to my brother, I'll kill you."

CHAPTER 43

METILAI

Croak leaned his head back, the damp from the stone not even registering.

Closing his eyes, he tried to slow his breathing. They'd returned him to his cell even more broken than when he'd first arrived, but he thought that owed more to the fact they hadn't sent a physician in this time. He knew his right arm was broken and he was fairly certain his right knee was shattered. So many breaks and sores, he was a giant throbbing heartbeat.

Except for the parts he could no longer feel.

They'd taken Orry shortly after they'd been captured. Croak had cried when he'd found out. He'd been unconscious at the time and when he'd come to, Orry was gone.

Groaning, Croak coughed weakly and shifted to sit up more. He was so tired, he kept slipping from the wall. The last time that happened, he'd smacked his already bruised jaw against the stone floor and lost two teeth.

"Croak."

Croak blinked. He turned his head as much as he could manage.

Xoran, Captain of the Imperial Guard, stood looking at him. Hands tucked into his sword belt, he sauntered closer to the bars.

"Come to finish me off at last?" Croak joked.

The captain remained silent, his gaze fixed on Croak. Croak stared back, a darkness settling within his chest, and he knew. From the slowly forming smile, Xoran's mask fell off completely. The dread slowly seeping into his heart squeezed the organ so hard Croak whimpered.

"I knew it," Croak whispered. A tear fell onto his cheek and he grimaced. Frustrated his body would betray him at the moment he most needed to appear unbothered.

"You know," the captain said at last, his scarred hands gripping the bars as he looked down at Croak. "I always liked your father. I did not want to kill him, but she said I must. It was the only way to take his place. That is the only thing I regret about all that's come to pass."

Croak did not think it was possible for him to feel even more wretched than he did in that moment, but Xoran proved him wrong. He stared in horror at the villainous shit who'd just confessed to his father's murder.

"You vile, miserable snake," Croak murmured, his voice cracking. "I knew we shouldn't have trusted you. I told her you'd show your true colors eventually."

"If only they'd listened to you," Xoran said, his voice unnaturally empty.

"Aye," Croak sighed. He closed his eyes and let the tears fall.

THANORAS HOUSE WAS THE LAST PLACE ORRY EVER THOUGHT HE'D END UP.

Again.

It was a nightmare while he'd been attending as a student, let alone a prisoner.

Sighing, Orry leaned his head back against the stone wall of his meager room. He'd lived in a room exactly like this while attending the cleric's college five years ago, and it didn't look like they'd changed anything. The walls still smelled of mildew, the curtains were paper thin and the bed covers had stains of unknown origins.

One day back and already Orry regretted his life choices. He closed his eyes against the sudden sting of tears as he thought on how angry Terena must be with him and Croak for getting into this situation.

So far, High Cleric Christos had not visited, although Orry knew he was here under the cleric's orders. He'd had no interactions with anyone other than whoever delivered his food and picked up his shit bucket. The door was locked from the outside. As hard as he tried to stay awake to catch whoever entered his room, Orry always jolted awake to find himself alone with a new bucket and a tray of food.

The door opened, jarring Orry out of his miserable thoughts and he quickly jumped to his feet. Heat flashed beneath his skin to stain his face red and he swallowed as High Cleric Christos entered the room.

The man was dressed in his black cleric's robes with his gold and red braided lanaso, a cord draped over his shoulders to signify his rank. Orry had a plain red one he never wore.

As the man regarded him through narrowed, dark green eyes, his thick brows quivered as if they had a life of their own. He followed the man with his eyes as he took a step around the end of the bed and closer to Orry. It took everything Orry had not to step back or flinch away.

"Do you know," High Cleric Christos said in his rough voice, his Roison accent thicker than Gabriol's. "I had no idea who you were until the day of Terena Luca's execution?"

He tilted his head in a way predator birds do. The movement was eerie and Orry suppressed another shudder.

Orry did not reply. He knew High Cleric Christos well enough—well, through what others have said, at any rate—to know his questions were usually rhetorical. Orry unclenched his hands to clasp them at his back instead. Nothing good ever came of anyone standing before this man showing weakness.

"I knew *of* you, of course," High Cleric Christos said with a sigh. "I shook your hand at graduation. And yet, before that day," the cleric shrugged. "The day of Luca's execution, I wouldn't have been able to pick you apart from the baker."

The cleric crossed his arms and Orry almost fainted at the abrupt movement.

Breathe, Orry. He's just a man. A very scary, powerful man. But a man. I bet he, too, used a shit bucket once. Maybe. Gods, please spare me from—

"You will tell me everything about the god, Terena Luca. If you fail in any detail, you will wish you'd never caught my notice."

Orry shook. He couldn't help it. An image of Ren in the dungeons flashed in his mind. Her swollen eye and bruised body. Orry did not doubt this man planned the same and worse for him if he didn't comply. And yet, he could not betray his friend.

Stiffening his spine, Orry lifted his chin an inch and met the cleric's gaze.

"Oh," the man said with a worrying smile. "You wish to play the hero? Very well. Let us begin."

RYDON PACED THE SMALL PANTRY AT THE BACK OF THE BOAR'S HEAD INN. His friend and the innkeep of this establishment, Eden, had let him in through the back entrance. He'd had the man send a note to Xoran earlier.

Sighing, Rydon turned and eyed the shelves, leaning in to sniff at a bunch of herbs hanging from a hook above the shelves.

"A little late to be out shopping."

Rydon's head swiveled around and he grinned at the speaker.

"Never know when you might need some rosemary."

Gabriol grinned back as they clasped arms. "Rosemary, huh? You plan on making some savory pies or something?"

Rydon shrugged as he tucked his thumbs into his sword belt. "Not a bad profession. Might look to switch soon."

Gabriol snorted. "Come. They're expecting you."

"What news?" Rydon asked as they walked. Huddled beneath his cloak, Rydon kept his head down whenever they passed others walking about. Daris and his men were not far behind. Once the City Watch caught sight of the Liodari, Rydon knew the city would be locked up tighter than a priestess's legs.

"The usual. One step away from discovery and execution."

Rydon snorted. "How many times have you clobbered some sense into Croak while I've been gone?"

Gabriol's steps faltered, and Rydon frowned.

"Croak's been captured," Gabriol said with a quick glance at Rydon.

Rydon's breath caught. "What?"

Gabriol nodded with a grim smile. "Aye. I'm not surprised it happened; the fool insisted on going to the cleric's old rooms and the Watch found them both. Ren is... beside herself. But the prince and Xoran came up with a plan to rescue him. Oh, and there's a fancy to-do tomorrow night so a bunch of royal pricks are at the castle."

"No wonder there was more security at the gates," Rydon mumbled. "I thought it was because of our victory in Ravos."

Gabriol laughed darkly. "It is both. The guests were already on their way but when General Peleon brought back word of their defeat, Emperor Solon had him and Xoran triple the guards within the palace and the city. I'm surprised no one snatched you up to conscript you."

Rydon ran his hand down his face and looked about. "Fuck that. I'd love to have been tested. So, who's attending this celebration? All the dukes and their wives?"

"And more besides," Gabe replied. "Terena said there are foreign dignitaries as well. I've seen a few uniforms I don't recognize. Also saw someone wearing Roison colors and a few from Offeni."

"What's going on?"

"Apparently, a month ago, the emperor named his youngest boy as his successor. Now that Prince Lerek's back from the dead, he wanted to have a big dinner to reinstate him as the crown prince and his heir."

"Perfect timing," Rydon grumbled, and Gabe flashed him a grin.

"Aye."

"How's she holding up?"

Gabriol shrugged. "About as well as can be expected, considering her brother's been snatched, the cleric too, although he was taken somewhere called Thanoras House, and her sister is in the hands of a deranged Olympian."

"Sounds like any other day to me," Rydon scoffed.

"Aye."

"Can you sneak me in now or should we wait for nightfall?"

Gabe shook his head, glancing over his shoulder. "I can sneak you inside now, but getting you to where Ren and the others are will need to be done later tonight. There's some sort of reception for the royals and other fancy guests, so everyone that matters will be in the throne room." He reached out and clapped Rydon's shoulder. "Your timing is uncanny."

They walked for a bit in silence. Rydon kept his gaze down, which was easy to do with how unsettled the news of Croak's capture made him.

"I'm assuming they took the boy to the dungeons," he said aloud. Gabe glanced back at him with a short nod. "Any chance you can sneak me in to see him?"

"No, not now. But if you're still around, you can help us get him out tomorrow night."

"Good. It bothers me more than I like, thinking of him down there. At the hands of the man who tortured Ren."

Gabe nodded again, ducking his head as he sighed. "Aye. Hopefully, he'll keep his damned mouth shut."

Rydon threw back his head and laughed, catching himself at the last moment when several heads turned in their direction. He lowered his head and walked faster. "That's about as likely as Ren having a plan that doesn't involve killing someone."

As they neared the castle, Rydon opened his mouth to ask something when shouts sounded ahead of them. They ducked behind a building on their left as soldiers rushed past, their armor clanging.

Exchanging a look, Gabriol leaned out of cover. A moment later, he moved back and pushed Rydon further out of sight.

"I don't know what's happened, but we can't go in this way."

"Let's wait then."

More soldiers rushed past, while others went toward the castle.

"Fuck." Rydon closed his eyes.

"What?"

"I think I know what's happened."

Gabriol lifted an ashen eyebrow as he waited for Rydon to continue.

Opening his mouth to answer, he was saved from doing so when a soldier passing nearby shouted.

"Spartans! Spartans at the gates!"

Rydon shrugged, a rueful smile on his face when Gabriol rolled his eyes.

THE DULL ROAR OF CONVERSATIONS IN THE THRONE ROOM MADE LEREK wince more than once. He'd forgotten how loud these events were.

As more and more dignitaries and their families arrived, Lerek wished he'd never returned. His face felt as if it was frozen in a satirical mien of crown prince arrogance mixed with feigned graciousness.

This is what he'd run from in the first place.

Lerek shuddered.

"Hello, Lerek."

Startled out of his reverie, Lerek pasted a smile on his face and inclined his head at Serephina.

His father's second wife was beautiful; dark haired with big brown eyes framed by thick lashes that made her seem innocent. She'd married his father after becoming pregnant with Adonis, Lerek's half-brother. Offeni by birth, Serephina had arrived in Metilai with a healthy dowry from her wealthy merchant father, looking for a titled husband. She landed the emperor instead.

Lerek shifted his gaze to the small woman who clutched his new sister in her arms.

"Greetings, Serephina," Lerek said, hoping his voice didn't sound as exasperated as he felt. "You look wonderful."

She smiled, a poisonous lift of her lips that never reached her eyes. No, those eyes held naked hatred instead.

"Well. For someone who's been dead close to a year, you look well."

Lerek inclined his head.

A moment of silence settled between them until a woman grabbed Serephina's attention, turning her away to speak with two men behind her. Lerek took the opportunity to leave.

It took some time navigating through the crush, but he made it out of an exit to the rear of the room and away from prying eyes. A shield of City Watch provided the cover he needed and he strode down the corridor eventually taking him to the royal residences.

When he finally made it to his rooms, Xoran was standing in

front of his doors, waiting. The captain turned at the sound of his footfalls, opening the doors for him.

"Did you get what we need?"

Xoran nodded as he closed the doors behind him. "Aye. I've already given them to Terena. At seven bells tomorrow night, they'll go to the great hall and blend in with the guards."

"Good," Lerek mumbled. He yanked on the front of his coat, which fastened higher up on his neck than he was used to. The uniforms for royal events were not meant for comfort, he knew, but it was barely tolerable.

Lerek cursed under his breath, thinking of how much longer he'd have to wear it. Only a few more hours today and then the dinner tomorrow.

"What else?" He paced the room. "I need to find out what Christos has—"

A loud banging sounded at the door. Lerek and Xoran exchanged a look as Xoran's hand went to his sword. He strode for the door and yanked it open to see one of his men standing there with a grim expression.

"Captain," the man said, his eyes flicking beyond Xoran to Lerek. "Highness. General Peleon and Emperor Solon need you both. Right now, in the council room."

"What's happened?" Lerek asked as he and Xoran immediately quit the rooms, following behind the guard as they made their way down the corridor.

All around, Lerek noticed servants and courtiers anxiously speaking or running every which way. There were no guards about.

"The Spartans are outside the city walls. Doesn't look like many, a couple hundred maybe, but the colors of the Spartan Liodari were spotted."

Lerek's head snapped around and he barely missed slamming into the balustrade when they rounded the corner to the staircase leading to the council room.

"Liodari? Are you certain?"

"Aye," the guard said. "Spotted them about ten minutes ago. The general has ordered more men on the walls near the gates but they haven't moved, nor have they sent anyone forward to speak."

Lerek exchanged a worried look with Xoran.

Was it Daris? Lerek had the crazy thought that the commander had found out Terena was there and had come for her.

Had Terena told him she was here? Was this a ruse to let her inside so they could ransack the city?

No. Lerek shook his head. He would not believe it of her.

"Have they sent anyone to speak with them?"

"I don't know, Your Highness," the man mumbled as they strode down the hall to the room. The hall was filled with Imperial Guard. There were more men from the Watch as well, all heavily armored.

Inside the council room, his father stood in front of a large, rectangular table with a section of the center painted to show the city of Metilai. Lerek knew the section could be turned over, where another map, this one of the continent, was depicted.

Men of various ranks and nationalities were inside, pulling Lerek up short. He'd never seen anyone other than his father, uncle, and their own military leaders in this room.

As he looked over the other faces, Lerek wondered at their inclusion. He had a feeling there was something else at play here, and not only the fact that they happened to be here for his succession feast and now were in the middle of what appeared to be a siege.

As soon as his father saw him, he motioned him over with a scowl. Despite the dark expression, he looked haggard.

Lerek had marked the changes in his father upon his return, knowing it owed to the events of the last year. The loss of one son and the disappearance of another. The war looming with the Spartans that, truthfully, the emperor had instigated. Throw gods into the mix, and Lerek no longer wondered what worries burdened his father other than the usual minutia of running an empire.

"No one's breached your walls in over a century," a man beside Lerek's uncle, Peleon, remarked. Lerek recalled meeting him earlier.

He had a smushed-in face with thick, dark lips and eyes constantly appearing as if he was squinting. Lerek could not remember where he was from.

"That's what you said a minute ago," the man continued, flinging a corpulent arm in Peleon's direction. "You have more than one exit out of Metilai. I daresay maybe even a secret exit. Let us make use of it now—"

"They won't attack," Peleon huffed, his face ruddier than usual. He looked as if he'd been holding his breath.

Glaring at the man who'd spoken, he added, "It's the vanguard, nothing more. If they attack now, we will easily rout them. No, they are waiting."

"For what?"

Lerek spun around to look at the new speaker, a man with golden curls held back from his face with a black strip of leather. His skin was tanned as if he spent much of his life outdoors, his grey eyes flashing with impatience.

"I do not know, Romulus," Peleon seethed. Lerek watched a vein in his temple throb. "Whatever it is, we'll be ready. In the meantime, we do not panic."

"We already know of your defeat at Ravos at the hands of the former tracker, Terena Luca," the man, Romulus, said. He looked around at the others, who nodded and mumbled in agreement. "And if the rumors are true, she had an army with her, led by the Olympian god, Hermes. Perhaps his army is on it's way here now."

The din erupting at his words made Lerek wince, despite the elation flooding his chest. His father shouted to be heard and his uncle screamed at a man near him, one of the Offeni royals.

"How is that possible?"

"I thought all the gods were killed? You said there was no truth to the—"

"SILENCE!"

Lerek watched his father as the room quieted slowly. The emperor's face was as red as an apple, his heaving breaths making his shoulders bounce as he glared at everyone.

"Terena Luca will be handled," his father said into the sudden stillness of the room. "And the dinner goes forward as planned."

A chorus of protests erupted, and for several long minutes, the din of the various conversations was loud enough to make Lerek's ears ring.

"And what of the rumors? What of Hermes?"

The emperor thumped on the table so hard, some of the war figurines on the map fell over. The room quieted as Lerek's father glared at them all.

"I look around this room, and I do not see leaders," he sneered, his dark eyes darting around at everyone. "I see muling babes, whining about rumors, crying about a tracker brat who is so insignificant, I'd forgotten all about her until her reappearance in Ravos.

"The only reason my men were there was to take back the prince! If General Peleon had stayed, I assure you, that rabble would not have won in Colinas."

"And what of the Spartans?"

Lerek's eyes darted to Romulus, the most outspoken of his father's guests. He must be more important than Lerek had first thought, although he could not place where he was from.

"You're worried about a hundred warriors? I have *thousands* under my command. Do you see me losing my composure?"

Sullen silence thickened in the room as Lerek watched his father's sneering countenance.

"You were all invited here for a reason, so you are all made aware of the situation. We will continue with the festivities as planned, regardless of the wolves at our gates. You will be assigned additional guards for the duration of your stay. Updates will be provided as needed, and if the situation changes, we have an evacuation plan ready.

"But we are not there yet. So, comport yourselves as men befitting your stations." His eyes narrowed to dangerous slits as his lip curled up. "Or you'll be the first ones thrown to those wolves."

CHAPTER 44

METILAI

The room Xoran had found for them was spacious, but had a musty smell. All of the furniture was shrouded when they'd first arrived.

Migela helped Cassandra pull them off the table and chairs. Vassori had gone into the bedchamber and snapped the curtains open, stirring a flurry of dust. She coughed as she ripped the coverings off the bed.

"It's too cold to open the windows!" Cassandra had snapped.

Vassori gave her a disgruntled look over her shoulder. "And it stinks in here. A few minutes of discomfort won't kill you."

She crossed to the bed and grabbed the blankets off, hauling them to the windows to shake them out. Cassandra shivered, watching Vas go about her work with a mutinous look on her face.

"You know, not all of us are from places so cold it'll freeze your nose off as soon as you step outside. Some of us are from climates with beautiful, sunshine-filled warmth, where birds sing and the water is so crystal clear you can see the colorful fish darting about."

"Where is that?"

"Troy," Cassandra grumbled, her face falling as her thoughts drifted away. Terena sat in a chair at the table in the adjoining room, her head in her hand as she watched the two argue.

"Never heard of it," Vas said as she took the pillows over to the windows. She grabbed a brush from the vanity nearby and wiped it on her pants. Using it to beat the pillows, she glanced over her shoulder at Cassandra. "Where is it?"

Cassandra sighed. "It's... not in this world."

"What?" Vassori snapped upright, dropping her arm and the pillow as she regarded the seer. "What's that mean?"

"Cass is from a world called Earth," Terena called out, her head slipping into her palm. She shrugged when Vassori gave her a quizzical glance. "She was Apollo's lover apparently, although she never did tell us the whole story."

"Well," Vas flapped her arms out after tossing the pillow. "We've got time now. I want to hear more about this place that was so beautiful you left it to come here."

Terena chuckled as Cassandra crossed her arms in fury.

"I didn't choose to come here," Cassandra snapped.

"Then why are you here?" Vas flashed her a skeptical look before turning back to the bed. Flopping down on it, she crossed her booted feet and wiggled her brows expectantly.

Terena looked up at Cassandra from her contemplation of her fingernails when the silence stretched. The woman had a haunted, faraway look in her eyes and the hand she raised to the necklaces dangling from her neck shook.

"There was a war," Cassandra said in a low voice, and Terena leaned forward. A sense of inevitability settled around them. Terena exchanged a look with Migela, who sidled closer to the seer.

"I am not Greek," she continued, swallowing. "I am Trojan. My father is... was... King of Troy. And aye, a more beautiful city you've never seen. In my years here, I've not seen a city to rival its splendor.

"When the Greeks invaded, I was in Apollo's temple. I ran." She rubbed at her forehead. Her voice was small, shaking. "I wasn't fast enough."

Migela moved to sit beside Cassandra, her hand wrapped around the woman's arm.

"Cassandra..." Terena started before her mouth went dry.

The seer shook her head and tears slipped from her eyes as she aggressively wiped them away.

"By the time Agamemnon, one of the kings of the Greeks who invaded my country, brought me to my father, I..." She wiped again at her face and shuddered. "Apollo had forsaken me. *I* was the one violated. *I* was brutalized by those men, but Apollo punished *me*."

Terena gripped her hands together so tight they shook.

"He could not take away my gift," Cassandra continued, her voice breaking, "so he altered it instead." She laughed bitterly. "He raged at my infidelity. He wouldn't even listen to me, even when I pleaded with him, telling him I loved him. The god made it so no one believed my visions afterward."

Lifting her gaze at last, Terena was struck by the rage blazing in the woman's slate blue eyes.

"Do you know what it's like, to see the ruin of your home, the deaths of your family and countrymen, and not be able to do anything but watch as it happens? I warned my father. I warned my brothers." She shrugged. "No one believed me."

"How did you escape?" Vassori asked, sitting up in bed as she stared at the seer.

"Believe it or not, one of the authors of our demise was my savior. The goddess, Athena, favored the Greeks during the war, but she was angry when she'd seen them defile me. And angry with Apollo for punishing *me* for it. She arranged for my freedom. I cannot explain the details but, suffice to say, she helped and now I am here."

Terena's fury was a living thing, twisting and churning in her gut. She hated that a few cowardly men had taken away her friend's dignity, her safety, her power.

One of the most fearless women Terena had ever known,

Cassandra hid her gifts behind a playful, irreverent mask, numbing her trauma with drink and magical herbs. Despite how they'd met, Cassandra was one of them now, and Terena would ensure nothing like that ever happened to her or any of her friends.

Cassandra's soft, ragged breathing was the only sound in the room for a long time. Her small hands shook, and she clutched at the fabric of her skirt.

Migela reached out and covered them with her own. When the assassin lifted her gaze, her eyes were glassy with tears. Her hands flew, signing faster than Terena could decipher.

"What are you saying? Slow down—"

Cassandra whimpered, covering her face as a sob wracked her. Terena rose from her seat, alarmed.

After a moment, Cassandra lowered her hands. Her face was bleak. She reached out and hugged Migela, whose tears flowed freely now.

"What happened?" Terena demanded, taking a step closer to the two women. Glancing up at Vassori, the tracker shrugged, equally baffled.

"Migela," Cassandra started, her voice cracking. The assassin looked up at Terena, her hands flying again as she signed something else. Terena didn't understand everything she said, but she understood one of the words.

Killed.

"Migela," Cassandra said again and took a deep breath. "When she was a child, her village was attacked by soldiers on their way to her country's capital. They attacked her family, killing her father and two brothers. They cut out Migela's tongue because she started screaming while they raped her mother. When she was old enough, she tracked down those men and killed them all. It's why she became an assassin."

Fury writhed through her insides, and Terena hung her head. Lifting her head at last, she looked at her friend.

"I am so sorry for what you went through, Migela. I'm glad

you've avenged your family. Those men deserved everything you did to them. And we will avenge you, Cassandra. We cannot make those men pay for what they did to you," Terena said to Cassandra, her throat tight as she snapped out the words. "But, I can make Apollo pay. And the day he and the rest of the Olympians return, is the day I honor this vow."

Cassandra swallowed and hung her head for a moment. She remained stiff as Migela continued to hold onto her hands.

Despite the tears falling unchecked, Cassandra's expression was harsh now, her jaw tight and her eyes gleaming with resolve.

"Aye," she whispered, smiling ruefully. "I know you will. Because I've seen it. And when that day comes, I will be at your side. I'll be at your side through it all."

THEY SETTLED FOR THE NIGHT, TERENA TAKING THE BED AND INSISTING IT was no bother for Cassandra to share the bed with her.

Vassori took first watch in the antechamber and Migela slept on the couch in the small common area.

Hours later, a sharp stab of pain in her belly made Terena pitch forward, her hands grabbing hold of the bedding on either side of her. She panted, blinking rapidly as another wave of intense pain speared through her middle.

Rolling off the side of the bed, she fell to her knees.

Terena gasped as another sharp ache stabbed her insides and she reached to clutch at her stomach. Cassandra's voice beside her was dull and unintelligible, as if she spoke underwater. As Terena panted, she saw Migela and Vassori run to her side, their mouths opened but she couldn't hear their words.

A million memories flashed behind her eyes. Most from this journey, but going backwards, further back before her earliest memory, back before she'd arrived in this realm. Tears fell as the memories bombarded her mind and she went back

back

back

back

to the first circle.

"YOU HAVE TO KILL HER!"

Terena swung her terrified gaze away from Sonah to Lerek.

"What are you saying? Stop! I'm not the—"

"Kill her, Sonah! Before she kills us!"

"Lerek, stop!" Terena took a step closer to Sonah, but stopped when her sister raised her bow.

Terena froze.

"Ren!"

Terena spun to see Daris sprinting toward her. He slid to a stop when he saw Sonah with her bow trained on Terena.

"Daris, this doesn't concern you," Sonah said, her voice hard.

Lerek pointed a finger at Daris and snarled, "You've done enough damage, Liodari."

"Sonah, please," Terena whispered, her eyes pleading with her sister. "Listen to me. He's lying to you."

"Sonah, put the bow down and listen to your sister!" Daris yelled.

"I've listened to her before and look where it got me! Lerek speaks true, Liodari. You dripped your poison in Terena's ear and now I cannot trust her!"

"Sonah," Terena's voice broke and she swallowed, her hands up. "I love you. I —"

"You love me?" Sonah seethed, the hand on the bow shaking. "You love me? You left me there to die! You let them—"

Sonah hung her head, her words ending on a sob.

Shame flooded Terena and she could not speak. Daris's hand folded hers within his warmth. She chanced a glance at him, but his eyes were on Sonah.

"You chose him *over* me!*" Sonah continued in a voice so filled with pain, Terena felt it break her own heart. She deserved Sonah's wrath.*

She'd failed her sister.

"You will always choose him! That's your fate!"

"No, no, Sonah—"

"You made your choice. Now face the consequences."

Terena ripped her hand from Daris's grip and raised both in front of her, her eyes going wide a second before Sonah released the arrow.

"TERENA!"

Terena's hands dropped from her head where she'd been clutching her hair, and she struggled to breathe. Strong hands clutched at her shoulders. She couldn't breathe.

Can't breathe!

"Terena, what's wrong? What's happening?"

She knew that voice.

Rydon?

Blackness filled her vision.

When she finally opened her eyes, Terena blinked up at Rydon, bent over her. His face was contorted. Angry. Scared? How was he even here?

"Thank the gods," he whispered, closing his eyes for a moment before he turned his hard gaze on her again. "What the fuck just happened?"

So much had happened. So much had changed in just a few hours. And now she was realizing that everything she'd ever done or will ever do might not matter.

Every one of the last circles was doomed from the start. Something—someone—was behind the sabotage. Someone who didn't want her and Sonah to succeed.

Despair and impotent rage warred inside her as she thought about how futile it all seemed.

How could she fulfill the prophecy if forces stronger than her conspired to stop her?

A moment of panic seized her and she thought again of what had happened to her in Ravos, when she'd lost control of her powers and destroyed half of the duke's men without thought.

Maybe whoever or whatever hidden force was working against her did so to stop her from becoming exactly what Duke Ravos claimed she was.

An abomination.

Terena's hands shook as she reached out to touch Rydon's face.

"I remember. I remember everything, Rydon."

CHAPTER 45

METILAI

After Gabriol had shared their plans with him, Rydon embarked on the challenge of getting out of the palace unseen. It had taken him an hour, and when he'd finally made it into the city proper, the journey to Daris's camp was even more difficult.

Shading his eyes against the late morning sun, Rydon found the door leading to the sewers they'd used a year ago to get Ren and Sonah out. Recalling the location had delayed him further, and by the time he came out near the river and circled around to the front, he was filthy and cold and in dire need of a bath.

Holding up his hands as he approached the encampment, one of the soldiers on watch grunted in acknowledgement and waved him in. Looking around at the additional men, Rydon tightened his jaw and lengthened his stride, his head swiveling about as he searched for the commander.

Rydon came to an abrupt halt when he spotted Daris standing with Hermes. They didn't seem to have noticed him and Rydon had the fleeting thought he should melt back into the shadows of the tents and make his way back into the city.

"Ah, there he is!"

Rydon closed his eyes and cursed Soros for his ill-timed greeting. The captain clapped him heartily on the back as everyone nearby looked over at them. Rydon cut a glance at Daris who watched him with a frown. Hermes, of course, had a face-splitting grin as if Rydon was the key to all the world's wisdom.

"Eudaemon, come!" Hermes raised his arm and motioned to Rydon, who could do nothing but drag his feet as he approached the god with Soros at his side.

"What news from the palace?"

"Everyone's shitting themselves, most like," Soros laughed.

Hermes ignored the man, a cruel glint in his eyes as he watched Rydon.

"Terena's inside, of course," Rydon said, parsing his thoughts to share only what would appease the god and not further endanger Ren. "They know you're out here but they are waiting to see if you've terms. Otherwise, they are hosting a feast this evening, to announce Prince Lerek's reinstatement as successor and crown prince."

"Aye, but," Hermes's mouth twisted. "How is my niece? Is she recovered?"

Warning bells went off in his head but Rydon kept his face blank. "Recovered from your... conversation with her back in Ravos? Aye, I'd say she's recovered."

Hermes gave him an amused, incredulous look. "I'll let that one go, Eudaemon, because I like you. I am referring to her ascension. Today is her nameday."

Rydon's heart stopped and then threatened to gallop right out of his chest. His eyes darted to Daris, who stared back at him with dawning horror. His face was as red as a harvest sunset, and he looked about as ill as Rydon must at that moment.

"When did you see her last? If you saw her this morning, you should've already seen a difference."

Rydon hoped his face concealed his frustration. "In what way?"

Hermes laughed. "In the way that separates someone like me, from someone like you."

"I'm immortal as well," Rydon seethed.

"You know what I mean."

The underlying edge to the god's words was belied by his grin.

"She looked the same."

"No... uncontrollable rage? Changes in her appearance? Visions of previous circles?"

Rydon blanched and the god laughed.

"So she knows everything that came before. Good. I'll speak with her later, of course, but I'm curious. Did she say anything of interest? About any of it? Specifically, does she know how she was tricked into finding the shroud before she reached her majority?"

Rydon shook his head. When Hermes arched an eyebrow at him, Rydon sighed. "She did not mention anything about that, no."

"But..."

"But," Rydon glanced at Daris. "She said... Sonah tried to kill her in the first circle. And that Daris tried to kill her in the last circle."

Hermes turned his head and stared at Daris. "Interesting."

"Her appearance remains the same," Rydon added, pulling the god's attention back to him. "Was it supposed to change?"

"Depends on the god," Hermes sighed. "We'll have to catch up later. I have an assault on the city to prepare for."

Rydon's thoughts spiraled as he tried and failed to take in everything Hermes was saying. There was an ocean, swirling and turbulent, crashing through his head right now and he had the overwhelming urge to throw his head back and scream at the sky. Instead, he looked over at Daris. The commander's mouth hung open.

"Why would you assault the city?"

"I need to make an example of them," Hermes said as if talking to a child. "This is the beginning of a new era, Eudaemon. This is no longer the age of man. I am proof of that. Terena and Sonah are proof of that. Melanos—"

Rydon's jaw snapped shut when a large shadow to his left resolved into a scowling visage Rydon knew well. Melanos stopped next to Daris, his enraged countenance fixed on Hermes as the trickster god held out his arm and smiled at the newcomer.

"Melanos," he said again, turning to pin Rydon in place with a malicious grin. "Is proof of that."

In the sudden quiet of the clearing, Hermes looked around at the soldiers who'd stopped to listen in.

"They all thought they killed us. When we Olympians left, the demigods and those favored by the gods were hunted and killed. Their families were hunted and killed. But man is arrogant." Hermes laughed, a maniacal chuckle raising all the hairs on Rydon's body.

"Mortals cannot kill gods. The gods left behind hid themselves," Hermes said as he pointed to Melanos. "They've lived on the fringes. Hiding their nature. Their gifts. No more. Our time has come. Tonight, we reclaim this realm, and all those who have fought against the gods, railed against the gods, prayed against the gods will learn what their defiance costs."

Hermes abruptly turned away, leaving them all in stunned silence. Melanos was the first to react, bounding forward, gripping Rydon's shoulder in a crushing grip that made him wince.

"Where is the goddess? Is she safe?"

Rydon nodded dumbly. Daris, too, came to stand before him, their small huddle the subject of low, murmured conversation from the soldiers nearby. Daris motioned with his head, and all three of them moved away to speak in private.

Following on numb legs, Rydon's thoughts shifted from everything that had happened to Terena and the others inside the palace. By now, everyone would know Hermes and his army were camped outside their city. Rydon wondered if Terena was already moving forward with their plan.

They stopped walking and Rydon glanced up, realizing they stood in front of the commander's tent.

"What do they have planned?" Daris asked.

Rydon smoothed down his beard. "Croak is in the dungeons. He and the cleric were found almost as soon as they arrived. Orry is somewhere else. Some college. I don't recall the name. The prince has a plan to get Croak out, but he needs Ren to distract the emperor at the feast he's planned. All the guards will be there. If she holds them off long enough, Lerek and Gabriol will sneak down to the dungeon to get him out."

"How?" Daris snapped. "They'll still be stuck in the palace—"

"Lerek has a plan for that as well, although, he wouldn't elaborate."

"And Terena was fine with that?"

Rydon shrugged, nonplussed. "I guess. She trusts him, at least."

Daris colored as Rydon watched him. They were silent, with Melanos's giant frame blocking them from anyone's prying eyes.

"Why did they come to Metilai in the first place?"

Startled, Rydon glanced up at Melanos and shrugged. "That was the plan all along. Before we left Olympia, Hermes said we'd meet up here. But I know she wanted to come because of something she figured out about the prophecy. She said something about it back in Ermanel when we found the prince. And Cassandra was adamant that—"

"Who's Cassandra?"

"The seer," Rydon said with an uncertain glance at Melanos. At the blank look on the god's face, Rydon grunted with impatience. "She was with us in Ravos. Blonde woman. About this tall?"

As Rydon gestured, a grin broke out on Melanos's face.

"Aye, the little one who was draped all over you. Are you together, then?"

"What?" Rydon spluttered, feeling his face heat. "No, we are not together. She's not... I'm not..."

"All right, what did the seer say about Metilai, then?" Daris cut in. "She was adamant about what?"

"That she follow Lerek. Join him in Metilai. She seemed to think we'd find an amulet here. An amulet with a terrible power. Something about twisting people's desires until they've ruined themselves and everyone around them."

Melanos snapped out his hand, clutching Rydon's forearm hard enough to make him wince. When he looked up at the god to loosen his grip, Melanos's eyes were wide with alarm.

"The Amulet of Kaïra? It's here?"

Rydon frowned. "Aye. I guess. She seemed to think so."

Melanos cursed under his breath, which worried Rydon.

"So how do we help?" Melanos asked, dropping his hand to stand akimbo. "We cannot allow Hermes to find that amulet."

"The emperor searches for it as well," Rydon grumbled. "Ren struck a bargain with Xoran, the Captain of the Imperial Guard, to find it. Who knows what nefarious plan Solon has for it."

"Wait," Daris said, shifting so Rydon was forced to look over at him. "You allied with Xoran? Wasn't he one of the ones trying to kill Ren back when you first met her?"

Rydon shrugged and chuckled mirthlessly. "I said much the same to Ren at the time. Although, he's proven trustworthy, thus far. As has Vassori. She and Ren have gotten close over the last few weeks."

"Vassori is the tracker? What's she have to do with this?"

"She's Xoran's sister."

Daris stared back at him for a moment, incredulous.

"Someday, I hope to hear more of what happened to you all before we found each other again."

"For now," Melanos added with a scowl, "we need to find a way inside. Perhaps we can help with Croak's escape."

"I think I have a way."

Startled, they all took a step back as Sonah ducked out from Daris's tent.

SONAH STRUTTED TOWARD THE FIRST PART OF HER PLAN: HERMES.

The god was inside his tent, the largest in the encampment. He'd left her alone for most of the journey to Metilai, although she caught him more than once staring at her. She wondered if he was still upset over her defiance at Lethe, but the way he looked at her was more frustrated confusion than annoyance.

Sonah squared her shoulders as she approached, the two soldiers posted outside eyeing her warily. She'd not voluntarily been in Hermes's presence before, and Rydon had worried her sudden interest would instantly alert him to her hidden agenda.

While it was a worry, it wasn't what preoccupied Sonah right then as she gave both of the guards a tight smile and asked to enter.

"What are you doing?"

Sonah winced. Turning, she pasted a smile on her face she hoped wasn't as sickly-looking as she felt.

"Leander." Sonah greeted the shifter, her eyes searching his face. She wanted to reach out to touch his beautiful face now bruised and swollen from the beating he'd received from Hermes's men at Lethe.

The shifter, however, stared down at her with hard eyes and a strange look she didn't understand. Averting her gaze, Sonah looked to the guard beside them who watched with a frown.

"What are you doing here?" she asked.

"What am *I* doing here?" Leander motioned with his chin. "What are you doing here? If Hermes has asked to see you, I'm coming with you."

"No." Sonah cut off her objection, swallowing past the urge to stomp her foot. Her eye twitched as she looked up into Leander's green eyes. Those beautiful orbs were now surrounded by swollen lids and the right one had blood on most of the white of his eye.

Leander crossed his arms and moved closer.

Sonah refused to step back.

Opening her mouth to tell him to leave, Sonah was preempted by Hermes's bellow for her to enter.

"I hear you out there, niece."

Sonah rolled her eyes and pursed her lips. Leander was looking at her with such determination, she balled her hands to fists and turned, her movements jerky as she slapped the tent flap aside and entered. She didn't hold it for Leander.

Hermes was seated at a large desk which was oddly out of place. How the hells had he brought it with? Sonah didn't recall a wagon cart in their convoy.

As she glanced around the spacious tent, she noted the gilded candelabra stands and a bed—a *bed*!—with gorgeous velvet blankets that looked black but as she neared saw were a deep ruby.

"Leave us," Hermes said to the two men who flanked him. When she turned to face him, he was eyeing Leander pointedly.

Leander lifted his chin and stared back at Hermes. Clasping his hands in front of him, his face set, he remained silent.

"Aye, Leander," Sonah said, cringing as her voice sounded an octave too high to her ears. Modulating her voice, she added, "I wish to speak with Hermes alone."

Leander's eyes snapped to her and she tried not to cringe at the mess they'd made of his face. He shook his head.

"I will not leave you alone." He turned back to Hermes. "I heard what you did to her sister, lord. My... patron would not like it if I failed her."

Sonah blinked. What?

A thunderous expression flashed across Hermes's handsome features before he smiled at Leander.

Shifting his intense gaze to Sonah, Hermes motioned with an elegant hand for her to speak.

Taking a deep breath, Sonah hoped Leander wouldn't fuck this up for her.

"I want an escort into the city," she started. Leander swiveled his head to her, about to object. "I want Rydon and Daris to accompany me—"

"Let me stop you right there," Hermes said in a bored tone. "First, you're not going anywhere near the city until we've secured it with our victory. Which will be very soon. Second, Daris is not going anywhere. He's mortal now and—"

Sonah gasped. "What? How? When?"

"Oh, right!" Hermes chuckled, slapping his hands on the desk as he rose. "I forgot! Happy Nameday, niece."

Nonplussed, Sonah gawked at the god. "Huh?"

"Aye, not as exciting a day for you as it is for your sister, but still! You're eighteen now, how does it feel?"

The blood leached from her body. "What?"

Hermes waved a hand as he tutted. "I know, I know. Your time will come, though! Today, Terena is immortal and, with her powers, we'll soon take the city."

"And... and... Daris?"

Hermes's lips twisted and a flash of ire raced across his eyes before he lowered his gaze. He came around the desk and leaned against the front, crossing his ankles.

"Daris is no longer a eudaemon. So, I don't want him going into the city ahead of the fighting. I still have some... work to do with him."

"Well," Sonah spluttered, her mind racing as her plan fell apart. Cursing under her breath, she squared her shoulders and looked up at the god. "You—you make him immortal then! Now!"

Red tinged the god's cheeks and he pushed away from the desk.

"Leave us," he snarled at Leander. This time, Sonah nodded at him and, thankfully, he left without a word of protest.

Hermes stared at her a moment before shoving a hand through his hair. His dishevelment was uncharacteristic and she frowned at the rare glimpse of vulnerability from this powerful being.

"As you so eloquently put it earlier, my dear niece, my powers are limited. I don't know why, so don't ask. I suspect it has to do with you and Terena but I'm not sure. I've spoken with Melanos as well, back at Lethe, and he confirmed he's similarly afflicted. Although, he hasn't been feeling as... murderous as I have of late."

Sonah gaped at him. "So, what's that mean? What—how do we fix it? We need to fix it! We can't start a war with the emp—"

"We will deal with it later," Hermes snapped. "Your sister's powers should be enough. Whatever it is, it's not affecting her. I was with her in Olympia for a month before we came south. She was powerful then. Far stronger than a god before ascension. Terena will win Metilai for us, and we will figure out the rest when the time comes."

"I need to go."

Hermes frowned at her but Sonah wasted no time, turning and lunging through the tent before Hermes could respond.

She felt him shadowing her steps and she raced ahead, weaving her way through the warriors and their tents, her heart in her throat threatening to choke her as she fought the sobs rearing their ill-timed heads.

CHAPTER 46

METILAI

"May I speak with you?"

Terena looked up at Gabriol in surprise. "Of course."

He looked over his shoulder at Vassori, who stood near the door, waiting. They were about to leave for the emperor's celebration feast and Terena was more than ready.

Fidgeting with her costume, she frowned, hiding her impatience behind a neutral mask as Gabriol sauntered closer. She nodded at Vassori to leave them and she and the other women moved away to give her and Gabe some privacy.

Stopping in front of her, he wiped a hand down his beard, his eyes darting around as if thinking.

"What is it?" Terena prompted.

He looked up at last and the expression on his face was one she'd not seen from him before.

A look her father usually gave her right after she'd done something wrong.

"Ren," he started, his eyes sympathetic. "I know you're under a lot of pressure. I cannot imagine the things you're dealing with and now that you're a god in truth, I know the road for you will only become more difficult."

"Aye," she said with a swift nod.

"But I beg you, do not forget your humanity. It will temper your actions when you need it most."

Terena narrowed her eyes. "What are you talking about?"

Gabriol sighed. "I'm talking about Ravos. I'm talking about how you destroyed those men without mercy, and," he held up a hand when she opened her mouth to respond. "And aye, you said that happened without conscious thought, but now that you have the use of your powers, I caution you to use them wisely. There is a reason mortals went to war with the gods. There is a reason why the emperor and many others have killed any gods left behind after the Olympians were banished. Fear. They fear your kind. Do not justify their beliefs. Please. You endanger yourself and you endanger your family if you continue down that path."

Terena warred with her body to keep calm. A part of her understood what he was saying, while another part fumed at his judgement. So much had changed within her in the last year, more so in the last few hours that she struggled to keep herself sane.

Always different, even in childhood, and yet her father and her family had always grounded her, tempered her impulsive tendencies. Now, it was her new family—Gabriol and Rydon chief among them —that took over that responsibility. She owed it to them, to the memory of her father and her mother who taught her right from wrong, to listen to Gabriol now.

"We're about to go into a room filled with people who would sooner kill you than try to understand who you are as a person," Gabriol went on, his eyes searching hers. "The man who already tried to kill you and your sister will be in that room and I am begging you to restrain yourself."

Terena scoffed. "Has Cassandra said something to you?"

"No, why?"

Suppressing a smile, she glanced over at the door where the seer was huddled close to Migela. "She said something similar to me the other day."

"We're only looking out for you," Gabriol said, the low timbre of his voice soothing and she sighed as his words washed over her. "We love you, Ren. I hope you know that."

When she felt more in control of her emotions, Terena laid a hand on his cheek and smiled.

"I love you, too. I wouldn't be here without you and Rydon, you know that. I'm humbled by your support and your faith in me, and I hear you. I do. Thank you. For sticking by me, for believing in me, and for protecting me. Even from myself. You're right, at times I have lost sight of what is right, and I will do better."

"I know you will," Gabriol said, holding her hand against his cheek.

"If we don't leave soon, we'll not be able to blend in with the other arrivals."

Terena rolled her eyes as Vassori's words cut through her moment with Gabriol. Pulling him into a hug, she kissed his cheek and thanked him again before turning to stride for the door.

The din coming from the ballroom reached them as soon as they descended the main staircase to the grand hall. Terena wasn't bothered, but she caught Cassandra wincing as they neared the double doors. Imperial Guard were posted on either side, their expressionless faces unmoving as guests came in and out of the ballroom.

Terena and Vas were both dressed as City Watch, while Migela and Cassandra wore dresses they'd found still hanging in the armoire in the room Xoran had stashed them in.

When Terena first saw the outfit Cass had put on, she'd frowned. The dress looked familiar, but she'd quickly dismissed it as unimportant while Cassandra tugged and tugged at the bodice to accommodate her bust.

Glancing over her shoulder, Cassandra gave her a tight smile when she caught Terena's gaze.

Turning back, Terena held out her hand as she waited for a large group to pass them. Walking quickly, they blended in with the group and strolled into the ballroom without raising any alarms.

"The emperor knows how to throw a party," Cassandra mumbled when they stopped walking. The group they'd gone in with were chatting with other guests already inside, their shrill laughter making Terena frown.

She motioned to the women with her head and they followed as she moved away from the thick crowds clustered in the middle of the massive room. Leading them to the far side, Terena nodded when they passed another Watchman.

"I don't see the prince or my brother," Vas whispered as they slowly made their way to the dais. It ran the length of the back wall, long tables set up for twenty, which seemed excessive to Terena. Besides the emperor and his family, she'd assumed High Cleric Christos and maybe several of the more important foreign dignitaries would be seated there.

It mattered not. When the time came for her to reveal herself, she doubted anyone would stay on the dais besides Solon and Christos.

"If they're not here yet, they will be," Terena whispered back.

"I'll take a look around for them," Vas mumbled as she melted away.

Cassandra took a seat at an unoccupied table and popped something into her mouth. Terena suspected it was one of her special sweets that dulled her mind. She did not begrudge the seer the vice, but she worried she would lose focus.

As soon as Cassandra sat, a servant materialized with a goblet of wine and a plate of refreshments. The seer clapped her hands and grabbed the wine before the servant set it down.

"I'll take a turn around the room. Stay with Cassandra," Terena said to Migela, who nodded and sat beside the seer.

Keeping her left hand on the hilt of her sword, Terena scanned the room, ducking her head when she spotted Duke Elis with Duke

Ermanel. She pivoted and threaded her way through a group of women tittering over the handsome—

Someone bumped into her and Terena looked up in annoyance. Her mind blanked when she looked into the startled blue eyes of Henri, Duke Aurora. Terena moved away as he opened his mouth, disappearing into the crowd.

Putting a hand to her chest at the near discovery, Terena cursed. What the fuck was Aurora doing here? She hadn't heard about them being back under Heylisia's rule. Terena would ask Lerek about him the first chance she got. If that pompous shit had recognized her and dared to say anything, she'd find him and pluck out those baby blues he always batted at her.

While she fumed about Aurora, a commotion caught her attention near the dais. Narrowing her gaze, Terena saw Serephina enter the room with her son, Prince Adonis, at her side. He looked like a miniature Solon, poor thing. He wore a peevish expression on his little face, and he stuck to his mother's dress as if she'd had her seamstress pin him there.

Terena scowled and prowled forward, keeping to the side of the room near some of the Imperial Guard. High Cleric Christos loomed behind Serephina, tall and powerful with a pompous sneer on his lips as he listened to a man Terena did not know.

"Indeed," Christos was saying, his eyes drifting over the man to assess the room at large. "We are fortunate he has returned unharmed, although, I am worried about his continued affection for the traitor, Terena Luca."

Terena stilled. Cocking her head, she edged closer.

"I hear you do not believe she is a god, despite her actions at the execution you'd planned for her."

The man who'd spoken had a thick accent she could not place. He had numerous charms pinned to the front of his charcoal jacket. A tall woman with dark red hair piled up and clipped with a beautiful jeweled butterfly pin stood beside him with her hand tucked into the crook of his arm.

"The failed execution and the events surrounding it were greatly exaggerated where the traitor's actions are concerned," Christos responded. "Pure fantasy on the part of the citizens."

"And yet," the man with the numerous pins said, emphasizing his point with a finger raised, "I heard from some of your own Guard she used magic or god-like powers to escape."

Christos's lips pulled back in disgust. "Our Guard are too embarrassed to admit they were the ones that allowed her to escape. She had help. That's how she got away."

"Let us not bore Master Guerrine," Lerek said as he moved up to stand next to the foreign man. He glanced over his shoulder and Terena met his gaze. He gave her a slight nod. Turning back to High Cleric Christos, he held out his wine goblet. "If you'll excuse us, High Cleric, I must introduce the Master and his charming wife to Ambassador Bonum."

Terena moved back, melting into the crowd and made her way to where she'd left Cassandra and Migela. Cassandra was looking at her with a manic expression. Before she could walk over, drums began thumping.

Fanfare sounded, the sharp notes from the horns pulling everyone's attention and quieting the room. The Royal Bard swept into the center of the ballroom, his gleaming white silk suit threaded with gold and red. Tassels atop his shoulders shook as he waved to the crowd. Turning toward the dais, he bent low in a deep bow.

All eyes turned in unison and Terena swiveled to see Solon step onto the dais with High Cleric Christos at his side.

Her pulse raced as she watched the man who'd ordered her execution smiling benignly as everyone clapped. Bile rose in Terena's throat and she almost screamed with the force of her fury.

As the applause faded, Solon put his hand to his chest.

"Thank you all for joining me this evening. I... did not expect the event I'd originally invited you all to Metilai for would double as a joyous celebration for the return of my son, Crown Prince Lerek. It is a blessing from Gaia, and I am equally blessed to share it with you all."

Terena's brow furrowed at his words. According to Lerek and Xoran, that is exactly what this event had been for: Lerek's return. But as the crowd exploded into applause, Terena stared hard at the guests assembled at the tables on the dais. Some of them had come from countries far across the Black Sea to be here.

Fuming as realization dawned, Terena vowed to question Lerek at the first opportunity. He had better have an explanation about how these guests had gotten here this fast if Solon had only found out about Lerek mere weeks ago.

And why the hells Duke Aurora was here, too.

"Almost a year ago," Solon droned on, "someone I trusted and respected betrayed me in the most heinous way possible. But the old gods are benevolent and have returned my firstborn, Lerek, to my side. And while I mourn the loss of my second son, Isher, I am forever grateful to have Lerek restored to me and this empire. This is a celebration," Solon said with a grin as he looked around the room. "This is a celebration not only for his return, but to restore him to his birthright as heir to the Empire of Heylisia."

Terena looked around until she spotted Lerek, who waved a negligent hand at the raucous applause. When it died down, Lerek slipped away. Sighing in relief, Terena turned back as High Cleric Christos stepped up to Solon's side.

"But we are here tonight for another celebration. To honor the new allegiances formed this week, with friends near and far, to strengthen our empires, countries, and kingdoms, from enemies of mankind.

"We are on the cusp of a shift in our world. A dangerous shift that has prompted me to reach out to my peers near and far to join me in building a strong foundation to fight against the tyranny of the Olympian gods."

Gasps and the hum of murmured conversations sounded all around as Terena's blood heated.

The emperor held up a hand to quiet the room as he continued. "I want to assure all of you, as I've assured my new friends here." The emperor turned to acknowledge the men seated on the dais. Turning back to the crowd, he smiled. "The old gods have not forsaken us. We do not need to fear the return of the Olympian gods, if they're any left alive. Because the Titans provided us a weapon."

More gasps and excited chatter broke out. Terena took a step forward, stopping herself only when a Guard nearby turned toward her with a scowl.

"High Cleric Christos and his priests have been working tirelessly, translating the old texts, consulting seers blessed by the Titans, and have found a weapon to destroy the Olympians if they dare return to Elysium. They will know we will not be subjugated to their will! They will know, once and for all, *we will not! Bow! Down!*"

The crowd roared, everyone up from their seats as the ballroom shook with their cheering. It lasted a full minute before Solon could calm them enough to speak over their noise.

"No celebration would be complete without some extraordinary entertainment," the emperor said with an affected chuckle as he clapped Christos on the back. The cleric's top lip curled with disdain, but the look was gone before Terena could process what it could mean.

"It is no secret the traitors who perpetrated one of the worst crimes in our empire's history escaped our justice. But tonight, I am pleased to share we have caught one of the traitors and have brought him to face our justice right here, right now!"

Terena's heart stopped. Frantic, she searched the room for Lerek or Xoran. Migela and Cassandra were nowhere to be found either. Her blood boiled as she turned her attention back to Solon as he smiled and stepped aside. A commotion behind the dais drew his attention. Terena made her way slowly to the center of the ballroom.

If this maggot thought he could use her brother for entertainment, he was in for a long overdue lesson.

Her fingers tingled and the familiar red haze shrouded her vision when the Imperial Guard dragged their burden to drop at the feet of High Cleric Christos.

Someone pressed close behind her, and Terena stiffened as a voice she knew well whispered in her ear.

"You should have listened to your brother," Vassori said.

Terena spun around, but the tracker was already gone. She frantically searched the faces of those surrounding her, their gleaming eyes trained on the dais, hungry for the entertainment the emperor promised.

Swiveling back to the dais, Terena choked on a gasp. The bloodied face lifted, tears streaming down his face.

It was not Croak staring in mute shock at the gathering before him.

Terena clenched her hands as she stared up at Orry.

CROAK OPENED HIS EYES TO LOOK AT THE EMPTY PLATE SITTING ON THE ground. No one had come to get it or bring him another meal all day.

Rubbing at his belly, he contemplated all the things he'd do to the next guard if he came down and didn't bring with him something for Croak to eat. A slice of bread, at least.

He stilled as footsteps sounded on the flagstones. More than one set.

"Here he is."

Croak started. His stomach sank as he pushed away from the bars, his swollen face turning mutinous when he saw the woman in the dimly lit dungeon.

Serephina.

Flicking a glance at the men who followed her in, the sinking sensation in his belly grew worse. Dread slithered down his spine as he blinked up at the men before he shifted his gaze to Serephina.

"What is this?"

The woman, who always treated him with disdain and never actually spoke with him before, grinned at him.

"It's a rescue, dear! What else? I know you were expecting my Xoran but I wanted this moment for myself."

Croak rose slowly, his eyes darting between Serephina and the unknown arrivals. They wore black, nondescript clothes. He did not know them.

"And who are they?"

"Oh!" Serephina tittered, putting her hand to her mouth as if Croak had said something witty. "These men are here to take you away! Away from all of this." She waved at their surroundings.

"Where's my sister? Where's Lerek?"

"After you leave here, I'm afraid you'll never see them again."

Croak stepped away from the cell door as Serephina motioned to one of the men. He came forward with a key, unlocked the door and shoved it back.

The grating of metal on metal shrieked and Croak panicked. Two men came in and he fought against them, cursing his weakened state as they easily batted away his hands.

One man hauled him out and threw him to the ground. Croak cried out when he landed on his side. Another man grabbed his hands and bound them with iron shackles. Lifting him as easily as a babe, the men turned him to face Serephina.

He'd never seen a more cunning look on her pointy little face and that was saying something.

This woman was a viper.

"I sold you to these men," she said with a negligent lift of her hand. "You'll spend the rest of your days—however many that is—as a slave."

It took a moment for her words to sink in. Stunned, Croak gaped at the woman, then thrashed against the men when they pulled him away.

"You can't!" Croak shouted, terror crashing over him. His throat clogged with a sob as he fought to free himself. "You can't do this! Serephina! She'll kill you when she finds out! No! No! Get off me— get the fuck off me!"

Croak ranted and sobbed as he continued to fight, shouting expletives at the woman waggling her fingers at him.

"Don't you worry about your sister," Serephina called out as she disappeared from his sight. He could still hear her voice, and her words made him fight even harder.

"She won't survive what my Christos has planned for her."

Lerek gaped as Ormano Peredor, his childhood friend and Ren's confidant, dropped in a heap at the front of the dais. His eyes shot to Xoran, who watched the scene with a clenched jaw.

Moving closer to him, he hissed in the captain's ear. "Find Terena. Tell her to cause a distraction right now!"

Xoran didn't bother to acknowledge the order as he strode off behind the rest of the Imperial Guard, the men moving for their captain as he passed.

A buzzing sounded in Lerek's ears, drowning out whatever that pompous idiot, Christos, was saying as his eyes ranged about the crowded ballroom.

Hoping to spot Ren, his eyes instead found Cassandra, whose wide-eyed stare was riveted on someone to his left. Glancing over, Lerek frowned. He couldn't tell what had caused the frightened look on the woman's face.

When he looked over at her again, she was still looking at the same spot. Turning back, Lerek scowled as a woman he'd never seen before turned and stepped up onto the dais, her face ashen. She swayed a bit as she caressed the amulet at her neck, a beautiful emerald that sparkled as it caught the light. Lerek craned his neck when he saw another woman beside her.

Duchess Ovenno.

He made to move closer when everything went black.

A collective gasp sounded around the room, along with some titters quickly giving way to shouts and panicked movements the longer the darkness remained.

Lerek put his hands out as he went to the back of the dais, stumbling a few times as he moved past the Guard and the Watchmen to the spot he'd prearranged with Xoran to meet. Terena had told them she'd use a blackout to cause the distraction they needed while allowing her friend Vassori to kill as many of the soldiers posted about the room.

Someone bumped into him and Lerek pushed back when Gabriol caught his arm, snarling in his ear.

"Xoran ran off. I saw him head for the dungeons. Isn't he supposed to be with you?"

Nodding despite the pitch black surroundings, Lerek muttered to the mercenary to follow him as he led the way out of the back of the ballroom.

They left the darkness behind as they exited, striding down the hall to a hidden door in an alcove. Servants used these hidden passageways to move about the palace unseen, but Lerek and his brother, Isher, had used them as well, playing when they were younger and using them to sneak out of the palace when they were older.

They hurried through the narrow walkway, coming to a fork. Torches lined the walls at long intervals, the wan light just enough to keep them from stumbling, although Lerek knew these passageways like the back of his hand.

Reaching the exit they needed minutes later, Lerek ushered them through the lower kitchens, moving purposefully as servants stopped to gape at them.

The stairs to the dungeons appeared as they rounded the corner past the pantry Ren had hidden in days ago and Lerek quickened his pace.

"He's in the cell in the furthest part of the dungeons," Lerek murmured.

Grabbing a torch as they made their way to the back, he halted at the sight before him, confused. Behind him, Gabriol swore and unsheathed his sword.

"Welcome!" Serephina said with delight. Xoran stood behind her, sword drawn as he stared back at them, expressionless. Serephina clapped her hands, keeping them together as she brought them to her lips. She made a tsk and pouted at Lerek. "Someone's been naughty."

"What the fuck are you doing here?" Lerek snapped, eyeing Xoran and the five men flanking them with their swords readied.

"I was expecting you, silly," she said. Glancing at Xoran, she grinned. "You were right again, my love. I am sorry I doubted you." Turning back to Lerek she twisted her lips. "Prince Lerek, I had no idea you consorted with traitors and criminals."

Lerek's face flooded with heat as he held up his hand. The men beside Xoran looked familiar, but they wore black clothing, the bottom of their faces masked. They shifted uneasily as they backed away a step.

"I don't know what you're about, Serephina," Lerek said through gritted teeth, his anger rising the longer he eyed the woman. Her smile made him want to slap it off her face. "But I suggest you return to the ballroom and take your place beside the emperor."

"Oh ho," Serephina said, her hands dropping to her chest as she howled at him. "Listen to the princeling trying to sound like his father! Although—" Serephina's mouth compressed and her eyes lost all humor—"You will never be like your father. Because you'll never be *emperor*. I found out about your ill-advised plan, again," she said with a glance at Xoran. "And I sold the boy. You'll never find him now. *She* will never find him." Serephina flicked her hand. "Kill them both."

Gabriol rushed forward, catching one of the masked men unawares. The man brought up his sword at the last moment. Serephina jumped back and one of the men escorted her away.

Lerek yelled and swung his torch at Xoran when he came at him. In his panicked state, he stumbled backwards, nearly falling over. His left hand landed on the wall, catching himself as Xoran stared grimly at him.

"I knew it," Lerek said, his voice quivering as he lifted the torch and backed away. "Gods, I knew I shouldn't have trusted you."

"It was inevitable," Xoran said as he swung again. Lerek lifted the torch, crying out when Xoran's strike easily disarmed him.

Lerek continued to step back, one hand on the wall as he extended the other before him. He wasn't sure why he thought it might stop the captain.

"Why?"

Xoran prowled closer, his face impassive. "I made a vow to her. Long ago. And this is what she demanded of me."

Lerek exhaled, his eyes darting over Xoran's face as he fought to understand. "Who? Serephina? You and her—"

"You should've stayed dead."

Lerek glanced behind Xoran, seeing Gabriol hack at another one of their assailants before snapping his gaze back to the advancing captain. He raised his arm, fear gripping his heart tightly and cried out as the man swung his sword in what was sure to be the last thing Lerek would ever see.

It never came.

Xoran stared blankly at him, the sword protruding from his belly confusing him when he glanced down. He looked back up at Lerek, and his expression eased into acceptance as he dropped to the flagstones.

In the sudden silence of the room, Lerek blinked away the sight of the dead captain and looked up to see the strange, redheaded mercenary who traveled with Terena glaring down at him. Gabriol came up behind him, clapping the warrior on his shoulder.

"Rydon?" Lerek asked, his voice shaking.

The man's scowl deepened. He bent forward and thrust out his hand to help Lerek up. Rings bit into Lerek's fingers and he grimaced against the pain of the man's iron grip.

The mercenary stood eye to eye with Lerek, but his expression turned quizzical.

Before Lerek could ask again, the man spoke in a deep, gravelly voice.

"Where's Croak?"

CHAPTER 47

METILAI

As soon as Terena realized Orry was the entertainment Solon promised his guests, all the light from the room vanished, blanketing them in deepest black.

Guests screamed and rushed about like headless chickens. Terena shoved her way toward the dais as the darkness disappeared. The sudden brightness made others around her cry out, and Terena ripped off her helm. Throwing it across the room in her rage, she snarled as Christos and Solon gaped at her.

She stood alone in the center of the ballroom, the guests huddled together trying to get even further away. Her eyes searched for Vassori, but the tracker was nowhere to be found. Her eyes returned to the dais.

To Solon.

"Get her, you fool!"the emperor screeched at an Imperial Guard closest to him, and the man rushed forward.

Terena snapped out her hands and the Twins formed in them, the short swords flashing red, crackling with the power of fiery lightning.

Before the guard raised his arm, she stepped forward, bringing her arms in and slashed out. His head flew up in the air before following his body down to the ground.

Screams and cries renewed as the guests fought to get further away from her.

"You know," Terena said, glaring at the terrified emperor, a red haze at the edge of her vision. "I was going to let you live. For Lerek's sake. I was going to make a scene and leave once I had my brother back." She scoffed. "But you couldn't leave well enough alone, could you? You didn't heed my warning all those months ago. You did not learn from what I did to Duke Ravos's men. No, Emperor. Instead, you took my brother. You took my friend and... you tortured him?" Terena swallowed. "He's done nothing to you! Bringing Orry before these... these sycophants, for what? To harm me? Is this how you rule? Picking on the weak? He's a fucking cleric! He doesn't—"

"Ren!" Orry shouted, his face a mess of multicolored bruises, the right side of his jaw swollen so badly he lisped. "He has it! I'm sorry! I'm so sorry, I couldn't—"

High Cleric Christos grabbed Orry's hair and yanked his head back. Terena lurched forward as Christos screamed something unintelligible and swiped a blade across Orry's throat.

Terena's breath caught, watching in horrified denial as Orry grabbed at his neck, blood all over his fingers and down his wrists as he fell, his body twitching.

All around her, people cried out, pushing and shoving to get away as Terena's heart shattered. Her frame shook, head to toe, as her mind fought to make sense of what her eyes were seeing. Blood roared in her ears but she stood rooted, staring.

Orry stared back at her, the light leaving his eyes as his lips parted.

In stunned silence, Terena looked up at High Cleric Christos, whose wicked grin widened as he pulled a young woman in front him. She cried out and stumbled, and Terena watched her dispassionately. Her blonde hair shook as she moved, torn from its pins, and her arms, marred with bruises, flailed against Christos. The girl sobbed, fighting against the cleric's hold as he screamed at her to use her amulet. Terena glanced down at the jewel resting at the woman's chest.

An emerald amulet.

Chaos raged around her and Terena finally understood.

Terena roared, the sound ripped from her soul. Her body levitated, her hair lifting and crackling like a roaring fire, every inch of her skin alight as her eyes blazed with red heat, blocking her vision for a moment.

Terena whipped her hands out over and over, releasing the short swords at the dais. More blades materialized in her hands, red phantom swords, thrown with all her might as she raged.

Landing with a ground-shaking boom on one knee, Terena lifted her head to glare up at the dais. She smiled at the emperor laying there, multiple wounds bleeding profusely as he stared at her in mute horror. High Cleric Christos was nowhere in sight.

Terena stood, stalking toward the dais and the dying emperor. He held up a feeble hand, squeezing his eyes shut before opening them up to beseech her.

"It's all coming to pass," he whimpered when Terena crouched before him. "Everything she said. I thought I could stop it. He said we could stop it."

Terena gazed at the fallen emperor with disdain. She spared a glance around as the room emptied, someone finally having opened the doors.

"Where is Christos?"

Solon exhaled and blood oozed out his mouth. He licked his lips, his face pale as he lifted fearful eyes. He shook his head and cried. "We are doomed. We are doomed."

"Aye," Terena said without inflection. She summoned one of her swords and with a quick twist of her wrist, slammed it into Solon's chest. He wheezed, his eyes going wide.

He whispered something and she leaned in to hear. Pulling back, she frowned down at him. He was still.

Terena turned away from the dead emperor, fresh tears blurring her vision as she moved over to Orry. Her friend's eyes were still open, glassy and unseeing. His face was white beneath the fresh bruises and she prodded at his shoulder. A sob escaped her throat and she almost choked trying to stop the overwhelming rush of agony.

Standing abruptly, Terena threw her head back and roared. Every candle and torch snuffed out, leaving the room darkened once more.

"CHRISTOS!"

Rydon ran with Gabe behind Prince Lerek, bursting onto a chaotic scene when they reached the great hall. People screamed and ran every which way. There were only a handful of guards, City Watch by the look of their uniforms, all of them shouting at each other and the people as they tried to gain some kind of order. It was impossible.

The prince led them to the grand ballroom, the doors on the ground in a broken mess of splintered wood and metal. The interior of the room was dark and an ominous feeling shuddered through Rydon as he gripped his sword tight.

Stopping short at the sight before them, Rydon blinked. A moment later he was running.

"Ren," he said, crouching beside Terena's sobbing frame. She was crouched over someone, her body shaking with the ferocity of her cries and she wailed anew when he tried to pry her away.

"No!" she shrieked, thrusting her arm out. The force of it knocked him back on his ass.

Gabriol and the prince came up on the other side of her, Lerek's eyes wide and his mouth hanging open as he stared down at Ren. He dropped to his knees, his eyes welling as he reached out a tentative hand.

Terena snapped forward, ready to bite his hand as she shrieked again. "Don't you fucking touch him!"

As if realizing who he was, Ren blinked stupidly at the prince before she looked around, a crazy gleam in her eyes as she swiped a hand over her face.

At last, she spotted Rydon and threw herself into his arms. Great wracking sobs shook her body, and he tightened his hold, burying his hand in her hair as he tucked her head into his neck.

A long time passed before Ren lifted her head and sniffed, snot and tears marring her features.

"Where is he? Where is Croak?"

Rydon glanced up at Gabe. He'd gotten an abbreviated version of what happened in the dungeons, but he waited for Lerek to speak.

Prince Lerek sat back on his haunches and spread his hands in a defeated motion.

"I'm... I'm sorry," he said, his voice cracking.

Terena stared at him a moment. She began breathing heavily, fast, her chest rising and falling alarmingly as Rydon tried to comfort her.

"What? What?" Terena whimpered, clutching Rydon's sleeve with one hand as she wiped furiously at her face. "Tell me!"

The prince hung his head for a moment. Everything seemed suspended. Rydon swore under his breath at Lerek's cowardice.

"He's been taken," Gabriol said, trying to soften his words with an awkward pat on her shoulder. Ren jerked around, her eyes confused.

"Taken? Taken where?"

Rydon glared up at the prince who was watching them, dumb-struck. "Well?"

"I don't... I don't know. I... we got down to the dungeons and he was already gone. Serephina—"

Terena moved, jumping to her feet as her eyes focused, glaring daggers at the hapless prince. "Serephina? What's she to do with my brother?"

Lerek exhaled and shook his head. Rydon cursed again. The prince was in shock.

He grabbed Ren's sleeve to turn her attention back to him.

"Xoran betrayed you. Us. I don't know the details but he must have told her of our plans. She said she sold Croak and then left her men to kill Gabe and Prince Lerek."

Terena became so still, Rydon exchanged an uneasy glance with his friend.

"She sold him?"

Rydon winced at her whispered words. "Aye."

"Where? To whom?"

Rydon glanced at the prince again and gave a short shake of his head. "We don't know."

Terena turned to Lerek who stared back at her as if she'd just spat in his face.

"You don't *know*?"

Lerek shook his head vigorously. Rydon rose to his feet. Gabriol ran to the doors with his sword drawn as shouting and cries rang out, getting closer.

Ren laughed. The laughter grew in volume until she threw her head back, eyes shut.

She screamed at the ceiling and every window in the room blew out.

Lerek's hands shook, shielding himself from the spray of glass as he huddled near Orry's body.

Silence thickened around them after Terena's rage died down, and he glanced up to see her crestfallen face looking down at the ground, her shoulders slumped in defeat.

"Hermes is here!"

Cringing at Gabriol's shout as he barreled back toward them, Lerek got to his feet slowly. He spared a glance at Terena.

"We need to go. Now. He's here."

"How close?" Rydon asked, bending to pick up his discarded sword. Lerek flexed his hands as he swung his gaze between the men.

"Close. They've sacked the city."

"Fuck!" Rydon scrubbed his hands up and down his face, before turning to scowl at Terena. "We need to get you out of here. Now. Go with Gabe. I've got to get out there and stall him. I promised Daris I'd find a way for him to get inside before the others do but it looks like it's too—fuck!"

Lerek flinched at Rydon's outburst, backing away several steps.

"Take Ren—hey!"

Lerek turned frightened eyes on Rydon as the man snapped his fingers in Lerek's face.

"What?"

"Take her out through the dungeons. You know the way?"

Lerek nodded. "Aye."

"Good," Rydon grumbled turning his attention to Gabriol. "Where's Cassandra?"

Gabriol glanced around the remnants of the once magnificent ballroom and scowled. "She was here, with Migela. But I've not seen her since I've been with the prince."

Rydon groaned. "I'll find them. Take Ren and the prince and go. Don't worry about getting word back to us, we'll find you."

"Sonah—"

"It'll have to wait, Ren!" Rydon shouted as Terena started for the doors. He grabbed her by the elbow and spun her back. "We will find you. I'll keep her safe. I promise you."

Shouts outside the doors sounded and Lerek's head swiveled to the doors.

"What was that?"

"Fuck." Rydon smothered a shout as he cursed. "They're here. Go. Get her out of here now."

Gabriol grabbed hold of Terena's arm and hustled her away as Lerek stood rooted to the spot. More shouts sounded behind them and when Lerek turned his gaze back to the dais he stilled.

He hadn't noticed him before. Lerek took a tentative step closer and his chin shook as he took in his father's lifeless body.

At a shout from Gabriol, Lerek shook himself out of his stupor and gave his father one last look.

"Goodbye, father."

Turning, Lerek ran after the others.

Something was happening.

The ground beneath them shook and he exchanged a look with Melanos. The god was frowning as if he knew what was coming but before Daris could ask, Hermes shoved his way between them, a manic grin transforming his features.

"Take the city!"

His roar triggered answering shouts from his men and they rushed forward, the thunder of hooves deafening. Daris and Melanos were a moment behind, heads low over their mounts as they careened toward the gates.

Hermes held out a hand as they neared, and the gates burst into thousands of pieces.

The next half hour was a blur of blood and madness. Daris fought beside Melanos and the Liodari, his movements precise, his kills swift. The power he felt now was unlike the immortality granted to him by Athena. No, this was something else.

This was Melanos.

The God of Heroes fought beside them, infusing them with added strength and courage as he'd done back in Ravos.

"To the palace! Push on to the palace!"

Daris gutted the man he fought, looking around when he heard Soros's shout. The captain and a score of men ran through the streets, shouting and yelling with swords raised.

"We have to get there before Hermes!" Daris shouted to Melanos. The giant god smashed the head of one of the Heylian soldiers, pointed to Daris and nodded. He knew Melanos was still worried about Bethana, but the moment Hermes had focused on Metilai and sacking the city, the nymph was no longer in danger. Leander would watch over her and Sonah.

When Sonah had come tearing out of Hermes's tent earlier, she'd made Rydon go to the palace in place of Daris. He'd objected, only to have Sonah yell at him he was no longer immortal, and Ren would kill her if he died because of Sonah. Rydon had agreed, even as Daris chaffed at being left behind.

He was a warrior, ready to die for Terena, and no one would stop him.

Melanos had stopped him with a bonk to his head from his giant, meaty fist. By the time Daris had come around, Rydon was already gone.

As they made their way through the city now, Daris spared a thought to the carnage surrounding them. This was worse than any he'd seen in battle before, and he scowled at the bodies littering the city streets as they neared the palace. Most of the casualties were ordinary citizens. His blood boiled as they passed yet another woman with deep wounds, dead eyes staring into the night.

"How will we get inside?" Melanos yelled over to him as they ran.

"Rydon will come out. Be ready."

Just as they approached the palace gates, another quake shook the ground beneath them. Daris stumbled as Hermes cackled ahead of them. A second later, they all dropped back as every window in the palace exploded.

CHAPTER 48

METILAI

Rydon ran through the corridor outside of the ballroom, the masses racing around him in every direction. He shouted, calling out Cassandra's name as his head swiveled around, his eyes wild, searching for the seer. His pulse roared in his ears, mixing with the shouts of frightened royals, nobles and servants, everyone unfortunate enough to be trapped inside while Hermes's men raced toward them.

"Rydon!"

He whipped around and his eyes widened, his heart squeezing as Cassandra screamed his name. At last, the bodies parted and he saw Migela shoving her way toward him with Cassandra clutching the assassin's waist.

Rydon's relief was immediate, and he became lightheaded. Stumbling forward, he threw his arms around both women, dropping a kiss on Cassandra's blonde head.

He growled and roared at people to move as he shouldered his way back toward the ballroom with Cassandra sheltered close to his body.

When they were safely away from the press of those trying to escape, Rydon turned to address Migela, but the little seer grabbed hold of his tunic, her grip surprisingly strong.

"It's not Sonah! I mean, it *is* Sonah but not *your* Sonah!"

Rydon could not make sense of what she was saying and when he glanced at Migela, the assassin's hands flew in the language of the mute. He lifted his hands in surrender, his mouth dropping open. Migela huffed in frustration.

Cassandra whirled him back to face her and he blinked down into her slate eyes. "I think Vassori betrayed us! I saw her! I saw her speaking to that woman and she called her Sonah! She said, this way, Lady Sonah. And then the woman turned, and it was not our Sonah! It was a different woman but she had the amulet, Rydon! The Amulet of Kaïra! She was wearing it, and they called her 'Lady Sonah'!"

Rydon did not know what to make of her rantings but he grabbed hold of Cassandra's arms and shook her gently.

"Listen, listen! Right now, I need you and Migela to follow me out of here. Terena and Gabriol are waiting in the dungeons for you and I—"

Migela snapped her fingers at him and then started doing her hand language.

He shook his head in frustration. "I don't know—"

"She says she knows where the dungeons are and she can take us there herself," Cassandra snapped, her eyes flashing up at Rydon.

He nodded. "Good. All right, go now. I have to get to Hermes before he finds Ren. Go!"

The women took off and he watched them run to the far side of the ballroom. Before he turned away, Cassandra looked over her shoulder. Their eyes caught and held until Migela grabbed her and shoved her through a door and out of sight.

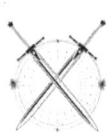

TERENA SHOOK GABRIOL BY THE SHOULDERS, HER EYES WILD AS SHE PLEADED with him. "I don't have anyone else I can trust with this! It has to be you, Gabriol, please!"

Lerek hung back near the archway in the very back part of the dungeons, his vacant gaze on the ground. Cassandra and Migela held each other as Terena gazed up at Gabriol.

They had arrived a few minutes ago as Gabriol was about to go back up to search for them. After exchanging brief hugs, they had made their way toward the exit when Terena grabbed Gabe, stopping him.

Gabriol shook his head, his eyes falling away from her. Terena choked back a sob. She thrust her hand beneath her leather armor and pulled out the oilcloth-wrapped shroud, shoving it against Gabriol's chest.

He balked and shoved it back at her. "I am not the heir! I'm not even a god! How can I possibly open the portal and—"

"Please," she moaned. "The prophecy only spoke of the heir bringing the gods back to glory. Nothing about how they actually come back to Elysium. Go to Hekate's temple and open the portal. Here," Terena held the shroud against Gabriol's chest while she fished inside her cloak. From the inside pocket, she pulled out a gold armband and held it in front of her. Gabriol held onto the shroud as he scowled down at her.

"Take this with you," she said, her voice breaking as she shook the adornment at him. "When you find my mother, she'll know you speak true if you show her this. It belonged to her brother, my uncle. Please Gabriol. You must warn her. Tell her about Hermes. Tell her everything I told you about the previous circles. Someone has sabotaged us from the beginning and you're my only hope to find out who."

"How can I go back?" Gabriol asked, huffing in frustration. "I can't use this to open the portal! I won't even know what to do—"

"You will," Terena said emphatically, nodding her head as she narrowed her eyes. "Remember what Orry said? Hold up the shroud and speak the words. I have to believe there was a reason you were with him when he read of it in the priestess's journal. I'd hoped it would be Orry going back, but he's gone and I *need* you, Gabe. Please, help me."

Gabriol looked around as if lost, shaking his head. Terena wanted to scream. They had no time for this, but if Gabriol didn't leave now, she had a horrible feeling all would be lost.

"I have no one else, Gabe. If you don't do this, we're going to lose. I trust you. Please go. For me. Please."

Gabriol reached out hesitantly and took the armband from her, slipping it over the sleeve of his tunic. Terena watched his movements, a strange calm settling over her as she saw the band fit snuggly against his bicep.

Like it was made for him.

She exhaled and gave him a watery smile. Tears slid down her cheeks and she wiped at them angrily as she stepped away from Gabriol.

"I promised Rydon I'd get you out of here! I can't—"

Terena snorted, wiping her nose on her bracer. "You can. And you will. I'll be fine. I'm a god, remember? Your only concern now is getting north as fast as possible. Get to Hekate's temple and do not hesitate. Open the portal."

She turned away, bringing her hands up to rub at her eyes. Her breath fogged out in front of her and she quickened her steps.

Gabriol was about to disappear through the door leading to the secret corridor Rydon had used earlier to get inside, when Lerek called out.

"I'm going with him."

Terena arched a brow and shared a look with Gabriol when he turned back. "What? Why?"

"I can do more than just sit in a palace all day, Ren," Lerek said. He looked away, lips pressed tightly together, before turning back to her. "A lot of what's happened started because of me. I know it won't make up for it, but I'd like to at least help in any way I can."

Lerek turned to Gabriol. "You'll be going through Thalos?"

"Aye," Gabriol said, his eyes shifting between Lerek and Terena.

"Heylisia controls the port, and the bridge is guarded by River-men. The only way they'll let you cross is with me. Peleon isn't letting anyone cross. Now that Ravos is back with the empire, he's not taking any chances with soldiers defecting to join Hermes. They'll kill you if you try to cross the bridge."

"There is no more empire," Terena said bitterly. "Hermes has sacked the city and I'm sure is sitting on the throne right above our heads at this very moment. It won't be long before word gets out across the continent."

"You're wrong," Lerek bit out, his eyes intense as he stared back at Terena. "*I* am the emperor now, and I will take this city back. But for now, I'll go north with Gabriol and do this. For you. For my city and my empire."

Terena sighed and waved a hand. "I—Gabe? It's up to you."

Gabriol was silent for a minute, eyeing Lerek as if he was something nasty he'd stepped in.

"Please," Lerek muttered. "Please let me help. I can do this."

After a very tense and awkward silence, Gabriol gave Lerek a curt nod. "Fine. But I'm not going slow because I have the crown prince with me. We'll ride hard and sleep outdoors."

"You'll have the *emperor* with you," Lerek corrected Gabriol and shrugged. "And, aye, I understand."

When Gabriol went through the doorway, Lerek made to follow. Terena rushed forward, grabbing hold of his arm.

Turning, Lerek looked at her, then smiled sadly.

"Don't get yourself killed," she said as heat rose in her cheeks.

Something passed over Lerek's eyes and made her step back. Before she could, Lerek bent his head and kissed her roughly. He pressed his forehead to hers, the heat from his words fanning her cheeks. "I love you."

The ache those words spiked in her heart made her pull away. Tears stung her eyes, and she averted her gaze.

She did not say the words back to him.

Lerek stood there a moment more before striding off with brisk steps until Terena knew they were both gone.

Pressing her hand to her chest, she sighed and closed her eyes.

"Terena."

Opening her eyes, Terena turned to Cassandra. The seer's eyes were red-rimmed. "Ren, I think... I think Vassori betrayed us."

Terena's hand froze in front of her face as she stared at Cassandra. The moment Vassori had spoken to her in the ballroom flashed in her mind and she recalled what the tracker had said.

"What did you see?" Terena's voice was quiet as she stared at the blonde.

Cassandra glanced at Migela, who nodded grimly.

"Do you remember my vision? Of Sonah wearing the amulet? The Amulet of Kaïra?"

"Aye. I saw it."

"You did?"

Terena nodded once. "On a blonde girl. High Cleric Christos found it somehow. And I think the girl wearing it is the real Sonah Yahn."

"What do we do?" Cassandra wailed, clutching the necklaces at her chest. "We have to get it back somehow! Why was Vassori with her? How—"

Migela signed with her hands and Terena opened her eyes to watch her.

She shook her head in response. "No. I am not going anywhere. I am going to find Vassori and make her talk. And then I'm getting that fucking necklace."

"No!" Cassandra's eyes widened in horror as she shook head. "No, no, Hermes will be up there by now. We have to leave. You cannot go up there!"

"I will not cower," Terena seethed, her heart beating a painful tattoo within her breast. "I am a god in full now. He can try to hit me again, but this time I swear by the Fates he will regret it. Sonah's up there and I will not have her at his mercy."

Terena strode back through the dungeons as Cassandra continued to beg her to stop. She and Migela trailed after her and Terena took the winding steps up to the first floor of the palace.

As soon as they neared the great hall, Terena's steps faltered, taking in the crowd of warriors standing there.

Hermes's men.

They hadn't yet noticed her and she curled her lip as she watched them celebrating by tearing up the palace.

"Ren!"

Terena spun around. Was her mind playing tricks on her? That was Sonah's voice. Right?

"Ren!"

Terena took off running, following the echoes of Sonah's shouts, stopping in front of the throne room. Her eyes widened when she spied Sonah.

Cursing, Terena took a few steps forward, hands clenched at her sides. Sonah spotted her and made to run to her when Hermes pulled her back roughly. A man nearby shouted, trying to get to her but froze in place mid-stride. Hermes dropped the hand he'd held up toward the man and turned to Terena, a playful grin on his lips.

Hermes cupped a hand to his mouth and called out, "Look who I found!"

SONAH SWALLOWED AS SHE CAUGHT THE STRICKEN LOOK ON TERENA'S FACE. She didn't come any closer, standing near the doors to the throne room and looked back at them. Migela, the assassin she'd met at Lethe, stood outside the threshold, uncertain, her hand on the hilt of her dagger.

Hermes draped an arm over Sonah's shoulders, the heavy appendage making her dip a little as she scowled up at the god.

"Come, Terena. Your sister awaits."

Still, Terena did not move. Sonah made to remove Hermes's arm, but it was like trying to move a boulder.

"If it's me you want," Terena called out, "I'll come. But only if you let Sonah go."

"Where is the tracker?"

Terena's eyes narrowed. "Who?"

Hermes leaned forward. "Don't be coy. She was with you in Ravos. Bring her here."

"Vassori's gone," Ren said in a loud voice.

"What?"

Ren shrugged, her eyes shifting to Sonah. Giving her a small smile, her sister turned her attention back to Hermes. "You're surprised? She betrayed me. And she also has the Amulet of Kaïra. How did she know where to find it, I wonder? Perhaps you told her? Was that your plan all along? Why you wanted me to find her?"

"I was ready to forgive you for your insolence back at Ravos," Hermes snarled. "But I cannot forgive incompetence. I wanted *you* to find her because she asked *for you!*" He stepped off the dais, hands balled at his sides.

"Well, now she's gone and so is the amulet."

Hermes looked like he might faint. Sonah edged away from him.

"Vassori has the amulet?"

"Aye," Terena said, her gaze shifting to Sonah. "And someone who can wield it. The real Sonah Yahn."

"Impossible," Hermes said, his face slack.

"And yet," Ren scoffed, spreading her arms as she sneered. "Cassandra has seen it."

Hermes's head snapped up at that, looking beyond Ren, searching the room. "Bring the seer forward. Now!"

Sonah's gaze caught on the blonde woman struggling against her captors as they brought her toward the dais. Ren lunged for them, grabbing hold of the woman's hand before they were torn apart by more of the god's soldiers.

The woman was thrown to the ground, her sharp cries loud in the cavernous room. Rydon shouted and sprang forward, as did Ren. Both were stopped before they could reach her.

The woman raised terrified eyes to Hermes when he stepped forward to loom over her.

"Hello, Cassandra," Hermes murmured, his silken voice soft. "What a surprise to find you here."

The woman averted her gaze.

"You've seen the amulet?"

The woman nodded. "Aye."

"And the woman who has it? Is what my niece says true?"

"It is."

Hermes threw back his head and laughed.

Startled, Sonah looked over at Ren, who frowned at the god's mirth.

"Well. We'll deal with that shortly. For now…" Hermes gestured to some of his men.

Sonah turned, curious, her eyes widening when they brought in Leander.

Sonah's movements became frantic. What had he done to Leander? She turned to Rydon, who stood beside Daris at the bottom of the dais. "Rydon! Help me!"

Rydon's face was pained as he lifted sad eyes to Sonah. Daris looked downright murderous.

"Let me go," Sonah said, tugging at the god's arm.

Hermes laughed. To Terena he said, "You know I won't do that, dear niece. Why don't you stop whatever foolishness this is, so we can all enjoy our victory."

"Let her go!" Terena screamed.

Sonah gawked at her sister when the room shook.

"Daris!"

The commander pulled his gaze away from Ren and frowned at Sonah.

"Please, help me!"

Daris spared a glance for Hermes before he said, "I'm sorry, Sonah."

"Rydon! Please—"

"Don't waste your breath, child," Hermes said. "I hold the mercenary as long as I hold you. And the commander... well, let's just say his life is now bound to me."

"What?" Sonah gasped, her head swinging from left to right. Both men looked angry, but beneath, she saw the frustration that ate at them. The way Rydon would not look over at her, the high color in his face as he continued to look anywhere but at her.

And Daris. His face was thunderous, ready to unleash a storm. He looked to be in so much pain, Sonah felt a momentary sympathy for him.

Then she got angry.

"You two are the most useless warriors a lady could ever have the misfortune of surrounding herself with!" she grumbled.

Turning back to Terena, who paced near the center of the room, she yelled, "Don't do it, Ren! I'll find a way to get free and then we'll make him sorry! He can't hurt us!"

Hermes chuckled and leaned close to her ear. "You won't get free, little niece. And you're mistaken, because I *can* hurt you, remember? I can hurt your pet wolf, here. So do not test me."

"You wouldn't dare," Sonah seethed.

Hermes smiled cruelly. "You want to play? I warn you; I'm too strong and you're not strong enough."

Sonah snapped around and snarled at him. "We both know *that's* not true. Or did you forget our conversation outside the city?"

Hermes's sneer faltered and he snatched hold of her arm.

"Let her fucking go!" Daris yelled.

Sonah turned her head to see him struggling against whatever hold Hermes had him under. He almost broke through the invisible bonds, the veins in his neck straining, muscles bulging, and she gasped at his raw power.

"Oh not you too, Commander," Hermes chuckled, although she noted the uncertainty in his expression. Hermes had zero problems holding onto Sonah as she struggled against his grip. "Terena, look, even your lover is moved to speak up at last! Rydon!"

Before Sonah knew what he was about, she yelped when Hermes dropped his arm and shoved her toward Rydon. She stumbled into him, glaring daggers at Hermes as Rydon wrapped her in his arms and moved her away. Leander was still frozen in place, his face and neck red with exertion as he tried to break free of Hermes's control.

Rydon tried to calm her when she struggled to get to Terena, crying in frustration. Terena stood still with her hands balled at her sides, her face scarlet and her lips thinned to the point they disappeared.

"Now," Hermes said, stepping down from the dais in a leisurely fashion as he made his way to Daris's side. Sonah balked when Hermes grabbed Daris and hauled him bodily in front of him, steadying the Liodari commander with a chokehold on his breast-plate. Daris struggled, his face identical to her sister's in color and temperament.

"Perhaps I'll take your lover's other eye?" Hermes mused, a dagger in his hands faster than Sonah could blink. Renewing her screaming and yelling, she switched the focus of her cries to Hermes, begging him to release Daris.

Daris stood there, his eyes downcast as Hermes held the tip of his blade to Daris's left eye. "Maybe I'll just slit his throat. What say you, niece? Despite your pretty request, I've yet to make him immortal. Shame..." He turned back to Terena, an innocent smile on his face.

Sonah blanched and her head snapped around to her sister. Terena rushed forward, hand outstretched and her face stricken with terror.

"Stop!" she screamed, her chest rising and falling rapidly with her breaths. Her wild eyes shifted between Hermes and Daris.

"I won't hurt Sonah," Hermes said conversationally, then clicked his tongue. "But I have no issue with killing your lover. I'm curious how far you'd let me go before—"

"I'll come with you!" Terena shouted. Her voice cracked and Sonah's heart broke to see the pain on her face. Tears flowed freely as she looked at the god with hate in her eyes. "You filthy piece of shit, I will come with you!" She yelled out that last part so fiercely, Daris's face lifted at last.

"Don't you fucking do it!" Daris shouted, his voice desperate. He fought against Hermes's hold. "He won't hurt me! Don't you fucking do it, Ren!"

"Awww! I am *moved*! Sincerely, the love between you two, I mean..." Hermes pounded his chest as he tilted his head. "I feel it. Right here. Terena—do you see what you've inspired? It's almost enough to make me let you all go, but... alas, I don't think I will."

"You coward," Terena said, her voice shaking with rage and fear. Her eyes sparked red as she glared at the god. "Let him go."

"You see," Hermes said with feigned sincerity, belying the anger in his glare. "I would, but I can't. He bound himself to me."

"What? Why? He's my—"

"He *was*," Hermes tutted, his expression contrite. A wicked smile transformed his face and Sonah shuddered as she watched the inter-action. "He's mine now."

Terena's nose scrunched. Daris's face blanked, but Sonah saw his body shaking against whatever hold Hermes had over him.

"What? That makes no sense. You don't need a guardian."

Hermes stood there with a self-satisfied smile on his face.

Terena's eyes shot to Daris, standing like a stone sentinel at the god's side. Rage rolled off him in waves as he looked away from her. Terena shuddered.

"Daris," she called out, her voice little more than a whisper. She'd moved closer, standing near the center of the room.

Daris's body shifted infinitesimally, straining against something they could not see.

"What did you do?" Terena's voice broke.

"I'm waiting," Hermes said in a tone devoid of feeling.

Terena's eyes snapped to him, mouth open.

"Why?"

Hermes watched her in silence. Sonah swore for a moment that disappeared in a blink, regret and panic passed over his features before they hardened.

"I learned it from your commander," Hermes replied as if sharing a fun fact. "He took your sister, and here you are, back in his arms. Well, almost. I wanted *you* back. So I took your lover."

The bastard had the audacity to hold out his arms, tilting his head as he smirked at Terena.

"Now, you're back in *my* arms."

"You sneaky shit," she said softly but in the tense silence that followed, they all heard. Sonah closed her eyes.

The insult transformed Hermes from playful god into wrath personified.

Sonah called out to Hermes but her words were cut off with Rydon's hand over her mouth. He bent close to whisper in her ear and she shivered.

"You will pull his attention away and Terena will have you to worry about as well. We will help her, I promise you, but keep still for now."

Hermes bent closer to Daris, speaking to him in hushed tones and Rydon pulled his hand away at last.

The soldiers around them shifted, and Sonah flinched when Rydon's grip tightened. The soft hiss of several swords leaving their scabbards filled the room. Hermes moved away from Daris to retake his seat on the Heylisian throne.

Daris did not move.

Sonah bucked against Rydon, frantic as the men approached Ren.

"Hush," he said. "If you keep quiet, he won't put those on you as well."

Two men behind them grabbed hold of Daris as another soldier moved toward Terena with manacles that glowed faintly, a sickly yellow color that smelled, if the look on Terena's face was anything to go by.

Daris struggled against the men who held him in place as he screamed at Hermes, obscenities she'd never heard him utter before. Terena lost all color and dropped to the ground when the manacles were in place. One soldier bent and lifted her over his shoulder, the heavy metal chains thudding and dragging on the ground as they left.

"Stay close to me, Sonah," Rydon whispered. "The first chance I get, I'll get those fucking shackles off her and get you two away."

Sonah panted, her struggles against Rydon exhausting her and she slumped against him, grateful for the strength of his arms and the quiet words he whispered to her. She knew Rydon was only doing what Hermes, as his liege lord or whatever, told him to. She also knew that as her eudaemon, he would not let her come to harm. But she was still frustrated they were so helpless against Hermes.

Daris surged forward, intent on getting to Terena but Hermes did something with his hand and Daris froze again in the same manner as Leander. Her eyes shot to the shifter who remained standing in the exact spot he'd been in since Terena arrived.

"Ren!" Daris shouted and Hermes whipped his head around, surprised. "Ren! I'll get you out! I love you, Ren! Hold on! Hold—"

Hermes backhanded Daris. The commander fell to the ground

and Sonah cried out. He was so still, she feared Hermes had killed him.

The god moved back to the throne and sat, a gold staff as tall as Melanos forming in his hand, two snakes winding around as wings emerged at the top.

"Please don't let him do this," Sonah begged Rydon, her throat clogging with emotion. "Please, Rydon."

"There's nothing we can do right now, Sonah," Rydon said gruffly, his grip easing as he glared at Hermes. "The time will come when we fight back. But not now."

CHAPTER 49

METILAI

Terena's eyes remained closed even as the scrape of boots sounded outside of her cell.

The heaviness of the adamantine shackles went beyond the strange metal, its energy seeping deep into her bones. The suppression of her powers felt as if her very blood was slowly draining from her body, and it took her a long time to lift her heavy lids to face Hermes as he stopped in front of the iron bars.

Confusion furrowed her brows as she stared at the stranger standing there.

Not Hermes, but she knew the man was a god. Now that she'd ascended, she could feel his otherness like an itch she couldn't reach.

In silence, she watched him as he in turn gazed at her, sable brows furrowed and lips puckered as if watching a curiosity in one of the traveling circuses of Osta.

He took a step closer, wrapping long, elegant fingers around one of the bars as he peered down at her.

"You submitted to him for your sister," the god said in a voice that rumbled through the quiet. Terena winced, moving to adjust against the damp wall at her back.

When she did not respond, the god tilted his head and frowned. "How far would you go to protect her, I wonder?"

Despite the cuffs draining her power, Terena's adrenaline kicked in and she surged forward, snarling at this stranger who dared question her loyalty to Sonah.

"Let me out and I'll show you."

The man nodded and dropped slowly to his haunches. The light was fickle, moving unnaturally so that his face remained hidden in shadows. The only thing she could see was the glitter of his dark eyes and the strange silver snaking across his pupils, like Hermes's eyes. She could barely see the square cut of his jaw as he lifted his chin.

"You can let yourself out," the god said after an uncomfortable silence. "Those shackles were not meant for you. Or your sister."

Terena snorted. Lifting her arms as high as she could, she shook them at the god. "They seem to be holding onto me just fine."

The man's gaze shifted from the shackles to her face, and he frowned. "Have you tried?"

Blinking stupidly, Terena had no response. Looking down at the cuffs, she was about to speak when he sighed.

"I should not be here," he said softly as if to himself. "But I had to see her again. And then when he put you down here..."

Terena screwed her lips in confusion. What was he talking about?

"Your friends will come for you. But you can free yourself. You are more powerful than you know. Hermes is afraid of you. He's afraid of... your sister. And he's afraid of me."

He rose, moving away from the bars. Terena shifting, trying to stand, but she was too weak.

"Who are you?"

The man glanced at her over his shoulder. Everything about him was hidden by shadows, as if they coated his very skin. She could see nothing of his features beyond the cold glitter of his dark eyes and the shine of his black hair.

"We will meet again, daughter of Ares."

Terena lifted onto a knee when the man evaporated before her eyes.

RYDON SNUCK OUT OF HIS TENT TO LOOK FOR DARIS. HERMES THOUGHT TO punish him, Daris, and Sonah by making them sleep outside the palace where the rest of his army was encamped. Or perhaps he thought it better to keep them far from the dungeons where Terena was being held. The shifter, Leander, was in the palace, far from Sonah, ensuring her continued compliance.

As Rydon moved, shouts sounded from the southern side of the camp. Slowing, Rydon frowned, turning his head as he strained to hear what was going on.

Seconds later, firelight arced above him, hitting tents and blazing to life. Rydon cursed, pivoting and racing for Sonah's tent. The interior was dark, and he stumbled to a halt before he saw the shadowed lump of her body. She was asleep, curled up on her side with furs tucked around her.

Lunging forward, Rydon dropped to his knees, grabbing the furs and tossing them before grabbing hold of Sonah's shift and yanking her toward him. Yelping, Sonah's arms flailed out, one hand catching him on the side of his jaw.

"Sonah! Get up! We're under attack!"

Sonah mumbled something incoherent, but Rydon ignored her as he hauled her up beside him. He searched frantically for her clothes.

"Where the fuck are your clothes? Get dressed! Hurry! Meet me in

Daris's tent. Sonah!" Rydon grabbed the girl by her shoulders as she rubbed at her eyes and yawned. How the fuck could she sleep so soundly after everything?

He gripped her chin, his face so close to hers he could see the whites of her startled, puffy eyes. "Listen! We're under attack. Get to Daris. West of here, two tents over."

"Wait, what?"

Rydon shouted a curse, dropping the tent flap as he turned back to her. "Get fucking dressed! And get to Daris! Two tents over. Go west!"

"Which way is west?"

Rydon closed his eyes and clamped his mouth shut. The shouts outside the tent were growing louder. Closer. Someone rushed past, and Rydon spared a glance over his shoulder before he waved his arm at Sonah.

"Turn right outside your tent," he bit out through clenched teeth. Without another word, he strode out of the tent. Rydon was jarred by a running soldier, grabbing the man's breastplate instinctively and hurling him out of his path.

He took off running, weaving through the tents as he made his way back to the palace. If he could use this attack to rescue Terena, they could leave with Sonah and the others while Hermes dealt with whatever the fuck this was.

Skidding to a stop, he gawked at the sight before him. An enormous wolf tore through the camp, cutting down Hermes's men. More wolves appeared, running and grabbing up any soldier in their paths.

Just as Rydon made to turn away, he spotted a giant of a man fling a soldier toward him. Ducking at the last moment, Rydon shot back up as the man sailed over him, and a smile broke out on his face as the giant turned and Rydon saw who it was.

"Melanos!"

The god pivoted, his eyes darting around, and Rydon called out again. Stifling the curse that came to his lips, Rydon raced between tents, dodging past men fighting off the terrifying wolves. Water surged over a group of soldiers to his right, swallowing them up and sweeping them away as the water moved unnaturally toward more of Hermes's men.

Rydon stared for a second before turning to run.

"Melanos!"

The god spotted him as Rydon stopped running and clapped him on the shoulder, almost knocking Rydon down.

"Where the fuck have you been?" he yelled up at the god as another of Hermes's men rushed toward them. As if swatting away a gnat, Melanos scowled at the soldier and batted him away with one meaty arm. Turning back to Rydon, the god grinned down at him.

"Eudaemon!"

"What happened to you? I thought you were with Hermes." Rydon spread his arms, baffled but still very glad to see him.

"I am never with Hermes," he replied. He turned, grabbing hold of two soldiers who rushed at them, cracking their heads together. They dropped at their feet, and Melanos pulled Rydon away. "After we took the city, I went back for Bethana. When I returned, I heard of Hermes's actions. Fucking snake."

"I'm glad you're with us," Rydon said clapping the god on his broad shoulder.

Melanos looked back at him with a frown. "Only because our interests align at the moment. I am here for Terena and Sonah only."

"Then our interests indeed align," Rydon said, motioning with his head as he led the way through the fighting. Melanos followed him warily. "Who's with you? I saw wolves destroying Hermes's army. Where's Bethana?"

Melanos winked at him and pointed. Rydon narrowed his eyes and frowned. A mass of water moved in a cyclone, engulfing a soldier while his screams filled the air.

"Where? I see nothing but water... where the fuck did water come from?"

"You are looking at my bride. *She* is the water. Bethana is a naiad.

A water nymph. And one of the wolves is Leander. The rest are my Relics. Remember Sonah's plan to get you and the commander inside the palace before we took the city?"

"Aye," Rydon said. She'd wanted Melanos to use his Relics to distract Hermes and his men while Daris and Rydon snuck away. Instead, she'd come running back to them after meeting with Hermes to tell them Daris wasn't going. That didn't go over too well with the commander.

"My Relics are causing havoc out here. And with Bethana and Leander's help, hopefully the distraction will buy you and Sonah time to get Terena out of the palace."

Turning back to the god, Rydon held out his hand. "Terena's down in the dungeons. I can get in, but I need you to help distract the guards inside while I get her out. I've already told Sonah to go to Daris's tent. Once we get Terena released, we'll go get Sonah and get the fuck out of here."

They reached the entrance to the dungeons and made their way down. He worried Melanos might be too big to fit inside the narrow corridor but the god kept up just fine.

As they reached the cells, Rydon ducked back behind cover. It was too quiet. There should be guards down here.

Rydon turned to look back at Melanos. Frowning, the god moved past him. Moving to catch up, Rydon stopped short at the sight before them.

Half a dozen guards lay dead at Ren's feet. Melanos chuckled and reached out to embrace her.

When she pulled away, Ren turned to Rydon with a grin.

"What fucking took you so long?"

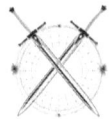

"Can you walk?" Rydon asked.

Terena lifted her head, still feeling the affects of the adamantine, the metal ore used to weaken the gods.

"Aye, I'm fine," she said, but the pallor of her cheeks put the lie to her words.

"How'd you break out?"

"Long story."

"We have horses outside," Rydon said. "I'll get Daris and Sonah and meet you—"

"I'm not going anywhere without Sonah," Terena said firmly, her words garbled. She hocked and spat out blood, lifting weary eyes to look between her friends. Rydon watched her in stoic silence but Melanos's face was nothing but violence.

"We're all going together," he responded.

They exited the dungeons and walked toward the horses tethered a few feet away. As Rydon pulled Nyx's reins free, rustling sounded behind them. A shout at their backs made Terena lurch forward, her hands grabbing onto her saddlebags.

"They're here!"

Terena's heart stuttered. Rydon shouted, blocking her from view as Hermes and his men rushed forth. The sound of metal hitting metal rang out as Hermes's men engaged Melanos.

Terena's hands whipped out and her short swords materialized.

"No!" Rydon shouted, pushing her back toward Nyx. "You'll only endanger her further if you go to her now! He'll only imprison you again and again until you submit!"

Terena looked beyond him at the soldiers fighting against Melanos. Her blood surged, begging her to turn and fight.

"I'll get Sonah," Rydon called out as he moved toward the fighting, unsheathing his sword. "I swear it!"

Terena watched until Rydon entered the fray.

Turning, she sprang onto Nyx's back and took off. Terena looked back over her shoulder. Hermes's men surrounded Rydon and Melanos.

She cursed and turned forward, bending low over Nyx as she whispered, "Fly, girl, fly!"

They tore through a copse of trees beyond the rear palace gate.

The ground sloped down and she veered right. Grass and low shrubs flattened beneath Nyx's hooves and they finally reached the flat lands between the city and the sea.

Nyx needed no more urging as she raced across the plains. Terena whooped as the wind tore through her hair, laughing even as tears streamed from her eyes and into her hair.

Her victory was short-lived as thunder sounded behind her. Terena glanced over her shoulder and swore as soldiers bore down on her.

She muttered encouragement to Nyx, her heart racing in time with Nyx's hooves. Her head swam, and nausea roiled in her empty belly, clawing its way up her throat so she choked back bile.

Shouts sounded behind her, and her pulse ratcheted up. Terena kept glancing back and panicked as the men seemed to gain on her. She could tell from the change in the air they were close to the sea now.

More shouting rang out behind her, and Terena urged Nyx ever faster, her heart plummeting at how close the soldiers were. She thought someone bellowed her name, and for a moment she swore it sounded like Daris.

But that couldn't be. He was with Sonah.

Wasn't he?

Bending low over Nyx's neck, she panted. The thunder of hooves drew closer.

Heart hammering against her ribs, Terena blinked, staring ahead. Realization dawned slowly as the horizon drew closer and closer. Nyx kept up her breakneck speed. Too late, Terena pulled on the reins to stop her.

"Terena!"

Her name on the wind was the last thing she heard before Nyx flew off the edge of Heylisia.

"Terena!"

The scream tore from Daris as he watched her disappear over the cliff. He yanked on his mount's reins and the stallion reared up.

As the mighty hooves stomped back onto the ground, Daris leaped from his horse and ran, dropping to his knees at the cliff's edge.

For long seconds, the only sounds in the misty dawn were the thudding of his heart and the hooves of the horses at his back. He didn't want to believe what he'd just seen. How could this happen? He'd been coming to get her. To tell her he'd do what she wanted. To show her how much he loved her by agreeing to her request.

To break their bond.

Daris put a hand to his chest, certain his heart was breaking. The pain was unbearable and yet he deserved it because he'd failed her.

As he watched the horizon, his chest on fire and his soul screaming inside him, he blinked, trying to make sense of what had just happened.

He lurched forward to look at the beach far below and reared back when a large, black shape erupted into the sky before him.

The cries of the men behind him filled the silence, but all Daris could do was stare at the sight in disbelief.

Nyx flew through the swirling mist, sleek, black wings spread wide as she banked left with Terena bent low over her back.

Daris fell back, raising his hand to shield his eyes against the sunrise. Nyx's form swerved, a shadow before the morning sun, and flapped her massive wings, soaring away.

"Ren," Daris whispered and swallowed.

ƐPILOGUE

HEKATE'S TEMPLE

The land surrounding the temple was eerily silent. There was no wind rustling through the trees. The snow was untouched: no rabbit, fox or bird prints to hint at any wildlife about.

As Lerek trudged behind Gabriol, he wondered again if the Roison could actually call up the portal to the realm the gods were banished to. And if he was successful, what if something—someone—came through? Lerek had a very basic understanding of swordplay. Unlike his brother, Lerek had preferred to study history and politics over martial arts. He hadn't worried before because there was always someone with him well-trained in warcraft.

Even now.

Turning his gaze to the mercenary, Lerek glared at his back. "Do you even know where we're going?"

Gabriol didn't respond. Lerek sighed and tried again. "What if—"

"The oracle told me what I needed to do," Gabriol muttered.

Lerek's mouth dropped open. "What? When? It was Terena—"

"When we rescued her in Messene."

Gabriol slowed down and Lerek quickly caught up to him, his narrowed eyes locked on the Roison's face. He had a shuttered look as he stared ahead, but Lerek thought he seemed troubled.

"She told me Terena would ask something impossible of me. And when that happened, I was to say yes. And when I was ready, I would know exactly what to do."

"How do you know this is what she meant?"

Gabriol laughed harshly and shook his head. He glanced at Lerek and shrugged. "Terena's never asked anything of me that I thought was impossible. Until she asked me to come north to Hekate's temple and open a portal to the world known as Earth and find her mother."

Lerek nodded. "Aye. I guess that qualifies."

"Indeed."

"But you told her you didn't know how."

Gabriol's face when he glanced at Lerek was bleak. "I hoped to dissuade her."

They walked for a time in silence. After a while, Lerek squinted at something on the horizon.

"Look!"

He pointed and ran ahead, his face breaking out in a wide smile as he saw columns come into view. Gabriol hurried, stopping beside Lerek as they gazed up at the haze-shrouded temple, the sun blocked out by the trees.

The greying marble was home to climbing vines and bird nests in the pediment. The temple looked as if it hadn't been used in decades, perhaps centuries, and yet as they stepped inside, the small antechamber was immaculate.

Lerek crept behind Gabriol. The antechamber opened into a wide circular room with old braziers against the walls and an altar in the middle. Lerek stepped closer, eyeing the remnants of candles and small vials, some still filled with spices. Tarnished keys and scraps of paper with writing so faded Lerek could only see a few letters, lay beside the candles.

Gabriol pulled the shroud from his jacket. The braziers around the room came to life, bursting into flames and bathing the temple in light. Lerek jumped, covering his mouth with a shaky hand as he stared wide-eyed at the braziers and then at Gabriol.

He was gratified to see a similar look on Gabriol's face. Lerek shuddered.

"How did that just happen?" Lerek whispered.

Gabriol turned in place as if searching for the answer. "I don't—"

He stopped abruptly, his body stiff as he held onto the shroud in his fist. Lerek took a tentative step closer to the mercenary. His skin itched with the certainty they were no longer alone, and yet there was no one else in the temple.

"What is it?"

Gabriol turned his head so slowly, Lerek had the uncanny sense he might not be the one controlling his own body. When Gabriol spoke, Lerek felt certain he was right.

"Achandia," Gabriol said in a voice so unlike his own, Lerek stepped back a few paces. He clutched his cloak and stared at the mercenary.

"Achandia," he said again, this time in a whisper as if speaking to himself.

He lifted the shroud, holding it aloft in both hands, the fabric sheer and bathed in the glow of the braziers. Lerek watched as Gabriol whispered in a foreign language, his mutterings growing more intense the longer he spoke.

Something cool brushed the back of Lerek's neck, and he jumped, grabbing his neck as his head whipped around, searching for the reason.

The fire in the braziers grew, and the room was almost uncomfortably warm. The hairs on Lerek's arms rose, and he scratched at his forearms.

Birds took flight behind him. Lerek spun around to see the shadows of the birds, their cries fading away to leave behind an eerie silence broken up by Gabriol's chanting. They disappeared as if only shadows.

"Gabe—"

Lerek turned and blinked. The fire in the braziers went out.

And Gabriol was gone.

"Gabriol!"

Lerek lurched forward, his eyes wide as he stared at the spot Gabriol had stood, then stumbled around the altar, the smell of the fire still in the air but the mercenary was nowhere to be found.

LEREK STARED AT THE SPOT WHERE GABRIOL HAD BEEN STANDING. REALIZING his jaw hurt because his mouth hung open, Lerek snapped it shut, his mind whirling with what he'd just seen. All his life, the legends of the gods that had ruled this realm had been just that: legends. Stories they'd all been told to explain away the unexplainable.

And yet he could not deny what his own eyes had seen these past few months.

Lerek lifted a shaking hand to rake through his already disheveled hair. The quiet permeating the temple was unsettling, expectant. Glancing around, Lerek felt an overwhelming need to leave. He took a step back, his eyes darting over the marble columns and faded mosaic tiles. As if hurried along by instinct, Lerek turned, striding across the empty chamber and down the steps onto the snow-covered ground.

Lifting a hand to his chest, Lerek's breath puffed out in thin wisps of smoke as he cast his eyes about the lonely winter landscape for his mount.

Lerek pursed his lips and took a step as the ground rumbled

beneath him. He spread his arms for balance, crying out as a sharp snap of wind crackled behind him.

Spinning around, Lerek gawped at the sight of the swirling vortex that disappeared as swiftly as it had formed. Lerek stared at the man who stumbled forward, a giant with bronze greaves over thick leather sandals.

As he rose to his full height, dread speared through Lerek as the man's bronze breastplate flashed in the weak sunlight, turning to face him. Ash-blond hair flowed onto the man's large shoulder plates, a deep red cape settling around him like a sentient being as the man flexed his immense arms above bronze and blood-red studded vambraces.

Stepping forward, the giant's steps made the marble tremble at his feet, and Lerek's gaze widened as he trembled.

Hazel eyes, threaded with red lights swirling over the irises, stared at Lerek. The man's mouth twisted into a sneer as if the sight of Lerek disgusted him.

Lerek thought his heart might have stopped.

Long minutes passed. Then, the giant stepped close enough Lerek had to tip his head far back to look up at him. A fine shudder ran through his frame.

"Bow, mortal!"

Lerek's body moved without thought, sinking to his knees with his head bowed.

Quaking, Lerek dared not move.

"Where is my wife?" the giant asked in a voice that would give Lerek nightmares for the rest of his life.

Before he could respond, the giant grabbed hold of Lerek's hair, snapping his head back to glare down at him. "Where are my *daughters?*"

Lerek's mouth worked, but speech eluded him. He was a mass of shaking limbs, and he could not form a coherent thought to save his life.

"Speak!"

"My—my—"

"SPEAK!"

Lerek felt something warm and wet slide down his breeches. Tears slipped out of the corners of his eyes as he gazed up at the terrifying giant.

"I don't—I don't know—"

"Where is Achandia?"

"I don't know who that is," Lerek whimpered, gasping as the giant ripped more of his hair from his scalp when he tightened his grip. "I don't know who that is!"

Lerek was shoved back onto the snow. Lifting his hands up defensively, he shied back as the towering nightmare before him seemed to grow larger.

"Then you are of no use to me."

Lerek felt a fresh wave of terror when the giant reached back, lifting a sword that looked like it was forged in the underworld, sparking with red lightning.

"Wait! Wait!" Lerek begged, scrambling back across the ground, his feet slipping in the wintry mix of dirt and snow. "I can help you!"

The giant snorted, bringing the tip of his monstrous sword to Lerek's panting chest.

"I am Ares, God of War," the man snarled, his wrathful eyes swirling with a strange red light, and Lerek felt his insides melt. "I need no mortal's help."

And with that, red lightning crackled as he swung his sword.

Acknowledgments

It's surreal I'm writing another one of these! I have a load of folks to thank, first and foremost my family. My husband David, who has no idea what I'm saying half the time when I talk about my books, but still my biggest champion. I love you, babe.

My children, Colin & Noelle, who love me despite my craziness, and who believe in me even when I don't. I am so proud to be your mother.

Thank you to my sister, who still carries around one of the first copies of the first book before it was even called From the Ashes of Gods lol. Antoinette—you're my Sonah, and I am not who I am without you.

Thank you to my bestie Elena Mendez, who is always ready to cheer me on no matter how small my accomplishments. Oh, you wrote 100 words today? Let's go celebrate! I love you for always being there for me.

A special thank you to Courtney "Coco" Hale, who continues to be one of the most influential people in my life with her wisdom, her insight and her belief in me. I love you, lady.

Taylor Dux - you humble me with all your gracious praise. You are a bright light in a dim world, and I hope you never lose that. Thank you for being so supportive and cheering me on - I love you.

My lovely VMW ladies—Katie Murray, Megan Munster, Taylor

Lavelle, Bethany Sage, and Ashley Kania: you continue to be a source of pride, support and escape for me. You are some of the strongest, smartest, beautiful and talented women I've ever had the good fortune of knowing and calling my friends. I love you all so much and am grateful to have you all in my life.

During the writing of this book, I also found my people. Chicago Authors IG besties, I am so grateful we found each other!

Thank you to all the professionals who made my book look AMAZING! Shepengul - thank you for the beautiful map, which is even more beautiful in this book. SeventhStar Art - so grateful for the stunning cover, which I cannot stop looking at! MgsDesiigns - I appreciate your patience with me so much. The artwork you created for my scene breaks and chapters for each of my characters is so good I had to add it to all the editions :). Jessie Cunniffe - thank you for the fabulous blurb; I never could've done that. It's perfect!

To all my betas, Dolores Avram, Debbie Samoson, Andrea Roberts, Verna Regier, Taylor Dux & Jen Curry - your feedback made this book even stronger. Thank you so much for your thoughts and insights and for being my guinea pigs...

Jordyn McCoy - I cannot thank you enough for all your patience, guidance and cheering on (and keeping me on task). I cannot wait for this to sell a million copies (even half a mil, I ain't greedy) so we can work together full time!

Thank you to my amazing street team, the Liodari - Andersen, Rachel Underhile, Morgan Prince, Autumn Morgan and Brianna Sall.

And finally, a huge thank you to you, my readers. This world came to me in a fever dream and in sharing it with you I have found myself. You cannot know how much it means to a writer when readers tell us how much they loved the characters and the world and the stories we create. I am so humbled and appreciative of your support and I hope to bring you many more stories set in Elysium.

By the time this releases, it'll be one year since we lost our precious little Carlos, who always hung out with me in my office while I wrote. I know you did it because you love me and were bored out of your mind, but now I have no one to share my Cheetos with. It makes me smile to think of you up there somewhere peeing on the corner of an angel's couch.

Carlos
2011-2024

ALSO BY KATERINA SPEERS

THE EIGHTH CIRCLE SERIES

From the Ashes of Gods

About the Author

Katerina Speers grew up in the Chicago area where she currently lives with her husband and children. When she's not writing, Katerina can be found reading a book, playing video games or enjoying movies at the theater.

instagram.com/katerina.speers

goodreads.com/katerinaspeers

tiktok.com/@katerinaspeers

www.ingramcontent.com/pod-product-compliance
Lightning Source LLC
Chambersburg PA
CBHW020648110726
47901CB00001B/93